Also by Elizabeth Chadwick

THE CONQUEST
THE CHAMPION
THE LOVE KNOT
THE MARSH KING'S DAUGHTER
LORDS OF THE WHITE CASTLE
THE WINTER MANTLE
THE FALCONS OF MONTABARD
SHADOWS AND STRONGHOLDS
THE GREATEST KNIGHT
THE SCARLET LION

DAUGHTERS
OF THE GRAIL

Elizabeth Chadwick

sphere

SPHERE

First published in the United States of America in 1993 by Ballantine Books
First published in Great Britain in 2006 by Sphere
Reprinted in 2007 (twice)

A CIP catalogue record for this book
is available from the British Library.

ISBN 978-0-7515-3899-1

Papers used by Sphere are natural, recyclable products made from
wood grown in sustainable forests and certified in accordance with
the rules of the Forest Stewardship Council.

Typeset in Horley OS by Palimpsest Book Production Limited,
Grangemouth, Stirlingshire
Printed and bound in Great Britain by
Clays Ltd, St Ives plc
Paper supplied by Hellefoss AS, Norway

Sphere
An imprint of
Little, Brown Book Group
Brettenham House
Lancaster Place
London WC2E 7EN

A Member of the Hachette Livre Group of Companies

www.littlebrown.co.uk

ACKNOWLEDGEMENTS

In the paragraphs below this one, readers will see the original acknowledgement written in 1993 when *Daughters of the Grail* was published in the USA. To that acknowledgement, I must now add my gratitude to the team at Little, Brown for giving me the opportunity to rework this novel and see it once more in print. My thanks go to my editors there – Barbara Daniel, Joanne Dickinson and Sheena-Margot Lavelle.

I would like to thank all the people who helped me in writing *Daughters of the Grail*. Indeed, without them, *Daughters* would not have been written at all. Tony Sutcliffe first set me the challenge and introduced me to the triumph and tragedy of the Cathars. My research was aided by my good friend Alison King, and our discussions over numerous cups of coffee provided me with valuable insights into my characters.

I want to thank my husband, Roger, for standing over mountains of ironing without complaint whenever the need has arisen. Greater love hath no man. I have also appreciated the support of my parents who have come to the rescue with childcare services and freshly baked cakes when there have been more tasks in the day than I have hands.

I owe many thanks to my agent, Carole Blake, who has been with me every step of the way – usually ahead, smoothing the ground. A special thank you goes to Pamela Strickler and Lesley Malin Helm at Ballantine. *Daughters* is as much their project as mine. Together we have planted, nurtured and pruned. I am proud to have them as editors.

CHAPTER 1

THE BLACK MOUNTAINS OF THE HIGH LANGUEDOC, SUMMER 1207

Bridget knew her mother was dying. The golden life force that should have shone steadily within and around Magda's body was a pale flicker, and her injuries did not respond to the surge of healing energy from Bridget's hands.

Outside the mountain cave in which they were sheltering, a summer storm raged across the High Languedoc. Bridget felt the lightning within herself and saw its vivid flicker through her hot, tired lids. She had been born during just such a storm, and the power of the lightning was in her veins. It was a sacred life-gift, a manifestation of the forces of the One Light. But tonight it came to take her mother.

'Don't leave me,' Bridget whispered in a tear-choked voice. 'Please don't go; I'm so afraid.' She bent her cheek to her mother's hand. The fingertips were crusted with blood, only raw flesh where trimmed pink nails had recently been. The slender wrists wore weeping red bracelets where manacles had abraded the skin. Those wounds would have healed in time, but not the one upon Magda's forehead where the priests had branded her to the bone with the sign of the cross she had refused to kiss. Witch and heretic, they had called her; foul devil's whore. Her poor mother, who had never done or wished anyone harm in her life.

Her mother's eyelids fluttered and lifted. 'You have many years to live,' she whispered, 'and a duty to fulfil; you are the last of my line.' Her throat moved as she struggled to swallow. Bridget helped her to sip from a small wooden cup filled with water from the spring at the back of the cave.

Magda drank, although most of the liquid dribbled down her chin. Her grey eyes were wide and bright, all her remaining life force concentrated in their gaze. 'You must find a consort when the moon time is right to seed your womb. That is the way it has been since the great stone circles were raised, before the holy thorn was planted.'

'But Uncle Chretien . . .' Bridget started to say, and cast an involuntary glance over her shoulder towards the dark cave mouth.

'Your uncle will not stand in your way. He is a Cathar, and for him it is necessary to be celibate; but he knows it will not be that way for you.'

Bridget listened for the sound of footsteps outside, but heard only the wind hissing through the stunted trees on the mountainside and the lash of the rain. Her uncle Chretien and his companion Matthias had gone to find shelter for the horses. There was no room in the cave, but Matthias had noticed a derelict goat shed lower down the slope. Although it was closer to the village, no one was likely to be abroad to see them in this weather.

The fire she had kindled earlier was dying, and her mother's hand resting in hers was icy. Bridget set more firewood on the embers. Closing her eyes, she reached down inside herself and drew forth her life energy in a lightning-bright thread. Flames surged beneath the outspread hand she passed over the fire, leaping as if on strings to her command. The strange animal paintings on the cave walls rippled with an illusion of life in the clambering flare of light and contrast of shadow. Bridget knew if she sank deeper into her trance, she would see small, olive-skinned men marking the walls with fire-blackened sticks, painting pictures of their prey to invoke success in the hunt. She would hear their sacred chant and taste the smoke of their fire, burning where hers now burned.

Flame to flame, she felt the connection before she withdrew her hand and turned once more to her mother. 'It is so difficult to bear,' she said softly, and heard her own voice echo off the walls with the forlorn note of a lost child.

Magda lay more motionless than the paintings. Although her mother's lips did not move, words entered Bridget's mind with precise clarity. 'The path of our bloodline has never been otherwise. Always you will find stones cast in your path, but if you turn them over, you will find the love and courage to endure.'

A tremendous flash of lightning sundered the night, shaking stones loose and rattling them down the mountain-side. Thunder crashed overhead, and, as the echoes surged around the cave, Bridget felt the warmth of a kiss upon her cheek and then on her brow in tender blessing.

'Mother!' Bridget's anguished cry mingled with the tail of the thunder and outlasted it, but Magda did not respond. Her abused, exhausted body was slack and lifeless – an aban-doned shell. Bridget whimpered, then stifled the sound behind compressed lips. Her mother was with the One Light now, was free of pain and persecution. The only reason to weep was for herself.

She kissed the bruised, hollow cheek and gently removed a silver amulet from around her mother's neck, hanging it around her own where it clinked softly against an identical token – an incised design of a six-pointed star within which a dove rose out of a chalice.

At the cave entrance, she heard masculine voices raised against the storm. One was rich, deep and confident. The other, lighter voice bore the exotic tones of Outremer. Soaked to the skin, the two men stooped under the low overhang at the cave entrance and entered within. Their conversation ceased as their eyes fell upon Bridget. Her uncle Chretien sucked in his breath as his gaze went from her to the still form by the fire.

'May she walk in the Light,' he said compassionately. 'She had a perfect spirit.'

His smaller, grey-bearded companion approached Magda's body and crouched on his heels. His right hand was badly mutilated, missing two fingers and a thumb, the stumps a puckered, angry red. He touched Magda's glossy black braid with his remaining fingers.

'She was still so young,' he said in a voice that was close to breaking. 'They should have taken me instead.'

'They would take us all if given the opportunity.' A deep weariness in his eyes, Chretien opened his arms to Bridget and, with a small, wounded cry, she ran into them, pressing herself against him, uncaring that he was drenched from the storm. She had always known the path she trod was lonely and dangerous, but never had she felt it so keenly as now.

Later, after she had washed and prepared her mother's body for burial, Bridget sat before the fire, a cup of fortified wine between her hands, and looked through the smoke at the two men who were now her only family – Matthias the scholar and Chretien, her father's younger brother. For six years she and her mother had been travelling with them, visiting the villages to preach the Cathar way and offer healing and comfort to the sick. As their fame had grown, so had the hostility of the Roman Church, to whom Catharism was a cancerous heresy to be excised at all costs.

Her father had been of the Cathar persuasion. He had died of a fever when Bridget was ten years old, but at least in his bed and unpersecuted. Cathars had been able to move openly then, without fear of being harried by the Church of Rome. Now it was a different matter. Her gaze flickered to the body of her mother, shrouded in a threadbare blanket.

When the songbird was gone, all that remained was an empty cage.

'When the storm has passed we must leave,' she said to the men. 'There is nothing for us here.'

Chretien looked troubled. 'Where will we go? Only the remote high places such as Roquefixade and Montségur are safe these days.'

As he said 'Montségur', a vision of a castle engulfed by fire flickered across Bridget's inner eye. She saw a night sky crowned in lightning and heard the cries of hundreds of people raised in suffering. 'No, not Montségur,' she replied with a swift shake of her head. 'We still have many friends who will give us shelter and protection.'

'And I must obtain fresh parchment and quills,' Matthias said. Unconsciously he rubbed his mutilated right hand with the fingertips of his left.

Chretien nodded, but his frown remained. 'Niece, I would be happier if you stayed in the mountains. There are too many prying eyes in the towns of the plain.'

'No,' Bridget answered with resolution. 'It is not yet time. If I retreat from the world now, I will not find the father of my child and it was my mother's dying wish that I take a mate.'

Chretien looked into the fire without speaking, although his jaw tightened. Bridget sighed softly. To Cathars such as her uncle, begetting a child was the trapping of an immortal spirit in sullied flesh. To her mother's more ancient religion, it was a sacrament. She knew that while Chretien disapproved, he would not press her to change. In equal respect she did not seek to persuade him of the necessity of her cause.

In the lingering silence, another image blinked across her mind – of a vigorous, sturdy woman in her middle years, red-cheeked, with heavy braids of iron-grey hair and a huge, toothy smile. 'We will go to the lady Geralda at Lavaur,' she said with quiet decision. 'She is a staunch Cathar and she will succour us for the moment.'

Chretien raised his hand to rub the heat of the fire from his face. 'If you will not go into the hills, then Lavaur is perhaps the next best alternative,' he said with a reluctant nod. 'Matthias?'

Bridget heard Matthias's hesitant agreement, and knew that with or without the men's approval, she was going to Lavaur. The town itself was not important; she had grasped nothing of its essence in her vision, but the road leading there was. A feeling tugged at her core, twisting and tightening her soft inner organs as if the child her mother desired her to bear were already kicking in her womb. As she pressed her hands to her flat stomach, the feeling vanished, but not the certainty that the decisions taken now were all-important to the future.

CHAPTER 2

Displaying prudence beyond his twenty-one years, Raoul de Montvallant covered the Venetian goblet with his palm and shook his head at the squire who leaned to replenish it. It was not that he disliked the wine; indeed, on a different occasion he would have drunk as deeply as every other young man present, but tonight he had good reason for remaining sober.

He slid a restless glance at that reason – his bride, Claire, to whom he had been betrothed since childhood. He had last seen her when she had a gappy smile and mud upon the hem of her gown from splashing in the bailey puddles after a summer rainstorm. Her smile today was dazzling and complete. The hem of her gown was embroidered not with mud, but with lozenges of gold thread glittering against a background of sumptuous green samite. Her hair, brushed down to proclaim her virginity, glowed like silk on fire, and Raoul wanted to run his fingers through its ripples to discover if it was as soft as it looked. She kept darting him swift glances, her eyes the rich brown of woodland honey. Raoul tried to think of something to say that would not seem trite or banal, but found himself at a loss. The beautiful creature at his side bore no resemblance to the skinny girl he remembered. The knowledge they would soon be alone together, in bed and naked, robbed him of all coherent thought.

Although he had no vast experience of women, Raoul had

sometimes visited the maisons lupanardes of Toulouse, where one of the whores had taken a fancy to teach him that there was more to pleasure than the brief, rough simplicity of his first encounters. Claire, however, was innocent, a virgin, unlikely to help him if he fumbled. She was also very desirable, and he was hot for her to the point where he doubted his own control. He reached for his cup, remembered it was empty for that very reason, and rested his hand flat on the table instead.

'Champing at the bit, eh?' laughed Father Otho, the priest who had officiated at their marriage in the castle's dusty, neglected chapel. 'I don't blame you – I wouldn't mind saddling her up myself!' He bit into an apple comfit and chewed lasciviously.

Raoul clenched his fist and thought about punching it into the priest's overfed face. Father Otho was a lecherous glutton, caring for his own pocket and pleasure above the needs of his flock, who, through his slovenly mismanagement, were few and indifferent. 'Then it is a good thing you are sworn to celibacy,' Raoul snapped.

The priest belched. 'There's always room for interpretation, I say. To know sin, you have to wrestle with it first. That's it, boy, fill it up, fill it up!' He gestured imperatively to the squire, then raised his brimming goblet and leaned towards Raoul's father. 'A magnificent cellar you keep, my lord!'

Berenger de Montvallant gave Otho a tepid smile that didn't reach his eyes.

'And he'll drink it dry before the night is out,' Raoul muttered to his father as the cleric's attention settled on a pretty maidservant attending the bride.

'If he weren't my second cousin and I hadn't promised his father I'd give him a living here, I'd have turned him off long ago,' Berenger said with a grimace. 'Is it any cause for wonder that the Cathars flourish among us when lard-tubs like him rule the clergy?'

Raoul watched Otho's pudgy hand crawl over a dish of sugared almonds, grasp, convey to wet lips and cram into greedy mouth. His gorge rose and he looked away. Three pilgrims had just arrived in the hall, their cloaks and broad-brimmed hats dusty with travel. Alein, his father's usher, found them a place to sit among the crowded trestles near the door. There were two men, one in his forties, the other about ten years older. Seating herself between them and thanking Alein with a warm smile was a young woman. The bones of her face were too strong for beauty, but there was something beyond her looks that was totally arresting. Filled with curiosity, Raoul studied her, wondering where she had come from and where she was going. Pilgrims occasionally stopped at Montvallant on their way to Toulouse, but usually they claimed hospitality at the church in Villemur.

A serving maid leaned across the trestle to dish out bread and wine, hiding the young woman from Raoul's sight. He craned his neck, trying to keep her in view. The musicians who had been playing softly through the various courses of the feast changed their tempo, and the lively strains of a traditional jig filled the hall. His father nudged him.

'Are you not going to dance with your bride?' Berenger teased. 'People are waiting for you to lead her out.'

Raoul became aware of the expectant stares of the wedding guests. Flushing with chagrin, he hastily rose, and, turning to Claire, extended his hand to assist her to her feet. Blushing, she placed her slender fingers in his. The new gold of her wedding ring shone like a promise. Raoul forgot the pilgrim woman as he led his bride to the cleared space on the floor, forgot everything but the feel of her supple body lightly touching and leaving his as they stepped and turned in the age-old patterns of celebration.

'More bread, Bridget?' Chretien offered his niece the basket of small loaves.

She smiled a refusal. 'I couldn't eat another morsel.'

Leaning her elbows upon the trestle, she watched the dancers with wistful eyes. Theirs was another world, one that she could glimpse but never dwell within. Part of her longed for the colours, the revelry and carefree exuberance that cared for nothing beyond the moment. Sometimes it was very hard to be who and what she was.

The dancers swirled towards her, the young bridegroom trapped in a group of other young men. He was laughing as he tried without any great effort to escape their clutches. Bridget's breath caught at this closer sight of him. She felt the magnetism of his vigorous young body and the joy surging through him. Her own body responded like a plucked harp string. She lowered her gaze to the board and stared at a dark wine stain on the wood, her heart quickening and her skin tingling with sensation.

The hall erupted with cheers and shouts, approving whistles and cries of encouragement as the groom was borne towards the tower stairs.

'What's happening?' Bridget asked a woman sitting at her trestle.

'What's going to happen, you mean!' the woman chuckled. 'Time for Lord Raoul and his bride to be put to bed to do their duty!'

'Ah,' Bridget said. That was why she had felt his vigour just now, but tonight it already had its focus. The new wife, surrounded by her women, was being led from the dais to a different set of stairs. She had the graceful gait of a doe, and the same shy, startled manner.

Silently, Bridget wished the couple well.

'Niece?' Chretien leaned towards her, a look of concern on his face. 'What is wrong?'

Bridget forced a smile. How could she say that her body was tingling with the desire to be in the bride's place tonight? 'I am overcome by all this bounty,' she said, 'and very tired. It is past time I sought my pallet . . . No, finish your wine. I would like a little space alone first.'

She pressed his arm, and absented herself from her uncle's shrewd scrutiny.

Outside, the warm evening air bore the scent of hot charcoal and cooked meat from the extra braziers burning in the courtyard. The sound of lute and pipe, the thrusting beat of tabors, followed Bridget relentlessly, pounding through her groin in dull waves of longing. She stopped to lean her forehead against the cool stone of the castle wall, and breathed deeply, seeking to be calm.

'Bridget? Bridget, my dear?'

She looked up to see a tall woman hurrying towards her. 'Geralda?' Bridget took a step forward and was engulfed in a strong, maternal hug.

'I have just seen Chretien and Matthias in the hall, and they told me I would find you out here. Let me look at you!' Still holding Bridget by the shoulders, Geralda of Lavaur examined her thoroughly. 'So much like your mother.' Tears shimmered in her dark hazel eyes. 'Chretien told me she had been killed. I'm so sorry.'

'She is one with the Light.' Bridget blinked on tears of her own. 'She was caught healing a sick woman in one of the hill villages by two travelling friars and put to the torture.' Her voice faltered. 'I miss her so much.'

Geralda's embrace closed around her again and Bridget shuddered within it, giving vent to a storm of grief and tears while Geralda held and soothed her like a child. Finally, drawing herself together, Bridget made a determined effort and pulled away.

'Did my uncle tell you we were on our way to you at Lavaur?'

'Indeed he did, and you are most welcome to stay. I have some new manuscripts I want Matthias to look at. The people will want to hear Chretien preach and visit you for healing. The friars will not dare to interfere with me!' Her eyes glittered with ferocity.

Bridget knew Geralda had every right to be confident.

Her brother, Aimery, was one of the foremost warriors in the South. Every right, and yet the flickering torchlight made dark hollows beneath Geralda's cheekbones and deepened her orbits with shadow, until her face became a skull.

Shivering, Bridget started to walk towards the small shelter that she and her guardians had pitched against the bailey wall near the main gates. Her feeling of foreboding increased as she and Geralda walked past the well housing. In a moment Bridget knew that if she allowed it, the vision would come with dreadful clarity and show her what she did not wish to see. She closed her mind, pushing the premonition away, squeezing it from existence. As a distraction, she asked about the wedding.

Geralda was only too pleased to hold forth. 'I've known Raoul since he was a babe in arms,' she said fondly. 'He's my godson, you know . . . or he was when I was of the Church of Rome. He and Claire have been betrothed since they were little – they seem well suited, don't you think?'

Bridget murmured that they did indeed. Her inner eye would not be denied and filled with another image, and she saw Raoul de Montvallant and his bride, limbs entwined upon cool linen sheets. Feverish body heat. As Geralda continued to gossip, Bridget watched the moon rise above the castle walls, haloing the sky with silver, and saw a man and a woman, saw light and darkness and fire.

CHAPTER 3

Shivering with tension, Claire stood in the bedchamber where she was to spend her wedding night. Embroidered hangings of scarlet, blue and gold adorned the walls and kept the draughts at bay, and where there were no hangings, the plaster was painted with a delicate tracery depicting flowers, vines and scrolls of leaf work and greenery.

The great bed of walnut wood dominated her awareness. Hangings of blue and scarlet damask were drawn back to reveal a coverlet of dark blue sarcenet worked with moons and stars of thread-of-silver. The maids had folded it back upon a bolster and sheets of pristine white linen awaiting the inscription of her virgin blood. If her legs had not been trembling with fear, she would have run from the room.

A servant had set an infusion of wine and spices to simmer over the hearth. Beatrice, Raoul's mother, drew Claire to the fire and bade her stand on a mouflon rug while the attendants undressed her.

'This is a happy day for me.' Beatrice kissed Claire warmly. 'I am more than proud to call you my new daughter.'

Claire tried to smile but her stomach was clenched in a hundred knots. She liked Beatrice, but she was no substitute for her own mother, Alianor, who was going to ride away tomorrow. Claire's anchor was now supposed to be her new family, but she felt as if she had been cast adrift on a wide and perilous ocean.

Thinking about Raoul made Claire feel queasy. What were they going to say to each other? Or were they going to talk at all? The maids were giggling as they scattered the bed with herbs to promote fertility. Claire was not ignorant. Alianor had taken her aside several weeks before the wedding to explain all about the joys and duties of being a wife. She had seen animals mating in the yard and cockerels treading hens. Once, in the stables, she had caught a groom raising himself from between the spread legs of a kitchen maid, so she knew how men were made when aroused. Her mother said the act was supposed to be a pleasure, but Claire could not imagine how. If there was supposed to be blood on the sheet in the morning, surely there would be pain?

Her attendants unpinned the gauze veil and chaplet of stiff gold flowers from her hair, and her mother took a comb to the chestnut-gold waves to tidy and burnish them. 'Child, you are beautiful,' said Alianor mistily. 'I'm so proud of you. I wish your father were here to see your wedding day.'

Claire swallowed, unable to respond. Usually she remembered her father, dead these past five years, with gentle, sad affection, but tonight she had room in her mind for nothing but her own fear. Obediently she raised and lowered her arms to the commands of the women, and watched the garments gather upon the clothing pole until she was naked. Near the fire, it was not cold, but her skin was covered in goose flesh. Cool silk slithered upon her shoulders as she was urged into a loose bed-robe, and her hair was rearranged over it in a sheaf of glowing colour. She felt numb. People spoke to her, but she didn't hear what they said.

The door burst open upon a rowdy shock of men, Raoul jostled in their midst and naked beneath his cloak. A din of noisy laughter and good-humoured jesting filled the room. Risking a glance at Raoul, Claire saw that his colour was high, and the smile on his face as fixed and nervous as her own.

Beatrice pressed a cup of hot wine into Claire's hands. 'Drink and take heart,' she whispered.

Claire raised the cup and sipped. The taste of cinnamon and hot red grape flowed over her tongue. Raoul joined her and taking the cup from her hands, set his lips to the place where she had drunk. He put his free hand lightly at her waist. The young male guests, and some of the older ones who were in their cups, cheered encouragement. Claire blushed. Raoul's palm seemed to burn through the thin silk robe into her spine.

Father Otho elbowed his way forward to perform the benediction that would cleanse and purify their marriage bed and bless any fruit that came of it. He was drunk, his black eyes glittering and unfocused.

'Well, well,' he leered at Claire, 'it hardly seems a moment since you were a tight bud on the stem, and now behold the open rose, ready to be well and truly plucked!' He pushed the thumb of his right hand into the clenched fist of his left in a gesture that was unmistakable.

Anger and shame welled in Claire's breast. Light jesting she could accept; it was all part of the nuptial tradition. Every bride and groom were teased on their wedding eve, but not by the priest, his face congested with drink and lust. Raoul started to lunge, but was restrained by his mother's grip on his arm.

Berenger de Montvallant said through his teeth, 'Father, I suggest you confine yourself to the words of the benediction.'

Otho tried to draw himself up, but only succeeded in lurching into one of the guests. 'No sense of humour,' he muttered, pushing himself precariously upright. His lower lip thrust out like a sulky child, he approached the bed and began the blessing. He slurred the words and used neither the correct order nor form before sprinkling the bed haphazardly with holy water. Breathing as stertorously as a mastiff, he presented Claire and Raoul with a cross to kiss.

Claire felt sick. She would not have been surprised to see the tip of a forked tail twitching beneath the skirts of Otho's habit. Unable to bring herself to touch the cross with her lips, she kissed the air above it. Raoul, too, kissed the air, his face taut with leashed temper. The gold clasp on his cloak flashed and flashed with his rapid breathing.

Father Otho belched. 'You can get to work now, lad,' he said. 'Let's have a good bloody sheet to show in the morning, eh?' His lewd amusement terminated in a squawk as Raoul seized him by the throat.

'A pity you won't live to see it!' he snarled.

Otho's complexion darkened. A rasping noise emerged from his windpipe, and he scrabbled at Raoul's fist, the veins in his forehead bulging. After a moment, Berenger intervened, and with an effort prised his son's grip from his victim's mottling flesh. Otho collapsed on the floor, clutching his throat and wheezing. 'Let him go,' Berenger said, 'you don't want to sully your wedding night with murder.'

'Don't I?' Flexing and clenching his hand, Raoul glared at the semi-conscious priest gasping at his feet.

Berenger gestured peremptorily to a couple of servants. 'Take Father Otho outside and leave him there to sober up,' he commanded. 'As near to the midden heap as his behaviour dictates.'

'Yes, my lord.' Grim satisfaction on their faces, the men lifted Otho and carried him out of the bedchamber, carelessly bumping his head against the wall on the way.

Berenger made apologies all around, his colour still high. 'Time, I think, and well past time to leave bride and groom in peace,' he said gruffly and ushered the guests from the room. Then he turned back to embrace first Raoul and then Claire with tenderness. 'You must not let this spoil tonight for you.'

'No, sir, you can be sure that I won't,' Raoul said with a forced smile.

The final guests departed, and the latch fell on the door. To keep herself from panicking, Claire went to the flagon the maid had left warming on the hearth and, tossing the cold dregs of her last cup on the fire, refilled the goblet. The hiss and splutter of evaporating liquid shocked the silence. Half in a trance, Claire stared into the jagged turrets of flame When she tasted the wine, it was like drinking the heart of the fire. Heat scorched her face, but she could not tear her eyes from the gashes of light and the prowling darkness behind.

Raoul returned from barring the door and was horrified to see her so close to the flames. Crying that she would set her robe alight, he hastened to draw her away. Claire blinked up at him through a hundred mirrored tongues of flame and put her hand to her forehead.

'Claire?' He held her shoulders and looked anxiously into her face

'I'm sorry.' She lowered her hand. Her head felt light, and at the same time far too heavy for her neck to support. 'It has been a long day, that is all.'

'In more ways than one.' Raoul grimaced. 'I swear I would have felt no remorse at strangling Father Otho.'

The memory of the way the priest had defiled her wedding chamber when he should have been blessing it added to her distress and weariness. An aching lump swelled in her throat, impossible to swallow down. She tried to bite back a sob, but the effort jerked her shoulders and gave her away.

'Claire, don't, I cannot bear to see you weep.' Raoul pulled her against his strong young body. Claire pressed her face to his cloak and stifled her sobs upon the prickly soft wool.

'I had a feeling of dread when I looked into the fire just now,' she whispered against the steady thud of his heart, 'as if the whole world was burning and I could do nothing to prevent it. I used to have nightmares about fire when I was little. Once a priest came to our castle and preached a sermon about the flames of hell that awaited all heretics. My mother said I did not sleep properly for months afterwards.'

'Priests!' Raoul said with disparagement. 'I know for

certain that hell must be full of them!' He pressed his lips to her herb-scented hair and nuzzled lightly down to her fire-hot temple. Cupping her face in his hands like a chalice, he kissed her salty cheek, the corner of her mouth and finally the softness of her lips. 'Ah Claire,' he said with a catch in his voice, 'you are so beautiful.'

His sea-blue eyes were bright and narrow, his breathing swift. Claire felt as if she were about to be devoured. The taut hunger in his expression frightened her, but at the same time a strange new excitement tingled through her breasts and loins.

Murmuring reassurances, his hands moved upon her body and if they were trembling with excitement, he knew where to touch and stroke to evoke response. He continued to kiss her – light butterfly kisses that explored her eyelids, cheeks and jaw. He nibbled her throat and sucked upon the hollow behind her ear until she shivered and gasped. Stealthily he reached to the tie on her bed-robe, and then his hands were inside, gliding upon her naked skin, drawing her hip to hip against him.

Claire made a small, panicked sound as she felt the thrust of his penis, hot as a branding iron against her belly. She tried to pull away, but he held her still, one hand upon her buttocks, the other stroking her hair and the valley of her spine.

'Don't struggle,' he pleaded. 'Dear Jesu, I'm as frightened as you are.'

Wide-eyed, she stared up at him, holding her breath.

'I promise, I swear to God, I'll try not to hurt you,' he said hoarsely. 'Please, I want tonight to bring us both joy.'

Claire swallowed. 'I want that, too,' she answered, her voice barely audible.

They stayed as they were for a moment longer, locked together in anxious uncertainty. Then Raoul swept her up in his arms and carried her to the bed.

CHAPTER 4

On Montvallant's battlements, Bridget filled her lungs with air that was still night-cold and, facing the place where the sun would soon rise, sat down cross-legged. Towards the east, the sky beyond the crenellations gleamed like the pearly interior of an oyster shell. Softly, she began to chant the sacred words that were the legacy of an unbroken female lineage more than a thousand years old.

As her voice rose and fell, the surrounding walls dissolved away. Light pulsed around her, changing hue, flowing into and filling her until her whole being was suffused with radiance. A single spear of sunlight burst through the gap in the merlon where she sat waiting. The pain was intense. Liquid fire consumed her body until she was brighter than the light itself.

The sky turned black and, as if from a great height, she saw a man nailed upon a cross. At the foot of the cross knelt two weeping women, one young and dark-haired, the other older but with a bone structure defying her years. A child clung to the rumpled skirts of the younger one, a little girl with eyes the crystal colour of Bridget's own and her name was Magda, daughter of Mary. Even if Bridget had not known this through the ancient traditions, passed down from mother to daughter, she would have felt her heritage in the very marrow of her bones.

Without warning the vision changed and suddenly there

was fire, harsh with smoke, and within it the cries of men and the bitter wailing of women and children. Instinctively Bridget recoiled, for the heat was so fierce that it seemed to singe her brows and hair. She was one with the fire – with all the people burning in the fire.

Through the flames the young bridegroom strode towards her, a sword in his hand, his expression torn with grief. He was so close that she could see the black chevronels on his gold surcoat, the tawny stubble pricking his jaw and the detail of the tears running down his face. Weeping, reaching out to him, his wife ran behind him, her chestnut-gold hair streaming down her back, her face smudged with bruises. The fire roared across the path, sundering her from him, and he came on towards Bridget alone, until he was kneeling before her. Their eyes met and she felt his gaze pierce her body. He laid his sword across her palms and she closed her hands over it until the twin edges cut her flesh and her blood trickled down the engraved fuller in a thin, scarlet thread. As the sun blazed in full glory over the horizon, she saw what was to be, and her high, wild cry soared from the battlements to strike the new day and shatter into a hundred echoes.

In the bridal chamber, Raoul tossed and moaned, beset by a nightmare. Images of fire and the flash of weapons beat across his mind. He heard screams of men in triumph and agony, the terrified squealing of horses, and knew he was fighting for his life. His sword arm was aching so fiercely that he could scarcely parry the blows raining down on him, and that in itself was strange because he had never tasted battle, let alone fought in one to the point of exhaustion.

A knight was riding him down, white light glaring from the edge of the sword as the horseman swung and struck. The blade sliced through Raoul's shield like a knife slicing bread. The world darkened, and through that darkness a woman's voice sought him, calling, pulling him towards the light. He could see her in the distance, black hair blowing in the wind and hands outstretched.

'Raoul, in God's name, wake up! Raoul!'

His terrified cry echoed in his skull as he ripped himself out of the dream and surfaced wide-eyed and gasping into the sun-flooded brightness of his marriage chamber. A woman's voice still called to him, but her hair as she leaned over him was golden chestnut, not black. 'You were dreaming,' she said, and laid her palm to the side of his face.

'Dreaming!' He shuddered. 'God's wounds, I've never been so frightened in my life!' He covered his eyes with one hand. He was soaked with sweat, the sheet clinging to his body like a shroud. Sunlight filtered through the waxed linen across the window arch, and he could hear his mother's doves cooing on the ledge outside. Claire was tousled and beautiful beside him, but he felt unnerved, as if an intruder had been rifling through his possessions.

'What happened?'

'I don't remember, only that there was a battle and a woman with long black hair who wanted something from me.' A shiver rippled through him. 'Jesu!'

'Perhaps it is because of what happened last night?' she suggested.

He lowered his hand, turned his head to her and frowned. 'Last night?'

Claire blushed beneath his scrutiny. There were many aspects to last night, not all of them unpleasant. 'The priest, I mean, Father Otho. Perhaps you dreamed about fighting because of that.'

'Perhaps,' he said in a doubtful voice and screwed up his face. 'There was a woman in pilgrim robes at one of the lower trestles who looked like the one in my dream.'

The rumbling of wain wheels and the cheerful shout of a guard drifted up to the window as the castle gates opened to the morning. Raoul threw off the damp sheet and sat up. The linen beneath him bore brownish smears of dried blood, and his shoulders were sore where she had gripped him at the moment of defloration. Claire was looking at him and biting her full underlip. 'I did not mean to be clumsy with you,' he said, struck by a pang of guilt. 'You might not see it as such, but it was a compliment to your beauty. I couldn't wait any longer.'

The lip came free and tentatively curved. 'It didn't hurt that much, only at first, then I forgot the pain.' She blushed again.

'Then you are not upset?' Tempting his eye, the blush descended towards her cleavage.

'No, I'm not upset . . . ' and then as he leaned eagerly towards her, 'a little sore, but I was assured by your mother and mine yesterday that it will quickly pass.'

Although there was no distress in her voice or attitude, he felt the slight tensing of her body, and checked himself. Perhaps this morning it would be better to confine his admiration to gentle words and caresses rather than engaging in another bout of lovemaking. Time alone was what she required now, and then time with other women. And he needed to recover from the vivid violence of his dream.

He kissed her nose and the corner of her mouth in light affection, and left the bed to don his clothes. 'I'll send in your maid,' he said over his shoulder as he went to the door.

Claire smiled gratefully and burrowed back beneath the covers.

When Bridget descended from the battlements, Chretien was at the outer well, filling the water flasks for the journey to Lavaur, and Geralda was giving him directions and saying her farewells.

'I would travel with you myself,' Geralda said, her voice full of regret, 'but I have promised Berenger and Beatrice to stay awhile at Montvallant. Besides,' she added with a rueful smile, 'the less attention you draw to yourselves, the better.

Journeying in my company would hardly make you anonymous.' Her gaze lit on Bridget, who had silently begun to help Matthias load their few belongings on to the horses.

'Perhaps you should rest here for another day,' she suggested. 'The Montvallants are sympathetic towards Cathars, and Bridget looks exhausted.'

Chretien opened his mouth.

'No,' said Bridget quickly before he could speak. 'It would not be wise. Two travelling friars will soon arrive.' She strapped a pack efficiently to her mount's crupper. 'I saw them in the sunrise.' She could have added that the time was not yet ripe for herself and Raoul de Montvallant. There was moon-blood between her thighs, and the groom had his new bride to sow with seed. Mindful, however, of her uncle Chretien's Cathar morals, she kept that particular information to herself.

'You have had a vision?' Chretien's voice was sharp with concern.

Bridget sighed. 'Several,' she said and, gathering the reins, mounted her gelding. 'Are you ready?' She turned towards the castle gates.

Chretien considered her thoughtfully as he settled across his own saddle. Making the sign of the Cathar blessing over Geralda, he followed his niece across the courtyard.

Matthias, bringing up the rear, paused as they passed a midden heap beside the gates. A priest lay snoring on his stomach, sodden as a joint of marinated meat. Matthias shook his head sadly, but without surprise. 'I doubt we'll ever be ready.'

CHAPTER 5

It was peaceful beside the river. In the midday heat, the trees
lining the banks of the Tarn provided welcome shade for the
picnickers who rode down from the castle to take their ease
by the water.

Most of the guests had departed Montvallant after the
wedding breakfast and the traditional parading of the
bedsheet stained with the bride's virgin blood, but a few had
lingered on, including Geralda of Lavaur and her brother
Aimery, who were old family friends. Aimery and Berenger
shared a passion for falconry and were keen to fly and
compare their hawks, whilst Geralda and Beatrice had a
year's worth of gossip to exchange.

A little apart from the older people, shielded from their
scrutiny by a screen of willow and ash saplings, Claire shifted
Raoul's head to pillow it more comfortably in her lap as he
napped. Her gaze dwelt upon the natural upward curve of
his lips, his dense gold lashes and the darker feathering of
eyebrow. Pleasure and fear knotted her belly. Dear Jesu, how
handsome he was, and all hers. It was as though someone
had piled her arms full of treasure, and while she marvelled
at her good fortune, she was also worried lest she drop it.

Her mother had left yesterday with tears and promises of
an early reunion. The parting had been desperately painful
for Claire. Although her new family had done their best to
welcome her and shown kindness, everything was still

strange, and there was so much to learn. Being a wife was very different to being a daughter.

She leaned back against the tree supporting her spine and watched sunlight weaving through the willow leaves, fashioning a trellis of green and gold; a faerie arbour for the lady and her knight. She heard Geralda's deep laugh, the splash of two squires horsing about in the river shallows, the startled cry of a moorhen.

Stealthily she reached towards a tall cluster of foxtail growing near her tree and nipped off a stem between her fingernails. Stifling a giggle, she dangled the plump seed-head over Raoul's nose. He twitched and raised a languid hand to brush away what he obviously thought was a hovering midge. Claire waited a moment and repeated the move, almost laughing as he swept his palm across empty air. She dangled her bait again, tickling, teasing.

With the speed of a striking snake, Raoul grabbed her arm, pulled her down and sideways, and rolled her beneath him, hands braceleting her wrists. A grin flashed. 'What are you going to do now?'

Claire wriggled beneath him and angled her head, inviting a kiss. 'Bargain for mercy?'

'Show me.' He released his grip so that he could brace his weight on one hand and caress her body with the other. They kissed. Her hands slipped beneath his tunic and she spread her fingers upon the damp curve of his ribs. Warmth flooded her body and centred in her loins.

'You drive a hard bargain, my lord,' she whispered against his mouth.

'I trust you to eventually soften my resolve.' He nibbled her throat and reached within her surcoat to fondle her breast. Just as he felt her nipple peak under his caress, Aimery's fluffy Pyrenean hound wagged up to investigate the disturbance. Raoul swore softly and tried to shove the dog away, but it only jumped boisterously from side to side and barked, intent on play.

A sharp whistle from Aimery brought the hound gambolling to heel, but the damage was done. Raoul sat up and squinted through the brilliant sunlight at his father's friend. Blushing furiously, Claire smoothed her rumpled garments.

Amusement glinted in Aimery's eyes. He ruffled the exuberant hound's coat. 'I am sorry,' he said in a cheerful tone of voice that gave the lie to his words. 'I can't stop Blanc from sniffing out game in the bushes when it is what he is trained to do.' He tugged a folded hawking gauntlet out of his belt and drew it on to his fist. 'Let your poor wife alone awhile and come and look at the paces of my new hawk.' He glanced over his shoulder. 'Your father's waiting.'

Seated around the picnic cloth, the women watched the men ride away, hawks on their fists. The lady Geralda clucked her tongue and laughed. 'Aimery's been desperate to show off that hawk to Berenger and Raoul all week. Never has such a bird existed before if you're to believe his praise. I tell you, he has driven me half-insane with all his talk of it!'

'So now you are wholly mad,' said Beatrice mischievously.

Geralda struck her friend's arm. 'Beatrice de Montvallant, you should be ashamed of yourself, teasing an old woman!'

'I thought that Cathars did not lie,' Beatrice retorted, eyes sparkling. 'You're not much older than me, and I have no intention of admitting dotage yet!'

'Ah, but you have Berenger to keep you on your toes and a new wife to tutor.' Geralda smiled inclusively at Claire. 'All I have is Aimery and his moulting hawks!'

'You have your faith,' Beatrice objected.

Geralda sobered at that, but her smile remained, deepening the seams at her eye corners. She glanced round at their attendants, but only Claire's maid Isabelle was within earshot. Geralda assessed the girl for a moment, then produced a small leather-bound book from the satchel she had brought with her. 'Now that the men have gone, let me show you something,' she said, her fingertips tracing the interlaced circles tooled in gold on the cover. 'Not that I'm hiding anything; Aimery's heard me read from this several times, but he's about as interested in it as I am in his hawks.'

'What is it?' Beatrice looked both curious and apprehensive.

'A translation of ancient writings from the Holy Land. A burgher at Lavaur brought some scrolls back from a pilgrimage he made to Jerusalem, and bequeathed them to me when he died. I'm having them translated into our own tongue by a Cathar scribe in my household. Listen.' Opening the book at random, she began to read in a clear, firm voice.

'"To know oneself at the deepest level is to know God. Look for God by taking yourself as the starting point. Learn who it is within you who makes everything his own and says, 'My God, my mind, my thought, my soul, my body.' Learn the sources of sorrow, joy, love, and hate. If you investigate carefully these matters, you will find Him in yourself."

'Is that not wonderful? And yet the Church would deny us.' Geralda's eyes shone with indignation 'If they could, they would burn every book not written in Latin and every book that disagrees with their narrow image of God.' She snapped her fingers. 'You don't need that useless priest of yours in order for your cry to reach God, Beatrice. Stand before Him as you are and He will hear you!'

'I have never tried to find God through Father Otho.' Beatrice shuddered. 'That would be like drinking wine out of a filthy cup.'

'Precisely!' Geralda struck the ground to emphasise her point. 'The priests serve the God of their own worldliness, not the one of simple truth! They tell us to believe in blood-guilt, in hell. If Jesus was sacrificed on the cross to take away our sins, why is there any need for a church? And if we are still sin-burdened, why was there a sacrifice at all? Such cruelty is not the conception of the God of Light.' She shook her head. 'Oh, I tell you, our consciences are ruled with fear and oppression, and when we try to free ourselves, we are punished.'

Beatrice laid a calming hand over Geralda's. 'You are lecturing to those who sympathise. I have long been a believer in the Cathar faith, and Claire comes from a family who welcome the Good Men into their home.'

Claire murmured shy assent. Her mother often gave food and lodging to travelling Cathar priests, although she wondered why they should be called Good Men when there were so many women among them. From these itinerant preachers she had learned that the Cathar way to the truth was to live a pure and simple life – prayer, celibacy and plain, meatless fare. The teachings of Christ were followed, but with a minimum of ritual. There was no Son of God, only the one bright light of the deity. His counterpart, the dark Rex Mundi, ruled the world and all its lusts, and was to be shunned.

Only the intensely committed took the final, austere vows and became Perfecti, but there were other levels for those who believed in the Cathar way and were not yet prepared to subject themselves to the rigorous discipline required. Some only came to it on their deathbeds, others after they had raised families and outgrown the passions of youth.

Claire had often toyed with the notion of becoming one of the Cathar Perfecti. She had dreamed of it the way other young women mooned over the images of knights in burnished armour and troubadours with smouldering eyes. A dream, but almost vivid enough to be real as she sat beside Geralda and Beatrice in the deepening afternoon.

'Would you read some more,' she requested softly, 'before the men return?'

The lady of Lavaur eyed her thoughtfully and Claire saw in her expression that Geralda had recognised a kindred spirit. 'Nothing would give me greater pleasure, my dear.'

* * *

On their return from the picnic, the women retired to the bower to refresh themselves. The men, when finally they tore themselves away from the hawk mews, made do with stripping to their braies and swilling themselves at the trough in the yard. Claire stood in the window embrasure and peeked out on Raoul, admiring his loose-knit grace and the play of his muscles beneath the sparkle of water droplets. Plucking a flower from a jug of marigolds set on the embrasure ledge, she tossed it down towards him. It missed, but the bright movement caught his eye. Glancing up, he smiled and blew her a kiss.

Claire ran down the tower stairs to the hall. At their foot, she was startled to see her father-in-law in the company of two black-clad friars and a sour-faced Father Otho. Hastily, she curtseyed, and lowered her eyes.

'Daughter,' the older of the friars saluted her in a cool, thin voice. A knotted scourge hung from his belt beside a set of wooden pater noster beads. One of his thumbs was almost obliterated by a chunky gold seal ring inlaid with a grey cameo. She fastened her eyes on the ring, too frightened to look up lest he read the guilt of heresy in her face.

Berenger's tone was formal and strained. 'Claire, my dear, will you tell Lady Beatrice that we have guests at the high table tonight – Friar Dominic and Friar Bernard.'

'Yes, of course.' She was turning to make her escape when Raoul walked nonchalantly through the tower doorway, his shirt and tunic slung over his shoulder; his bare chest beaded with water droplets, and a marigold tucked behind his ear. He, too, stopped short when he saw the two friars and Otho. His smile died and irritation flickered before he schooled his expression to polite neutrality. The moment the necessary introductions had been performed, he excused himself, sliding Claire an exasperated look.

She knew he had been on his way to see her, that without the presence of those dour black robes, he would have swept her into his arms and paid her for the marigold in kisses and love-play. Dismayed and anxious, she hurried back to the bower to warn Beatrice and especially Geralda about their unwelcome guests.

The presence of the two friars and Father Otho at dinner in the hall sullied what had until then been a day of pleasure. Friar Dominic dipped a piece of bread in the salt dish and gazed around his audience. 'I assume you have heard there is to be a crusade to put a stop to the Cathars unless Raymond of Toulouse curtails their activities himself?' he said, his stare sharp and searching. 'The call has gone out in the North.'

Berenger glanced at Raoul, who was holding Claire's hand. 'There has been talk of a crusade since I was my son's age, and that is further back than I care to recall. I doubt it will come to anything.' His gaze continued along the high table to Father Otho. 'The Church would do better to set its own house in order before it casts stones elsewhere.'

The friar's face darkened. 'Men are weak reeds. There will always be a need for reform, but the disgrace of the Cathar heresy cannot be permitted to survive.'

'Count Raymond would never stand for a French army on his soil.'

The younger friar ceased toying with the chicken on his trencher and raised dark eyes to Berenger. 'With respect, my lord,' he said primly, 'your overlord seldom bothers with anything if he has to make an effort.'

'He would make an effort if the French invaded.'

'But not for ridding himself of heretics,' retorted the young friar.

Berenger forced himself to remember that these men were guests beneath his roof and could only thank God, whichever one, that Geralda and Aimery had opted to remain in their chambers and not make it difficult for their host.

Friar Dominic made a silencing gesture towards his young companion. 'I made mention of a crusade by way of a gentle warning,' he said to Berenger. 'We are not here to preach at you. Truly, all we wish is a night's lodging, and perhaps a little information if it be in your power to give it.'

'Oh?' Berenger looked wary.

'We are seeking some heretics, whom we have heard are in the vicinity.'

There was silence. Beatrice paled and Claire pressed herself against Raoul, who gave her arm a reassuring squeeze.

'You mean the horse-faced bitch Geralda of Lavaur and her brother Aimery?' said Otho, wiping his sleeve across his mouth. 'Yes, they're here as Lord Berenger's guests. More than half the townsfolk are Cathar sympathisers and they're openly encouraged at the castle.'

'My guests are no business of yours,' Berenger said icily. 'I will not have them harassed in my house. Their beliefs are their own concern. If there are Cathars in this town, then I ask you who is to blame, Otho? Who would want you for a confessor?'

Friar Dominic raised his right hand and the light gleamed on the cameo ring. 'Lord Berenger, as you say, your guests are your own affair, although I would counsel you to have a care for your immortal soul.'

Berenger tightened his lips on his temper and silently promised himself that Otho's career as Montvallant's priest was finished.

'We are seeking two men and a woman travelling together,' continued the friar. 'One is known to be a senior Cathar Perfect, Chretien de Béziers; the other goes by the name of Matthias. He's a scribe from Antioch, two fingers and the thumb missing from his right hand. The woman is young, and some would say beautiful.' His lip curled with disdain on the final word.

The younger friar leaned earnestly towards Berenger. 'They are known to preach abominations that go even beyond what the ordinary Cathars would dare. They are minions of the Devil!'

Berenger shook his head and was relieved to say with a

clear conscience, 'I have neither seen nor heard of anyone fitting your description.'

Friar Dominic eyed him closely, then hunted his stare along the high trestle. 'Anyone else?' His scrutiny paused at Raoul, who blinked, then stared directly back, his face as blank as a clean sheet of vellum.

'I saw two men and a woman,' offered Father Otho. 'I do not know if they are the ones you are seeking, but the woman was indeed lovely, and the men wore Cathar robes.' He folded his hands over his belly and smirked at Berenger and Raoul.

'When was this?' Friar Dominic leaned forward.

'At the young lord's wedding. They had a shelter in the bailey near the main gates.'

Raoul said quickly, 'If you mean the ones who arrived late to the feasting, they were respectable pilgrims on their way to Compostela. I spoke to one of the men, and he said his name was Thomas and he came from Anjou.'

Otho began to splutter a protest and Berenger swiftly interrupted him. 'Would you care to explain to the good friars how you were so drunk at the wedding feast that you could not perform the words of the blessing at the bedding ceremony and had to be carried outside to sleep off your excesses? I doubt you could have remembered your own name that night. Raoul, I know, was stone-sober.' He turned again to the friars. 'Seek elsewhere for your heretics,' he said. 'You will not find them here.'

'Were those three people truly at Montvallant?' Claire asked Raoul later as they lay in bed, their limbs entwined in the aftermath of lovemaking.

Raoul nuzzled the top of her head. 'I saw them, yes.'

'Was the man really from Anjou?'

'I don't know. I never spoke to him. We were bedded not long after they arrived.' He was silent for a while, his hand trailing lightly over her damp body. Then he added softly,

'I would rather be damned for lying to those friars than I would for letting them set their claws into innocent people . . . and they know it.'

The night was warm. Between herself and Raoul there was a slippery layer of love-sweat, but instead of seeking the cool of the sheets, Claire pressed closer to him, feeling afraid. 'What if there is a crusade?' she whispered. 'What if the Pope does send soldiers to crush the Cathars?'

'What if the sky fell on our heads tomorrow?' Raoul took her fist, which was clenched against his chest, and kissed it open. 'As my father said, there has been talk of a crusade since time began and it has always amounted to naught. Stop worrying; the darkness always makes trouble seem greater than it is.' He licked and nibbled his way up her arm before transferring his attention to the swell of her breast. His other hand smoothed down over her belly, forefinger lazily exploring, until she gasped and arched.

But later, when she descended from the glorious pleasure of making love with her husband, the fear was patiently waiting to claim her, and the sanctuary of dawn was many hours away.

CHAPTER 6

The summer ripened to produce a burnished harvest.
Bloomy dark grapes and fat green olives were trodden and
pressed to extract their juices under a sky so blue that it
almost cut the eyes to look up. Men toiled from dawn to
dusk, scything in white fields, picking orchard fruits and
nuts, driving their animals to fatten on the glut before
slaughter.

Geralda and Aimery returned to Lavaur, but itinerant
Cathars came frequently to Montvallant, sent by Geralda in
the knowledge they would be welcomed. Extra hands were
always needed at harvest time, and the Cathars, in exchange
for food and lodging and a listening audience, were hard
workers.

Sometimes Cathar Good Men spent the night at the castle
itself and held prayer meetings in the courtyard. On other
occasions, Claire and Beatrice attended gatherings in the
town and the villages of the surrounding countryside. Raoul
and Berenger usually declined to go with them, being
tolerant of the faith but not as interested as their wives.
Indeed, Raoul even went so far as to grumble half-teasingly
to Claire that she was neglecting him in favour of their two
most recent Cathar guests, two leathery old men who stank
of goats.

Contrite, she abandoned her plans to attend the next
meeting and rode with Raoul instead to inspect the

harvesting, but gave her maid, Isabelle, leave to go and hear the Good Men preach, for of all the women Isabelle was the one most taken with Cathar ideals.

'You wanted to go with her, didn't you?' Raoul asked as they paused to water their horses at a stream meandering through the cherry orchards.

Claire looked at him obliquely. 'Not as much as I wanted to be with my husband,' she said diplomatically.

'Sometimes I wonder,' he murmured.

Claire was shocked by the underlying melancholy in his voice. 'You must not think like that!' She leaned across her mount and set her hand over his.

He glanced down at her gesture. 'Perhaps I don't want to share you with the Cathars,' he said. 'Perhaps I fear you will become one of them and I won't be able to touch you any more.'

'Oh, Raoul!' A lump in her throat, she tightened her grip, but he nudged his horse forward and she had to let go. Biting her lip, she urged the mare to follow and tried to think of something to say that would mollify him without compromising her own position. Perhaps on their return to the castle, she could soothe him in their bed, prove to him that however much she admired the Cathars, she admired him, too, and for the moment had no intention of taking any prohibitive vows.

She caught up with him in the heart of the orchard. Silvery-green pears bowed the branches, and the leaves rustled in the breeze. Sunlight and shade dappled both horses and riders. 'Raoul, wait,' she entreated. 'I want you to underst— What is it?' Her voice rang with alarm as he slapped the reins down on the grey's neck and once more lunged ahead.

Then she heard a muffled scream and a masculine curse. Something thrashed in the long grass among the trees ahead. Raoul drew rein and leaped from the saddle. Arriving in his wake, Claire pulled up her mare and gasped with horror and revulsion. Staring up at her and Raoul, his habit rucked around his thighs, was Father Otho, and beneath him, torn skirts at a similar level, was Isabelle. Her mouth was bloody and swollen. Bright weals burned her shoulders where her gown and shift had been ripped down to expose her breasts.

'She's a heretic!' Otho panted. 'The Devil's whore! She trapped me into sin!'

'The only Devil's whore I see is you!' Raoul choked. Seizing the priest, he dragged him off the girl and hurled him furiously to one side.

Claire dismounted from her mare and hurried to attend her maid, tugging down the bunched-up skirts, covering the girl's bruised breasts with her own light cloak.

Raoul glared at Father Otho. 'Pack your belongings now and get off the Montvallant lands.' His voice constricted with loathing.

'You have no right . . . ' Otho began, then swallowed to a stop as Raoul's sword half hissed from its scabbard.

'No!' croaked Isabelle as Claire helped her to sit up. 'Leave him. It is against the Cathar way to kill for any reason!'

'I am not a Cathar,' Raoul retorted, but rested his sword in the scabbard. 'You will be gone by sunset,' he said to Otho. 'I will come looking for you, and if I find you still here, I will make of you a eunuch and nail your balls to the church door as a warning to others of your ilk. Get you gone before I change my mind and do it now!'

Otho staggered upright, and tried to hitch up his dignity along with his gilded belt. 'Pierre de Castelnau, the papal legate, will hear how you nurture heretics!' he launched over his shoulder as he started to limp away.

'And I will gladly explain all he needs to know!' Raoul unsheathed his blade and took three steps forward. Father Otho abandoned his bravado and fled.

Claire helped Isabelle to her feet, one arm solicitously around her shoulders. The girl's olive complexion was sallow with shock but, apart from her bruises, she seemed otherwise unharmed.

Raoul returned his sword to its scabbard. 'What happened?'

Isabelle shivered. 'I went to hear the Good Men preach on the riverbank and decided to return by way of the orchard. He . . . he was waiting for me – he must have followed me and been biding his time.' She shook her head. 'He said he wanted to save my soul from damnation, and when I answered that I had no need of his intervention, or any priest's, he called me a witch and a heretic, and leaped upon me like a wild animal. If you had not ridden past when you did . . . ' She buried her face against Claire's breast and sobbed.

Claire hugged her and made soothing noises. 'Hush, hush. He'll never bother you again, I promise. Come, we'll take you home and I'll find some marigold salve for those bruises.'

'You can ride pillion behind me,' Raoul said.

Isabelle shuddered and clung more desperately to her mistress.

'Better still, behind me,' Claire said quickly, her understanding sharper than her husband's. To have come fresh and cleansed from a Cathar meeting and then to be assaulted by a slug like Father Otho was an outrage to the soul. Raoul's compressed lips and battle-hungry eyes exuded a powerful masculinity that was only adding to Isabelle's agitation.

'I suppose the mare has a gentler pace,' he said neutrally, but Claire did not miss the look of hurt that flickered across his face at the rebuff before he caught the palfrey and brought it to the women.

Raoul descended the stairs from the women's quarters and crossed the hall to his father who had recently returned from the hunt and was still wearing his hawking gauntlet.

'Is she all right?' Berenger asked. 'They told me what happened as soon as I rode in.'

Raoul nodded. 'Bruised and shocked, but recovering.'

'I heard what you said to Father Otho.'

'And I meant every word.' Raoul set his jaw. 'If I trod on your authority, I'll apologise, but for nothing else.'

Berenger tossed his gauntlet and cloak upon a settle bench. 'Otho's been given too many chances already. I would have done the same. I only wish it had not coincided with the results of this wretched papal council.' Going to the flagon standing on a nearby coffer, he poured cups for himself and Raoul. 'I met a merchant from Marseilles earlier today.' Berenger took a swallow of wine. 'He told me Pope Innocent has asked the King of France to back a crusade against our Cathars. The merchant said he'd travelled over the Alps with the Roman envoy. Apparently Innocent has written' – Berenger looked at the rafters – '"Let the strength of the Crown and the misery of war bring them back to the truth."'

Raoul grimaced. The news was disquieting, the words even more so.

Berenger sat down heavily on the bench, rubbing his knees. 'I've been ignoring the signs, hoping they'll go away, but there has been no easing of the pressure this time. Our Count Raymond is walking into a quagmire, and the only way back to dry ground is across a path of Cathar slain.'

'Would you persecute Montvallant's Cathars?'

Berenger snorted. 'How could I? Your mother sponsors them, my head groom's a convert, so is Claire's maid, and you have just thrown our priest out of his living to protect her!'

Raoul gazed uneasily around the hall where the shadows suddenly seemed darker. He had been trained in the art of war – what boy from a noble household had not? But it had been part of a wider education, a chance to work off surplus energy between the reading and writing, the ciphering, Latin and music. Saving this afternoon, he had never raised a sword against anyone in his life.

He turned away, but it was too late. Berenger had already

seen. 'Mayhap it will yet come to nothing,' the older man said.

'I am not a child!' Raoul snapped.

Berenger's smile was bitter. 'We are all children,' he said. 'Only we pretend ourselves into men.'

CHAPTER 7

SAINT-GILLES ON THE RHÔNE, WINTER 1208

The wind blowing down the Rhône delta had made the January evening as raw as an open wound and Raoul was glad of his cloak and the fleece lining to his calf-high boots. In the hall belonging to Marcel de Saliers, Raoul's second cousin, the conversation was loud, punctuated by wine-wrought laughter, but Raoul heard the discord of fear and saw the tension in men's eyes.

Two miles away at the palace of Saint-Gilles, Count Raymond of Toulouse and Pierre de Castelnau, the Pope's representative, were discussing their differences. Berenger, as one of Raymond's advisers, had left for the conference before dawn. It was nigh on vespers now and still no word had come.

> 'At sunrise there is light
> Love comes shining
> I am one with the brightness
> My lady wears a silver girdle
> Gleaming like the moon
> Love comes shining
> We are one with the brightness'

Raoul eyed the jongleur who was singing a spell over the people gathered around him, Claire among them. She was wearing her silk wedding gown and a gauzy veil bound in place by a silver circlet. Her chestnut braid, thick as a bell rope, hung to her hips. He imagined it unbound and herb-scented upon the pillow, or stranding over her rosy tipped breasts. The jongleur was making sheep's eyes at her, and she was giggling behind her hand like a little girl. Raoul's stomach churned with love and lust, and a touch of jealousy.

He turned at a nudge on his arm and found that his father had arrived in the company of a young Templar knight. The cold smell of the winter evening clung to their woollen cloaks.

'I thought you were never going to come,' Raoul said. 'It must be full dark by now.'

'It is,' Berenger growled. 'Darker than you know. Raoul, I want you to meet Luke de Béziers from the preceptory at Bezu. Luke's related through his mother to Marcel's wife, so that makes him our kin after a fashion.'

'Better still, it gives me a reason to claim hospitality here tonight,' Luke said as the two young men clasped hands. 'Count Raymond's in such a rage, I'd rather not sleep at the palace.' His dark eyes assessed the gathering with the wary thoroughness of a lynx.

'Has there been trouble?' Raoul asked.

Berenger laughed sourly. 'Hell would seem cold by comparison! It started off politely enough, I grant you, but they were soon at each other's throats. The legate said there would be no pardon for Raymond while he continued to nurture the Cathars in his bosom and freely employ Jews and other undesirables. Count Raymond tried to placate him at first, even said he would dig out the worst of the rot, but the legate would have none of it.' The anger in Berenger's voice intensified. 'He accused Raymond of perjury and oath-breaking. Raymond said he had come to discuss the matter, not to be insulted, and before we knew it, they were snarling at each other like a pair of curs in the street!'

'Raymond drew his dagger and threatened to kill de Castelnau,' Luke said.

Raoul stared at him in horror.

Berenger waved his hand. 'Oh, it was all posturing. Doing violence to the papal legate would be tantamount to Raymond cutting his own throat and letting the French lap his blood.'

Raoul made a face. 'Even so he must have been close to the edge. He never loses his temper.'

'Well, he lost it today,' Berenger said. He spread his hands. 'De Castelnau stormed from the palace in high dudgeon and Lord Raymond followed his example. Needless to say, he remains outside the grace of the Church, and the tensions are higher than the Garonne after a winter storm.' He rubbed his palm over his face. 'There's a bitter wind blowing tonight, and no place to shelter.'

As if his father's words had conjured the cold out of the air, Raoul shivered. Luke de Béziers excused himself and went in search of their host, prowling through the gathering with the grace of a cat.

'His father is a senior Cathar Good Man,' Berenger murmured from the side of his mouth, 'or so I have heard. He has told me little of himself and I did not want to pry.' He looked thoughtful. 'The Templars have a reputation for going their own way, regardless of Rome. It's a well-known fact that Cathar families send their sons to the Templars to be educated.'

Raoul shrugged, not seeing that it mattered, except that a warrior knight was a useful friend to have. Excusing himself, he started in the direction of the jongleur whose eyes were smouldering over Claire while he sang a suggestive song involving hands beneath cloaks and white naked bodies in flowery meadows.

That night Raoul slept badly. The bed was lumpy and uncomfortable, and they were sharing the chamber with several other guests, one of whom had a snore like the bass note of a cathedral organ.

Pressed to Raoul's side, undisturbed by the racket, Claire slept, bundled in her fur-lined cloak for warmth. He sighed and shifted, wondering how long it was until morning. The snorer turned over and the sound softened to a continuous rumble like a cat's purr. Raoul dozed. His mind became a mosaic of fireshot crystal. He thought he heard someone call his name from afar and, with a loud grunt, woke up again. Claire murmured and snuggled against him. Raoul stared into the darkness above his head, tantalised by the memory of the grey-eyed pilgrim woman – sitting at his wedding feast, dancing through his dreams, leading him through fire and storm.

'What's the matter?'

'Mmmm?' Raoul turned to Claire with the blank gaze of a dreamer. They were riding along the marshy banks of the Petit Rhône on the road to Arles. Raoul desired to visit a swordsmith there who had been glowingly recommended by one of their fellow guests at Saint-Gilles.

'I asked you what was the matter. You've scarcely spoken a word all morning.'

He moved his shoulders and said diffidently, 'It must be the lack of sleep.'

Claire frowned, certain his anxiety was not due to lack of sleep. He had been on edge long before they retired last night. Perhaps it was to do with the boldness of the jongleur; she knew Raoul had been both proud and annoyed by the attention paid to her. His kisses in a darkened corner before they retired had been hard with possession and desire. She mulled the thought for a while, and then set it aside. If jealous passion was the cause, he'd be paying her attention, not staring off into the distance. Another notion twitched her brows into an anxious frown. The conference at Saint-Gilles had broken up in discord. What if he knew things about the outcome that she did not, and was keeping them to himself? She had seen him talking to Berenger last night, both of them looking worried.

'Raoul . . . '

'Ssssh.' He raised an imperative hand.

Claire stared at him, then she too caught the sound of shouting, the clash of arms. They were approaching a fording point; such places were always susceptible to ambush by brigands and mercenary bands down on their luck. It was the reason Raoul was riding with a hefty escort of Montvallant troops.

'Roland, Ansil, stay here with the women!' Raoul snapped, collecting the rest of the men about him.

'Raoul, be careful!' Claire's heart began to thump. She knew he probably hadn't heard her, but her warning was a talisman that might keep him safe.

He spurred off at the head of the troop, but had not covered more than fifty yards towards the ford when a horse came galloping from the opposite direction, reins trailing. He swerved to meet it and made a grab for the loop of bridle. The dagged red leather cut into his fingers, but he held on hard, guiding the grey with his knees, and succeeded in bringing the runaway to a rearing stop.

The bit chains were gilded; so was the harness. The saddle-cloth was of kermes-dyed wool, the border edged with a design of crosses and crosiers in thread-of-gold, while the saddle itself was a sumptuous affair, ornate and thickly padded.

'Belongs to a priest,' said Giles de Lostange, one of the senior knights.

'Not just any priest.' Raoul gentled the trembling horse. It was a showy, highbred chestnut with a chalk-white blaze and hind socks. 'This is no meek ambler and just look at his trappings. Here, Philippe, take him to my lady.'

'Then who . . . ' the knight began, but was interrupted by the thunder of more hooves.

'Ware arms!' Raoul shouted. He swung his shield from his back to his left shoulder and fumbled his arm through the two shorter leather straps.

Six armed riders came pounding up from the direction of the river and jammed to a halt as they saw Raoul's troop. One of them rode a handsome sorrel courser, trapped out as finely as the chestnut – most obviously a recent acquisition.

Raoul unfastened his helm from his saddle and settled it over his head, tugging it into place by the decorated nasal bar. His heart pounded in his ears, warring with the circling drumming of shod hooves. Without further pause for thought, he cried his challenge and spurred the grey, his knights bunching behind him.

The brigands declined to engage. Whirling their mounts, they fled at the gallop. The grey's powerful stride devoured the ground, but the horses in front had too great a start, and it soon became clear they would not be caught.

Upon the crest of a low flood-bank, Raoul gave up the chase and drew rein. What he saw on the slope to the river beyond stopped his breath.

'God's love,' he whispered. A loose sumpter mule cropped the grass close to a corpse wearing priest's robes. The linen alb was saturated with blood and the chasuble was missing. Two servants lay dead nearby, together with another priest and three soldiers. The contents of disembowelled saddlebags were strewn among the bodies like collective entrails. Already, in the pale winter sky, the buzzards were wheeling.

Raoul made himself ride closer. The scene reminded him of the butchers' quarters of Toulouse, only this time he was not looking at slaughtered pigs and sheep, but at men.

Nostrils flaring, ears back, the grey shied from a corpse. Raoul wanted to shy away too, to run and not stop until he reached the security of Montvallant's warm golden walls. Instead, he dismounted to examine the victims.

'There's one here still breathing, my lord!'

Raoul hastened across the smeared grass to where Giles had knelt to pillow the head and shoulders of a tonsured young cleric. Blood was seeping sluggishly from a bulging gut wound, and the man's face was pallid. Giles looked at Raoul and shook his head. 'Dying,' he mouthed.

Raoul crouched on his heels. The victim looked younger than himself, a rash of adolescent spots scattering the grey skin. 'What happened?'

The cleric's eyelids fluttered. 'Count Raymond's men,' he mouthed. He wanted . . . he wanted my master dead.'

'Your master?' Raoul recoiled, knowing what the dying cleric was going to say and not wanting to hear.

'Pierre de Castelnau . . . '

'Impossible! Raymond would never besmirch his honour with such a deed!'

'His men . . . saw them yesterday at Saint-Gilles.' The young man sagged against Giles's arm.

Raoul could not speak. He turned his head aside and spat. When he looked again, the young priest was dead and Giles was easing to his feet, his surcoat soaked in blood.

'Raymond would never be so foolish as to do this!' Raoul said in a choked voice.

'And who will believe him even if he is innocent?' Giles stooped to wipe his hands on the grass. 'A hundred witnesses yesterday heard him wish de Castelnau dead. Those men looked like mercenaries, and God knows Count Raymond has plenty of them in his employ.'

'And they come and go as frequently as whores in a public brothel!' Raoul retorted. 'Look at this; it's more than just murder.' He went to stand before what he now knew to be the body of Pierre de Castelnau. 'Look at him – no crosier, no ring of office . . . God's death, not even his robe and cloak! This couldn't have been done by Raymond's command!'

Giles stood up. 'It may be so,' he said tonelessly, leaving Raoul in no doubt that he was being humoured. Then his gaze changed focus and he made a swift hand gesture.

Raoul swung on his heel to see Claire sitting on her mare on the flood-bank, taking in the scene with appalled eyes.

'Dear God, Raoul . . . '

Feeling as if all the marrow had been sucked out of his bones, Raoul lifted himself wearily into the saddle and rode over to her. 'It is Pierre de Castelnau,' he said. 'He's been robbed and murdered. There's nothing we can do here except send a cart from the nearest village to collect the dead. They're all beyond help.'

Thunder rumbled softly in the distance. Claire's maid Isabelle was murmuring part of the Lord's Prayer to herself, over and again in the Cathar manner. 'Deliver us from evil, deliver us from evil, deliver us from evil.'

Raoul glanced towards the accumulating thunderclouds. Wind began to seethe through the grass, lifting and flapping the dead legate's garment, giving him the semblance of life. He doubted that a voice in the wilderness was going to hold back the storm about to be unleashed upon them, Cathar and Catholic alike.

CHAPTER 8

MONTFORT L'AMAURY, NORTHERN FRANCE, APRIL 1209

Simon de Montfort narrowed his eyes against the spring gale buffeting into his face, and fixed them upon the dark bulk of the keep rearing before him. A thirty-mile ride from Paris lay behind him and his troop, through weather that had grown progressively worse. He was tired and saddle-sore, but showed nothing of this as he waited for the guards to open the great gates. Besides, the news he bore from the French court was a counter to his weariness and discomfort. Ambition warmed him, buoying him up as he rode into the torchlit courtyard and dismounted. Sleepy grooms came tumbling from the stables to take the blowing horses. Stripping off his gauntlets, Simon walked towards the hall, his gait gaining pace as his saddle-cramped muscles began to ease.

Giffard, his squire, held aloft a pine torch to light Simon to the women's quarters on the floor above; a second, junior squire brought up the rear. His boots scuffed on the turret stairs. A woman pressed her back to the wall to let them pass, her white undergown lit to yellow by the sputtering torch.

Simon recognised his wife's maid, Elise. 'Is Lady Alais awake?' he asked.

'Yes, my lord. She sent me to fetch hot wine.'

He could feel the woman's nervousness. She fluttered like a bird cornered by a cat. Scornful, indifferent, he let her go and entered the room

Alais was waiting to greet him, a cloak thrown in haste over her chemise. Her fine, light brown hair was unbound; individual strands floating in the candle gleam betrayed a rapid, recent combing.

'Welcome home, my lord,' she said and curtseyed.

Simon raised her up and tilted her chin on his index finger to study her face. The light hazel eyes and sharp nose, the controlled mouth that seldom yielded to emotion of any kind. A falcon well trained to fly to the lure of his fist. 'Not for long,' he said and, releasing her, turned to the squires. 'Disrobe me,' he commanded. 'Then seek your beds.'

Alais busied herself lighting more candles and setting another log on the fire. Simon checked his impatience while the squires undressed him down to his shirt, braies and hose.

The youths bowed out of the room. Elise, having returned with the hot wine and given the flagon to Alais, was peremptorily dismissed by Simon. He coveted the privacy of this inner chamber. It was the one place he could shrug off his burdens and, like a man unbuckling his belt, let all confined tension relax. The servants had long since learned not to linger.

Alais presented him with a cup. He took it from her, feeling the heat of the wine through the silver, inhaling the spiciness of cinnamon and nutmeg in the steam. After one perfunctory sip, he set the drink aside. Free from the constraint of prying eyes, he pulled Alais against him and kissed her roughly, his hands busy with the lacings of her shift.

Simon was a born soldier, decisive, swift to act and react, and ruthless in pursuing any goal, be it fighting infidels in Egypt, keeping his own fiefs clear of brigands, or satisfying his physical needs after several weeks of abstinence in Paris. He was quite capable of self-denial, but he viewed his body as a piece of equipment; occasionally it had to be overhauled and rested in order to function efficiently.

'What did you mean "not for long"?' Emboldened by his relaxed attitude in the aftermath of release, Alais raised herself on one elbow and leaned over him.

Simon gestured to the flagon. 'A fresh cup wouldn't go amiss.' Arms pillowing his head, he admired her legs as she left the bed to obey his bidding. 'I've been invited to join the crusade against the Cathars as secular head of the army.'

She crouched to set a poker in the banked fire. Her back was turned, denying him her face to read, but he saw her hand pause on the poker handle, and her voice was not quite steady when she said, 'By whom?'

'Arnaud-Amalric, Abbot of Cîteaux. Although it was Burgundy who recommended me to him as all that was laudable in a Christian warrior.'

'Isn't Arnaud-Amalric the papal legate to the Languedoc?'

'He has been ever since Pierre de Castelnau took an assassin's spear in the ribs. We'll deal well enough together providing he remembers that I'm the soldier and he's the priest.'

Alais plunged the hot poker into the wine and brought the steaming cup to him.

He eyed her. 'What is the matter?'

'Nothing,' Alais said quickly. 'You surprised me, that's all. Are there not other lords who would wish to have the privilege of leading?'

'Of higher degree, you mean?' He gave her a warning look. 'Leave the double meanings to the diplomats. It's not a privilege.' He tilted the cup to his mouth. 'It's a pain in the backside. All Burgundy and Nevers want to do is prance along at the head of their troops and show off their best tourney gauds. When it comes to pitching tents in the rain and laying siege to disease-riddled towns with mosquitoes biting to death those parts not already killed by boredom, they'll turn tail for the comfort of home.'

'But surely you do not enjoy that kind of life yourself?' Alais said, drawing the coverlet over her shoulders.

'No, but I enjoy a challenge, and I have the endurance of an ox.' He contemplated his cup. 'I am made for this and they are not. They are great lords with the difficulties of government upon them – they cannot afford to become involved beyond a token commitment.' He rotated the cup thoughtfully. 'The army's to assemble by midsummer at Lyons. Burgundy's bringing five hundred knights, so is Nevers, and the contingents of Saint-Pol and Boulogne will be substantial too.' He gave a contemptuous snort. 'There are always thousands parading their arms at the start of a crusade and making brave speeches by the dung-load but less than a tenth will see it beyond the first two months.'

'So they are not worth having?'

'Oh no, they serve their purpose,' Simon said. 'But you don't use them to build your backbone.'

'You talk as if you expect this to be a long campaign.'

He shrugged. Her expression was neutral, but he sensed her annoyance. 'You don't rush a banquet,' he said, 'and the South is a feast fit for an emperor.' He placed a possessive hand on her shoulder. 'Or at least fit for the lord of Montfort l'Amaury.' Her skin had a silky gleam. She had borne four living children and two that had not survived. Breasts and belly might be a little slack from such toil, but she remained an attractive woman and in her mid thirties was still of childbearing age. Taking a handful of her brown hair, he twined it around his fingers, watching it take on gold highlights from the night candle. Then he tightened his grip and pulled her down to him.

'Simon de Montfort, you are an ambitious man,' she said huskily. He laughed against her mouth and kissed her hard before releasing her. There were still things he wanted to say; the first edge of his desire had been blunted, and he approved of self-discipline.

'Admit it,' he said. 'If I were the kind of man to covet the hearth, you'd not be so eager to please me.'

'Instead I never see you from one month to the next!' There was genuine grievance in her tone.

'I'll need you with me in Lyons to run my household before we ride down into the lands of Raymond of Toulouse.'

'Hah!' she sniffed. 'A camp follower!'

Simon chuckled. 'You have no need to complain. My pedestal is yours, and I know your pride and ambition are a match for mine. Besides' – he leaned to her ear, his breath a hot whisper – 'not every camp follower receives gold collars and bolts of red silk from Paris for their services.' He cupped her breast and caressed her nipple with the pad of his thumb. 'If you are good, you can have them before breakfast.'

'We can't,' Alais protested half-heartedly. 'It's still Lent. Indeed, we should not have lain together just now.'

'I have indeed been absent too long,' Simon growled. 'Confession and penance will deal with the matter of sin, but Lent or no Lent, you will do your duty to me.' He continued to stroke her breast. 'I thought I might take Amaury on this campaign with me. He's fifteen, old enough now for the experience of a battle camp. Tiltyard training is all very well, but it won't toughen him up like the real thing.'

'I am sure it would please him greatly, my lord,' she replied in a placatory voice.

'I'll speak to him at breakfast,' Simon said, pushed her down flat, and thrust into her.

CHAPTER 9

MONTVALLANT, TOULOUSE, SPRING 1209

'Berenger!' Raymond de Saint-Gilles, Count of Toulouse, clasped the lord of Montvallant in a vigorous embrace.

'Welcome, my lord,' Berenger drew his guest into the great hall, his own greeting tempered with caution. Berenger and Raymond had been squires together and their friendship was of long standing, although with overtones of liege lord and obliged vassal.

Raymond wore his years lightly. He had good bones and his olive skin was still tight upon them. He walked on the balls of his feet like an athlete and had a young man's love of gilding and grooming. It was rumoured that his black curls owed more to a subtle application of soot than to nature. If so, the camouflage was superb, for the fine-grained skin bore no telltale streaks or stains. His indolent lifestyle and love of luxury should have left him as fat and slack as a slug, but instead, in his red tunic, he was lean and vulpine.

Beatrice and Claire served the men with wine in the solar, and a pair of musicians was fetched to play music. Beatrice excused herself to stir up the household to provide a meal fitting for their guest, but when Claire made to help, she stopped her.

'No, my love, in your condition you must rest. Sit with your embroidery. I can manage perfectly well.'

'I'm all right, Mother,' Claire protested. The pregnancy had caused her very little discomfort thus far but Beatrice tended to fuss.

Under the pretence of a maternal scolding, Beatrice drew Claire to one side. 'I want you to stay here and listen to what they say,' she whispered. 'If I ask Berenger afterwards, or you ask Raoul, we'll only get half of the tale, and altered to make it palatable. I know Raymond de Toulouse of old. He can charm the very birds down from the trees, and to no good purpose!'

Bowing her head, Claire appeared to yield to Beatrice's insistence, and returned demurely to her embroidery frame. She felt Raoul's curious stare and flushed. She had never been good at deception.

'Do I gather that there is some good news to impart?' Raymond queried with a smile as he settled into a cushioned chair.

Blushing harder, Claire busied herself with her needle.

'In the autumn, my lord,' Raoul said proudly.

'My congratulations.' Raymond smiled, dismissively polite. 'You must send and tell me when the child is born.'

'Of course, my lord.'

Raymond looked down at his thumbs, circling one over the other as if their rotation represented the external workings of his brain. Then he lifted his gaze to Berenger and Raoul. 'I wish my own news were as happy as yours.'

Berenger said, 'We have heard that a French army is assembling in Lyons with the objective of destroying the Cathars.'

'Yes,' said Raymond. 'You have heard rightly.'

'And you want us to help you repulse the French?'

Raymond fiddled with a large cabochon ruby adorning one of his thumbs. 'Not quite. It would be easier for me to stand in the sea and command back the tide with the palm of my hand. The army is vast. Tens of thousands, my informants tell me, and from all parts of the North and the Low Countries.'

'Then what should we do – stand aside and let them do their worst?'

Raymond stopped twiddling the ring and straightened up in the chair. 'I'm taking the Cross myself, and I'm advising all my vassals to do the same.'

Berenger stared at his overlord. 'You want me to take up arms against my own people. Is that what you are saying?'

'It's not as simple as that.' Raymond grimaced at Berenger. 'You can stop looking at me as if I'd asked you to roast your grandmother over a slow fire.'

'Perhaps not my grandmother, but what about the Cathars on my lands?' Berenger's nostrils flared. 'Perhaps you would like me to roast them instead?'

'It won't come to that!' Raymond's gaze slipped from Berenger's.

'Oh, won't it?'

'What did you have in mind?' Raoul asked expressionlessly.

Raymond turned to him. 'Resisting the northern army is impossible. I have appealed to the Pope and I have promised to repent my ways – even down to the humiliation of a public scourging.'

Berenger hissed through his teeth and Raymond glowered at him. 'Yes, Berenger, I would rather be whipped by the Church in token of my submission than have the French trample over us all. I propose we all take the cross. If we are crusaders ourselves, then on pain of excommunication, they cannot touch our lands.'

'You think Pope Innocent will not see through such a ruse?' Berenger demanded with an incredulous shake of his head.

'That is what the public scourging will be about – proof that I am in earnest this time.' Raymond shrugged his elegant shoulders. 'It is inevitable that a few heretics will have to be persecuted, but we might be able to deflect the wrath of the crusade – from Toulouse at least.'

'Deflect it where?' Berenger asked.

'On to Roger Trenceval, of course, where else?' Raoul spoke up. 'His lands succour twice as many Cathars as those of Toulouse, and he is far too powerful a neighbour for his own good, or ours.'

Raymond drew himself up. 'I gave Roger Trenceval the opportunity to stand solid with me and repulse the northern army, and he refused. Whatever happens now is on his own head. Do not presume to judge me, young man. I have to do what is best for me and mine.'

Berenger sighed heavily and looked uncertain. 'You ask a great deal of us, my lord.'

'I would not do so unless I had no other choice, you know that.' Raymond leaned towards Berenger, his voice liquid and persuasive. 'At least if we are part of the crusading army, we might be able to soften the blow.'

'How strong is the intention of their leaders?' Raoul asked.

Raymond made a face. 'Arnaud-Amalric of Cîteaux is a fanatic. As to the ordinary soldiers, I don't know. They're being led by some insignificant baron from Paris, Simon de Montfort. If I have read the situation aright, the bulk of the army will march down here, throw its weight around until harvest time, and then head for home.' His dark eyes shifted between father and son. 'It is the only way out of this bind, Berenger. I need your backing when I talk to my other vassals. You're dependable; they'll take notice of you.'

Berenger looked at the floor. 'Dependable,' he repeated, as if he were striving to grasp the gist of an insult. He shook his head. 'I am not proud to say it, indeed I half think I am damned, but for the sake of our friendship, I give you Montvallant's support.'

Raoul said nothing, appalled, but agreeing tacitly by his silence.

Claire stabbed her needle into the fabric and without a word, ran from the room.

Raymond looked startled by her sudden exit, then he

grinned at Raoul. 'My wife was exactly the same when she was having our son. Her maid used to follow her around with a basin.'

'I think there is more to it than that, my lord,' Raoul said with wooden composure, and excused himself.

He found his wife on the battlements, leaning against a merlon and staring across the orchards and vineyards towards the silver glide of the river.

'Make my apologies to the excellent Count,' she said in a tight voice. 'Tell him I am sick; it's the truth – sick to the soul!'

'I know, love, I know.'

She swallowed. 'Raoul, if you go to fight Cathars, I will never forgive you!'

He spread his hands towards her. 'I have no intention of harming a single Cathar, and neither has my father.'

'But Raymond has,' she said with a curl to her lip.

'We are backed into a corner, do you not see?'

She looked at his hands, at the graceful tapering fingers. How often had she seen them folded around the neck of a lute, coaxing harmony from the strings; how often had she felt their same persuasiveness on her body. It was an abomination to imagine them fisted around a sword hilt. 'All I see is that Count Raymond wants this northern army to crush Roger Trenceval for him.'

Raoul gave an exasperated sigh. 'Were you not listening to anything down there? Whatever we do, the crusaders are coming down on us. We can't resist, we have to deflect, and if Raymond does persecute a few Cathars, it is so that the others will survive. I like it no more than you, but we're caught in a cleft stick.'

'So we persecute a few for the good of the whole,' she spat. 'So which of our Cathars should we toss on the fire? Isabelle? Pierre the groom? What about the old woman who brings mushrooms to the castle?' Her voice dripped with rage, and she saw him recoil as if a flower had bitten him. The look on his face only goaded her further. 'Perhaps we could send for Aimery and Geralda; now, there's a thought!'

'Claire, stop it!'

'Why, is your conscience troubling you?'

He grabbed her roughly by the shoulders; she felt the bruising span of his fingers, and through them the shuddering of his own body. 'Yes,' he muttered thickly, 'my conscience is troubling me, and I am so frightened that I want to shut myself up somewhere deep and dark and never come out. I don't want to wear armour and wield a sword, but this isn't going to go away just for the ignoring. Ah God, Claire!' He sought her lips.

She responded fervently, filled with remorse for the words she had hurled at him. She was sick with terror at the thought of him going to war. The memory of the bodies on the banks of the Rhône still haunted her, the blood, the indecency of sudden, violent death. Raoul might be a knight, might be trained in the arts of war, but he was untried and he would be facing men of far wider experience. Her child might never know its father. 'Why?' she wept. 'Why must they interfere? What harm have we ever done to them?'

He stroked her spine and pressed his cheek to hers. 'We have made them envious and afraid. They have to destroy us before they themselves are destroyed. It is about power and greed and fear.'

Claire pulled away to look at him. 'Raoul, what about our Cathars?'

'They will have to worship less openly for a while. They can take refuge in those old caves in the hills above the vineyards.'

'And the Cathars who dwell on the lands of Roger Trenceval?'

He looked uncomfortable. 'We'll do what we can – stay our hands if nothing else. It's a difficult situation – so little room for manoeuvre.'

She blinked up at him through her tears, wanting to agree with him, but unable to bring herself to do so.

'Will you come back to the solar?' he asked gently, stroking away her tears on the ball of his thumb.

'I cannot.' She shivered with revulsion. 'Make my excuses, Raoul. In truth, I am ill.' She pushed out of his embrace and walked from the battlements. He stared after her, the wind stinging his eyes. When he followed her into the tower, the contrast between the clear light on the wall walk and the sudden blackness of the twisting staircase left him stumbling in the dark.

CHAPTER 10

'Do you ever think of returning to your mother's homeland?'
Geralda asked Bridget. The women were seated by the fire
in Geralda's bower at Lavaur, rubbing herbs that had been
dried the previous summer and autumn and putting them
into storage jars. The common, powerful aromas of sage and
rosemary mingled with the fragrances of dittany, juniper and
lily of the valley.

Bridget crumbled a sage leaf in her palm and gave Geralda
a wistful smile. 'Sometimes, yes, but it is a life I left behind
a long time ago. I was little more than a child when we
crossed the Narrow Sea.' Her gaze turned inward. 'I would
like to celebrate midsummer there once more, among the
standing stones, but I do not think it will come to pass.
Perhaps one day a daughter of mine will raise the cup in
my stead. I hope so.'

'Can you not see such things in the future?' Geralda asked,
openly curious.

Bridget turned her head towards the fire licking at the
logs in the hearth. 'Sometimes, but it takes preparation, and
I do not always court the sight. It is a double-edged sword.
Would you wish to know the time and manner of your own
dying?'

Geralda pondered before mutely shaking her head.

'No,' said Bridget. 'Neither would I.' Making a funnel of
her hand, she tipped the powdered sage into a jar and reached

for another sprig of dried leaves. 'But occasionally I have come too close.'

The women did not speak for a while after that, Geralda's garrulous tendencies checked by the undercurrent of sadness in Bridget's voice. Bridget herself used the silence to consider the direction of her own life. Since her mother's death, she had been drifting with the current, letting it take her where it would, but such a state of affairs could not last for ever. She had an obligation, a terrible duty to her bloodline to bear a child. Mother to daughter, the chain stretched unbroken for twelve hundred years, each link gleaming with ancient knowledge and power.

She had seen the way men looked at her; it would take no persuasion to have one plough her virginity and seed her womb, but she found herself reluctant to take that irrevocable step. There were several personable young men in Geralda's household from good Cathar families, but they did not call to her body in the way that the bridegroom at Montvallant had done.

Geralda said hesitantly, 'Is it true that you are descended from the Magdalene? Is that where your sight comes from?'

Bridget smiled. It was a question asked sooner or later by everyone who came to know her. 'A little of it perhaps, and yes, she was my ancestor, or so the story has been handed down to me. You will never find her tale in the Scriptures.' She could see that Geralda was bursting to know the details, but unsure of her ground were she to ask.

Bridget took pity on her. 'It is simple enough. She married James, the brother of the man the Roman Church calls the Christ, and bore him children. When the Christ was crucified, she and her family fled the Holy Land to find a new life. They came here, to these mountains, and settled – for a time at least. Then the persecutions began. The Christians wanted no claims of kinship to detract from the God-head, especially not female kinship – women of the royal bloodline descended from the Virgin and the

Magdalene. We were blasphemers, to be hunted down and exterminated.' Her voice grew harsh. Although she was talking of the distant past, her vision was filled with the image of her wounded, dying mother. 'And so it continues even unto today.'

'I'm sorry, I should not have asked,' Geralda said with anxious chagrin.

Bridget shrugged. 'The wound is there whether I speak of it or not,' she said. 'Do not blame yourself.' She continued rubbing the herbs. 'My family's descendants scattered. Some were caught and killed. Others settled into normal lives and forgot their heritage. My own branch travelled north to dwell among the Bretons and then crossed the sea to Cornwall. Ours has always been a female line, mother to daughter. We have the gift of healing, and some of us can raise the fire.' Bridget closed her eyes and stretched her palm towards the hearth. The flames licked up, green and gold, as if she had thrown a handful of crumbled loaf sugar on to the logs.

Geralda stared.

Bridget withdrew her hand and opened her eyes. 'It is not always so easy. It depends upon how rested I am, how my mind is prepared. And a fire already burning is much easier than a pile of wet sticks and leaves.' She sighed with melancholy. 'I am one of the few left with such skill. Most are either dead, or the learning has lapsed among their kinfolk.'

Geralda started to speak, then stopped and looked at the door with widening eyes.

Turning, Bridget saw a young Templar knight standing on the threshold.

'Luke?' Bridget sprang to her feet, her sadness forgotten. 'Oh, it's good to see you!' Hastening across the room, she clasped his hard hands and kissed his cheek.

'And you, too, cousin.' His smile was uncertain, as if not often used. He approached Geralda, who had also risen, and was studying him with raised eyebrows.

'Madam, forgive the intrusion into your most private

domain, but your steward said I might find you here and make myself known.'

Geralda inclined her head. 'If you are known to Bridget, then you are most welcome,' she replied. 'Cousin, you call her?'

'Yes, madam. My father is Chretien de Béziers. I understand you are sheltering him beneath your roof, and Matthias the scribe, too.'

'You seem remarkably well informed,' Geralda said with acerbic amusement, and indicated that he should be seated.

He did so, making sure out of habit that he could see the door and that there was room to swing a sword. 'We communicate when we can,' he said, his eyes following Bridget as she returned to her stool.

She felt the intensity of his regard. Like Chretien, Luke was vowed to celibacy. A pity, but she would not push him to break it for all his suitability to be her consort. 'Your father and Matthias are visiting in one of the villages,' she said. 'But they'll be back before dark.'

Luke nodded. 'I have news for you, both good and bad,' he said. Geralda poured him wine. He took it from her courteously enough, but glanced quickly at Bridget for direction.

'If you want me to leave the room, I will,' Geralda said, her eyes full of reproach.

'No, no.' Bridget motioned her to stay. 'Our news is yours, too. Luke?' she prompted him.

He drank, then rested his cup on his thigh. 'The good tidings are mainly for Matthias. Our preceptor at Bezu has some more documents for him to translate – ancient manuscripts from Outremer, recently brought by one of our brethren.'

'And the other tidings?' Bridget felt the heat of the fire burn her cheek. She dared not look into the flames for fear that she would see more than the simplicity of a domestic fire. But as she turned her face from the hearth, her stare was trapped by the gleam of the wine in Luke's cup. Dark

as spilled blood, shimmering like a river with each beat of
his heart.

'The northern crusaders are mustering at Lyons. We stand
on the brink of war. It will only take one small push to send
us tumbling over the edge . . . ' He paused, his expression
filling with concern. 'Cousin? Bridget?'

She heard his voice as if from a distance, and felt his
anxious touch on her arm, saw the drink splash as he moved.
Blood of grapes trickled over his hand like a wound, spilling
to the rushes, spattering her gown.

'I fear we are already in the flood,' she gasped, and covered
her eyes, squeezing out the visions crowding upon her.

The stars seemed so close that Raoul felt he need only reach
out his hand to pluck them from the sky. Cool and silver,
they cast blue light over the horse lines near his tent where
he had stopped to feed his destrier, Bausan, a handful of
grain. The stallion had a minor foreleg strain, and Raoul had
applied a poultice that Montvallant's head groom swore
always worked.

The night was so beautiful it made his throat ache. He
wanted the stillness, the silence, to last for ever. He did not
want to think about the morning and the order that had been
issued by the northern battle commanders to march on the
defiant city of Béziers.

Simon de Montfort was not, as Count Raymond had airily
dismissed him, 'some insignificant baron from Paris', likely
to turn for the comfort of home as soon as the grain ripened
in the fields. In the short time that the armies of North and
South had been united, Raoul had seen the true calibre of the
man and realised how badly Raymond had underestimated
him. De Montfort knew how to command men, how to coordinate and control. Against de Montfort's iron will and fist,
Raymond was exposed for the lightweight he was. No matter
that he had done penance and sworn allegiance at Saint-Gilles
to the Church, he was neither believed nor trusted by the

leaders of the crusade. De Montfort had made it clear that if Raymond put so much as one foot out of line, Toulouse would be the next city to receive a visit from the northern army.

Raoul stroked Bausan's spotted golden hide and stared into the distance, his heart sick within him. He had no desire to go to war against his fellow southerners for a cause that bore so few particles of goodness or truth – a cause that was an excuse for the likes of Simon de Montfort to plunder the Languedoc for their own gain.

He leaned his forehead against the destrier's tawny neck, seeking comfort. Only two weeks ago that comfort had been the softness of Claire's shoulder and breast as she breathed beside him in their bed. It had been the tiny flutterings of their child growing inside her womb. It had been the sight of Montvallant against the sunrise, enduring stone and familiarity. Now he was separated from all that, perhaps for ever. When he closed his eyes, he could see Claire standing at the castle gates, tears streaming down her face, her arms around his mother. There was more to their grief than the fact that their menfolk were riding away to war. It was the nature of that war. 'Like attacking one of your own limbs,' Claire had said.

Like cutting out your own heart, Raoul thought, and turned to watch Arnaud-Amalric, Abbot of Cîteaux, and the papal secretary, a monk named Milo, walking together towards de Montfort's tent. Some men did not have hearts to cut out.

'How's the stallion?' Berenger asked when Raoul returned to their fire.

'The poultice is working well. He'll be rideable on the morrow.' Raoul sat down on a stool and unhitched his sword belt. He had worn his sword constantly since joining the campaign, trying to accustom himself to its weight and feel. Familiarity had begun to settle upon his body; only his mind recoiled.

Nearby, some northern soldiers were playing dice,

gambling for the favours of a camp slut and tossing a wine flask between themselves. Their language, so different from Occitan, grated on Raoul's ears.

Father and son exchanged glances without comment. To bring their concerns into the open would be like turning over a corpse to expose a host of wriggling maggots.

'Raymond stopped by while you were gone,' Berenger said. 'He says the Toulouse troops are to be held in reserve. Any frontline assault has to come from de Montfort's men.'

'De Montfort's orders?'

'Yes.'

'We're not to be trusted.' Raoul stared at his sword belt. The gold wire decorations still gleamed – new and untempered. What he would give for a patina of experience now. 'De Montfort's not so far wrong. I do not believe I could bring myself to press an attack with zeal. If it's our task to take care of the camp and the baggage, I'll be relieved.'

'If it was left to conscience, we wouldn't be here at all,' Berenger growled. 'I'm not proud to admit that we're only here to save our hides.'

'Our hides being more sacred than our honour,' Raoul said bitterly. 'We may yet have sacrificed both. The crusaders won't stop at Béziers and the destruction of a few Cathars. They are just whetting their appetites for the feast to come – the entire South.'

Berenger fetched a pitcher of wine from a nearby trestle. 'I suspect you're right,' he said in a tired voice as he filled the cups and handed one to Raoul. 'I'm going to get sodden drunk tonight because it's the only way I'm going to sleep.'

Raoul took the wine from his father and stared into its blood-red depths. It was rough, peasant brew, as spiky on the palate as broken glass. 'How many cups between now and oblivion?' he asked.

In a simple shepherd's hut on the low slopes of the Corbier Mountains, Bridget laid her hand upon a child's sweat-drenched forehead. The willow-bark tisane had done its work, and beneath her palm, the infant's damp skin was cool to the touch. Bridget was aware of the shepherd kneeling behind her, watching her every move with anxious dark eyes, of his wife wringing her hands and biting her lip.

'Will he be all right, madonna? Will he get better?'

Bridget rested her hand on the boy's brow a moment longer, then rose gracefully and faced the parents. 'The fever has broken,' she said with a tired smile. 'He will live, but he still needs careful nursing. I will leave you the herbs you need and explain how to use them.'

The mother knelt at Bridget's feet, kissing the hem of her robe, weeping her gratitude, calling her 'Madonna' over and again. The shepherd crouched at his son's side and touched him for reassurance, then looked at Bridget. 'We can never repay you,' he said in a choked voice.

'There is no debt,' Bridget said softly. 'As my skills were a gift to me, so I give of that gift to you.' The words had been taught to her by her mother, and were ancient tradition, but each time they were spoken, she felt them shake off their dust and resonate.

'But, madonna, there must be something . . .'

'Nothing more than a crust of bread and a drink,' she replied, smiling. 'I have to be on my way soon.' Leaving them, Bridget ducked through the hut's low doorway into the early morning. The moon still hung in the sky, a thin silver crescent glittering against a pale aquamarine sky. Moths, like flakes of pale ash, flickered through air scented by herbs and summer growth.

Bridget inhaled deeply, replenishing herself in the cool air. The little boy had been very sick, and healing him had drained her. She needed peace, and time alone. Chretien would be here soon to take her back to the Cathar house down the mountain where they had been dwelling this past week. News of their presence always spread faster than a bird could fly. The shepherd was a second cousin to a maid in the Cathar household. Now he would pass the tale of his son's miraculous deliverance to his brother-in-law's cousin in the valley who had the lung sickness, and so it would continue. Again and again she was obliged to give of her gift. The people talked of payment and debt, but it was she who paid every time, as once her mother had done.

'You must never refuse those who come to you for help.' Bridget could still hear Magda's voice, clear and strong with emphasis. 'Break your body, break your heart, but never your sacred vows.' The words sounded so vividly in Bridget's mind that she gazed round in startlement, almost expecting to see her mother standing in the dew beside her. The eastern horizon was ribboned with gold, the moon as insubstantial as a ghost. Her straining eyes caught only the birth of the morning. Abruptly she returned to the hut and with a smile for the shepherd's wife, accepted the cup of ewe's milk from her hands.

CHAPTER 11

BÉZIERS, 22 JULY, 1209

Simon paused in the act of donning his coif to observe the trajectory of the boulder that had sailed out from the town walls and was curving down towards the besiegers. It hit the ground far short of the troops with a dull thud, dust rising from the impact. As well as stones, the citizens of Béziers had hurled mouldy vegetables and dung at Simon's soldiers, all landing well out of range. Unhurriedly Simon laced the coif.

'Missed again,' said his son Amaury.

'What does that tell you?'

'That they haven't got strong enough siege machines or the expertise to man them, sir,' the youth answered confidently.

Simon nodded with approval. Amaury was a good pupil, swift to learn if a trifle lacking in scope, but that would come with maturity. 'They think they are safe,' he said, 'and that is their weakness.'

Taunts and jeers rained from the defenders on the walls. Most of them were in Occitan, bearing more resemblance to Catalan than French, but a few were in the Norman tongue and unequivocal. Simon gave a wintry smile as he saw his son's ears redden. 'Let them have their petty pleasure,' he said. 'They will pay soon enough.' He turned to his destrier. The Lombard stallion was the colour of fresh snow with a mane and tail like an ice cascade. Simon had chosen the horse, knowing it would stand out on the battlefield.

'If matters change and I am sought, you will find me with Cîteaux,' he told Amaury as he swung into the saddle and set off through the camp. Now and again he paused to speak to the soldiers, enquiring of their well-being, assessing their morale. A string of small victories along the way from Montpellier and the capitulation of several minor southern lords had increased the loyalty and respect in which the troops held their commander. They looked for him now on his distinctive stallion, the fork-tailed lion on his shield always at the forefront – sure, strong and victorious.

Arnaud-Amalric of Cîteaux, papal legate to the troubled lands of the Languedoc, was sitting outside his tent discoursing with a small flock of agitated townsmen who were trying to negotiate a settlement that would leave their comfortable lives intact. With his grey curls and rubicund features, the legate resembled a decadant cherub. A power broker, he wanted as much from this campaign as Simon did, and that made them uneasy allies and jealous rivals.

Among the gathering, translating the southern tongue for the benefit of Cîteaux and his scribe, were two knights from the retinue of Count Raymond of Toulouse, Berenger de Montvallant and his son, Raoul. Simon eyed them with disfavour. They were typical specimens of the southern nobility – hostile, untrustworthy, sympathetic to heresy and with about as much fighting ability as he would apportion to one of his own squires in his first year of training. He reined to a halt before the little group and was scornfully amused to see the well-fed faces of the townsmen blench.

'What progress?' he demanded.

Cîteaux glowered at him. 'I told you they would not yield . . . except these few, and they're as much use as a pile of wet kindling!' He gestured contemptuously at the citizens. 'Ten thousand of them are still behind those walls, defying God.'

From the corner of his eye, Simon saw the younger knight clench his jaw and his fists. Rash whelp, thought Simon with disapproval, but he was not surprised. He knew how much the southern attitude clashed with the aims of the crusade. Well and good. Like the rest of their countrymen, the lords of Montvallant would either obey or be broken. He started to dismount, but had gone no further than freeing his feet from the stirrups when he heard a shout and saw Amaury cantering towards him.

'Sir, come quickly!' The youth's adolescent voice was cracking with alarm and excitement. 'They're attacking us over the river bridge!'

Simon jammed his heels back into the stirrups and spun the destrier in a dusty circle. 'Keep them under guard!' he bellowed at Cîteaux, indicating the bemused townspeople, and dug in his spurs.

'Attacking over the bridge?' Berenger said in disbelief. 'Are they mad?'

Raoul shook his head as he watched de Montfort ride away. He was frightened and ashamed to be frightened. He was also angry at the unconcealed scorn he had seen in de Montfort's eyes.

Cîteaux put the townsmen under guard and went to don his armour, pausing on his way to ask Berenger and Raoul with malice if they wished to be shriven lest they become involved in the fighting. His eyes glittered with malice.

'Thank you for your consideration, but we prefer to make our own arrangements,' Berenger replied icily. Raoul said nothing and stormed off.

The undisciplined element of Béziers, scornful of the northern army, had attacked a perimeter crusader patrol post, setting fire to some newly erected tents and killing an equerry. The incensed camp followers had reacted with vigour to the foray. Snatching up whatever weapons were to hand, improvising with tent poles and cooking implements, they had launched a counter-assault so ferocious that it had reversed the townspeople's rash attack and turned it into a panic-stricken rout. As the inhabitants struggled to close the city gates in the faces of their enemies, a corpse became wedged in the opening. The trickle of crusaders forcing their way into the city became a stream, a river, and then a torrent. Camp followers, mercenaries and foot soldiers poured into Béziers, swept onward from behind by the steel and muscle of the mounted knights. The invading forces flooded the streets, carrying all before them in a tidal wave of bloody destruction.

Fat legs barely straddling an Ardennes stallion, his cherubic features flushed with exultation, the Abbot of Cîteaux joined Simon to watch the punishment of the city that had dared to insult them. Simon rested his clotted sword across his thighs. 'Do we stop this slaughter now,' he asked, 'or do we give our men free rein throughout Béziers?'

'What do you mean?' Cîteaux gave him an uncomprehending look.

'The non-heretics,' Simon said with laboured patience. 'Do you want me to set aside a sanctuary for them? Do you want the wealthy ones – those who aren't already dead – to pay an indemnity and go free?'

Cîteaux stared at the butchered body of a woman sprawled near their horses. Blood crawled in the hot summer dust, dividing to become intricate rivulets, reminding him of the sacred mission with which he had been entrusted. Flies already danced attendance on the corpse. 'No,' he said softly. 'Kill them all. God will know His own.'

With deliberate care, Simon wiped his sword on his thigh and sheathed it. 'The decision is yours,' he said, squarely placing the responsibility on the legate's shoulders. Cîteaux was, after all, the nominal leader of this crusade. Simon was quite willing to let the slaughter continue. It suited his plans to have the battle for the first major city of the campaign escalate into a massacre. Other centres of population were likely to capitulate fast when they saw the fate suffered by those who resisted. It was useful, however, to let Cîteaux take any blame that might later accrue to the decision. Turning in the saddle, he spoke to Amaury and his squires.

'Relay the order through the city that no quarter is to be given, no one spared. Tell the commanders, too, that I want patrols organised to prevent looting for private profit. Gains will be fairly divided once Béziers is ours.

'Are you coming with me?' Simon asked Cîteaux as the youths saluted and rode away to their task. There was an slightest edge of mockery to his tone. 'Shall we see what we've gained for Christendom this day?'

Raoul struggled to control Bausan. The destrier was prancing and sidling, thoroughly unsettled by the proximity of the fires.

Raoul, his father and their troop entered the city on the final wave, and only when de Montfort's insistence had made it impossible for them to do anything else. De Montfort needed some men who were not entirely overcome with bloodlust and greed to regulate the others.

Raoul felt as if he had ridden through the gates of hell. Every building was ablaze, even the churches whose future the crusade had supposedly arrived to protect. Smoke roughened his throat and obscured his already impeded vision. Between choking black clouds and bright gusts of flame, he saw the bodies of people cut down as they tried to escape – young, old, mothers, fathers, infants. Bausan stepped delicately over the corpse of a woman lying face down in the street, her arms still clutching the baby she had been trying to protect. Raoul thought of Claire and their unborn child. 'No,' he said roughly, his voice breaking, and with it the fragile armour of pretence. His hands were as bloody as those of the man who had murdered this woman and infant.

Farther up the street his way was blocked by tangled yards of vivid green silk spilling from an open doorway. Sprawled across the fabric were the bodies of a looter and a townsman, each dead by the other's hand.

Berenger rode up beside Raoul. 'This is an accursed day for us all,' he said in a bitter, grief-stricken voice.

From a narrow alleyway between the houses, a small troop of northern knights emerged. Their leader, broad of build and hard of eye, drew rein before the bodies in the road. 'I see you've had the orders,' he said.

'What orders?' Berenger asked.

'No quarter to be given to anyone. The legate says that they're all to die for resisting us. Loot's to be brought to the camp, orders of de Montfort. Anyone caught stealing for his own gain pays like these stupid bastards here.' He signalled to one of his troop. The man dismounted and tugged the bolt of green silk from beneath the corpses. A dark red stain marred the fabric's shimmer.

The leader unslung a wineskin from his saddle. 'Thirsty work,' he commented, offering a drink to Berenger and Raoul.

Raoul choked. Berenger gripped his arm and forced it down. 'Our thanks, but we have our own,' he said.

'No stomach for this, eh?' The knight took a hearty swig. The wine overflowed his mouth and trickled down his chin like blood. 'Better toughen up fast. This is only the start.' Stowing the wineskin, he casually rested his hand on the sword at his hip. 'We'll take care of this and check the rest of the houses.'

Raoul's fingers trembled a fraction from the hilt of his own sword. He felt Berenger's grip tighten.

'Do you have an objection?' the knight drawled, glancing round at his troop.

'No.' Berenger swallowed and, before Raoul could react, booted Bausan in the belly. The stallion gave a startled leap forward. Berenger pressed his own destrier so close to Bausan that Raoul had no room to manoeuvre and had to continue riding away from the potential conflict to the sound of northern guffaws.

Furious, he rounded on his father. 'Why didn't you lick

their backsides while you were about it!' he cried. 'I am ashamed to bear the name Montvallant!'

Berenger's tension released itself in a single blow, the full force of his arm behind the hand that connected with Raoul's face. 'Don't presume to judge me, boy!' he snarled. 'You would have died for nothing back there – for a handful of worthless insults. He'd have taken you on the first cut!'

Panting, father and son stared at each other. A bell that had been tolling was silenced in midstroke, and in the space where the next note should have fallen, Raoul made his decision. 'I cannot be a part of this murder,' he said flatly, and reined about.

'Where are you going?' Berenger grabbed for Raoul's bridle and missed.

'Home. If I'm declared an outlaw, so be it.'

'Raoul, if not for the love of God, then for the love of your family, stop and think!' Berenger entreated. 'I am as revolted as you by what is happening here, but that is all the more reason to stay within the bounds of de Montfort's orders.'

Refusing to listen, Raoul continued to ride away.

Berenger spurred after him. 'What will happen to Montvallant if you desert now? What of your mother and Claire and your unborn child? Do you want to see this happen to them?'

Raoul halted beside a high convent wall, his knuckles white on the reins. 'You can stay with de Montfort if you want,' he said, chest heaving. 'Disinherit me, bring up my child as your heir – do what you will, the choice is yours. I am telling you that I have made mine.'

'Listen, you don't . . . '

From behind the wall, they both heard heartrending screams for help and northern voices raw with excitement and lust.

Raoul drew his sword. There was a door in the wall, usually barred with a sliding iron grille so that the nuns could inspect petitioners before admitting them to their precincts. Today the door gaped at a drunken angle and there was no one to prevent or question Raoul as he urged Bausan through the opening. The convent buildings were ablaze. Coffers, hangings, vestments and altar furniture were piled up in front of the guesthouse. A cart stood beside the loot with two oxen yoked before it and soldiers were busily stacking the cart with the choicest items. The nuns had been herded into a corner, and Raoul saw that there were children in their midst whom the sisters were trying to shield with their bodies.

A group of laughing crusaders were toying with the women, taunting and prodding them with their weapons and making lewd gestures. The screams for help had come from a young nun who had been singled out from her companions. One man knelt on her arms, another had spread her legs. A third, to loud cheers of encouragement, was hitching up his tunic and loosening the drawstring on his braies.

Raoul's blood boiled over. Drawing his sword, he spurred Bausan across the convent's herb beds and straight at the soldier about to commit rape. He swung the weapon, felt it connect with something hard, bite through to something soft, and then grate upon bone. There was a lot of blood, but his vision was already crimson and he barely noticed. Wrenching his blade free, he pivoted Bausan and struck down the second crusader who had been about to leap on him, and then the third. In the periphery of his vision he saw his father leading the Montvallant troops into the convent grounds and directing them against the crusaders.

The soldier sitting on the cart cracked a goad over the backs of the oxen. The beasts lumbered forward and the iron-shod wheels rumbled on the pitted earth of the yard. Raoul turned Bausan and brought him directly across the path of the straining oxen, blocking the way out.

The northerner leaped from the cart and fled across the compound. Raoul let him go and, dismounting, tied Bausan to the back of the cart. He hurled out the bulkier items of loot, including two coffers carved of walnut wood and a handsome oval bathtub, and when he had cleared sufficient space, he clambered into the driver's place. He had occasionally driven an ox cart at Montvallant during the harvest, but it had been a boyhood delight, part of the fun of summer. Now, in the midst of a city that was being expunged from the face of the earth, he was sweating as he turned the beasts in a clumsy circle and brought the wain around to the women who were huddled together like terrified poultry in a slaughterer's coop.

Berenger had dismounted and, with his hand pressed to his side, was talking to an elderly nun, who appeared to be in charge of the others.

'Are you hurt?' Raoul demanded.

Berenger gave him a twisted smile. 'It's nothing. The flat of a blade caught me in the ribs. My hauberk's split, but no worse damage.'

Raoul nodded, not entirely convinced. 'We can't leave the women here; you know what will happen. If they hide in the cart and I pull the cover over, they won't be seen. If anyone stops us, I can say de Montfort bade us save them to entertain his troops.' He frowned at Berenger's harsh breathing. 'Perhaps you ought to ride inside, too?'

'It's nothing, I told you!' Berenger snapped. 'It's taken my wind, that's all.' He turned to the nun. 'Sister Margaret, did you understand what my son said? We are going to try and take you to safety.'

'Yes, my lord, I understood.' Her voice was calm and her spine as straight as a lance. 'We are of the Cathar faith,' she said. 'I do not know if that will make a difference to your attitude.'

Berenger shook his head. 'I succour Cathars on my own lands. I have nothing against your religion.'

'We have a sister house in Narbonne,' she said. 'We could seek refuge there once we are out of the city.' Her lower lip suddenly quivered and she made a determined effort to tighten it. 'Although God in His goodness knows how long we'll be safe there. How can people who call themselves Christians do something like this?'

'It is what they call themselves, not what they are,' Raoul said from the cart. 'Will you speak to the others? We must leave quickly.'

She nodded and turned to the remaining nuns and their charges.

'We're outlaws of a certainty now,' Berenger muttered. 'As likely to be hunted down as these poor women.'

'You can still leave,' Raoul said defensively. 'I won't stand in your way.' Berenger gave a weary shake of his head.

'I can't. I'm as much trapped by my conscience now as you.' He went to mount his horse, but as he grasped the reins, paused and gasped.

'Sir?' Raoul threw down the reins and hastened to him in alarm. Berenger's face was grey with pain.

'I'm all right,' he said, although he patently wasn't. 'That last blow cracked a rib, that's all. You drive the oxen, I'll ride the escort. Go on, make haste!' Setting his teeth, he pulled himself across his horse.

Raoul's anxiety was far from allayed, but there was no time to make a fuss and, with a single look over his shoulder at his sire, he climbed back on to the wain and urged the oxen with his voice and the goad.

With Berenger leading half the Montvallant men before the cart and Roland commanding the rearguard, the small troop emerged from the convent and into the burning city. Buildings collapsed upon themselves, gushing flame and smoke. Animals ran amok, mad with terror and pain; so did people until they were stopped by sword and lance, by mace and club and dagger.

At the city gates where the crusaders had first broken through, a dozen guards had been posted to ensure that anyone leaving Béziers was on legitimate business and belonged to the crusading army.

Pikes clashed across the nose of Berenger's stallion, barring the way out.

'Where do you think you're going?' demanded the senior serjeant, eyeing the troop and the cart with disfavour.

Berenger shrugged indifferently. 'We were told to bring these women to the camp for the soldiers' pleasure.' He gestured at the cart, and when his hand descended, placed it on his sword hilt. 'Lord de Montfort's orders.'

'Women for the troops, eh?' The soldier raised his brows. 'First I've heard of it. The lads'll find all the skirt they want back there. I've no orders to clear any such cargo through these gates.'

'It's a special consignment for Lord de Montfort's commanders.' Berenger looked over his shoulder at Raoul, who had taken his hand from the reins and was reaching stealthily downward.

'Let's have a look at them, then.' The serjeant stepped up to the cart, tugged aside the curtain and stared within at the huddled women and children. 'This isn't—' he began, but that was as far as he got. Raoul's hunting knife drove through the inferior link mail of the man's ventail and punctured his throat. Blood spurted bright and hot. Raoul kicked the convulsing body off the cart and tossed the knife in among the women with the terse command that they use it if necessary. Then he grabbed his shield, drew his sword and prepared to fight the rest.

Up, down, parry, slash, turn and brace the wrist, present shield, left foot forward, right back. He knew it all from the lessons learned in the tiltyard and the occasional tourneys he had attended. But knowing was nothing without the experience of the ultimate trial of war. His breath started to rasp in his throat. His opponent swung low, aiming to shear off his leg at the knee. Raoul leaped. The blade clipped him, making him stagger, but his mail remained intact. He made his counterstroke, also aiming for the legs. The soldier's shield halted the blow, but Raoul used his own shield to batter at the man's face, and then he raised his sword again, this time stabbing upward between the slit hauberk skirts.

The soldier fell, but the scream of agony that rang out was not from his lips. Raoul spun in time to see his father being torn down from his horse by one of the gate guards. 'No!' Raoul roared, and sprinted to intercept the descending enemy blade. He clashed the man's sword aside with his shield and struck hard and low. Dark blood spurted and his opponent doubled over. Raoul straddled his father's body and, snarling like a wolf, fought off all comers.

Then Roland and Giles arrived and the remaining gate guards backed off. The street was suddenly and eerily silent, apart from the distant noises of fire and skirmish. Raoul threw down his weapons and dropped to his knees beside Berenger. All fingers and thumbs now, he removed his father's helmet. Berenger's face was grey, his lips and the tips of his ears blue. Purple shadows deepened his eye sockets and his face was drawn with pain as he strove to breathe.

'Where are you wounded?' Feverishly Raoul unlaced the throat of Berenger's mail hood.

Berenger moved his head from side to side. 'Can't breathe . . . ' he gasped. 'My chest . . . '

Sister Margaret descended from the cart and touched Raoul gently on the shoulder. 'Put him in the cart,' she murmured. 'I have some herbs and nostrums with me that might help him a little. And prayer might do some good too.'

'Prayer!' Raoul spat the word as though it were poison.

'It is man who has violated the word of God,' she reproved him. 'Prayer still reaches out beyond the darkness.'

Raoul barely heard her, his attention on his father who was now unconscious. 'Roland, take his legs, help me lift him into the cart,' he said.

Carefully, they raised Berenger and placed him among the women. Sister Margaret climbed in beside the stricken man and leaned to tend him.

Raoul wiped away the combination of tears and sweat on the leather cuff of his gambeson and returned to the driving board of the cart, aware that they still had to win past de Montfort's outer pickets and into the safety of the hinterland between Narbonne and the raging inferno that had once been a proud city called Béziers – and that they all might yet die.

CHAPTER 12

THE TEMPLAR PRECEPTORY OF BEZU, SUMMER 1209

The guesthouse at the Templar preceptory of Bezu was spacious and comfortable. It was a welcome haven for Bridget, who had spent the recent weeks following Chretien and Matthias from village to village, living in huts, caves, abandoned hill forts and forest clearings. Here, at least, she could rest for a time and renew her energy.

A glowing hearth, pallets freshly made up with linen sheets and good woollen blankets were luxuries beyond compare. An elderly Templar made them welcome, and when they had unpacked their few belongings and washed the dust from their feet, he took them to dine with the prior.

The meal was simple but substantial – baked vegetables and cheese, served with a tart sauce, small flat loaves of crusty golden bread, slashed across their tops, and good wine to wash it down. Bridget was invited to break the bread and bless it before they ate. The prior might be head of a preceptory of celibate warrior monks, but the Templars had always acknowledged in their most secret ceremonies that the Goddess had walked the earth long before the God. She was Ishtar, Isis and Astarte, she was the Virgin Mary and the Magdalene. If the Templars were celibate, it was out of awe for the deity, rather than from fear of being tainted.

Bridget felt the power of their belief settle upon her

shoulders like an invisible mantle. To the peasants of the hills she was simply a healer, to the Roman Church she was so dangerous that they sought her death, to the Templars she was the descendant of the Magdalene and the Virgin and to be revered. And to myself? she wondered as she ate and drank. What am I to myself?

When the meal had been cleared away, the prior brought a cedar-wood casket to the table and unlocked it with a key that had been threaded upon a cord around his neck. 'Since last you were here, another book has come into our possession.' His words were addressed mainly to Matthias. 'While you are staying here, perhaps you would care to make a copy.' With infinite reverence and care, he lifted a small leather-bound codex from the casket.

Matthias, with equal reverence, took it from him with his good hand and held it to the lamplight. The cover was made of hide that had been stiffened with papyrus and tooled with tiny golden crosses, each set within its own circle. He unwrapped the strip of thonging that was bound around the book. The pages were made of papyrus pasted together in two layers to give a smooth, strong writing surface. The script was a precisely executed Greek, although the language was not Greek, but Coptic.

Chretien looked on, curious, but not lit by the fervour that transfigured Matthias. His own gift was for oratory, for conveying a simple message to simple people, distilling the essence of such works into something they could understand. 'What does it say?' he asked.

The ring finger on Matthias's mutilated right hand trembled across a line of ancient lettering. 'It's a Gospel.' He raised his eyes to Bridget. 'The life of Mary Magdalene.'

There was a silence far longer than it took the reverberations of the uttered name to settle into the texture of the room.

Bridget gazed at at the small, battered book. Perhaps it did hold between its pages the proof to others that her word-of-mouth ancestress had truly lived and breathed. But it was something she had always known and, unlike Matthias, did not feel a need to prove. Besides, something was badly wrong. Although it was a July evening and the air as warm as new milk, she was cold. Matthias's voice, carefully following his finger along the Coptic letters, seemed to be coming from a great distance, and when she looked at him, the air between them shimmered as if with smoke.

'"And Mary Magdalene, kinswoman to the Saviour, went in great fear for her life and the life of her daughters, for they were persecuted for their close knowledge of Him, and for teaching His name amongst the people. And so they fled by night from their home and came with their kinsman Joseph of Arimathea to the shores of Brigantium, where they found succour."'

They were all startled by a sharp knock at the door. The prior himself went to answer it, and Matthias quickly closed the book, a look of fear upon his face. The moment of tension was broken as the prior murmured words of welcome and stepped aside to admit the young Templar knight Luke de Béziers. His face was grey beneath his tan, and his clothes powdered with the dust of hard riding. 'Luke?' Bridget rose from her chair to greet him, her eyes filled with worry.

'Béziers has fallen to de Montfort,' he said, and dragged his gaze from her to Chretien as though it were a dead weight. 'There has been a massacre . . . Everyone is dead, and the city is in flames.'

Bridget gasped as the earlier sensation she had felt became a bone-deep chill. Even before Luke had uttered the words, she had known what he was going to say, for she had plucked the images from his mind. She saw Chretien put his face in his hands. Béziers had been his home city for more than thirty years before he took the Cathar path, and his roots still clung there.

'I'm sorry,' Bridget said, tears filling her eyes, 'I'm so sorry,' and went to put her arms around him.

That night, lying on her pallet, the full moon streaming across her blanket, Bridget's thoughts wandered in the direction of Raoul de Montvallant, something that had not happened since leaving Geralda at Lavaur. At one time she had wondered if destiny had chosen him to be the father of her child, but as the seasons had passed and their paths had not crossed, she had pushed him to the back of her mind and half-heartedly begun to search elsewhere. Now, vividly, she could see his face again. She remembered her vision on the battlements of Montvallant, the tide of flame and the bloody sword. He had been at Béziers, of that she was sure, but what effect it had had upon him, she could not know – unless she sought him out. The thought quickened her blood. She saw again his vigour, the sea-blue of his eyes, the white edge of his smile. He was not dead, for the space he had occupied at the back of her mind would have been empty, and she could feel him pressing upon her consciousness.

Bridget closed her eyes and relaxed her body, her mind concentrating on the life force of Raoul de Montvallant.

Berenger opened his eyes. At first there was only darkness, but gradually he became aware of the light and shadows cast by a small clay oil lamp. Chinks of moonlight straggled through a warped shutter and ribboned the blanket at the foot of the bed. The air was close and still in the summer heat, and the room was pervaded by an unfamiliar, frightening noise. Slowly he came to realise it was the sound of his own lungs, labouring like worn-out bellows.

Where was he? He recognised nothing, neither castle nor camp. Pain stabbed through him with each breath. There seemed to be a crushing weight in the centre of his chest. He struggled with his memory, but it was as full of holes as an old, outworn blanket.

Something stirred in the shadows surrounding his bed, a darker shape, its garments whispering. For an instant he experienced pure terror, almost expecting to see the leer of a skull and a scythe in fleshless fingers as in the illustrations of the dances of death painted upon church walls. But then the lamplight fell across the features and he recognised Sister Margaret, whom he and Raoul had saved from the massacre of Béziers.

'Where am I?' His voice was a weak whisper. 'Where's my son?'

She entered within the range of his full vision. Against her dark blue robe a silver chain glinted. Attached to it was a small medallion in the shape of a dove. 'You are in the convent of the Magdalene, outside Narbonne,' she replied. 'Your son and your knights are lodged here, too. He would not leave you until pressed most strongly, but I could see he needed respite. I am keeping vigil in his place.'

Berenger struggled to hold her in focus, but his lids were as heavy as destrier shoes, the weight on his chest like a destrier itself.

'Drink.' She bent over him and put a cup to his lips. 'It will give you ease.'

He managed to take two or three small swallows. The brew was so bitter that he would have retched if he had owned the strength. 'How long have I been here?' He lay back against the pillows, spent. The lamp flickered and the room brightened and darkened by turns like a faltering heartbeat.

'We arrived here at noon after two days on the road.'

He knotted his brow, tried to remember, but couldn't.

'We were only challenged the once,' she added, 'and mercifully for us, they were soldiers from Toulouse and let us pass. The only people we met after that were refugees.'

Berenger closed his eyes. What place on earth was safe from de Montfort and Cîteaux? The cave-riddled mountains of the Ariège and Cévennes? Catalonia? Lombardy? Certainly not Montvallant and Toulouse. Perhaps, like his life, the life of the South was guttering out, all culture, colour, and intellect killed by the frozen wind from the North. He moved his head restlessly. The potion she had given him had dulled his pain, but he was not so foolish as to believe that he was in any way improved. He was having to fight for every breath and his vision was growing murkier by the moment. 'My son . . . ' he whispered. 'Please, will you fetch him?'

She set the cup down on a crude wooden chest, her gaze suddenly anxious. With a brief nod, she hurried out. Berenger closed his eyes and clung by weary fingertips to life.

'Sir?'

The voice was so young and frightened that it brought him back from the crumbling edge of the precipice. He forced his eyes to open, to look for perhaps the last time upon his son. The boy was haggard and bloodstained – no, not a boy any more, but a man. Transition by fire. He swallowed and tried to find the breath for what he had to say. 'You must return to Montvallant immediately . . . tend our defences. Your mother and Claire . . . get them away if it comes to the worst.'

Raoul nodded, tears gleaming in his eyes. 'We're leaving at dawn.' His throat worked and he looked down at his clenched fists.

'I won't delay you.' Berenger's mouth contorted. 'If I am so inconsiderate as to linger beyond sunrise, you must leave me . . . '

'Sir . . . '

'We make our farewells now . . . ' Berenger struggled to rise from the pillow to emphasise his point as the last of his strength ebbed away. 'Tell . . . tell your mother to remember the good years we had . . . not the bitterness of the lees . . . '

Raoul bent his head and wept openly then, not just for his father, but for everything that had been taken for granted and was now lost in the bloody destruction of war.

Berenger reached out and touched Raoul's sweat-stiffened hair in tender, grief-stricken farewell. 'All my life . . . ' he whispered, 'I tried to be a good Christian . . . I think . . . now . . . at the end . . . I want to take the consolamentum.'

Raoul looked up, his eyes widening. The consolamentum was, among other things, the Cathar version of the last rites. It purified and prepared the believer for a higher plane and was taken only by the seriously devout and by the dying, for whom austerity, celibacy and a meatless diet were no great trials. But to a Catholic, it was the path to everlasting damnation. 'Do you mean that?'

Again Berenger smiled. 'I've seen . . . the light.' Had the whisper not been so weak, it would have held a hint of irony. 'The nun . . . bring her now.'

Stunned, Raoul backed from the bed. Berenger had never displayed more than a passing interest in the Cathar faith. Perhaps because he could not have the last rites of a Roman priest, he was seeking the comfort of another form of ritual. Or perhaps it was a final act of defiance.

Sister Margaret was waiting outside the door, reading from a tattered copy of the New Testament. 'It is over?' she asked Raoul as he emerged from the sickroom.

Numbly he shook his head. 'He wants to take the consolamentum,' he said in a choked voice, and gestured her towards the open door. Then he saw her expression. 'You are not surprised?'

Carefully she closed the book and stood up. 'Many times I have seen it. The closeness of death opens our spiritual eyes.'

Raoul envied the belief and serenity shining in her face. His own soul was a wasteland of bitterness and uncertainty. She went silently into his father's room. Rubbing his hands over his tired eyes and stubbled jaw, Raoul slumped on the chair she had vacated and stared blankly at the outer door facing him. A homespun curtain was drawn across it to keep out the draught. A woollen cloak hung upon a wall peg. Beneath it a pile of untidily stacked willow baskets tilted to one side. A pair of worn pattens stood close to the threshold. Ordinary peasant items, speaking to him of an ordinary life that was more like a tale in a book than a present reality. The reality was the soreness of his abused, unwashed body, the dried blood on his surcoat and mail, the terrified scream of a child's nightmare as they jolted in the ox cart through the starlit night to Narbonne. His father's life slipping away . . .

He heard the nun murmuring, but his father's voice was so weak that the responses did not carry beyond the bed. The summer night was close and sultry, with no air to cool his sweating, sticky body. He pressed his cuff to his hot forehead and stinging eyes.

The curtain across the entrance suddenly stirred and the door opened. He looked up in dull curiosity, then stiffened with terror, for the door that had opened and the curtain that had lifted were superimposed upon a door that was still closed and a curtain that hung unmoving to the floor.

'Jesu's sweet life!' he croaked as the light started to shimmer around him. He wanted to leap from the chair and run, but he was paralysed by the white brilliance. A cool, herb-scented breeze blew on his face and ruffled through his hair.

And then she was in the room with him, aureoled by the light – the dream woman, her black hair blowing and her gaze locking with his. Raoul pressed himself against the hard back of the chair, trying to retreat into the wood. She wore a pale chemise, and around her neck was a red cord from which dangled a circular pendant. He could see the individual filaments of her hair, could have reached out and touched them had he not been rigid with fright. She looked at him and then into him. Raoul screamed, but the sound echoed inside his head, never uttered.

She gazed past him into the sickroom where Sister Margaret was leaning over the bed. 'Your father has joined with the Light.' Her voice was compassionate. She extended her hand. He did not feel her touch his face, but was conscious of the flow of her power tingling through him, restoring balance and energy.

Then she was gone. The door upon the door closed and blended with its solid counterpart. A milky residue of light hung in the air. Raoul swallowed. His throat was parched. He badly needed a drink, preferably some Gascon double-strength wine. Did Cathar nuns keep such a thing or would they consider it decadent? He stood up. Although he felt cold and shaky, the fatigue had ceased to burn behind his eyes, and his limbs were no longer leaden with exhaustion and strain.

Entering the bedchamber, he knew what he was going to find even before Sister Margaret turned to tell him, nor was he surprised to see that in death Berenger was smiling.

Bridget re-entered her body. There was a jolting sensation as essence and flesh were again made one, and suddenly she was fettered by the weight of bone, cocooned in flesh and warm, breathing skin. Pressing her hands upon the coarse linen sheeting, she felt the stalks of straw poking through the mattress. She stirred and turned over, her thoughts filled with the image of Raoul de Montvallant. She had seen the depth of his grief and confusion and knew she could help him. Her conscience reminded her there were others who needed her just as much, if not more.

'But surely, this once, I have the right to choose,' she murmured as, facing the shutters, she waited for the dawn to probe its way between the slats.

CHAPTER 13

MONTVALLANT, JULY 1209

'And here, my lady, I have an eaglestone all the way from Cathay, a talisman guaranteed to ease the travail of childbirth.' A crafty glint in his eye, the pedlar offered for the women's inspection an egg-shaped brown stone. The apex of the oval was clutched by four gold eagle talons on to which a ring had been soldered. Through this ring was threaded a silk ribbon so that the eaglestone could be tied to the wrist in the hour of need.

Beatrice took it from him and examined it curiously. 'I asked Berenger for one of these when I was having Raoul,' she said to Claire, 'but you know what men are, he kept forgetting. By the time he did remember, it was too late.' She passed it to Claire.

'How much do you want for it?' Claire asked, trying not to appear too eager.

The pedlar named an outrageous sum and justified it by repeating that the stone had come along the silk route, all the way from Cathay, the land where dragons still roamed at will. He expanded on that theme. The tale was entertaining and the women were in sore need of distraction from their cares. Claire offered him less than a third of his asking price and turned the stone over in her hand. It was cool and smooth, pleasant to the touch, and its heart winked with tiny speckles of gold.

She was in her sixth month of pregnancy and the baby

had been moving for several weeks, the first tiny flutterings becoming more vigorous each day. She had made new gowns to accommodate her girth and, like a nesting bird, had begun to gather the articles necessary for childbirth and mother-hood. It should have been a time of anticipation and pleasure as the sickness and fatigue of the early months yielded to a powerful, waiting calm, but Claire was frequently troubled.

Sitting in the bower, stitching swaddling bands, she would envisage the baby, tiny and helpless in her arms, sometimes with Raoul's sea-blue eyes, sometimes with her own brown ones; a boy, a girl, fair, dark. But then fear would burst her fragile bubble and her thoughts would take a different, disturbing turn. Would Raoul be home for her confinement, if at all? What was to be their future? She knew a pregnant woman was supposed to think benign, placid thoughts and receive no upsets if she was to bear a healthy, vigorous child, but what chance did she have, dwelling on a permanent knife edge?

They had received occasional letters from Raoul and Berenger, but all they contained was daily trivia, nothing of consequence. She and Beatrice had assumed from this that either there was nothing to report or, more ominously, that the men were keeping them in ignorance to prevent them from worrying. If so, Berenger and Raoul were deluded, for Beatrice and Claire only worried the more. They had heard rumours of skirmishes between the northern army and the forces of Roger Trenceval, their information coming without any reliability from men such as this itinerant pedlar. The last they had heard, the crusaders were marching on Béziers. Since then there had been silence. There was silence now. Claire realised with a jolt that the pedlar was regarding her expectantly.

'I'm sorry, what did you say?'

'Lady, I offered you the eaglestone for eight silver Raymonds.'

Was that a bargain? She did not know, and glanced at Beatrice for direction.

'Six and no more!' Beatrice snapped. 'I do not believe in dragons.'

The pedlar gave an exaggerated sigh and spread his hands. 'What can I do? It is a long trudge to Toulouse, and in the meantime I have to eat and buy myself shoe leather. You drive a hard bargain, my lady.'

'Rubbish and you know it!' Beatrice retorted. 'But in consideration of your fertile imagination, you can rest here the night. My steward will see that you are paid and fed, and show you where to sleep.'

'Thank you, my lady.' The pedlar flourished a bow first to Beatrice, and then to Claire. 'May you be delivered of a fine, healthy son,' he added, giving her a wink.

Smiling despite herself, knowing him for a rogue, Claire thanked him and turned towards the stairs, intent on putting the eaglestone away in her coffer. She had taken no more than two steps when she halted and looked towards the hall door. Her heart began to pound.

'Raoul!' Gathering her skirts, she sped down the hall and flung herself into her husband's arms, pulling his head down to hers, kissing him, weeping.

His embrace tightened around her, and he buried his face against her cheek and throat. She felt him shuddering, heard him groan her name, and when he released her, she was appalled at what she saw. It came to her that this was how he would look in old age, a frightening glimpse of what was to come, when he was only three and twenty. Her fingertips caught on some broken pieces of thread on his surcoat, and she saw that the crusader's cross she had so reluctantly stitched to it had been ripped off.

After a moment, he set her gently to one side, his attention upon his mother, who was watching the knights enter the hall, her gaze searching ever more frantically. Claire's hand went to her mouth as she realised what the expression on Raoul's face heralded. 'No,' she whispered. 'Oh dear God, no!'

'Where's your father?' Beatrice turned towards Raoul, her composure so stiff that it was brittle and Claire could almost see tiny pieces shattering from its edges.

'Mama . . . ' Raoul took a step towards her, his hand extended.

She ignored the gesture. Some knights had entered the hall bearing a litter covered by a pall, and she stared numbly at their approach, her eyes growing wider and wider. 'No, it is not true,' she whispered hoarsely, and began to back away, shaking her head. 'No, no, no!' The sound rose in an eerie, continuous wail that raised the hairs on Claire's nape. Before either she or Raoul could reach her, Beatrice had turned from the hall and stumbled back up the turret stairs, still screaming.

Biting her lip, Claire looked between her husband and her mother-in-law, unsure as to who was in most need of her care. After a hesitation, she followed Beatrice.

Raoul rubbed his face and swung around to the knights who were avoiding his gaze. 'Take Lord Berenger to the chapel,' he said wearily. Squaring his shoulders, he went after the women, knowing that the more you ran from death, the faster it gained on you.

Beatrice had fallen into an uneasy sleep, induced by the poppy syrup in wine Claire had given her.

'It was his heart that broke,' Raoul said in a low voice as he stood at the bedside. 'He never had a moment of ill health until this war tore him apart.'

Claire looked at him. He had told them very little, only that his father's body had been unequal to the task of bearing armour in the summer heat, but she knew from his stilted manner that he was withholding things from them.

She had persuaded him to bathe and eat. Divested of his armour, shaven and wearing a blue linen tunic, he looked more familiar, but he was still not the Raoul she had grown to love and depend upon during the two years of their marriage. A hard-faced stranger had come home to her from Béziers. When she had touched his hands, she had felt the unholy stigmata of sword-grip blisters, and when she looked into his eyes, they were empty.

He moved from the bedside and went to stand in the thick stone window embrasure. 'His end was neither swift nor easy,' he said. 'For more than two days I watched him die, and knew there was nothing I could do, that if the truth were known, he was better off dead.'

Claire saw him brace his hand on the stone, saw the pressure he was exerting, and felt afraid. She started forward, intending to offer him comfort, but before she could reach him, he began to speak in a low, clear voice.

Every detail of the Béziers campaign poured out of him like blood from a severed artery. Appalled, Claire listened to the tally of death and violence, rape and murder, and felt its stain seeping into her soul. He spoke of the men he had killed, and she heard the bitter triumph in his tone. Burning fluid filled her mouth. Choking, she dashed to the privy and was sick. When she staggered back into the room, Raoul's braced hand had clenched into a fist on the golden stone wall, and she knew that her husband was indeed a stranger.

CHAPTER 14

MONTVALLANT, AUTUMN 1209

It was savagely hot, and the thunderstorms too far away to refresh the air. Even Montvallant's thick stone walls were soaked with heat. The leaves of nettle, beech and plane trees wilted against a sky as blue and hard as a gemstone, the air so still that even an expended breath rippled the atmosphere.

Raoul lay on the bed in his chamber – not the same one he had shared with Claire for two years. That one had been barred to him for the past month as her time approached. She had shut herself away with her maids, his mother and the midwives; with swaddling bands, eaglestones and all the rituals surrounding childbirth. The only item missing from her encapsulation was himself, and he suspected the omission was deliberate.

He stared at the patch of sky framed by the double loops of the window arches. Blue, solid, opaque. What had happened to the promise? He thought back to his wedding day, to how lovely Claire had looked, how much he had wanted her. The Cathars believed that hell was here, that the earth itself was a cage to contain the trapped spirit, and Raoul was beginning to believe they were right. Only he did not have a deep enough belief or commitment to embrace that view with a whole heart.

Irked by his thoughts and the clinging, sticky heat, he shifted impatiently on the bed. Perhaps it would be easier after the baby was born. Perhaps the focus of a new life

would heal the breach caused by his father's death . . .
Perhaps he was a fool, wishing for the moon.

His mother had taken Berenger's death like a wound to
the soul and had retreated into herself, grief devouring her
substance and leaving her a husk, unable to withstand the
blows of daily life. Recently she had donned the plain blue
robe of a Cathar croyant and taken increasingly to reading
books in the vernacular sent to her by Geralda of Lavaur.
Claire, relieved that she was taking an interest in something, had encouraged her and in her turn been encouraged. His women, his family, had withdrawn into an inner
sanctum of their own and closed the door in his face. Did
they not know that he grieved, too? Or perhaps, because
of what had happened at Béziers, he was no longer
welcome.

His chest rose and fell against his damp shirt. Closing
his eyes, he willed the other woman to come to him.
Sometimes she did, a fleeting shadow skimming through
his dreams. He would feel her eyes on him, the trailing ends
of her hair, the light touch of her hands and her mind
brushing his like soft wing tips. Such sensations were never
more than a tantalising salute. Her visitations were unpredictable and intermittent, and even while they comforted
him, they disturbed him, too.

Of late, denied his marriage bed, he had taken to imag-
ining more than just her eyes and hair. He found himself
conjuring with thoughts of her hands on more intimate parts
of his body, and her mouth pressed to his. Once, in desperation, half out of his mind, he had visited one of his old
bachelor haunts in Toulouse. The whore had been experienced and knowingly amused. Young men with wives in
confinement were frequent customers of the maisons lupanardes that they had abjured nine months before. Eased, but
not at ease, Raoul had not gone there again.

The war relentlessly continued against the Trenceval
lands. Carcassonne had fallen after a brief siege when its

wells ran dry in the summer heat. Unlike Béziers, its citizens had been spared, Cathar and Catholic, but they had been forced to leave their homes and possessions to the victors. The Count of Trenceval had been taken prisoner and languished in a dank cell at Simon de Montfort's pleasure, his heir an infant of two years old.

Narbonne had preserved itself intact by purging its own heretics, among them the nuns whom Raoul and Berenger had rescued from Béziers. All of the women had died, burned at the stake for their beliefs. The day Raoul heard that news turned into the night when he visited the brothel. After the whore had finished with him, he had drunk himself into oblivion. But when he awoke to a grey dawn, nothing had changed. He thought his childhood had died at Béziers, but he had been wrong. It had died in a Toulouse whorehouse, an empty flagon overturned on the floor.

Raoul stared across the room at his hauberk where it hung upon its pole, the mail rivets bright from harsh scouring in a barrel of sand and vinegar. His sword was propped against the wall beside it, the tooled belt wrapped around the scabbard. Grim companions. Every day he practised in the tiltyard, developing muscles, perfecting technique. Daily he rode out on patrol and examined the castle defences for signs of weakness. Sometimes the sense of futility wearied him – he was David facing down Goliath and he no longer believed in miracles. On other occasions the anger came uppermost and seethed so violently that he no longer knew himself, and yet, at its receding, he was left with a growing residue of self-knowledge to which he clung like a drowning man washed up on a foreign shore.

Sitting up, he dragged off his wet shirt, balled it up, and used it to dry his damp body. His gaze returned to his sword hilt, to the iron pommel and its grip of plaited red and yellow silk. The shape and the colours throbbed at him, and the wall behind the weapon dissolved into white nothing. In the corner of his vision his hauberk, too, was pulsating, licked by tongues of silver flame. The taste of fear in his throat, he sat motionless, unable to look away.

Clearly and distinctly a voice said in his ear, 'The destroyers are coming; be on your guard.' For a fleeting moment in the pommel of his sword, like a reflection in a distorted mirror, he saw a vineyard and men on horseback locked in combat. Then, as suddenly as it had come to him, the vision was gone and the atmosphere was still. His chest hurt, reminding him to breathe. His eyes had been wide open for so long that they were watering. Outside he heard the shout of an irritated groom and the cheeky retort of his apprentice, but he knew he had not imagined the woman's voice murmuring against his ear. He had been shown his hauberk and sword, and warned.

Struggling back into his crumpled shirt, he threw open the door and shouted for his squire.

When he went to Claire's chamber, he was admitted somewhat cautiously by her maid. He saw Isabelle's eyes widen as she took in the detail that he was armed. Without a word he strode past her into the room. Two midwives and several women he did not recognise except to know they were new and Cathar watched him with a mingling of curiosity and fear. That the lord of the castle should enter this room accoutred in his armour spoke of trouble too close to their haven.

Beatrice was stooping over a coffer, putting away linen, and Raoul noticed how thin she was. Her haunches were two bony hillocks against her dark mourning gown, and the fabric was gathered in heavy pleats by her belt.

Claire sat near the narrow, arched window, fanning herself and reading. She wore neither veil nor wimple, and her braids were pinned high on her head to leave her nape cool. He saw the graceful curve of her neck, the little loose wisps of chestnut hair, and his heart filled and overflowed.

When she saw him, she jumped to her feet with a gasp and put down her book. 'Why are you wearing your mail? What's wrong?'

'Nothing, I hope, but I suspect there may be a raiding party on our lands.'

'You suspect?' She searched his face. 'Has the patrol sent word?'

'In a manner of speaking. I need to go and see for myself.' Taking her by the shoulders, he pulled her against him and was stung as he felt her flinch from contact with the cold steel rivets of his hauberk. 'Do you shun me now?' he asked. 'When I am trying to protect you?'

'It is not you I shun, but what you are becoming!' she answered tearfully. 'I watch you swinging your sword in the yard, I see the look on your face, and I fear that you are no different from them.'

'If you had ridden with them, you would not be so right-eous,' Raoul said bitterly and, releasing her, headed towards the door before he said other things he would later regret.

Biting her lip, Claire watched his choppy stride. Before he reached the door, she called to him, 'Raoul, have a care.'

He stopped, took a deep breath. 'And you,' he said without looking round.

She watched him leave, her throat tight, her back aching from holding herself rigid. The door closed behind him. Overwhelmed by a terrible sense of loss, she began to cry, her sobs wrenched from deep inside her. The women clus-tered around, exclaiming, trying to comfort. She felt their love and concern, but it meant nothing and she only wept the harder. She felt a strange, bursting sensation in her pelvis and water gushed down between her legs, splashing the rushes, soaking through her gown. Her womb felt as if it were tied inside her by a score of tight knots.

'The child is coming,' cried one midwife to the other. 'Quickly, help my lady to bed!'

The brief shade of the beech trees gave way to the scantier cover of twisted olive, dark cypress and holm oak as Raoul's troop climbed away from the castle and its harvested vine-

yards and barley fields. They headed east on the heels of
Roland's earlier patrol, which had ridden out on its daily
inspection of the Montvallant lands. Sheep droppings, dry
and crumbly, were pressed into the nibbled grass by the
hooves of the passing destriers. The aromatic scent of crushed
thyme and marjoram filled the the air. Daisies and pink
soapwort splashed the crevices. The sky sagged with heat.

'My lord, are you sure this is right?' Giles drew level with
him. 'Would it not be better to turn north?'

Raoul did not answer, concentrating instead on guiding
Bausan over the terrain as it grew steadily more sparse. Farther
up the slope, above the path they were following, were some
caves, well hidden from casual scrutiny and which he knew
were currently being inhabited by a group of itinerant Cathars.

'Do you believe in premonition?' he asked abruptly.

The knight looked startled. 'Never thought about it,' he
said and wiped his gambeson cuff over his trickling face.
After a pause, he glanced at Raoul. 'Why do you ask?'

'I heard a voice in my ear and I saw Roland under attack.'
Raoul's tone was wooden; he dared not trust it to emotion.

'When?'

'Just before I summoned you and the men.'

Giles muttered softly beneath his breath. Had he been a
dog, his hackles would have stood on end. 'Sometimes the
squires scare each other witless telling tales like that after
curfew,' he said disapprovingly.

Raoul made a face. Now that he had started, he could not
stop, even if Giles was not a sympathetic listener. 'When
she first revealed things to me, I thought I was going mad,'
he confessed, 'but then they happened. On my wedding
night she came to me in a dream and showed me Béziers in
flames. And I saw her again when my father was dying, only
then I was wide-awake, and she touched me.'

'She?'

Raoul nodded. 'There is a glow about her, as if she is filled
with light.'

Giles shivered. 'I've heard about demons in female form who suck out a man's soul through his loins while he sleeps,' he said dubiously, 'Perhaps you are possessed. You should talk to a priest.'

Raoul's lip curled. 'I'd rather remain possessed than let one of those crows sink his talons into my soul!'

'A Cathar, then.'

Raoul made an impatient gesture. 'Leave it,' he said. 'You don't understand.'

They rode in stony silence until they came to a fork in the path. The left one led up to the caves, becoming little more than a goat track and petering out before it reached the summit. The right wove down into the valley, usually a tranquil scene of vineyards and cultivated fields, irrigated by a stream that meandered its way between the hills to join the Tarn. Today that tranquillity was sundered by the flash of armour and the clash of weapons as Roland's outnumbered patrol fought to hold off a larger raiding party of knights and serjeants.

Giles looked askance at Raoul. 'Holy Jesu,' he muttered, and made the sign to ward off evil.

Raoul pulled his mail coif over his arming cap, laced it, and buckled on his helm. His gut was queasy, but the sensation was not as intense as it had been on other occasions. Experience was like another cutting edge on his sword blade, and anger was the burnishing. Not that his sword would be his first weapon. The initial attack would be launched by horse and the full thrust of a twelve-foot lance.

Raoul brought the weapon over, resting it on his thigh and across Bausan's pale mane. He fretted the destrier back on his hocks and drove in his spurs. 'For Béziers!' he howled, and charged.

The force of the attack hit the main skirmish and splintered it apart. The knight Raoul had singled out was flung from the saddle, spitted through his hauberk like a roasting fowl. Raoul wrenched the lance head free and swung to meet a challenge on his right. His opponent battered away the bloodied lance tip with his shield and chopped with his sword, splintering the haft.

Raoul threw down the broken lance and drew his sword. He struck and manoeuvred, gashing his opponent's shield arm to the bone. The knight tried to back out of the fight, but Raoul followed through hard, rising in his stirrups to bring down his sword and finish it. The man pitched from the saddle and his stallion bolted. Raoul lashed the reins down on Bausan's neck and spurred him into the thick of the battle.

Clods of dry earth and straw churned up by the destrier hooves turned the air into choking dust. He found himself matched against an older man, powerful and battle-wise. The shock of the blows raining upon his shield sent fierce ripples of pain up Raoul's arm. Gasping, he commanded Bausan with his thighs. The horse disengaged, and a blow that should have taken off Raoul's right arm at the shoulder went wide.

While the knight was still off balance from the missed stroke, Raoul darted into the attack again, cutting two swift blows, neither of which did serious damage. Vision throbbing with red and black stars, Raoul redoubled his efforts. His adversary's horse stumbled beneath the onslaught, and the knight was thrown and trampled.

Sweat blinded Raoul's eyes. His pulse roared in his ears. He gulped for air, unable to take it in fast enough to serve his starving lungs, and yet he dared not pause for respite. His sword arm was burning; his shield felt like a lead weight as he commanded Bausan with his heels, turning him once more into the vicious centre of the mêlée. 'For Béziers!' he howled again, reminding himself of what was at stake, and pushed his will beyond the limit of his body. 'For Montvallant!'

When he regained his awareness, he was standing in the churned-up ruins of the barley field, his sword raw and clotted in his hand, his surcoat splashed with blood and his helm on the ground at his feet. Bausan, his tawny hide brown with sweat, was being cooled at the stream with the other destriers. Corpses littered the field, several Montvallant men among them.

Farther across the field, a pair of his serjeants had taken a prisoner. Raoul swallowed, but his throat was so dry he choked. He stumbled to the stream. Before he could drink, he had to put down his sword. The state of it churned his stomach, but he forced himself to clean the blade on the barley stubble before sheathing it from sight.

He pushed down his coif and, scooping handfuls of the clear, running water, sluiced his hot face and sweat-soaked hair. Then he drank several slow mouthfuls, disciplining himself not to gulp.

The serjeants arrived with their prisoner, a knight in his late middle years, sporting a full grey moustache and beard to compensate for the lack of hair on his scalp. His surcoat was parti-coloured crimson and brilliant yellow, and his sword belt was as fancy as a strip of gilded gingerbread. The knight first bowed, then drew himself up. 'I am the seigneur Giroi de Saint-Nicolas, commander of a reconnaissance detail attached to Burgundy's army,' he said. 'You will find me worth the ransom.'

Raoul squared his shoulders. 'That remains to be seen,' he said in a cold voice. 'I am Raoul, seigneur de Montvallant, and this is my land. What I want to know is who you are, where you are from, and why you were plundering my lands and attacking my men like a common brigand? I am a vassal of Count Raymond of Toulouse, not of Trenceval.'

'I had orders,' said Giroi de Saint-Nicolas. His scalp glistened with drops of sweat.

'From Burgundy?'

The knight cleared his throat. 'You are on a list of known rebels compiled by our commander-in-chief, Simon de Montfort. The word is that you turned traitor at Béziers, that you aided some heretics to escape, and in so doing, murdered other crusaders.'

Raoul's jaw tightened. 'How many Cathars did de Montfort permit to walk free from Carcassonne in return for coin and property?' he demanded. 'More than the pitiful score of women and children I rescued, for certain!'

The prisoner shrugged. 'I only repeat what is said of you.'

'And you came all this way to plunder my lands because of that?' Raoul arched an incredulous brow. The knight did not have sufficient men with him to be the advance guard of a siege party, and he could hardly envisage the great Count of Burgundy sitting down before a minor town like Montvallant when larger cities remained to be conquered. 'You find me worthy of such attention?'

'We were travelling north and foraging for supplies.'

'North?'

'It was always understood that our Count would return home once the Cathars had been taught a lesson,' Giroi said with defensive dignity.

'One they have learned very well, but not in the manner you hoped,' Raoul replied, his mind dwelling on the interesting news that Burgundy had quit the field. So it had begun. The great northern army was going home for the cold season.

'De Montfort remains, and you will gain nothing by taking up the sword against him,' said the knight as if reading Raoul's thoughts.

'Oh, I well know de Montfort,' Raoul said, his lip curling as he remounted Bausan. The northern commander would cope efficiently, whatever the numbers of his army, but there were bound to be limitations. Winter would at least provide the beleaguered South with a respite, perhaps even a chance to regroup.

'He is no longer just seigneur de Montfort L'Amaury,' added Saint-Nicolas as he was granted the courtesy of a horse, although his hands remained securely bound. 'He's the nominal Viscount of Béziers and Carcassonne, and you are deluding yourself if you think the Trenceval line will ever rule again. I advise you to make your peace with him before it is too late.'

There was a bitter taste in Raoul's mouth. 'The peace of the grave,' he said with loathing. 'This has never been a holy war unless the gods have been those of possession and power.' Leaving the Burgundian knight, he trotted to the head of his troop. His body ached from the violence of battle and his mind had become a dull blade, sawing at matters that it did not have the ability to dissect.

By the time they arrived at Montvallant, the shadows were lengthening. Raoul clattered beneath the gatehouse portcullis and entered the bailey. Grooms ran out to greet the returning soldiers, as did relieved members of the garrison and several wives. Claire's maid Isabelle was waiting for Raoul, her dark eyes bright with news. 'My lord,' she said, coming to his stirrup as he prepared to dismount, 'you have a son.'

CHAPTER 15

CARCASSONNE, WINTER 1209

It had started to snow again, fine flakes driven slantwise by a bitter wind. Shivering, Bridget drew her cloak more closely to her body and fumbled in her satchel for a honey and raisin cake and her flask of sweet wine. Five miles to the east across the dusk-blue snow, torchlight twinkled on the walls of Carcassonne, the city that was now the centre of Simon de Montfort's web. Eating her honey cake, Bridget stared at the city towers rising in dark silhouette against the frozen landscape.

Chretien halted beside her and sighed. 'Once we were guaranteed a welcome in Carcassonne,' he said sadly. 'There were more safe houses than I could count on my fingers, but no more. Now they go in fear of de Montfort and Cîteaux . . . and who can blame them after Béziers?'

Bridget touched his arm in quick sympathy and turned her tired mount around. Two more hours of riding would bring them to a village where the Cathars were still welcome and their safety guaranteed. From there they were bound northward, to Toulouse and Geralda for the remainder of the winter months. It was never safe to remain in one place for too long.

Bridget's mare had been reluctant to head back into the wind, and now suddenly she shied, whinnying with fright. Bridget gripped with her thighs and tightened the reins. And then she saw the body lying at the roadside beneath a light dusting of snow. It was moving, lifting an arm to gesture weakly for help. The mare backed and sidled, her ears flat to her skull, and Bridget was hard-pressed to keep her calm.

Chretien dismounted and stooped to the figure, gently turning it by the leading shoulder. 'It's a priest,' he said, 'a black friar,' and momentarily recoiled.

Bridget dismounted from the mare, keeping hold of the reins as she joined her uncle. Her stomach churned as she looked upon the ashen, cadaverous features of a young friar. Blood was trickling from a jagged cut on his forearm where he had landed upon a sharp stone hidden by the snow. He had been bleeding for some time, for his aura was weak with impending death. It was also murkily unbalanced. Like Chretien, she recoiled. Men such as this had murdered her mother and mutilated Matthias.

'Can you do anything for him?' Chretien asked, his tone carefully neutral.

Never had Bridget been so tempted to say that she could not. In another hour the priest would be dead of blood loss and exposure, and better so for the world. And yet it was her sacred duty to preserve life, and she had no right to withhold her skills. For what the priests had done to her mother, she would have passed on by, but for the tenets of her mother's belief, she laid her hand upon the friar's wound. 'I do not know that it is my belief any longer,' she murmured as she summoned the healing energy from deep within her, and concentrated upon the man's damaged flesh. In her mind's eye she received a sudden image of a mountaintop crowned by the sacred lightning fire and the priest staring towards the summit with the predatory eyes of a wolf.

The bleeding slowed and stopped. Feeling chilled to the core and shaken, Bridget removed her hand. 'He will live,' she said with a shudder, 'but we will have to bring him with us.'

'And jeopardise the villagers?' Chretien shook his head. 'We cannot.'

'It is either that or take him to Carcassonne.'

Chretien chewed his lip and stared over his shoulder at the way they had come. 'I suppose we must bring him to de Montfort's lair,' he said reluctantly at last.

The young friar groaned softly and opened his eyes. They fixed and then widened upon Bridget, and his chest heaved.

'Lie still,' she soothed. 'You are safe now and help is at hand.'

'*Ave Maria, Regina Caelorum*,' he whispered, and fainted away.

'What did he say?' Matthias cocked his hand behind his ear.

'He saluted me as Mary, Queen of Heaven,' Bridget said wryly. 'He is like all his kind. So near and yet so far from the truth. If I told him the truth, that her blood is mine, he would burn me for a blaspheming heretic.'

Simon gnawed the trimmed end of his goose-quill pen, a deep frown linking his brows. He felt bone-weary and, despite the lynx-pelt robe across his knees and the beaver-skin lining to his cloak, he was cold. Whoever said that the southern winters were mild was a liar. Several times he had been caught in the snow; indeed, there had been a blizzard howling when Albi had surrendered. The Haut-Languedoc was a series of sugarloaf humps on the horizon, and at night, the howling of wolves sounded like the wailing of lost souls.

Not that Simon permitted either wolves or weather to hold him back. Snow, rain and hail were concealing mantles through which a small army could move to take an unsuspecting enemy, and he had need of every ruse at his command.

Roger Trenceval had died in prison of dysentery, and Simon was now Viscount of Béziers and Carcassonne, a title that sounded impressive but was in fact so precarious he felt as if he was tempting fate every time he signed himself thus. In defiance, he did so with a bold flourish.

Despite his drastically reduced army, he had commenced the winter season with some success. Limoux and Albi had both surrendered to him, as well as a complement of smaller towns. But then the sharper local barons had started to realise how few men he actually had, and had pursued rebellion with renewed vigour. Simon had been forced to give ground, and although he had lost nothing strategic yet, he had been compelled to yield several minor fortresses to the rebels.

Infected by the insurrection, the Count of Foix, a former reluctant ally of Simon's, had turned against him and refused to let him mount garrisons on any of his territory. Pedro of Aragon, Simon's theoretical suzerain, would not accept his homage or recognise his titles. As far as the King of Aragon was concerned, the Viscount of Béziers and Carcassonne was Roger Trenceval's infant son, and Simon had no credibility. Simon might not have his back to the wall, but he was close enough to feel the stones constricting his sword arm.

He stared at the logs in the hearth, lit red from beneath and flaking to grey. It was pear wood, aromatic and clean-burning. A pair of alaunts dozed before it. Giffard, who should have been polishing Simon's spurs, had fallen asleep with his mouth open. It was late. The triple candlestick near his hand was knobbed with strings of congealed wax, and the candles had burned down very low. Leaning over the parchment to write, he discovered that the ink had dried on the end of his quill.

Muttering impatiently, he retrimmed the quill with his penknife and sought the ink horn, determined to finish this letter to Pope Innocent.

The lords who took part in the crusade have left me almost surrounded by the enemies of Jesus Christ who occupy the mountains and the hills. I cannot govern the land any longer without your help and that of the faithful. The country has been impoverished by the ravages of war. The heretics have destroyed or abandoned some of their

castles, but they have kept others which they intend to defend.
I must pay the troops that remain with me at a much higher
rate than I would in other wars. I have been able to keep a
few soldiers only by doubling their wages . . .

Simon paused again to gain control of the frustration that
was running away with his pen, and tipped wine from the
almost full flagon into his cup. He drank slowly, spacing
each swallow. When his mind was calm, he finished the
letter, sanded and sealed it, and put it on the pile of documents waiting to be dispatched. Then he drew a fresh sheet
of parchment towards him and wrote to his wife. It was a
commander's letter to a quartermaster – brisk, efficient and
lacking in sentiment; nor, when Alais received it, would she
expect any. Yet he missed the silver flash of her needle in a
quiet corner, her solicitous regard for his welfare, her pride
in his accomplishments. Had the winter season not been so
fraught with difficulty, and had he not needed her to raise
support for him in the North, he would have kept her with
him at Carcassonne.

He finished the letter. The wine had made him light-
headed. Leaving Giffard to sleep, Simon wound his way
slowly down to the great hall, intent on finding a hunk of
bread and sausage to sustain him through at least another
hour of letter-writing.

Here, soldiers and officials were still going about their
business. Simon ordered someone's squire to bring him food
and, rubbing his hands, walked slowly to the warmth of the
fire.

Even before Simon had reached the comfort of the hearth,
there was a disturbance at the lower end of the hall as two
guards entered, bearing between them the unconscious form
of a Dominican friar. They approached the fire, but hesitated when they saw Simon.

'Come,' Simon beckoned.

Snow melting from their cloaks, the men set the friar down

before the hearth. His garments were sodden and water from his tonsure trickled down his ashen face.

'Three pilgrims brought him to the gate, sir,' explained one of the guards, wiping his nose on his sleeve. 'Said they found him on the road in the snow with an injured arm. Put his foot in a rabbit hole, so they think.'

Simon grunted. 'Foolish to be abroad in this weather,' he said. 'All right, back to your posts. Fetch my chaplain on your way and let him attend to this man.'

'Yes, sir.'

The soldiers trooped out. At Simon's feet, the young friar groaned and licked his lips. His eyelids fluttered open, revealing irises of a brown so dark that they were almost indistinguishable from the black of the pupil.

'I saw her,' he croaked, focusing hazily on Simon. He extended a shaking hand to clutch at the hem of Simon's tunic. 'I saw her on the road.'

'Saw who?' Simon looked down at the young friar's grip and felt unease prickle down his spine.

'The Blessed Virgin, mother of our Lord Jesus Christ. She appeared to me in a vision and told me that I would be saved.' The young man released Simon's robe and struggled to sit up. 'I know it was her. She wore a blue cloak and her body shone with light, and when she touched my arm, the pain disappeared!'

'You were brought in by three pilgrims,' Simon said. 'Perhaps you ought to wait for my chaplain before you say more.'

'You do not believe me?'

'I believe that you are suffering from shock and exposure,' Simon said evenly. 'Certainly you may have seen something, but you will be better able to judge reality once you have recovered.'

'I saw her, I tell you, I saw her. Do you think I would not know?' Tears filled the young Dominican's eyes. 'I had fallen on a sharp stone and was bleeding my life into the snow

when she came to me and put her fingers over the wound –
look!' He pushed up the saturated sleeve of his habit and
exposed his thin white forearm to Simon. The flesh was
bisected by a jagged red slash, deep and cruel, but it was not
bleeding. 'It's a miracle!'

Perhaps, thought Simon, the bitter cold itself had
stopped the flow. Then again, like Saul on the road to
Damascus, perhaps the young friar truly had experienced
a holy presence and been miraculously saved. Such things
did happen. Being a pragmatic man, wary of mysticism,
Simon preferred to reserve judgement for when the invalid
had fully recuperated from his ordeal.

Returning to his chambers with a platter of food, he
dismissed the friar from his mind and settled down by the
fire to finish his writing.

CHAPTER 16

TOULOUSE, SPRING 1210

Outside the great hall of Count Raymond's palace on the south side of the city of Toulouse, Raoul unbuckled his sword belt, handed his weapon to a guard, and strode into the room on the heels of the steward who announced him.

Raymond did not rise from his seat on the dais and bounce down the room to greet Raoul as he would have done only six months ago. That kind of optimism had been knocked out of him by the endless shock of warfare and Rome's icy rejection of all his recent attempts at conciliation.

Raoul's stride, however, was purposeful. He had learned that to hesitate was to make men take less notice of him because of his youth, indeed to dismiss and patronise him as Raymond had once done at Montvallant. The Béziers campaign and the months since then had taught Raoul his own value, and beyond that, his values.

He bent the knee before the dais, but rose the moment he was commanded and looked Raymond straight in the eyes. Raymond had been absent from his lands all winter, attempting to muster support in France and forgiveness in Rome, with success in neither venture. His face revealed the disappointments. Lines that had once been lightly etched were carved deep into skin now sallow and missing its vital glow.

'Welcome, Raoul, and thank you for coming.'

It was not the Count who spoke the formal words. Raoul

turned to regard the youth who, with guidance from his advisers, had ruled Toulouse during Raymond's winter absence. In the time-honoured way, he, too, was called Raymond, but to avoid confusion, he had been known to familiars from birth as Rai. He was a pleasant youngster who showed signs of being less indolent than his father, having inherited from his Plantagenet mother a streak of Angevin dynamism. But he was only fourteen years old, and raw to politics.

Wearily Raoul inclined his head and took the chair and the cup of wine that were offered.

'I was sorry to hear about your father,' the Count said. 'We had been friends since childhood; I was a groomsman at his wedding to your mother and I helped them celebrate your birth.' He shook his head and picked up his cup. 'I thought we still had many years and grey hairs left to share.'

'He was at peace when he died,' Raoul gave Raymond a challenging look. 'He took the consolamentum.'

The cup halted on Raymond's lower lip. He stared.

'He asked for the Cathar rites, and they were bestowed on him by a nun we rescued from Béziers. I learned later that she . . . that she was burned during the persecutions in Narbonne. I believe my father took the consolamentum in defiance of all that we witnessed in Béziers, but I know he also found peace.'

Raymond continued to stare. 'Are you of their persuasion?'

Raoul smiled sourly. 'Does it matter, my lord? We are not being harried for our beliefs, but for our lands and titles and our freedom.' Bleak humour glinted in his eyes. 'Are you going to clap me in irons and confiscate my possessions? Is that why you wanted to see me?'

'Of course it is not!' Raymond sounded both offended and shocked that Raoul should think such a thing. He held out his hands in a gesture designed to disarm and placate. 'We know you acquitted yourself well at Béziers, and since then you have destroyed a Burgundian raiding party on your lands.' He paused to let the flattery sink in. The pause was so deliberate that it served to increase Raoul's suspicion and he neither relaxed nor smiled.

Raymond cleared his throat. 'We need to organise and train fighting men to repulse de Montfort. Now that reinforcements are arriving from the North, he's gone on the offensive again. Toulouse is less than fifty miles from his boundaries.'

'You want me to help you organise resistance to de Montfort?'

Raymond nodded. 'We've started recruiting men from the towns and from the families whom de Montfort has dispossessed. We also have some Gascon and Spanish mercenaries, and we've been promised aid from the Count of Foix.'

Raoul said nothing. He looked down at his hands. Once, not so long ago, they had been soft and manicured, the right thumbnail cultivated for dalliance with a lute. Now his palms were as hard as boiled leather, and his damaged nails were clipped short, almost to the quick. A glance at the Count's hands showed him that the ruby cabochon ring still glowed on Raymond's thumb like a clot of fresh blood. Everything came back to blood, even his dreams of the grey-eyed woman.

Frowning, he looked up. 'I was declared a rebel at Béziers and my lands forfeit. Housing and training men will only compound my crime.'

'It will also strengthen your position and make you less of a tempting morsel to be swallowed in one gulp.'

'Indeed,' Rai interrupted with devilish grin, 'none but de Montfort and Cîteaux will dare tackle you.'

'Is that supposed to reassure me?' Raoul demanded but almost smiled in return. 'My lords, I accept your offer, assuming, of course, that you are prepared to pay the wages of the men you billet upon me and any expenses I incur beyond my feudal dues. I think it best if we know where we stand.'

The Count extended a pleading hand. 'Your feudal oath I can have for the acting of a ceremony, but I must know that it goes deeper than the mere mouthing of words.'

Raoul bit back the retort that his father had died proving his loyalty to the house of Toulouse and that he himself had been branded an outlaw. He knew what Raymond wanted, and that it was impossible to give. He was not Berenger, and the halcyon summers the Count and his father had enjoyed were thirty years in the past.

'My lord, I realise that honour is as difficult to find these days as a virgin in a brothel, but I hope that mine is still sufficiently intact that you do not doubt it.'

Raymond lowered his arm. The lines bracketing his mouth deepened. 'I doubt everything.'

There was a brief, strained silence. 'How is your wife?' Raymond asked. 'You have a son now, so I hear.'

If Raoul's expression had been guarded before, now it became as impenetrable as an enclosed jousting helm. 'It was a difficult birth, my lord, but Claire has recovered well and Guillaume is a fine, strong infant.' His voice softened as he spoke of his son. Guillaume was his at least, even if he seemed to be losing Claire.

'That is most excellent news; I am pleased for you.' Raymond's voice was over-hearty. 'If you want a foster home for him when he's ready for squirehood, you need look no further than my own household. I will be delighted to have him.'

Raoul gave a strained smile. 'Thank you, my lord,' he said courteously, knowing he would not send Guillaume into the house of Toulouse for training unless he was forced.

The rushes carpeting the floor of the Cathar meeting room in Toulouse were strewn with fragrant herbs and gilded with sunshine. Numerous bolts of fabric were stacked around the walls for the warehouse belonged to a wealthy mercer. Flemish broadcloths and plaids, striped damasks and sarcenets from Marseilles, Italian silks in glowing gemstone colours provided an opulent backdrop to the compelling voice of Chretien de Béziers.

Seated among the congregation, Claire felt a tingle run up her spine as she listened to him speak and absorbed the simple message of love and compassion he was conveying. Glancing at the rapt faces of the other listeners, she was assailed by a poignant rush of emotion. Here, in this sun-filled room, it was so easy to believe and to belong. She could live in this moment for the rest of her life.

Chretien de Béziers ceased speaking to drink from a wooden cup of water on the table beside him. While he rested, a young woman took his place.

'That's her,' whispered Isabelle to her mistress. 'That's the one I saw at the meeting yesterday.'

Claire shifted the warm weight of her sleeping son into the crook of her other arm and studied the Cathar woman. She was small and slender with a neat braid of glossy black hair and golden skin that caught and reflected the light. Her eyes were a clear, pale grey, her features fine but strong; however, her true presence lay beyond mere physical traits.

When she spoke, her voice was low and clear, so controlled that she did not need to raise it to make herself heard. 'Even Pope Innocent and the Abbot of Cîteaux have the ability to find the Light within their hearts if only they would search.' Her gaze held the crowd, and it was as if she spoke to each person as an individual. 'Even Simon de Montfort.'

There were angry mutters from some members of the audience.

'Even Simon de Montfort,' she repeated with emphasis.

Claire perceived a radiance around her like the glow from a beeswax candle, steady and bright.

'Do you see it, my lady?' Isabelle whispered excitedly.

A tiny thrill ran up Claire's spine. She shushed her maid and stared at the radiance while it expanded from its source to fill the entire room with a golden luminescence before slowly subsiding like rings fading from a ripple in a pool.

The woman smiled in reassurance at the staring, awestruck congregation. 'Do not be afraid,' she said. 'It is only that the glow of my spirit is more easily perceived. Everyone carries this within themselves, and they can learn how to set it free.'

She sat down quietly in a corner and Chretien de Béziers resumed his sermon.

The meeting ended as was customary with a recital of the Lord's Prayer and the laying on of hands. The bolder members of the congregation clustered around Bridget to speak to her, and although the meeting had officially ended, still many people lingered to talk among themselves or to Chretien de Béziers and an older, grey-bearded man with a mutilated right hand, who had not taken part in the sermon.

Claire knew she ought to leave. By now Raoul would be back at their lodging after his visit to Count Raymond, but she was reluctant to depart this atmosphere of warmth and companionship for the tensions of her marital hearth. Besides, she was curious about the Cathar woman, and wanted to know how the glow of spirit she had seen could be set free in herself.

As she pinned her cloak and adjusted her wimple, Guillaume woke up and started to cry with hunger. Claire seized upon the excuse to remain in the haven a while longer. Retiring to a corner of the room, she unlaced her bodice and put Guillaume to her breast, her modesty sheltered by her cloak. She had chosen to suckle him herself rather than hand him over to a wet nurse. He was her child and he would take his sustenance from her. He fed vigorously. He was securely swaddled to ensure his limbs would grow straight. She looked at his working jaws, at his skin so fine that it was almost translucent. His eyes, a warm, caramel-brown, reflected her own as he returned her scrutiny. Gently she traced the line of one feathery eyebrow and felt a deep surge of protective love.

'What a beautiful baby.'

Claire lifted her head and met the crystal gaze of the Cathar woman.

'How old is he?'

Claire did not ask how the woman knew Guillaume's gender. 'He was born in the autumn,' she murmured. *And my husband wept at my bedside, his surcoat soaked with the blood of the men he had killed.* The words sprang into her mind unbidden, and as surely as if she had uttered them aloud, she saw the Cathar woman's brows move in response.

'May I hold him?'

After a brief hesitation Claire gave him to the woman.

Bridget cradled him and spoke to him softly. 'You need not fear for your son,' she murmured to Claire. 'His life will be touched by this war, but his destiny lies beyond it.'

'You can see the future?' Claire asked with a mingling of eagerness and fear.

'Distantly. Each person chooses the path he takes, but I see your son's road with all its branches attaining full manhood, and he will have offspring of his own.' She touched his soft cheek.

'The Cathars teach that the world is evil; I can see that,' Claire said haltingly. 'But if I become one, do I have to renounce everything? It would kill me to be parted from Guillaume.'

Bridget shook her head. 'Of course you do not have to renounce him. Only the elect are called upon to go so far, and even then there is room for difference of custom. Chretien de Béziers is my uncle, a strict Cathar, but he loves and cares for me as I love and care for him. You must not feel guilty for the love you bear your son . . . or your husband.'

Claire gasped. 'Do you see everything?' Her lower lip trembled. 'Are we all soul-naked before you?'

Bridget gently returned Guillaume to Claire's arms. 'Not everything. If I wish, I can draw a veil across my perceptions. Indeed, sometimes it is necessary, otherwise I would go mad.' She deliberated for a moment, then added, 'I was at your wedding with my uncle and our companion Matthias. You would not have noticed us because we arrived late to claim a night's hospitality. I felt the attraction between yourself and your husband then, but I think that somewhere between then and now you have lost sight of each other.'

Claire bit her lip. 'Raoul has taken to the sword for his comfort since his father died. I do love him, but to see him taking pleasure in the spilling of blood sickens me. I . . . ' She stopped speaking and made a small gesture. 'You can see all this anyway, so why am I shaming myself by telling you?'

'There is no shame in unburdening your troubles.' Bridget set a compassionate hand on Claire's shoulder. 'Sometimes I long to do the same. It can be so lonely even when there are people all around you. It is too easy to reach out and touch nothing.' She looked sad. 'The spilling of blood is for his conscience, not yours. Perhaps part of his taking comfort in warfare is the fact that you are shutting him out. I have felt . . . '

'Felt what?' Claire demanded.

Bridget shook her head. She had felt his need, his longing, unsubtle and fierce. 'I have felt his loneliness,' she temporised. 'I say to you that you have time to grow and consider all paths before you take your own road. For now, your doubts make a decision impossible.'

'How long must I wait?'

'Live each day as it comes, and when the time is right, you will know.'

'How?' Claire beseeched her. 'How will I know?'

'Because you will not need to ask.' Bridget gave her an enigmatic, sad smile and started to turn away. 'Go home to your husband now. He is becoming anxious.'

She watched Claire give Guillaume to the maid and go quietly, almost chastened, to the door. Equally subdued, her head bowed, Bridget sat down to recover her own composure. It was difficult to offer impartial advice when the future, whichever branch was chosen, was a vast sheet of fire.

CHAPTER 17

MONTVALLANT, SPRING 1211

The forge attached to Montvallant's armoury was a dragon's den of red and black shadows – hotter and sweatier than a brothel bedroom, according to Jean the armourer, a pithy sixty-year-old who retained as much brawn in his arms as a man half his age.

The youngest apprentice was working like a demon with the bellows to keep the fire fed with air while Jean's adolescent son stood over an anvil, beating a lance tip into shape with a round-ended hammer. Sweat shone on his corded forearms and in the hollow of his strong young throat. Jean himself sat in the adjoining, cooler armoury, pitcher of wine to hand as he fashioned hauberk links from strips of wrought wire.

Raoul flexed his shoulders, testing the altered coat of mail for ease of movement. The rigorous training of the past year and the attainment of full physical maturity had increased his breadth so that the hauberk fashioned for him at the age of twenty was no longer the meticulous fit it had been at Béziers.

A troop of horsemen clattered into the ward. The leading horse was a red chestnut with distinctive white stockings, and Raoul recognised it even before he recognised its rider. It was more than a year since he had seen Aimery de Montréal, and in that time the man's hair had turned from iron-grey to white. His sister Geralda rode beside him on a dappled mare. Raoul remembered that she had written in the winter, promising to visit his mother, who was ailing with a coughing sickness. Half-pleased, half-apprehensive, he went to greet them.

Aimery met Raoul with a strong handclasp and looked him up and down. 'I see you've already heard the news,' he said grimly.

'What news?' Raoul had been about to kiss Geralda, but now he stopped and looked round.

'Then you don't know. I thought when I saw your armour . . . ' Aimery's voice tailed off.

'I was trying the fit of an altered hauberk,' Raoul said dismissively. 'What news?'

'Cabaret's fallen,' Aimery said. 'Pierre-Roger yielded two days ago to save his skin. De Montfort's on his way to take us with his entire summer force.' His tone was apologetic, as if he felt personally responsible for the information. 'I thought you knew.'

Raoul shook his head with bitter disbelief. 'I told Count Raymond months ago not to let de Montfort drag out negotiations through the winter, that they were a ruse and come the spring we'd pay for it.' His eyelids tensed. 'We should have gone on the offensive. We should have hit him and hit him again while he had no troops.'

Aimery sighed. 'It is easy for you to say that, Raoul, but Raymond is no warrior and he truly does desire reconciliation with Rome. He's caught by the balls.'

'I understand that,' Raoul acknowledged on a quieter, but no less astringent note, 'and I also understand that unless we organise ourselves, de Montfort will emasculate us all.'

'Geralda's going to take the consolamentum, you know,' Aimery said. 'She's deeply committed to the Cathar religion.' The men were seated before a brazier in the solar, their armour removed and a half-empty flagon sharing the table with a platter of dried fruit.

Raoul stretched out his legs towards the brazier's warmth. 'What about you?'

Aimery smiled and shook his head. 'I'm too set in my ways to pass the tests demanded of a fully fledged Perfect. I eat meat, I still enjoy the pleasures of the flesh, and I'm a soldier. Too many sins and not enough remorse to forswear them. Geralda used to argue with me about such things all the time, but these days she accepts that we're different.'

Raoul gave a heartfelt sigh. 'Claire and my mother are much drawn to the Cathars too. We have a large community at Montvallant. I'm always stumbling over their meetings.'

'And you resent them?' Aimery asked shrewdly.

'God's bones, I don't know!' Raoul said in exasperation. 'What they teach is no sin; indeed, they're probably right. This is Satan's domain, and living a pure life is the only way to break your chains, but . . . ' He grimaced. 'It is because of the Cathars we are having to fight – they gave the French the excuse they needed.' He dropped his gaze from Aimery's scrutiny. 'Also they have come between myself and Claire. It is not as difficult for you. Geralda is your sister.'

'Ah.' Aimery raised and lowered his brows in sympathetic understanding.

'It's not as bad as it was a few months ago.' Raoul contemplated his cup. 'I've grown accustomed to it now, found other things to occupy my time, and Claire, too, has compromised. We manage very well providing we stay in each other's shallows and don't go wading out of our depth. And I have Guillaume. He compensates for much.'

A sombre silence fell, both men constrained by the limits of the depths and shallows that Raoul had just mentioned.

In the women's chambers above the hall, Geralda clucked over Beatrice with sympathetic concern. 'You should take hore-hound syrup for that cough,' she said. 'I'll send you some.'

Beatrice gave a wan smile. 'It has gone too far for that to

be of much use.' She concealed her bloodied kerchief in her sleeve. 'Nor do I desire to fight it. The consolamentum awaits me very soon, I think.'

Geralda studied her keenly, but said nothing. Claire returned from settling Guillaume in his cradle.

'Asleep?' Geralda asked.

'Yes, at last!' Claire laughed. 'He's so inquisitive, hates to think he's missing something!'

'Raoul was just like him at that age.' Beatrice's gaze was misty with reminiscence. 'He led us a dance, I can tell you!'

Claire gave her a fond look in which there was an under-current of concern. Distant memories seemed to be the most rewarding part of Beatrice's life these days, and she appeared ever more willing to dwell in them and let the present pass her by.

'He still does,' Geralda said, 'if the look on your face earlier was any indication.'

'I don't like to see him wearing armour.' Beatrice compressed her lips. 'He knows it, but it doesn't make any difference.'

'He's a man grown now, with a son of his own. You cannot rule him as you did when he was a child,' Geralda cautioned. 'I know how hard it is to see your loved ones take the path of war, believe me, but I also know that if you push too hard, you will push him away.'

Beatrice stared at a wall hanging, depicting a hunting scene. 'It will not matter soon,' she said.

Geralda sighed but neither contradicted her nor sought to argue her out of her mood. Instead, she laid her hand over Beatrice's. 'I have a favour to ask of you. It is no light matter, and I will understand if you choose to decline.'

Beatrice's attention diverted from the doomed deer on the hanging. 'You know you need but name it and it is yours.'

Geralda smiled. 'And that makes it the more difficult.' She drew a deep breath. 'I have some Cathars staying with me at Lavaur. The Pope is desperate to destroy them above all other members of the Perfecti. May I direct them here to Montvallant as a place where they will be succoured if they have need?'

'Of course you may!' Beatrice said, with a glimmer of her former fire. The louder use of her voice caused her to break off, coughing, and fumble in her sleeve for her kerchief.

'Who are they?' Claire asked over her shoulder as she hurried to fetch Beatrice a cup of hot wine.

'Have you heard of Chretien de Béziers?'

Claire felt a thrill of recognition and looked eagerly at Geralda. 'I heard him preach in Toulouse last year. He has the most wonderful voice – like a warm sable cloak.'

Geralda laughed at the description. 'I'll tell him that; he'll be flattered!'

'There was a young woman at the meeting, too. She admired Guillaume and spoke to me for a while.' Claire's colour heightened as she remembered the content of the conversation. 'I felt that she could see through me as if I were made of glass.'

'Ah,' Geralda said, nodding, 'that would be Bridget. She is not a Cathar, but she, Chretien and Matthias have long travelled together. Matthias translates holy texts and Gospels from the old tongues into Catalan and Occitan. A few years ago, he was captured by papal spies and put to the torture. They cut off the pen fingers of his right hand as a warning. Bridget's mother they murdered by branding her forehead with a molten cross.'

Claire put her hand to her mouth in shock.

Geralda looked pensive, a rare expression for her. 'Bridget is the most important of the three. She is a healer of extra-ordinary skill, and claims descent from the Magdalene and the Virgin. Rome cannot afford to let her live.' She gave a vigorous shake of her head. 'I should not have asked you. There is too great a risk involved.'

'I do not care what the risks are if I am able to thwart the men who killed my husband.' Beatrice took the cup Claire handed to her and drank from it in fast swallows like a soldier. 'Of course you must send them to us.' A tint of pink seeped into her cheeks.

'If you are sure.'

Claire set the flagon back down upon the hearth. 'Raoul is already an outlaw in the eyes of the northern lords. It will make little difference to our standing with them should we harbour three more Cathars among those already here. Perhaps it is the other way around. Perhaps Montvallant will not be safe for them.'

Looking tired, Geralda closed her eyes. 'Child,' she said, 'nowhere is safe any more.'

CHAPTER 18

MONTVALLANT, MAY 1211

Raoul nuzzled his lips against Claire's shoulder and played with a strand of her tumbled chestnut hair. The bed curtains enclosed the two of them in shadowy warmth and it was almost possible for him to believe there was nothing outside this early morning haven – that his life was whole. Almost. Beyond the protection of the hangings, the world prepared to intrude. He could hear the stealthy movements and whisperings of Claire's maids and Guillaume's high-pitched babble.

Making a conscious effort to ignore the sounds, he kissed Claire's throat and mouth, the dimple in her chin, stroked the soft curves of her body. The caress was not urgent but the languorous aftermath of pleasure recently taken. She was often reluctant at first, but he had learned to be cunning, to choose his moment and then to ply her with teasing and cajolery, with a musician's delicate touch on her sleep-drugged body so that by the time she was fully awake, her stimulated flesh was reaching for release and nothing else mattered.

'I ought to go,' he murmured, making no attempt to do so. Claire said nothing, passive now beneath his stroking fingertips. After a while he raised himself on one elbow to look at her. She was staring up at the stars painted on the canopy, her mouth rosy and full from his kisses, the love flush still mantling her body, and her expression so haunted that it cut him to the quick.

Uttering a soft oath, he sat up and pushed aside the bedclothes. 'Perhaps I ought to take a concubine,' he muttered.

Claire flinched and her eyes met his in misery, making him feel guilty, and then all the more angry for his guilt. 'What is wrong? Why do you no longer take pleasure in lying with me? Is it because of the Cathars?'

'No, never that!' Her voice held a note of alarm. 'Do not turn against them because of me! I will never refuse you!'

Raoul felt as if she had struck him full in the face. 'I do not want you out of your fear or sense of duty,' he said stiffly. 'I want you to come to me as you used to do when we were first wed. You never touch me any more, or find excuses in the day to seek me out. The approaches are all mine. I feel like a beggar standing at a castle gate seeking crumbs of comfort from a table beyond my reach.'

Claire swallowed. Tears glittered in her eyes. 'This war,' she choked out. 'It has changed everything. I feel like a beggar, too. I love you, truly I do!'

Outside the bed curtains, a maid spoke in surprise to someone at the door. The voice that replied was young and light, but undeniably masculine, and it held a note of agitation.

'We'll talk later.' Raoul was unsure whether to be irritated or relieved by the interruption. Perhaps the crumbs were so few and far between because there was no longer a table spread from which to provide them. Pulling on his braies, he parted the curtains and looked at his squire, who was hovering on the threshold.

'Mir, what is it?'

The youth shouldered past the maid. 'My lord, there is a messenger to see you from Lavaur. He says that it is most urgent.' Mir gestured over his shoulder towards the door.

Raoul saw the glint of mail in the stairwell and knew that for Mir to bring the messenger above to the private quarters, an armed one at that, the news must be deeply urgent. 'You had better admit him,' he said. Tying the drawstring on his braies, Raoul indicated a south-facing alcove built into the thickness of the wall where Claire usually sat to do her embroidery.

The man whom the squire ushered into the room was heavily travel-stained. A grey rag of bandage was tied around a head wound and splotches of rust from his hauberk marred his surcoat. 'I nearly did not get through their pickets, my lord,' he said huskily, and swayed where he stood.

Raoul gestured him to sit on the low stone bench cut into the wall. With his own hand he brought the flask of double-strength Gascon wine from the cupboard and poured a generous measure into a cup. The messenger took a long, grateful drink, wiped his mouth and looked at Raoul. 'De Montfort has laid siege to Lavaur and is on the verge of breaking it. His troops are filling up the moat with soil and brushwood faster than we can empty it, and we cannot stop the sappers from mining the wall. Lord Aimery and Lady Geralda beg you to come to their aid before it is too late.'

Raoul frowned. 'I have troops, and well trained at that, but I don't have the numbers to tackle de Montfort's army.'

Guillaume toddled unsteadily into the alcove, a wooden toy grasped in a chubby fist. Raoul scooped him into his arms and looked at the messenger over the child's flaxen hair.

'But enough to tip the balance of the siege if you add your strength to Lord Aimery's. The whole area is being laid waste. I beg you, my lord, please help us!'

Raoul deliberated between duty and obligation. The men were not his; they were held in trust for Raymond of Toulouse, but appeal to Raymond would waste valuable time, and knowing his overlord's tendency to prevaricate, he might well be refused. 'I'll come,' he said with sudden vigour. 'Give me a moment to break my fast and arm up, and I'll have the men on the road before prime.'

'Thank you, my lord, thank you!'

Raoul grimaced. 'Do not expect miracles,' he said brusquely. Brushing his lips against Guillaume's curls, he set him down. Colours suddenly dulled. Glancing out of the unshuttered window, he saw that clouds had obscured the sun.

Claire watched Raoul buckle on his sword belt, adjust the scabbard at his hip, and reach for his shield, the background a bright egg-yolk gold on which the Montvallant chevronels stood out in a contrast of stark, black lines.

She hated to see him in armour, for it was a reminder of how she was losing him. Each time he returned to her from a battle, a little bit more of the Raoul she had loved was obliterated. She saw the steadfast gentle courage of the Cathar way, and the grim, blood-filled curse of the path of war. She could not bear to see Raoul's feet so entrenched upon the downward road, to feel the distance growing between them. And today it was for Aimery and Geralda that he was donning his armour and losing another small piece of his soul. She could not condone; she could not condemn. And so she witnessed in miserable silence.

He seemed to capture the drift of her thoughts, for he glanced up from checking his weapons and met her eyes. 'It may be, if we arrive in time, that we can hold them to a truce and save those within Lavaur from another Béziers,' he said.

She nodded stiffly.

'Whatever you think, I do not relish fighting for fighting's sake. If there were another way – a tenable one – I would take it.'

Claire swallowed. 'Do you think I do not know how difficult it is for you? Do what you can for Aimery and Geralda . . . and guard yourself.'

He folded her in an awkward soldier's embrace, hard with iron rings and the curved jolt of shield edge, the fierce thrust of a sword hilt against her ribs. She clung to him, accepting and returning his scratchy kiss.

'Come home safe,' she said. 'Come home whole.'

He kissed her again, embraced Guillaume and, with a final look, hurried away to his men.

Assailed by a sense of loss that bordered on grief, Claire climbed to the battlements to watch him mount up and ride out.

A storm was coming. Bridget felt its imminence raise the delicate hairs at her nape and tingle through her body. Far away, she detected the flicker of dry lightning and tasted its metallic essence. There was danger, too, a long, dark tunnel with only the barest glimmer of light at the other end. Lavaur would fall. Standing upon the battlements, she could see the twinkle of the crusaders' campfires and thought that they seemed almost as numerous as the stars. The smell of death was in the wind, but she hadn't the courage to search her mind and find out whose. If her road ended here, then so be it. The presence of the storm was surely an omen.

A light wind fingered her hair, stroking it back from her brow almost maternally. She closed her eyes and lifted her face skyward like a child.

'Bridget?'

The voice seemed to come from a distance, and it was with a great reluctance that she lowered her head and looked round. Geralda stood behind her. She was wearing the simple, dark robe of a Cathar Perfect. A plain white wimple covered her hair. Earlier that evening, Chretien had administered to her the sacred Cathar rite of the consolamentum, but for all that, Bridget saw no serenity in Geralda's eyes.

'There are so many of them.' Geralda came to the wall and stared as Bridget had done at the enemy campfires encircling Lavaur. 'Aimery says they will attack at dawn and we will be unable to hold them off.' She beat the palm of one hand frustratedly against her skirts. 'I am not afraid for myself, but it distresses me that I have failed to keep you from harm.'

'You have done all you could; do not reproach yourself.' Bridget touched Geralda's shoulder. 'Be at ease. Dawn will bring what it brings.'

Geralda chewed her lip. 'Aimery told me he had sent a messenger to Raoul de Montvallant, asking for aid. If only we knew if he had reached him.'

The name entered Bridget like a bolt of lightning, and images dazzled across her mind in rapid succession. Raoul de Montvallant astride a rearing golden warhorse, sword held skyward in defiance. She saw him standing naked, buffeted by the rain, his erection straining against his belly. His eyes were narrowed against the storm and his face was harsh and glorious with lust. She was facing him, and she, too, was naked, her dark hair plastered to her breasts. 'He will come,' she said in a breathless voice. 'Even now he is riding to us.'

'Praise be to the Good God,' whispered Geralda, and her worried expression eased slightly. 'I will tell Aimery.'

Bridget leaned against the battlements for support and withheld the rest of her knowledge. What would it benefit Geralda to be told he would come too late to save Lavaur?

The sky clouded and darkened as Raoul led his men towards Lavaur. Lightning flickered over the forested hills to the north in a sky the colour of sword steel. No thunder pursued the flashes of light and no rain fell. The assault on the senses was silent and unnerving.

They halted for the night in a small hamlet straddling the road and it was an eerie experience. Fearing the approach of the crusading army, the inhabitants had fled into the woods with their portable goods and their animals, leaving their houses empty shells, but so recently deserted that the essence of habitation still lived and breathed. It was like bedding down with ghosts, unsettling both men and horses.

All night the lightning blinked silently across the sky, now close, now distant, and a dry, fierce wind gusted over the land, causing shutters in the village to slam and doors to creak. The strange atmosphere sent tingles down Raoul's spine and throbbed in his temples, making it impossible for him to sleep. Finally, tense as a mountain lynx, he prowled outside and took over the night watch from one of the pickets.

He had not encountered the dream woman for several months, but tonight he could feel her in the storm-lit darkness. He stared until his eyes burned and he reached out with every particle of his mind, but she remained tantalisingly out of his grasp.

At dawn the wind dropped, but the lightning continued to flash. The sky was metallic, charged with power, and the weight of it was like a lump of brazen metal pulsing in his skull. His men made their ablutions and broke their fast in silence. Before full light they had kicked out their fires and were once again on the road to Lavaur.

As they approached the town, the sky changed to a dull bronze. Although the wind had died, Raoul recognised the stink of burning wood, burning fields and burning meat. No one who had been at Béziers would ever forget that smell and what it signified.

'Ah, God!' wept Amaury's messenger. 'We are too late!'

'Perhaps it is just the outskirts,' said one of Raoul's knights, offering words of hope without any conviction.

Tight-lipped, Raoul moved his troop off the road and continued his advance towards Lavaur with increased caution. After a few miles he halted the men in a stand of pines bordering the road and, taking Giles, went to reconnoitre ahead. Keeping to what cover they could find, they continued to ride parallel with the road and eventually came upon a procession of baggage wains, cooks, craftsmen and general camp followers, all heading toward Lavaur. Simon's army had struck camp and was on the move.

'What now?' muttered Giles.

Raoul narrowed his gaze in the direction of the town. The stench of smoke was powerful, but not as powerful as the certainty pounding in his temples 'We join them,' he said and squeezed his thighs against Bausan's flanks.

'Have you lost your wits?' Giles's voice rose an incredulous octave. 'We'll be butchered!'

'Who is to stop us? They're common northern camp followers, taught to tug the forelock to anyone riding a destrier and wearing spurs. They'll think we're part of the rearguard detail. If we don't disillusion them, we'll be safe enough.'

A muttering, reluctant Giles followed Raoul out of the trees and on to the road, but Raoul was right in his assessment that they would go unchallenged. The only difficult moment came when a pimp tried to interest them in his girls and had to be persuaded with the sharp end of a lance to try his luck elsewhere. After that, they rode right up to the town walls without incident.

Just inside Lavaur's main gate, their eyes were drawn to the remnants of a collapsed gibbet with bodies heaped around it. These were the soldiers of Lavaur's garrison, their armour stripped and their naked bodies hacked and mutilated. Raoul saw that the intention to hang the men like common criminals had been thwarted by the broken gibbet, so sword and axe had been used in lieu. Slumped against the gibbet, the rope still around his neck, his shirt saturated in his lifeblood, was Aimery, his stare fixed on the buzzards wheeling overhead. The smoke tore at Raoul's eyes, forcing him to blink, but the image was branded forever in his mind.

'Let us go!' cried Giles with revulsion. 'There is nothing we can do, and I have no desire to join these poor souls!'

'No!' Raoul snapped, swallowing his gorge. 'Not yet.' He urged Bausan further into the town, towards a rising noise of cries and shouting. Blaspheming, Giles spurred after his lord.

They came to a square where a throng of townspeople had been herded and held at bay by mounted soldiers. A procession was being led across the square by priests, a huge bronze cross carried on high, silk banners of Christ in suffering fluttering to either side. Behind the banners, his crosier held in his fist like a weapon, walked the Abbot of Cîteaux, his corpulent form barnacled by a magnificent gemstone chasuble and his face aglow with triumph.

In contrast, the roped line of men and women shuffling in his wake, prodded and spat upon by the crusaders, wore plain homespun robes in dull colours: Cathars and condemned to death but they wore expressions of triumph, too. Their bodies were about to burn, but their spirits were on the verge of release. Bringing up the rear were yet more priests bearing torches to light the faggots.

'Dear God.' Giles swallowed.

'Which one?' Raoul asked cynically. 'Cîteaux's God, or the Cathars'?' He scanned the prisoners, but could not see Geralda among them.

A Cistercian monk, his cowl pulled over his face, was pushing his horse through the crowd, forcing a path for his two companions and a laden pack mule. Raoul's sliding glance stopped and jerked back to the horse of the first monk. It was a lean red chestnut with a white blaze and four distinctive white stockings.

'That's Aimery's courser!' he said with fury. 'That priest is riding Aimery's horse!'

'Doesn't take them long, the vultures!' Giles spat over his mount's withers.

'Stop them!' An imperative bellow rang out from the far side of the square, and there was a sudden flurry and churning in the crowd as several knights and serjeants strove to thrust their way towards the monks. Whips lashed at the tardy. Shod hooves kicked. The leading destrier was silver-white, and its rider's shield bore the device of the de Montfort fork-tailed lion.

'Christ in heaven, it's Simon de Montfort himself, and he's seen us!' Giles croaked, turning his stallion about. 'My lord, this is folly. We must go!'

Raoul caught Giles's sleeve. 'It is not us they are after,' he said. 'It's them.' He pointed at the monks.

Giles looked nonplussed.

'Geralda asked me to shelter three important Cathars when she was at Montvallant. I hazard they're not monks at all. You're right, we mustn't tarry.'

'We can't . . . ' Giles began, but Raoul was already cutting across the edges of the crowd, dovetailing his path to meet the hurrying fugitives. A sidelong glance showed him that de Montfort was gaining, but not as quickly as the warlord might have hoped, for the press of people was still hindering him, in some cases deliberately. That was remedied when de Montfort drew his sword and used not the flat of the blade, but the sharpened edge to cut his way forward.

'Quickly!' Raoul snapped to the monk with the pack mule as Bausan came abreast of him. 'Follow me!'

Grey eyes glinted within the depths of the cowl. Smooth brown hands gathered the reins and turned the chestnut.

'Stop them!' The furious command resounded again. 'I'll have your balls for ballista missiles if you let them escape!'

Near Raoul, a soldier blinked round, obviously wondering who was shouting and at whom. Before he could make up his mind, a burly townsman deliberately started a brawl with his neighbour, thus distracting the northerner's attention.

Raoul led his charges down a cobbled alleyway, across a smaller open space, and then squeezed along a dark entry towards the light of a house garden on the other side. Halfway down the entry, the mule with its bulging load, by now bringing up the rear, became stuck. There was no room to turn. Raoul rode on to the end, dismounted, and hurried to the beast. His heart was hammering as if it would burst through his ribs, and not because they were being hotly pursued. A cowl might conceal all but the sparsest gleams of skin and eye, but he recognised his dreams made living flesh and bone.

'Leave the mule,' he said urgently, 'we'll travel much faster without it.'

'Impossible!' one of the other monks said, raising his right hand in negation, and Raoul saw that two fingers and a thumb were missing. 'If Cîteaux or de Montfort lay hold on what is contained in these bundles, they will destroy everything, and it cannot be replaced. Nor would it prevent them from pursuing us to our deaths. We are the guardians and we know too much.'

'The mule will hinder us,' Raoul insisted. 'If you must bring the baggage, let it be divided among the horses, and quickly.'

The man opened his mouth to argue.

'Matthias, do as he says.' The woman touched her companion's sleeve. 'The danger is too close.' She nodded at Raoul, and set about dismantling the mule's baggage herself.

'Be careful,' moaned the little man as Raoul cut the straps securing the bundles when he could not reach the buckles. 'Some of those writings are over a thousand years old!'

'Do you want them to go up in flames?' Raoul snapped. 'Here, take these down to Giles and your friends, and thank yourself for the lesser of the two evils!'

Matthias clutched the bundle Raoul thrust at him as tenderly as a mother with an infant. 'You do not understand,' he said as if to a barbarian, and made haste down the entry.

Once they were able to move the mule down the passage, they finished transferring the load in the open light of the garden beyond. Raoul watched as the woman secured a portion of the mule's bundle to her mount's crupper. Aimery's restive, highly strung stallion stood as contentedly as a cheeseseller's nag beneath her hands. Raoul stared at them. They were tanned and slim, unadorned by rings, the nails clipped short, so ordinary that they could have belonged to any peasant girl in the Languedoc; and yet they sent a pang through him. Lowering his eyes, he completed fastening his share of the load behind his saddle.

'I assume from your mounts and your disguises that you are the Cathars who were lodged with the lady Geralda?' he asked as he remounted Bausan. 'That chestnut was Aimery's favourite.'

'Indeed we are,' said the taller man, who had thus far hardly spoken. 'I gave her the consolamentum yestereve when we feared that the town would fall. At least she came to the Good End, even if the manner of it was terrible.'

'Then, like Aimery, she is dead?' Raoul looked at him in dismay.

'She lives in the Light,' Chretien answered firmly.

Raoul thrust his feet into his stirrups and wondered how he was going to break the news to Claire and his mother. He thought of the picnic by the river in the summer of his marriage. The memory was still strong, the colours bold, but it felt more like an illumination from a manuscript than an event that he had lived. 'What happened to her?'

The Cathar met his gaze with steady compassion. 'They threw her down the town well and stoned her to death. She denied them entry to the castle – stood in the gateway and read a sermon to Cîteaux himself. I implored her, but she would not come with us. If we are here now, it is because she sacrificed herself so that we might escape.'

Raoul closed his eyes. Poor, forthright, garrulous Geralda in whose spacious lap he had sat as a child. His own son had cuddled there too, lulled to sleep by her singing voice, which had been as soft as her speaking tones were harsh. He thought of Aimery and the butchered garrison by the town gate. 'Why are you so important?' he demanded harshly. 'Why do they hate and fear you even above the hatred and fear they have for other Cathars?'

'Because—' the woman started to say, and broke off,

looking towards the mouth of the entry. 'They are coming,' she said breathlessly. He followed her cowled gaze. The entry was empty. He could see tufts of grass growing out of the stonework and the deserted narrow street at the other end. A cylindrical gleam caught his eye, and he realised that he was looking at a document tube lying against the darkness of the wall where it had been dropped while they were freeing the mule from its load.

Cursing, he dismounted and ran to fetch it. In that same moment the street beyond the entry was suddenly aswirl with horsemen and running soldiers. Raoul closed his fingers around the tube. A crossbow quarrel whirred close to his head, struck the wall and rebounded. Others followed, bouncing and clattering, missing him by a miracle. He thrust the document tube through his belt and, as the entry darkened with soldiers, ran back to Bausan, vaulted astride and drew his sword to cover the retreat of the others.

The garden gave on to a narrow alley which was already filling with soldiers sent round to intercept them. With a single blow of his sword, Raoul chopped off the latch of a gate set in the opposite wall and charged Bausan through. They hastened through an orchard, past an empty stable and a ransacked house, and shot into the next street. A handful of mercenaries who had been looting the building emerged to confront the escapees.

Raoul and Giles clashed with them. By now both men were sufficiently battle-hardened to take on the extra man without depending on fortune's blessing to keep them alive. They had learned that honour in battle was not the same as honour outside it. Kill a horse if you must, kick a man in the balls, throw sand in his eyes, strike him when he was down. After the victory, then you could afford the gilding of chivalry if it was your whim.

One soldier was killed outright, two more wounded and the horse of the fourth brought down. The fifth and sixth men fled the exchange. Above their heads the sky rippled with lightning. Raoul and Giles wheeled their mounts and ushered their charges before them. A sharp right turn, a zigzag, and in a moment the city gates came into view, complete with drunken gibbet, dead men and buzzards. The birds no longer circled in the sky, but were settling to feed. Bridget stared for a moment at the carnage, then drew a deep breath. 'They are only shells,' she murmured. 'Without the spirit, there is nothing. Let us go.'

The last of Simon's camp followers were still straggling into the town as Raoul led the way out. Curious looks were cast by some, but the serjeant in charge of the guard was too busy arranging details with the pimp whom Raoul had encountered earlier to take much notice of two knights escorting three Cistercian monks on their way. As far as he was concerned, Cîteaux's spies and envoys were always coming and going at speed.

Raoul and his company were trotting past the plundered remains of ramshackle houses built outside the protection of the town walls when they heard the shouts behind them as their pursuers burst through the gateway like huntsmen on the trail of a deer. The five put whip and spur to their mounts. Raoul knew he had a good but not invincible lead. With twenty fighting men chasing two, if the distance was closed, death was inevitable.

He tried to remember how far back he had left his men and the safety of numbers. The distance seemed enormous and the leading white stallion of their pursuers was gaining with every stride. Behold a pale horse. Raoul felt as if the space between his shoulder blades was a target upon which his enemy's eyes were fixed. As he rode, he started to shout the rallying cry that would summon his men, hoping against hope that they were close.

'À Montvallant! À Montvallant!'

The road ahead remained empty. Behind them the hoof-beats were thunderous. The three horses the Cathars were riding were fresh from their stalls – but the destriers had been pushed for two days in haste to reach Lavaur and were heavier of bone than the rangy hunters.

'Ride on!' Raoul cried to Matthias, who was abreast of him. 'We'll slow them while you make your escape!' He signalled to Giles and spun Bausan in a dusty arc to face the oncoming riders. Several times in the last hour he had expected to die; now death was such a familiar companion at his shoulder that he felt neither anticipation nor dread.

De Montfort's stallion filled the world, its nostrils red caverns, foam spattering from the bit, hooves striking sparks from the road. The shield concealed the joining of horse and man so that they appeared to be one beast. Simon de Montfort, Rex Mundi's soldier. Steel and muscle and the eye of a grim reaper. Behold a pale horse. Raoul charged to meet him, flinging his gage in the face of death. Snow-silver and mottled gold, the horses jarred together. Bausan twisted sideways. De Montfort's sword hacked a chunk out of Raoul's shield and Raoul's blade rebounded off the glossy surface of de Montfort's. Altering his grip, de Montfort prepared for the killing blow but his mail-clad arm never completed its deadly sweep.

A fork of lightning stabbed down to earth, dazzling the fighting soldiers, striking two of de Montfort's men dead in their saddles. Horses reared, shied and bolted. The leaf tips of the trees on either side of the road burned like votive candles, and rags of yellow and orange flame danced over the surface of the grass. A new, acrid smell of burning overlaid the charred stench from the town.

'Montvallant!' came the cry from more than a score of throats. 'Montvallant!'

Amid the shock at the lightning strike, Raoul felt exultation as he saw Roland, Mir and the rest of his men filling the road as if conjured out of the storm. However, no more than perfunctory blows were exchanged as de Montfort bellowed at his men to retreat. It was plain that to continue fighting in the midst of a dry storm of these proportions was suicide. Both northern and southern troops backed off from the encounter, not even bothering to utter the usual rhetoric and threats as they hastened to take cover.

Two hours later, Raoul's troop arrived at a small but still inhabited hamlet and stopped to water the horses and eat. They were offered rough red wine and dark bread with pressed goat's cheese. For the Cathars, who ate nothing of animal origin, there was thick garlic and bean pottage to accompany the bread.

While Mir watered Bausan at the village trough, Raoul sat on its stone edge and put his face in his hands. He felt as if his bones had had their marrow sucked out. One arm throbbed where a sword blow had slipped past his guard and, although the rivets of his hauberk had held, he had been badly bruised.

'Here,' said Giles gruffly. 'Best eat something. You're the same colour as this cheese.'

Raoul eyed the hunk of bread and crumbly curds piled on top of it. His stomach lurched. 'I'm not hungry.'

'That's the reaction setting in,' Giles said with the comfortable surety of experience. 'Always does when a man goes beyond himself as I saw you go today. I'll put it in your saddlebag in case you want it later.' Biting into his own food, he started to leave.

'You saw and did the same things.' Raoul raised his head to look at the knight. 'Doesn't it sicken you?'

Giles paused and frowned at his meal, then turned round with a shrug. 'I'm pretending that this has been an ordinary day out on an ordinary patrol,' he said. 'I'm pretending I don't remember. Sooner or later that defence will crack, but by then it'll probably be safe to get drunker than hell and cry my guts out . . . those I haven't spewed up.' Turning away again, he carried on walking.

Sick to the soul, Raoul knuckled his eyes and stood up. Near the trough, some villagers had gathered around

Chretien de Béziers to listen to him read aloud from his vernacular copy of the Gospel of Saint John.

'"And this is the judgement, that the light has come into the world and men loved darkness rather than light, because their deeds were evil. For every one who does evil hates the light and does not come to the light lest his deeds be exposed. But he who does what is true comes to the light that it may be clearly seen that his deeds have been wrought in God."'

Raoul was still too benumbed by his reaction to all that had happened to be astounded at the rocklike tenacity of the man's faith. The words poured over him, meaning little, but the Cathar had a voice of such rich beauty that it caught and held him like a shaft of sunlight, and the spell was only broken when one of his men claimed his attention with a question. Raoul went to deal with the query, passing Matthias, who was muttering anxiously to himself and checking his precious bundles of manuscripts. When Raoul was finally free again, he saw the woman standing apart and went to join her. She was drinking a cup of the rough village wine and had pushed down the cowl of her habit so that for the first time he could see her features clearly.

Hair black as midnight hung down her back in the manner permitted only to unmarried women and virgins. Her eyes were mist-grey without the diamond clarity he remembered from his visions and her face was pale with exhaustion. When she did not acknowledge him, lost in her own thoughts, he cleared his throat. 'I do not even know your name,' he said softly, 'although you well know mine, I think.'

She took her gaze from the horizon where she had been watching the storm clouds retreating south, and rested it on him instead. 'It is Bridget,' she answered before raising her cup and finishing her wine. When she spoke again, it was more than half to herself. 'I'm so tired. Sometimes I wonder if it would be simpler to give in, to let myself be captured and killed, but then the knowledge would die with me, and I made a promise.'

Raoul had no idea what she was talking about, but he did know she and her companions were in desperate need of succour. 'There are caves in the hills near my castle, and you should be safe there, for a while at least, if you want to stay,' he said.

Bridget hesitated, then shook her head. 'I thank you, but we are intending to go to Foix, to the mountains. Raymond-Roger of Foix is well disposed towards the Cathars, and some of the valleys there are so remote they barely see a single shepherd from one season to the next.'

Raoul felt relieved and disappointed by her decision. He would have willingly given her his protection, but he was conscious of the dangers, both from external forces and from Bridget herself. It would be like living within the lightning to have her so close and yet so far. 'We will escort you there – make sure you arrive safely.'

She gave him a strange look and her eyes were suddenly crystal-bright. 'Then thank you,' she said. 'We accept your protection.'

That look, the timbre of her voice made Raoul swallow. He gazed at her mouth, at her wine-moist lips, at the gentle throb of her pulse in her throat. The beat of his own was harder, more rapid, coursing into his groin with exquisite discomfort. 'It is time we moved on,' he said abruptly. 'De Montfort will be on our trail now the storm is passing over.'

Bridget watched him go to his knights and issue orders concerning their new destination. Her body was liquid with anticipation. She could have refused his aid and sent him home to Montvallant and his wife, but she would be sending him to certain death. This way he had a chance to live, and in return, she would only ask of him a single gift.

When Simon returned to Lavaur, Cîteaux's soldiers were prodding through a heap of hot ashes in the field outside the gates where the town's Cathars had been immolated. They were searching for any larger bones that had survived the flames in order to grind them to dust. The broken body of the lady Geralda was still down the well, no one having had sufficient bravery to approach Cîteaux and beg its removal, although Simon knew she would have to be taken out before she started poisoning the water.

Leaving his stallion with a groom, Simon strode into the keep. A dozen petitioners were waiting for him, among them local lords tendering their submission and adjutants requiring orders. His son Amaury was dealing with some of the less important matters. Seeing his father, he rolled his eyes meaningfully at the dais, where Cîteaux was enjoying a meal of pigeons in wine sauce.

Simon paused for a moment, mentally preparing to do battle. Then, squaring his shoulders, he stalked up the hall to the dais, scattering servants and retainers.

Cîteaux looked up. 'You lost them!' he accused, wiping his greasy fingers on a napkin. 'You had them in your clutches and you lost them!'

Simon reached the trestle, braced his arms on its edge and leaned over the legate. 'Vent your spleen on me, priest, and it will be your last act on this earth!' he snarled. 'Were it not for the sharp eyes of my own men, they'd not have been flushed from cover in the first place! Your own soldiers were too busy throwing stones down a well and clapping their hands at the bonfire!'

Cîteaux's complexion darkened to match the gravy. 'How dare you threaten and insult me!' he blustered. 'I warn you I'll . . . '

'You'll what?' Simon asked with a contemptuous lip. 'Excommunicate me like Raymond of Toulouse? I think not. Sour your gut as it may, you need me to do your soldiering!' Simon thrust himself away from the table. 'Besides, I haven't lost them. I know where to find your heretics and their mentor.'

'Where?' Cîteaux sat back.

'They're in the company of Raoul de Montvallant,' Simon

said. 'Fought with us at Béziers, but turned rebel with a vengeance. My guess is that he was riding to Lavaur's aid and when he realised it was too late he snatched those Cathars from under our noses instead.' He took a cup from an attendant. 'Time and past time I paid a personal visit to Lord Raoul's home,' he said before tossing down the wine in six fast swallows.

CHAPTER 19

FOIX, MAY 1211

Seated at the high table on the dais, Raoul watched the jugglers toss their painted wooden batons from hand to hand, but although his eyes followed every twirl and turn and graceful arc, his thoughts were far away, and it was only his position as a guest of Raymond-Roger, Count of Foix, that kept him in his place.

At the centre of the table, presiding over the meal, the Count was deep in conversation with one of his knights, but now and then Raoul was aware of the astute black gaze flickering in his direction. Raymond-Roger of Foix had taken Bridget, Chretien and Matthias under his wing with alacrity. To Foix, the Cathars were a symbol of resistance, a rallying point against the northern crusading army.

Here in the mountains, Simon de Montfort was feared, but contempt was still the dominant emotion, together with the belief that in the end he would be beaten. Only last month, so the Count had told Raoul, the knights of Foix had ambushed several hundred of de Montfort's German mercenaries in the forest of Montgey and slaughtered them to a man. If the Cathars were going to be safe anywhere, it would be in these mountains marking the foothills of the great Pyrenean ranges.

Raoul's mind and body dwelt upon Bridget. He knew so little about her, only that she was strange and beautiful and in terrible danger. He desired her so strongly that even thinking of her provoked a physical reaction. She had not attended the evening meal in the hall, but he could feel her presence. Knowing how close she was and yet how far, set him on a fine edge.

'I assume,' said Foix, leaning across and interrupting Raoul's tortured thoughts, 'that you will be returning to your overlord?'

Making an effort, Raoul focused on the Count. 'Yes, my lord. Now that de Montfort has taken Lavaur, all the lands surrounding Toulouse are open to his attack, including my own.'

'And Count Raymond, has he the spleen to fight back?'

Raoul was not surprised to see the glitter of contempt in Foix's eyes. Few if any of the southern lords believed Raymond of Toulouse was capable of holding his ground. 'What choice does he have?' Raoul answered with a shrug. 'The Church refuses to believe he's repentant, and de Montfort's not open to negotiation while he's winning. He wants Toulouse for himself. Count Raymond must either resist or die.'

Foix mulled this over for a while. Then he looked at Raoul. 'Will you bear a letter to your overlord when you leave?' He laughed sourly at Raoul's startled expression. 'It is time to forget old rivalries. We must unite to survive, and we must fight back. There's only one language that de Montfort understands – the sword!' He smacked his palm decisively on the board.

Raoul thought that the sword was the only language Foix understood, too, the reason Foix and Raymond had never seen eye to eye. 'Willingly I will take a letter, my lord, but—'

'Excellent!' The Count directed a squire to refill Raoul's cup. 'De Montfort's bitten off more than he can chew and we're going to be the ones to make him choke. I'll send out messengers to Comminges and Béarn at the same time.' His expression filled with eagerness. 'What can you tell me about the current state of de Montfort's army from what you saw at Lavaur?'

'Apart from the fact that he's lacking a few hundred German mercenaries he was expecting from Carcassonne?' Raoul asked with a smile.

Foix's laughter resonated along the trestle. 'Should you ever need a roof, you'll be welcome to dwell under mine,' he said. 'You're a man after my own heart.'

Raoul wasn't so sure about that, but he joined the laughter anyway before settling down to discuss details.

Finally managing to escape the hall and its ebullient lord, Raoul climbed to the battlements to breathe fresh air. Below the great keep, most of the town slept, an occasional glimmer of torchlight winking from a bawdy house or tavern and reflecting on the dark surface of the River Ariège. Alone, but comforted by the unobtrusive, familiar sounds of the guards on watch, Raoul paced the wall walk and tried to think of nothing. As he approached one of the towers giving on to the walkway, he saw a woman standing in the shadows, her dark cloak embracing her body, her hair a flowing gleam like a river at night. His breath caught and his stomach knotted.

'I did not see you in the hall tonight; I thought you had retired,' he croaked, his throat suddenly dry.

'Only to my devotions.' A smile, no more than a ripple of starlight, crossed her face. 'There will be storms tomorrow, do you not feel them?' Without waiting on his answer, she added, 'I have a boon to ask of you before you leave Foix.'

'You have but to name it, my lady.'

'There is somewhere I have to go tomorrow without my uncle and Matthias. Will you take me?'

Raoul's stomach lurched. Averting his face, he pretended to pick at a loose lump of mortar on the crenellations. 'Where?'

'It's a hill fort a day's ride from here, mostly in ruins now. Long ago it was a sacred place.'

'And it is important to you? I thought the Cathars had no affinity for material ties.'

'It is not important to me for material reasons.' She faced him. 'I do not know if you will understand this, but sometimes, even after people have gone, the essence of their hopes and prayers remain behind. And I am not a Cathar like my Uncle Chretien. I was not raised as one, nor have I taken their vows.'

'So how do you come to be travelling in the company of two senior Perfecti with every priest in Christendom decrying you for heresy?' He leaned against the wall, pressing his hands into the cold reality of the stone, seeking its reassurance.

She stared beyond him towards the darkened hills. 'My father was Uncle Chretien's brother and a troubadour. He took service with Richard Coeur de Lion and followed him to Outremer. My mother was a healer who treated my father for a wound he took at the siege of Acre, and he settled with her in England.'

'Did she have the same skills as you?'

'Not as powerful as mine, but yes, she had them.' Bridget's expression grew distant and sad. 'Sometimes they are a great burden – when I see things I would rather not.' She took a slow, steadying breath. 'My mother taught me all she knew about healing – showed me how to channel the power. After my father died, we left England and visited the old holy places – Carnac and Compostela, which used to be called Brigantium after my namesake. Then we came to Béziers and sought out my father's family. My Uncle Chretien was already a practising Cathar Perfect, and Matthias was living with him then, too.'

Bridget made a troubled gesture and her eyes shone with moisture. 'Four years ago my mother was captured and killed by the black friars. My mother claimed descent from the Magdalene and from the Virgin Mary. The Roman Church is afraid that I will proclaim it to the world. They would destroy me for blasphemy, for the threat I pose to them. Matthias has the written proof of my bloodline.'

'So that was why he was so anxious about his manuscripts in Lavaur?'

She nodded, and took a moment to compose herself. 'I can see from your face that you do not know whether to believe me, or to think me deluded.'

'I have never met anyone like you,' he said hoarsely. 'What makes you think I am worthy company to be your escort tomorrow? If you knew what I was thinking, you would not be standing beside me now, let alone asking me to accompany you on a journey.'

'I know the kind of company I desire,' she murmured, and smiled up at him through wet lashes. The night settled around them like another cloak. Slowly, almost as if daring himself, he took his hand from the stone and reached out to touch her face, then her hair. He curled his grasp loosely around a thick strand and followed it down until his knuckles brushed over the peak of her breast. Finally he reached her waist and encircled it. She stood perfectly still, her eyes wide and her breathing rapid. He drew her against him, and she swayed into his arms, pliant and responsive. The darkness of night became the darkness of arousal, their bodies pressed together, mouth upon mouth and the tactile seeking of fingers.

He stroked her body, touching her, exploring her. Bridget made soft sounds and clutched him, her head thrown back. He cupped her buttocks and pulled her against him, letting her feel how much he wanted her. Desperate notions of throwing her down on the wall walk and thrusting into her coursed through his mind. Not even on his wedding night had he been so aroused. He swallowed a groan of pure lust.

Boots scraped on stone as a guard climbed the stairs on his rounds and Bridget struggled against him.

'Not here, not now!' she panted and, with a final wrench, freed herself from his grip and stepped away.

Breathing hard, Raoul leaned against the wall for support. All the strength in his body seemed concentrated in his groin where he was as hard as a sword hilt. 'I could die of wanting you,' he said in a trembling voice. He could hear the guard coming closer and silently cursed the man.

Bridget's eyes flickered in the direction of the sounds, and then returned to Raoul as if drawn by a magnet. She took a hesitant step forward, then two back as he reached for her again. 'No, wait until tomorrow,' she panted. 'The phase of the moon must be right.' She hurried away from him along the wall walk. On reaching the turret entrance, she looked over her shoulder and gave him a long look that made him shiver to the bone.

The guard passed him on the wall walk with a nod of greeting and a curious look in his eye. Raoul nodded stiffly in reply and returned to the pallet Mir had prepared for him in the hall, but it was a long time before he was able to sleep. He thought of Bridget, of how she had haunted him since his wedding eve, and how she was no longer a vision, but a warm, living, breathing woman. Inevitably he thought of Claire, of the unbearable closeness and the unbearable distance. His lids tightened, he tossed on the pallet, but he did not change his mind. For better or worse, the die was cast.

The road to Bridget's hill fort wound upward through forests of beech and pine, home to the boar, the brown bear, the wolf and the brigand, although Bridget and Raoul were troubled by none of these. Glimpses through the trees showed them snow still dusting the peaks of the Plantaurels even though it was early summer. Behind the white crests, the sky was as dark as slate and zigzagged by lightning.

Raoul had queried the wisdom of spending a night in the open when the weather was threatening to unleash terrific violence upon them but Bridget had given him an oblique look. 'There is nothing to fear, we are a part of it,' she had said, and her eyes as she spoke were the diamond-grey of his visions.

At noon they stopped to rest the horses. Bridget refused the bread and figs that Raoul produced from his saddle roll, and even a flask of the Count's excellent wine, contenting herself with water from the stream where their mounts were dipping their muzzles.

He ate his own food without tasting it, drank the wine without appreciation, and studied the seething bank of cloud amassing in the direction they were heading. Had Bridget's manner not been so strange and aloof, he would have suggested they return to Foix. Instead, he said nothing, aware that he did not have to speak; she could see every particle of him, as though his substance were made of glass.

Throughout the afternoon, they pressed on through valleys gashed by steep waterfalls, the trees clinging to the hillsides with roots like claws. The pines became sparse and small, giving way to hardy bushes and scrub. Outcrops of limestone thrust through the forests like giant bones, pitted with the dark sockets of ancient cave entrances. Once, in the distance, they saw the lithe, tawny shape of a lynx. It swung its head in their direction, took their scent, and vanished into the scrub. A herd of feral goats grazed on the steep slope of the mount where the ruins pushed up from the sparse grass like jagged teeth from their gums. On a tongue of rock, the dominant male regarded his territory with unnerving yellow eyes, his horns magnificent ridged curves, thick as young trees.

The fortress had been deserted for hundreds of years. Birds and animals, snakes and lizards had made homes in the limestone walls, and grass sprouted from every opportune crevice. A gust of cold air like a huge hand pushed Raoul through the ruined gateway. A marmot shot from beneath Bausan's hooves and scurried across the grass-choked ward. Desolation stalked the ramparts and ruined buildings. Overhead the sky was full of the coming storm.

Dismounting, Raoul looked round for a sheltered place to tether the horses and make camp for the night. The remains of a stone hut caught his attention, but a closer inspection revealed that at least one wall was in imminent danger of collapse. Shaking his head, he led their horses into the lee of the main curtain wall and tethered them to a holly oak tree that clung tenaciously to life among the crumbling stones. He supposed the horses would survive the night well enough where they were, but it was poor accommodation for himself and Bridget. This place must be special that she would seek it even in the face of such weather.

Looking over his shoulder, he saw her standing at the eastern edge of the broken ramparts. The rising wind carried to him the sound of her voice singing, although he could not make out the words, or even the language. His spine tingling, he attended to the horses unsaddling them, throwing blankets over their rumps and giving each of them a measure of grain. As he worked he was aware of Bridget standing out in the open, the wind whipping her garments against her body. His unease grew, and with it a gathering excitement.

He cast his glance round again, searching for somewhere to make a fire that would not flatten in the wind. Finding nothing, he left the horses and went to Bridget where she stood swaying in a state of half-trance. He started to touch her and changed his mind, confining himself instead to bellowing through the wind. 'We cannot stay here; there's nowhere to keep dry if the storm breaks. We'll die of cold!'

Her crooning ceased. She stood quite still, breathing deeply, then, obviously making an effort to retrace a mental path to the mundane, turned to him. 'There is a cave,' she said. 'It is too small for the horses, but there is room enough for us. Bring our packs and I will show you.' Without waiting for him, she started towards another, smaller gateway at the far end of the fortress. Dragging her gown through her belt, she scrambled over the pile of rubble in the entrance with the agility of a mountain goat.

Set into the hillside, the cave opening was concealed from the casual observer by an abrasive screen of juniper bushes.

Forcing them aside, Bridget crouched and entered. There was a sound like heavy rain on a tile roof and Raoul leaped backward, startled by the bats she had disturbed. A living twist of smoke, they streamed away in the direction of the fort. Bridget laughed and he managed a weak grin himself. He had to bend double to enter the cave. When he straightened and took a gulp of air, the smell of bat droppings and musty stone was so powerful that he nearly retched. Dim light filtered down through a smoke hole and there was a long-disused hearth immediately beneath it. Coughing, hand across his mouth and nose, he gave Bridget an eloquent look from his eye corners.

Her expression was preoccupied, for she was too deeply enmeshed in her own thoughts and emotions to notice anything as commonplace as a bad smell. Her gaze swept the small cave, and she picked her way delicately across it to a small ledge near the rear wall. 'My mother and I once sheltered here,' she murmured. 'It was shortly before we went to Béziers, to my uncle Chretien, and I was fourteen years old. She saw that I would return.' Reaching on tiptoe, she brought down a small lamp of red clay and a sealed container of oil.

Raoul found a relatively clean part of the cave floor and unhitched his sword belt. After one brief glance in his direction, Bridget coaxed the tinder to light and set it to the wick on the lamp. Light and shadows danced to life upon the smooth sides of the cave. Raoul felt as if he were caught inside a pulsating womb, the distant roll of thunder like the beat of blood around an unborn child.

'I'll fetch firewood before the storm breaks,' he said, and went back outside.

Bridget set about unpacking their saddle rolls. She laid out their blankets on the floor to one side of the hearth and set their eating bowls close by. Not that she intended eating anything herself. The fast was part of the ritual, opening the spiritual pathways. She could feel the power of the mystery tingling through her veins and gathering in the bowl of her hips as if she were already great with child.

When Raoul returned with a fat bundle of dry sticks, she had cleared the hearth of detritus and kindled a small fire in anticipation of the larger one to be built. Its smell was aromatic with herbs.

His glance lit on the blankets spread together and then upon her as he put the kindling down near the fire. 'We would have been more comfortable if we had stayed at Foix, and I doubt your uncle is deceived by any of this secrecy,' he remarked, only half in jest.

She set a small pot over the fire to simmer and scattered into it a handful of leaves. Hawthorn and white lily, fertility plants sacred to the Goddess; cherry laurel and hemp, the plants of visions. 'My uncle knows why I am here and my purpose, which is far more than that which I see in your eyes.'

Raoul sat down cross-legged opposite her and returned her stare. 'And what do you see in my eyes?' he asked softly.

'A child and a man, a girl and a woman,' she answered. 'Light and darkness and fire.' She took the pot from the fire in a fold of her cloak and poured the steaming contents into a cup. 'Drink,' she said. He hesitated. 'It is only a tisane that my mother taught me to brew,' she murmured to encourage him. 'It will not harm you.'

He eyed her with dark amusement. 'I did not think that you had brought me all this way to poison me.' Taking the cup, he drank. So did Bridget, but sparingly, and urged most of it on him. Then she sat down beside him and threw more wood upon the fire, adding more herbs.

The smoke clouded up, scented like incense and blossom.

'Last night at Foix,' Raoul ventured, 'you said that the phase of the moon must be right . . . that it was important? How so?'

'Women's bodies work to the ways of the moon and the tides. If they have the knowledge, they can tell when their wombs will quicken and when they will lie fallow.'

'That seems a very great power to me.'

'It is the power of choice.' She unwound her heavy black hair from its braid, and removed her gown, tunic and shift, her eyes never leaving his. 'Tonight you will sow your seed on fertile ground; tonight we will make a child between us.'

She saw him swallow, saw the look in his eyes as they travelled over her naked body. 'Then the power is mine, too,' he muttered with a hint of challenge. 'If I so wished I could withhold that gift.'

A half-smile curved her lips. 'And do you so wish, Raoul de Montvallant? Is that why you have come this far? Do you wish to go and sleep beside the horses? I will not stop you.'

He looked at her for a long moment, and then, breathing harshly, he began fumbling out of his own garments. 'No,' he said. 'I do not wish to sleep beside the horses.'

She leaned forward and set her mouth on his, her breasts grazing his chest, one arm around his neck, the other descending to his groin. Drugged by the smoke, exalted by the violence of the weather outside, she had no inhibitions.

She felt him, hot as a brand, swollen with need, heard him gasp. His hands, hard from the wielding of sword and spear, were infinitely gentle as they stroked between her thighs, but she needed no coaxing.

'Now,' she panted, guiding him home. 'Let it be now!'

He pierced her and she cried aloud with the twin sensations of pain and fulfilment. She was the sky and he was the force of the rain. She was the earth and he was the white-hot stab of the lightning. Closing her eyes, wrapping her legs around him, she let the force of the storm take her up so that she became a whirling particle of its vast element – the brilliance of pure sensation possessing her body and removing it from her control, and then the slow spiral down. And before she could grasp anything of self, the spiral reversed and returned her again to the vortex of the storm and the power of the surging life force.

*   *   *

Early morning brought the high-pitched twittering of the bats returning to their roost, ignoring now the presence of strangers in their abode. The smoke from the fire was a narrow twirl, unscented by any herb, and the light of day glimmered through the hole in the roof and entered obliquely through the screened cave entrance. By its light Bridget turned her head and studied the sleeping man. His arm lay across her, his hand loosely upon the red cords around her neck from which hung the two dove and chalice pendants. Well, perhaps it was appropriate. He had given her the means last night to fashion another such cord. She looked at his thick golden lashes, the sensuous curve of his mouth, and her heart ached. What could she give him in return? Only the bitter revelation of something she had known even before she brought him from Lavaur, and that he would discover when he went home.

Her eyes swept his body, admiring the lean contours of muscle and sinew. How easy it would be to stay here with him in dalliance, learning all the subtleties of the new mystery she had discovered – that he had led her to discover. And what would he recall of last night? Her lips curved poignantly. A man and a woman, light and darkness and fire. Gently she removed his arm from across her body and sat up. Her hair was a wild tangle over her breasts and shoulders. Quickly, quietly, she braided it as best she could, donned her chemise and gown, stuffed her belongings into her own saddle roll and, with a final look at Raoul, went silently from the cave. It was easier this way. If she stayed until he awoke, he would want to talk, to cement the bond they had forged last night, and that could never be. His heart and soul were not hers, and his body had only been a brief lending of the male life force. It had been fine and beautiful. That was what she regretted leaving behind.

It had stopped raining. The sunrise twinkled on the wet grass, covering the fortress ruins in a wash of gold. The air smelled of juniper and thyme and new young shoots. Bridget placed one hand lightly on her belly, feeling an affinity with all things growing. Humming softly to herself, she began climbing towards the fort.

Opening his eyes, Raoul stared across the empty space beside him at a fire that had gone out. Gradually he came to his senses, his memory floating into place piece by little piece. His eyes widened and he looked around the cave, discovering that he was alone. For a wild instant he thought he had been dreaming again, but when he sat up to don his braies, he saw the dried blood smearing his groin and thighs. But if last night's intimacy was not an illusion, where was she and why had she gone?

He fumbled into his clothing and went outside. A morning alive with birdsong sparkled at him, the sky and land cleansed of dust. The sun stroked his face. Shading his eyes with the flat of his hand, he stared around, but saw nothing save a family of ground squirrels grooming in the new warmth, and a lone lammergeyer high in the blue.

Feeling bereft, he stooped back into the cave and packed his saddle roll, returning the tinder, flint, oil and lamp to the shelf for the use of others who might happen this way. As he climbed back to the ruins on the summit, he wondered if they had begotten the child that she had wanted. Surely so, for she had the gift of seeing and last night her body had drained his dry.

'Why me?' he had asked her as they lay close, the sweat cooling upon their bodies. 'Why choose me?'

She had smiled, tiny creases appearing at her eye corners. 'I could say that it is because you are the most handsome man I have ever seen, and that would be the truth, but not all of it.' She had moved her hand slowly over his chest and abdomen, exploring the contours of muscle. 'Once, long ago, I saw you and wanted you,' she murmured, 'but the time was not right. You have a strong life force, Raoul de Montvallant, and a will of iron that runs straight and true.

I want these qualities for a child of mine. Her life will not be easy.'

'Her life?'

She had taken his hand and traced his palm and finger-tips over her belly to the moist juncture of her thighs. 'Her life,' she had said, and shortly after that they had ceased to talk.

His horse waited in the lee of the wall, and he saw that Bridget had fed and saddled him. Braided into Bausan's mane was a red cord from which hung a small silver disc bearing the device of a dove and chalice. He recognised it as one of the tokens Bridget had worn around her neck even while they made love. Smiling, feeling slightly less bereft, he put the cord around his own neck and tucked it down inside his tunic.

On riding into Foix that evening, it came as no surprise to Raoul to discover that Bridget, Chretien and Matthias had departed the moment she returned. He was told she had only paused to change to a fresh horse, and no one knew where the trio was bound. No messages, no hints.

Curious glances followed Raoul, but he ignored them. His troops saw the set of his jaw and knew better than to ask questions. Even Giles and Roland, who called him friend as well as lord, left him well alone.

The following dawn, Raymond-Roger of Foix handed over to Raoul the letters intended for the Count of Toulouse. His dark eyes gleamed with relish, for he had no need to bridle his own tongue.

'I gather it wasn't a success?' he needled as Raoul put the packets inside his travelling satchel.

Raoul's mouth tightened as he donned his gauntlets. 'My lord, with respect, that is a private affair between myself and the lady.'

'Oh, hardly private,' provoked Foix with a grin. 'Chretien de Béziers was somewhat vexed to discover you and she both gone. He spent the night before last in prayer for his niece, but I warrant you and she were worshipping at a different kind of altar entirely!'

The second gauntlet in place, Raoul clenched his fist to ease the leather and contemplated striking Foix in the mouth. But then Foix, for all his crude manner, had only spoken the truth, and Raoul knew his own conscience was on the raw. Carefully he unclenched his fist and turned round. 'Doubtless the lady will give her uncle all the reassurance he needs,' he said impassively. 'Whatever the lord Chretien's misgivings, he knew our destination. Thank you for your hospitality. I'll make sure Count Raymond receives your letters with all haste.' He bowed to make an end of the interview.

'And I wish you Godspeed.' Humour tugged at the other man's mouth as he gave a formal response to Raoul's formal farewell. 'Remember what I said. There's a place for you here among my own knights should you wish to stay. I know a good horse and a good man when I see one.'

'Thank you, my lord,' Raoul replied when he could be sure his voice would not betray him. 'You are generous.' Bowing out into the bright summer morning, he swung into the saddle and turned his troop for home.

And a little to the north, as the sun climbed in the sky, Simon de Montfort went for the enemy's throat and struck at Toulouse.

CHAPTER 20

MONTVALLANT, MAY 1211

Guillaume wailed and hit out with his small fists as Claire and Isabelle struggled to hold him still while they finished rubbing viscous brown walnut oil into his skin and hair.

'Hush, oh, hush!' Claire pleaded, unable to bear the sound of his cries but knowing that disguising her son as a goatherd's child was his best chance of survival. She looked in grief at the transformation from blond angel to grubby urchin. An old blanket had been found at the bottom of the press, and a frayed homespun tunic discarded from one of the kitchen boys had been cut down to fit him.

Overwhelmed by her love and her terror, she clutched Guillaume fiercely to her bosom, kissing him and weeping.

'My lady, it is not too late for you to come with us,' quavered Isabelle, tears shimmering in her eyes.

Claire shook her head. 'No, I cannot leave Beatrice. She's too weak to travel, and in Raoul's absence I am responsible for Montvallant. Here, take care of him . . . keep him safe for me . . . ' She gave Guillaume to her maid. Standing on the threshold, Pierre the groom was waiting. 'Go now, quickly. I'll join you later if I can.'

Unable to watch Isabelle leave with Guillaume, Claire turned away, her eyes squeezed tightly shut. Her heart was dying as surely as the soldiers had died on the town walls when de Montfort had brought his army down on them fresh from plundering Lavaur. She could not blame her people for yielding when threatened. With Raoul absent, they had no commander to coordinate resistance, and they knew what had happened at Béziers and at Bram, where the entire garrison had been mutilated. Apparently Raoul had been too late to save Lavaur, but had rescued Geralda's three important heretics from the town, literally from beneath de Montfort's nose. The lord Simon wanted them handed into his custody or else . . .

Claire's stomach dissolved. How could they give him what they did not have? 'Raoul, where are you?' she whispered. The crusaders held the town. If she refused to open her gates, de Montfort had threatened to raze Montvallant and do on a smaller scale what he had done to Béziers.

She entered the main bedchamber. The fire had been built up to a huge blaze to keep the room warm. In the great bed that was hers and Raoul's, Beatrice was propped up on half a dozen pillows. Her complexion was bright, but it was the radiance of fever, not the bloom of health. Her ravaged lungs were faltering badly now, the specks of blood on her kerchief had become blots, and her exhaustion grew worse daily. Her mind had started to wander. Sometimes she would speak to Berenger as if he were with her in the room. Claire did not even think of burdening her by telling her what was happening.

She stood at the bedside. The heat of the room beaded her brow with sweat, but Beatrice's skin was clammy. Her mother-in-law's eyes flickered open, smudged with the fatigue of living on death's edge. 'Light the candles,' she whispered to Claire. 'The night is closing in early today.'

Claire did what she could to give Beatrice ease, and when the sick woman had fallen into a restless doze, went down to give the order to open the gates to the crusaders. They came, row upon row, two abreast, their banners snapping in the hot wind, their armour shining like a shoal of netted fish. Their horses churned the dust into a white haze so that they rode into Montvallant's bailey as if out of a dream. A white stallion paced forward and the knight upon its back stared round, assessing the defences. Then he lowered his gaze, narrowed it upon Claire, and beckoned with a raised mail mitten.

Her foreboding verging on terror, Claire advanced to tender Montvallant's submission to Simon de Montfort. Her chatelaine's keys were held across her palms, but she had no intention of kneeling to present them.

De Montfort held his stallion on a tight rein and looked at her with the same hard gaze that had perused her castle walls. Claire forced herself to return his stare and felt as if she had been seized in a vice and squeezed until she could not breathe. This was the man who had overseen the massacre of Béziers and the atrocities at Bram and Minerve, who had taken Lavaur and watched its Cathars burn, and who was now going to do the same to the Cathars of Montvallant, perhaps including herself.

'It is your husband's submission I require,' he said huskily.

'He is not here, my lord; I offer you the keys in his stead.' Claire compressed her lips and, out of sheer, terrified bravado, raised her chin.

De Montfort frowned. He gestured and a young knight dismounted to take the keys from her hands.

'Your husband has a penchant for running away.'

'At least he does not steal other men's lands,' she retorted. 'I count him worth ten of you.'

'Do you indeed?' De Montfort curbed his sidling horse with one hand and examined the keys the young man passed up to him. He looked again at Claire. 'Then perhaps it is time you were taught to value differently. Giffard, escort Lady de Montvallant to her chamber and make sure she stays there.'

The squire grasped Claire's arm. She tried to shake him off, but his grip was of steel. The white afternoon heat, the enemy soldiers, the oppression of de Montfort's gaze, all combined to buckle her knees. She had to cling to the squire

to keep herself from falling at de Montfort's feet, thus making
it easy for him to take her away.

'Berenger? Berenger, where are you?' Beatrice's fever-bright
gaze wandered the chamber.

'It's all right, Mother, hush, I'm here.' Claire sat down
on the coverlet and clasped the sick woman's reaching hand.

'Berenger?'

'No, Mother, it's Claire? Are you thirsty?'

A frown shadowed Beatrice's flushed brow. 'I can feel
you!' she whispered. 'Beloved, I know you are here.' Her
hand tightened upon Claire's then slowly relaxed; her eyelids
drooped and her words died to a mumble.

Beatrice drifted into an uneasy sleep and Claire gently
released herself from the older woman's febrile grip. Her
chest hurt as she fought not to weep aloud. She wanted to
howl her fear and anguish at the rafters, but knew it would
disturb her mother-in-law. Besides, an armed guard stood
outside the room with his ear to the door, and she refused
to give him the satisfaction of hearing her.

Sniffing, wiping her eyes, Claire went to the pitcher and
tipped the last of the wine into a crude wooden cup. De
Montfort's men had looted the fine flagon and goblets,
leaving her utensils from the kitchens in exchange. The wine
tasted sour, but it had been standing in the pitcher since
before dawn, and it was past compline now. From darkness
to darkness, she thought, and no glimmer of light in between,
although the day she had just endured had been the longest
of her entire life.

In agitation, Claire paced to the shuttered window. If she
looked round, she would see the logs blazing in the hearth,
warning her of the fate awaiting all heretics. Before they had
locked her in here with Beatrice and stripped the room of all
luxuries, she had seen the priests among de Montfort's
troops. Beside Simon's personal chaplains she had noticed a
smirking Father Otho. There was also a young black friar

with a fanatical gleam in his eye whom she recognised from the first months of her marriage when he and another priest had come seeking Geralda's three heretics. Now, apparently, he was a member of de Montfort's retinue.

The door latch rattled and she leaped to face it, eyes wide, her empty cup falling to the rushes.

'Lord de Montfort wants to see you,' said the young squire whom she had heard the others call Giffard. He was hard-eyed like his master, and no older than herself.

'Why?' She put one hand to her throat.

'If you please, my lady. He dislikes to be kept waiting.'

If she pleased? And what would happen if she refused? Both the squire and the guard on the door were well fed and muscular, and it would be no difficulty for them to drag her wherever they desired.

'My mother-in-law is sick; I dare not leave her for too long.'

The squire indicated the door and looked impatient. Smoothing her gown, raising her chin, she followed him down the twisting stair to the solar. He banged on the door, waited for his lord to acknowledge, and then ushered her into the room.

De Montfort was sitting in the chair that had been Berenger's favourite, its cushions worn but comfortable, the wood bearing the patina of age and polishing. His broad, soldier's body occupied every inch of it.

'Come in, my lady,' he said, and dismissed his squire with a nod and a brief gesture of the hand not holding a cup of wine.

Claire took two tiny steps forward. Her spine was so stiff with the effort of holding herself together that she was shaking.

Without haste he put his cup down, unfolded himself from the chair, and prowled across the room until he stood over her. 'Where is your husband?' he asked.

Claire felt trapped by the domineering bulk invading

her space. Her teeth chattered with terror. She shook her head.

'You are deluded if you think silence will help you,' Simon said.

'I do not know,' she said in a thin whisper.

'Cooperate with me and your town will not be destroyed. Otherwise . . . ' He shrugged and gestured. 'You should know by now what happens to those who collaborate with heretics.'

She bit her lip. 'I do not know,' she repeated.

'By the rood, tell me!' Simon grasped her shoulders and shook her. Her head snapped back and her wimple tumbled askew.

The violence restored a spark of feeling. 'I tell you, I do not know!' she sobbed. 'Leave me alone!'

Beneath the pressure of his fingers, Simon felt her terrified trembling. Her hair spilled down her back, webbing his hands with the scent of lavender. His wife's hair was fine and straight, her braids not much thicker than the width of his thumb. This between his fingers was a lustrous river of fire. He was intensely aware of her full lips, the curve of her throat, the swift rise and fall of her breasts, and with that awareness came hard, hot arousal.

Simon prided himself on his control, on his ability to refuse the whores and courtesans whom his own officers used to satisfy their appetites. He had Alais, and as often as not she was within riding distance, but it had been a long time between visits and she was very close to birthing the child conceived last autumn. He discovered that, for once, he wanted to give his lust free rein, to ride its wildness until he was spent. It was his right to take, to be avenged on Raoul de Montvallant for what had happened at Lavaur.

His hands tightened in her hair and he set his mouth on hers. She jerked, tried to scream, but he sealed her voice in her throat with the pressure of his kiss and forced her back against the wall, jamming himself against her. Her struggles filled him with an eager need to subjugate. He would brand her for ever with his mark as if she were a runaway peasant.

He took her savagely on the rushes of her own solar floor, her gown bunched up around her waist like any common whore, her arms pinioned, her body invaded by his male force, flattened by his weight as he surged into her. His thrusts raged deep, violating, imprinting. He tasted the salt of blood on her lips as his mouth crushed down on hers, grinding, grinding, hands bruising her flesh, digging bone-deep. As he jammed into her for the final time and his seed pulsed within her, she represented to him the entire lands of Raymond of Toulouse. Raped, subjugated, sown with his will, never to be southern again.

'It doesn't matter about your husband!' he panted, still at his limit within her. 'Let him run, let him hide. It is only a matter of time.'

CHAPTER 21

MONTVALLANT, JUNE 1211

Still as a millpond, the Tarn reflected a solid silver moon. Raoul loosened the reins to let Bausan drink and stared across the water at the light-frosted lands beyond the river's gleam. Montvallant. His home. Crushed beneath a northern fist while he had been riding in the opposite direction to Foix.

The town itself remained intact, but it had been severely purged. The bodies of the garrison rotted on the walls, and the church bell, which had scarcely been swung in the last five years, now called the people to enforced mass and tolled an early curfew. Soldiers, wearing the hated red cross on their surcoats, were billeted upon the inhabitants. De Montfort had established a mercenary camp in the town, showing the people of Montvallant what happened when they supported a rebel lord.

Time and again Raoul relived his folly after Lavaur. Instead of returning to Claire, he had pursued a dream and gained nothing but the temporary gratification of his body at the expense of the fabric of his daily life. The bulk of his troop was swelling the garrison at Toulouse, where every man was needed to fight off de Montfort's sustained assault. ...ul had brought a few picked knights for this night recon- ...ds over which less than a month ago he ...ossession. *Je voi bien tuit perdu ai* – Now ... So the jongleur at Foix had plaintively ... stolen. On that thought Raoul spoke softly to the horse and urged him into the gleaming dark water. Ripples arrowed the stallion's legs and breast as he thrust against the current. Behind him, Raoul heard the soft plash of the other horses entering the river. Bit chains muffled, they rode across moonlit fields, through vineyards and orchards, and took the track towards the caves where Montvallant had given shelter to the itinerant Cathars of the Agenais.

Crickets chirred in the silence. Rags of cloud drifted across the haloed moon. The men shunned the light, their cloaks worn over their armour and their faces blackened with mud. Keeping to the shadows, they climbed the hill and took the narrow goat track to the caves near the summit. Raoul felt his heart sink, for they were deserted, their fires several days cold. An overturned cooking pot, eating bowls with the food still in them and a solitary shoe told their tale only too well. Montvallant's Cathars had been discovered, and therein died his hope that Claire, his mother and Guillaume had been able to shelter among them, undetected.

Dismounting, he squatted beside the dead fire, rubbing the ashes between his fingers. A different cave and a different fire held his inner vision, and his feeling of guilt increased threefold.

'Listen,' Mir whispered urgently. 'Someone comes.'

Raoul wiped his hand on his surcoat and rose to face the direction of the squire's stare. Silently, he inched his sword from its sheath and made urgent hand gestures to his men.

Their breathing swift and shallow, the men listened to the sound of other breathing, loud with effort as whoever it was strove up the rocks towards them from the direction of the town. The scrape of shod hoof on stone sounded clearly across the stillness of the night. A woman's voice spoke in the darkness and a man panted a reply. The tongue was southern and Raoul relaxed slightly but remained backed into the shadows.

The starlight shone on dark horsehide and sparkled on

bridle trappings. As the rider reined to a halt before the cave, Raoul recognised Claire's bay mare. His heart sprang painfully against his ribs, but the woman who dismounted wore the coarse weave of a peasant and was smaller than Claire.

'Isabelle?' Raoul stepped from the shadows. She screamed and her companion's knife flashed and then halted in mid-motion.

'Lord Raoul?' Pierre the groom thrust his head forward and peered into the darkness. The knife flashed again as he sheathed it in his belt. Covering his face with his hands, he started to sob. 'You are too late, my lord. De Montfort himself came at the head of hundreds of men. We had no choice but to surrender.'

Isabelle drew back the edge of the blanket in her arms to show Raoul his sleeping son. 'My lady bade me disguise him as a peasant child. We clothed him in homespun and rubbed walnut dye into his hair lest its fairness attract too much attention, and Pierre and I escaped with him.'

Raoul took Guillaume into his arms. An aching lump constricted his throat and he had to force his voice through it to speak. 'What happened to your mistress?'

'She was taken prisoner, my lord, and your lady mother with her. The soldiers burned the Cathars and forced us all to watch, and then they took Lady Claire and Lady Beatrice away – no one knows where.'

Pierre wiped his face on his sleeve. 'They came up here,' he croaked, 'straight up. They knew where the Cathars were hiding and they dragged them out and brought them to the town. God's true light, I never want to see such a sight again.' He touched the hilt of his knife and his voice hardened. 'It was Father Otho who betrayed them to the soldiers. The whoreson returned with de Montfort's troops and set about wreaking vengeance. He had people dragged out of their houses and beaten in the streets. He demanded to be the torch-bearer when the Cathars were tied at the stake.' Pierre's face twisted with revulsion. 'I knew he would come looking for Isabelle as soon as he was free of his duties, so I bided my time. For all that I am a croyant of the true religion, I do not repent that I killed him, and it was quicker than he deserved.'

'I would have done the same,' Raoul said flatly. 'And you know nothing more of Lady Claire and Lady Beatrice?'

'No, my lord. After they had been forced to witness the burning, they were put in a litter and taken away under guard. One of de Montfort's knights feasts in your hall, and the town is overflowing with crusaders and mercenaries. De Montfort is using it as a supply camp. There is nothing you can do.'

Raoul clenched his jaw. For a moment the anguish and guilt gripped him so powerfully that he could not think.

'We were making our way to Agen, to Lady Claire's mother,' Pierre added, 'but first we came up here to see if anyone was left . . .'

'Agen,' Raoul said huskily, fixing on the name, while comprehension blundered back into his mind. 'I'll escort you there. De Montfort's troops are everywhere.'

Isabelle held out her hands for the child. 'Shall I carry him, my lord?'

'No,' he said softly. 'Let me have him.' Cradling his sleeping son, Raoul mounted his stallion and felt his loss all the more keenly for the saving grace of this warm scrap of life in his arms.

Perched upon a steep, pudding-shaped rock, its lower slopes forested in pines, the fortress of Montségur was the foremost Cathar stronghold in the Ariège. Isolated, imposing, it was a haven for the persecuted, and daunted those who had no calling.

A strong wind buffeted Bridget as she paused to stare at her destination. The sky was a boiling mass of dark clouds above the castle. She would bear her child here and watch her grow in wisdom and strength. This place would succour them from a hostile world – for the immediate future at least. She set her hand lightly upon her belly, and felt with pleasure the fluttering throb of the new life quickening within her womb. *See, Mother, I have fulfilled my promise. Your grand-child grows inside me, a daughter of the Light.*

Chretien left Matthias sitting on the grass where they had stopped to eat their noontide meal, and joined her where she stood on the narrow mule track, watching the blending of castle, crag and clouds. She turned to him with a wistful half-smile. 'I was thinking of my mother,' she said, 'and missing her. When I see these mountains, I feel that I can touch her spirit, that she is watching over me.'

Chretien returned her smile and drew a deep lungful of the pine-scented air. 'She loved Montségur. It is fitting that you should come here.' He set his arm around her shoulders, and she leaned her head briefly upon his shoulder. Chretien had said very little about her pregnancy. Their views differed; neither would ever argue the other into a state of change. He had accepted the inevitable, and offered her his support, if not his approval. If a child was to be born, then let its path be a true and holy one. Matthias had been more openly pleased at Bridget's news, but then to Matthias, Bridget's fruitfulness was a continuation of the bloodline whose path he had traced and recorded for so many years – a light that still burned despite all efforts to quench it.

Montségur. A place both of kindling and of quenching, quiescent now, couched in power. *I will raise up mine eyes to the Light, and I will drink of its bounty. It is my heritage, my life and my death.*

'Come,' she said to Chretien, pulling away from him. 'There are still many miles to travel before nightfall.'

CHAPTER 22

A wild November wind buffeted the four-horse travelling wain that was bearing Alais de Montfort and her ladies towards the town of Castres for the winter season.

The endless swaying and bumping of the wain as it lurched out of one rut and into another made Claire feel sick. The furs and pelts with which the women had surrounded themselves to keep the draughts at bay smelled mustily of long storage in the clothing chest.

Seated next to Claire was a wet nurse, her ample white breast straining the jaws of Alais de Montfort's four-month-old son as he sucked lustily. Alais's daughter Amice, aged nine, nursed a straw doll on her lap and crooned to it. The sight made Claire feel ill. Shutting her eyes, she repositioned the padded cushions that were supposed to absorb the jolting of the cart, but the grinding ache persisted in the small of her spine. Beneath her ribs, the child kicked and wriggled continuously, reminding her with each punch and thrust of its conception upon the floor of Montvallant's solar.

Simon de Montfort had not touched her since that night. Indeed, he went out of his way to avoid her and regarded her burgeoning belly with as much revulsion as Claire did herself. She knew he had spoken of the rape to his confessor, for the priest treated her as though she were anathema. From the sermons with which he had lectured the household over the past months, she understood that Simon had

been exonerated of all blame and that she was the sinner –
a heretic harlot who had used her wiles to seduce an innocent man. The criticism had all been implied, and only
those involved understood the full meaning. Alais remained
in ignorance. She thought Claire's child was of the seed of
Montvallant. Many times it had been on the tip of Claire's
tongue to tell Alais the truth, but on each occasion she had
restrained the words, knowing her own vulnerability.

De Montfort had delivered her and Beatrice into Alais's
custody. 'Spoils of war,' he had told his wife in an offhand
manner. 'Tainted with heresy, the pair of them, but not
beyond redemption. I trust in your skills to lead them back
to the fold and prove to Cîteaux that it can be done.'

Claire looked through her lowered lashes at Simon's neat,
self-satisfied wife. Her thin brown braids were concealed
beneath a wimple bordered with gold lacework. Samarkand
sables trimmed the dark blue cloak, and several fine rings
adorned the thin, predatory hands. The notion of redeeming
a pair of heretical southern noblewomen had appealed to the
lady Alais. She was a devout Catholic, and for her own pride
and Simon's approval, determined to succeed.

Beatrice had cheated Alais's endeavours by dying within
a week of being taken prisoner, but de Montfort's
indomitable wife had ensured that Raoul's mother was
shriven at the end so that at least her soul could review its
errors in purgatory rather than being condemned to everlasting damnation.

Claire was determined that Alais would not claim the
victory with her. She knew she had to be cunning. Open
rebellion was not the way. To all intents and purposes, Claire
had become a meek, biddable mouse. She listened to what
Alais and the chaplain said, she attended mass regularly, and
she prayed with the rest of the women. They were not to
know that as she faced the altar, the stone chapel floor chilling
her knees through her linen gown, she was praying not to
their corrupt, earthbound God, but to the being of Light

worshipped by the Cathars. And the more religious observances Alais made her perform, the brighter shone Claire's inner rebellion.

They stopped at a monastery to water the horses and refresh themselves. Lord Simon, Claire was told, intended pressing on while the daylight lasted and desired to waste no time. She saw him from a distance as she stepped down from the women's cart. He had dismounted and was talking to the prior. Even from here she felt the weight of his personality bearing down upon her. As if sensing her scrutiny, he turned his head towards her. His stare narrowed as it dropped to her belly. Abruptly he turned his shoulder and bent a deliberate ear to the prior. Trembling, Claire followed the other women to the guesthouse. Bile rose in her throat and she was sick in one of the herb borders planted against the stone wall. If only she could vomit up the seed growing in her belly.

A small boy tugged at her gown and pushed a cup of water into her hand. 'Gentian says you're poorly because there's a baby growing inside you,' he said seriously.

Swallowing, Claire straightened up and looked at the child. Another of Alais's prolific brood of children. Simon de Montfort was as potent as a bull. This one, his namesake, was about four years of age, a serious little boy with gold hair darkening to brown and green-flecked hazel eyes. Claire, despite her hatred of his father, her misery and her grief, had been unable to bring herself to shun the child, and over the months of her captivity had even developed a fondness for him. His presence subdued the pain of losing Guillaume to a dull ache. Besides, it gave her satisfaction to know that the bond between herself and young Simon irritated his mother intensely.

'That is indeed part of it,' she said and, to please his anxious gaze, sipped the water.

'Will you be better soon?'

She forced herself to smile. 'I think so.'

He tilted his head to one side, assessing her. 'I have to ride in the cart when we set off again. Amaury says I can't sit on his saddle any more because I fidget too much. Will you tell me a story?'

Claire knew how much Simon loved to settle down in a comfortable lap and listen to tales until the teller was as hoarse as a bear. But today she was not sure of her stamina.

'The one about the brave knight and the wicked dragon?' he asked hopefully when she did not reply.

Claire bit her lip. The brave knight was always golden-haired and blue-eyed with a smile to pierce the clouds. The dragon, had the child but known, was his own father. 'In a little while perhaps.'

He considered her, his hazel eyes narrowing in uncon-scious imitation of his father's. 'Do you promise?'

Claire opened her mouth to say that she would not be persuaded into promising anything, but was forestalled by the appearance of Friar Bernard. He claimed to have been saved from death in a winter blizzard outside Carcassonne by the Virgin Mary herself, and that it was a sign of divine favour that must be repaid with crusading zeal. He made Claire's flesh crawl, and she could not stand to be near him.

'Your mother has been looking for you, boy,' he said to Simon. 'We are waiting to bless the meal.' He glanced distrustfully at Claire as if he suspected her of fomenting heresy with a four-year-old.

'I . . . I was feeling unwell,' she faltered. 'Simon brought me a cup of water.' She laid a protective hand on the child's shoulder.

'Mayhap you wanted to avoid the blessing,' hissed Friar Bernard.

'No, Father, that is not so. The babe makes me ill. I will come now.' In her own ears, her voice sounded breathless and afraid.

The friar gave a contemptuous grunt. 'It is Eve's curse that women bear children in pain and suffering.' He eyed her rounded belly with distaste. 'It is a heresy to think that it should be otherwise.'

'Yes, Father.' Meekly lowering her eyes, Claire ushered little Simon into the guesthouse. At her back, she could feel the friar's stare boring into her, replacing the marrow of her bones with ice.

Chapter 23

Within a small hut built upon the lower slopes of the mountain, Bridget crouched, controlling the pain with her will as she bore down to push her baby into the world. She was alone for the ordeal because she had wished it that way. She had food and water, and there were women at the fortress who took it in turns to check upon her welfare.

The pain came, wave upon pulsing wave, but she did not permit it to overwhelm her. Instead she envisaged a flower bud ripening, swelling and splitting open in wonderful colours. Her fingers sought the wet crown of her baby's head. She supported her elastic perineal muscles and panted shallowly, resisting the urge to push. On the next contraction, the head was born, followed by the slippery little shoulders, and finally, in a gush of fluid and blood, the tiny, perfectly formed body.

'Magda,' she whispered. 'Your name will be Magda, as was your grandmother's and her grandmother's before that.' And when Bridget had cut the cord with a knife of sharpened flint, she put her new daughter to her breast so that the infant's suckling would more quickly deliver the afterbirth.

The pain was relentless. Claire bit down on the block of wood that one of the midwives had forced between her teeth, the tendons cording in her throat. Someone pressed a moist

cloth to her brow and a voice murmured soothingly in her
ear. Between her thighs, hands probed and her spine arched
at the intrusion.

'Well,' she heard Alais snap, 'how goes it?'

'Slowly, madam. The child is big and the opening is not
widening as fast as it might.'

'Is she strong enough?'

The senior midwife made a seesawing motion with her
hands, which Claire saw as the contraction faded and she
opened her eyes. 'It depends upon how the baby's head is
lying, and that I cannot tell until she has opened further.'

'Hah!' Alais said impatiently. 'Inform me as soon as you
have news.'

Claire heard the fading swish of her skirts and gave a sob
of relief. She did not want to bear this child conceived of
violation, but the less she cooperated with the midwives, the
greater became her pain and the more they forced potions
down her throat and pried between her legs. The baby's head
pressing down the birth channel gave her a powerful urge
to push. She resisted it, wondering how long it would take
her to die. It was late February and spring clearly on the
horizon, but snow had fallen overnight and continued to sift
lazily down. She could see it distorted through the heavy
grey glass leaded into the window embrasure. Remote and
cold. If only she could detach herself from the struggle and
join the swirling flakes in the nothing-white air.

Another contraction built and crashed over her with such
force that she felt as if she would burst, and she screamed
Raoul's name. Where was he? Dead? Alive? And Guillaume,
what of Guillaume? The not knowing tortured her. Oh, my
child, my child, the born and the unborn. And as the pain
swallowed all thought and reason, the midwives returned to
pat and murmur and probe at her.

Simon de Montfort stretched out his saddle-cramped legs
and, uttering a deep sigh of relief, took the goblet of

strengthened wine from his wife's hands. His gaze was heavy with fatigue as he studied the room – the tapestries from Béziers, the candlesticks from Carcassonne, the goblets and comfit dishes from Lavaur. The proof of his victories was piled around him like a dragon's hoard. Even his wife's working gown was made of silk and her wimple coruscated with gold embroidery. However, they were all summer gains. He seldom brought anything to Alais except his exhaustion in the winter months. This time she had refused to go north with the departing army and, despite the hard fighting and some losses, Simon had felt secure enough to let her have her way.

He glanced briefly at his two eldest sons, who were still gorging themselves on the meal Alais had ordered to the chamber. Amice had squeezed between her brothers, demanding their attention as Alais, in her own fashion, was demanding his. She was dutifully waiting on him when a maid or a squire could as easily have performed the task of pouring his wine and serving him honey tarts.

'What is it?' he asked, his voice edged with irritation

Alais put down the rock-crystal flagon. 'Claire de Montvallant was delivered of a son just before vespers,' she said. 'The babe is lusty, but the mother's condition is cause for concern. She refused to push him out until the midwives threatened her with Caesar's cut while she still lived. When she finally did deliver him, he tore her badly.'

Simon's gut swooped. 'Why do you come to me with women's business?' he growled, using anger to shield his guilt. 'Think you I have an interest in such trifles?'

Alais's expression stiffened, but he judged her look a reaction to his manner, not an awareness of the child's paternity.

Her voice when she replied was low-pitched and controlled. Leaning over him, she refilled his cup. 'My lord, I desire to take the baby into my household and bring him up with Richard and Simon.' He raised it to his lips and took a long swallow. It was simple; all he had to do was snap a refusal and walk away. She knew better than to argue with him. But he had been raised to acknowledge responsibility and despised any man unable to take the consequences of his actions. He was already ripe with self-disgust over the matter of Claire de Montvallant. Nine months ago he had succumbed to his lust. He still felt the pulsing hunger whenever he looked at their lovely southern hostage, and was filled with bewildered anger at his own reaction.

'Show me the child,' he said abruptly, and stood up.

Alais gave him a startled look but led him with alacrity to the chamber where their own offspring slept. Richard, seven months old, was asleep in his crib, tightly swaddled for the night. Beside him on a pallet lay Simon, his thumb close to his mouth, freckles sprinkling his nose.

Alais laid her hand upon his sleeve and smiled with tender pride.

Uneasy, Simon shook her off and went to Mabel, Richard's wet nurse, who was seated in a corner suckling a newborn infant. The woman started to rise, but he gestured her to remain seated and stood over her to look upon the result of his lechery. She showed him the infant, which bawled in protest at being plucked from the squashy, milky comfort of her breast. In the dim light of the oil lamp, the baby's hair and eyes were dark and its puckered skin yellowish.

'Has he been named?'

Behind him, Alais smiled. 'As soon as the cord was cut,' she purred. 'I thought that Dominic was appropriate. Friar Bernard baptised him.'

He glanced at her sharply. Her expression was smug. The infant, however he developed, was branded for life with the name of one of the most feared and energetic opposers of Catharism – Dominic Guzman, founder of the order of preaching friars.

'If I cannot save the mother's soul, then I will save the child's,' she said, her eyes fixed upon the baby as the nurse returned him to her breast.

Simon was not deceived by his wife's piety. While he did not doubt the sincerity of her intention, fostering the child would salve her pride at not having control of Claire de Montvallant's wayward soul. 'Where's the mother?'

Alais led him into another chamber, separated from the main nursery by a heavy curtain. Fumes of incense clung to the folds and still pervaded the room, speaking of the recent presence of a priest. On the wall a crucifix was illuminated by a cresset lamp bearing three pools of flame. Lying on a pallet, the sheets drawn up to her chin, was Claire de Montvallant. Her form was so still, her breathing so shallow, that Simon thought for a moment she was dead. Her hair, bright with all the russet tones of autumn, was spread abroad on the pillow and framed a face of ice-white fragility. He remembered the feel of her lips, her frantic fight to throw him off, the rake of nails down his face as he pinned her down and thrust into her.

Alais turned to the midwife. 'Does she still bleed?'

'Only that which is natural, madam,' replied the woman with a nervous glance at Simon's impassive features. 'God willing, she will live.'

'God willing,' Simon repeated under his breath, and started to turn away.

'Whether she lives or dies, I want the child,' said Alais.

'Do as you please,' he said thickly. 'It is your business, not mine!' He almost ran from the room.

Alais stared after him, a perplexed frown on her face.

Chretien stooped over the fleece-lined basket near the hearth and peered down at his great-niece. She was awake and her eyes, a myopic infant-blue, examined him tenaciously. He touched her hand with a gentle forefinger. She opened and closed her tiny fist and gave a prodigious yawn.

'It seems a long, long time since I saw Luke lying in his cradle like this,' Chretien murmured. 'My brother was fighting in the Holy Land, and I was the master of an estate in Béziers. A different world.' He raised his head to look at Bridget, who was stirring a pot of soup over the fire, her silky black hair caught in a simple knot at her nape. 'Does Magda's father know that he has begotten her?'

'He knows why I lay with him,' she said warily.

'She is going to be fair, like him.'

Bridget said nothing, and scattered a handful of herbs into the soup.

'So you choose to raise her alone?' Chretien persisted gently.

Bridget suppressed a sigh. 'Raoul de Montvallant is a fine man, but he has needs and responsibilities far different from mine. I could hold him, I could keep him, but we would each be imprisoning the other. The soul must have its freedom – as you are always saying.' She smiled at her uncle and took some wooden bowls from a shelf. 'I could not raise Magda in a better place than Montségur. She will have the best and wisest of teachers.'

'And you will raise her as your mother raised you, and her mother before that?'

'I will.' Bridget ladled soup into the bowls and set one of them down before her uncle. 'And if she does not walk that particular path, you will show her the Cathar way.'

Chretien frowned at her from beneath his brows. 'And the ways of the world?'

'Those she will learn for herself when the time comes.' She put a spoon in his hand to terminate the conversation. 'Now, eat, and tell me how Matthias is progressing with his translations.'

CHAPTER 24

THE AGENAIS, SEPTEMBER 1213

'Papa, watch! Watch me!' Excitedly the child dug his small heels into his mount's sides. The pony, which was as small and fat as a pig, obliged by wheezing into a trot for ten strides, before throwing up its head and stopping, eyes showing a white rim. 'Did you see, I'm a knight!' The little boy waved his toy lance at the watching man.

'A preux chevalier indeed,' Raoul said, taking the old pony's bridle.

Guillaume rested the lance across his thigh in imitation of his father and sat upright. 'When can I have a proper horse?'

Raoul's lips twitched. 'When your legs have grown long enough to sit one.'

Guillaume considered the reply. He looked at his feet, which just about straddled the pony's fat, barrel sides. 'When I'm four?' he asked hopefully. He was four next month.

'We'll see.'

'Can I have a ride on Bausan now?' Before Raoul could deny him, he added, 'Grandmère said you'd let me.' He wriggled down from the pony and fixed Raoul with a beseeching brown stare. 'Please.'

Guillaume looked so much like Claire that a lump came to Raoul's throat. Stooping, he lifted the little boy in his arms and tried not to think this might be the last time he ever touched or played with him. Living by the sword inevitably meant dying by it, too. How he hated the day before a parting.

Tomorrow at daybreak he was due to leave for a rendezvous with other southern troops near the crusader-held town of Muret. De Montfort was trapped within and an alliance of troops led by King Pedro of Aragon, the Count of Foix and Raymond of Toulouse were confident of defeating him and bringing his rule of blood to an end.

'Can I come and see the soldiers?'

Raoul seated Guillaume before him on the saddle and slid the bridle between his fingers. 'No, not this time,' he said gently.

'We're going to win, Grandmère said so!' Guillaume twisted round to look up into his father's face. 'Then we'll get back our land and Mama, won't we?'

Raoul swallowed and ruffled the child's hair. 'Yes,' he murmured. 'We'll get them back.'

Reassured, Guillaume forsook the future for the pleasure of the moment and bounced in the saddle. 'Make him gallop!' he cried.

And Raoul did, as if the speed of the horse could outrun his cares.

Later, a drowsy Guillaume cuddled on his knee, Raoul looked across the firelight at his mother-in-law. She was sewing a tunic for her grandson, and he could tell that she was straining to focus in the dusk. Her eyes were the same warm brown as Claire's and Guillaume's. In her youth he knew that at least one troubadour had written a song praising her beauty – 'Na Alianor al Bel Cors'. Lady Alianor of the lovely body. The recent years had taken their toll on that. She was haggard and careworn these days, with deep lines scoring once smooth skin.

As if sensing his scrutiny, she raised her head from her needle. 'You are worried about tomorrow,' she said.

'I do not like leaving Guillaume behind. I know he is in good hands with you, Alianor, and he is happy, anyone can see that. It is just . . . ' He grimaced. 'I want to live to see him grow up.'

Alianor put her sewing to one side and fixed him with an anxious stare. 'Simon de Montfort is going to be defeated,' she said. 'He is facing the greatest force ever assembled against him, and led by the King of Aragon himself!'

'True,' Raoul said, 'but fighting is what he does best.'

'You have to defeat him,' Alianor said fiercely, tears filling her eyes. 'If you don't, I might never see my daughter again . . . if she still lives.' She looked at her sleeping grandson. 'The poor lamb,' she whispered. 'What have they done with his mother?'

Gazing down at Guillaume, Raoul felt the crack in his heart break wide open. Claire's loss was like a permanent but not mortal wound. He had learned to live with it, but the pain was constant and sometimes unbearable. 'I know you think it strange I so seldom mention her,' he said unsteadily to Alianor, 'but it is not because of a lack of care . . . It is because I care too hard and too deeply to find the words for what I feel.' Careful not to jolt Guillaume, he rose and carried him to the small truckle bed at the side of the room. Not the least of what he felt was guilt, but he would not admit such a thing to his wife's mother.

In the tent of King Pedro of Aragon, candles burned to augment the light of a young dawn. A large moth blundered around one of the flames. The King shot out his fist, snatched the insect and crushed it to iridescent dust against his muscular thigh.

'This is what we do to de Montfort the moment he rides out of Muret!' His eyes flashed around the ring of battle commanders assembled in his tent, daring anyone to challenge him. He had overindulged in wine and bed sport the previous evening and his temper was foul.

The Count of Foix vigorously agreed with him. He and Pedro of Aragon were men of similar outlook.

The light voice of Raymond of Toulouse entered the debate like a flagon of meltwater tipped on hot coals. 'I still say we should wait for him to attack us, not go out and meet him head-on,' he said. 'We're in a strong position here. I say stay here and pin him down with crossbows from behind our defences.' He swung to his own advisers for confirmation.

Arms folded, Raoul acknowledged the soundness of his overlord's reasoning even while he recognised that fear was more than half the motivation for Raymond's caution.

Foix had seen it, too. 'Ah, God!' he jeered. 'All the enemy has ever seen of you is your arse in retreat!'

The knights of the Ariège and Aragon hooted their appreciation of the crude but accurate sally.

'Peace!' The King's face flushed with temper. 'We gain nothing by these infantile exchanges.'

'There are no second chances with de Montfort,' Raoul said into the silence Pedro's glare had engendered. 'Lord Raymond is right. It would be better to hold our defensive positions and wait.'

'Bones of Christ, our army's twice the size of his!' roared Foix. 'I say strike him down now! I've not come to cower behind barricades like a woman!'

'Our armies usually are twice the size of his,' Raoul retorted drily.

'Aye, and always running in the opposite direction!' sneered Foix. 'I thought you at least were made of sterner mettle. Don't you want revenge for your wife?'

Raoul's jaw tightened. 'I am not unwilling to fight, my lord. All I say is that caution is advisable.'

Foix gave a derisive snort, but looked away from Raoul.

'We take your point' – Pedro of Aragon made a gesture of acknowledgement – 'but I agree with my lord of Foix. We gain nothing by dithering behind barricades. De Montfort will believe we fear him and are reluctant to engage, and it will only boost his morale.' He stared round the tent at his commanders and senior knights. 'When the French whoreson moves, we go to meet him!'

Cheers exploded on the tail of his declaration and men pounded the trestle with their fists until the candlesticks toppled over.

Raymond glared round the gathering. 'Then you go without me!' he snarled, and shouldered his way out of the tent. His son Rai and his adjutants followed on his heels to the accompaniment of howls of derision and cries of 'Coward!'

Tears of humiliation and fury shone in Raymond's dark eyes as he mounted his horse. 'I am right!' he said vehemently. 'I know I am!'

And who would believe him on his past record? Raoul wondered as he mounted Bausan. Raymond had cried wolf once too often. Riding away to sulk in camp would not enhance his reputation. 'Do you want me to keep my men on alert or stand them down?' Raoul asked in a neutral tone.

'Do what you like with them!' Raymond snarled. 'I care not!' He set spurs to his stallion's flanks and galloped away towards his camp.

Rai winced at the dust kicked up by his father's disappearing entourage. 'It will take all day for his temper to cool,' he said ruefully.

'He is in the right and they won't listen.' Raoul felt both pity and irritation for his liege lord. He was still unsure whether to ride after him or stay where he was.

'What's more, right or not, they're going to win a great victory and make him look even more of a coward,' Rai said grimly. 'He will have nothing left.' He looked sideways at Raoul. 'Go back to them, Raoul. Break a lance for Toulouse; you're carrying our honour today . . . what's left of it.'

Spreading out the parchment, Simon gestured Amaury to weight it down with the stones piled at the end of the trestle. A squire set a platter of cold fowl and a flagon before Simon, and departed on another errand. There were so many armoured knights in the room that it seethed and glittered like a fisherman's bulging net. They were the line commanders of Simon's army, the men upon whom he was relying to turn Muret from a potential defeat into a resounding victory.

Simon's demeanour as he broke fast, donned his mail and briefed the men was brisk but relaxed. Their position was difficult, but not hopeless, and keeping the confidence of his knights was essential. Tearing a leg off the fowl, he took a bite and pointed the joint at the parchment. 'Aragon is assembling his troops here on this rise to the north. This stream is protecting his right flank, and the marsh his left, so not only does he have the advantage of numbers, he also has the advantage of ground.' He stared round the gathered commanders to make sure they were following him. 'What makes these advantages null and void are the factors in our favour, namely God, as Bishop Foulquet will assure you when we join the muster in the main square, and southern incompetence. They have no cohesion. Each man is fighting for himself alone. We have the discipline they lack, and therefore we have the fighting edge. This battle is ours if we keep our heads.' He paused to take another bite of the fowl, to chew powerfully and swallow, as if the food represented his intentions on the battlefield.

'I propose we form three squadrons. William, you will command the first, and Bouchard the second. I'll take the reserve. We're going to charge them in three waves without giving them time to recover between each impact. Apart from coordinating the attack, your task and that of your seconds will be to keep the knights in line. I don't want our impetus becoming broken up in hand-to-hand glory fights. You hit them, you roll over them, and you crush. After that you can indulge in feats of arms if it is your need.' He tossed the chicken bone to a lurking hound and wiped his fingers on a napkin before donning his surcoat. 'It will be hard and bloody, I won't lie to you, but I know we can seize victory.

Let arrogance carry the day, not Aragon!' He grinned at his own weak pun.

The hearty laughter it drew from the assembled commanders was out of all proportion to the jest, but it served as a relief from tension. Since Simon was a man who seldom made jokes, they took it as a good omen and left the castle for the market square in a confident mood.

The fair-haired little girl toddled over to the crouching Templar knight and giggled at him.

'So you are Magda,' Luke de Béziers said, and swung her up in his arms. The child squealed with laughter before placing a curious hand on the chain-mail hood coiled around his neck. Luke grinned. 'She is the image of you, apart from the hair.'

'No, she is the image of my mother,' Bridget said.

'How old is she?'

'She will be two at the feast of Candles in the spring.'

Luke nodded. Bridget could tell that he wanted to ask about Magda's father, but was uncertain of her response. She was uncertain herself. She still thought of him. Once or twice she had even been tempted to seek him out, but her duty to Magda came first. She told herself she had only borrowed him for a night. His body and heart were not hers to keep but rightly belonged to another woman.

'What brings you to Montségur?' Bridget fetched two stools from her hut and placed them in the warmth of the autumn sunshine. 'Have you come to visit your father?'

Still holding Magda, Luke sat down. 'That is part of it. I've brought Matthias some more books to translate, and news of the outside world for those who want to hear it – but most of you at Montségur don't.' He smiled ruefully. 'I do not blame you.'

'Montségur is a haven,' Bridget said. 'The people here have eschewed the world; they have no need to hear news of it.'

'Have you eschewed the world, too?'

'While Magda is so young, it is necessary. I still travel to the local villages to heal, and sometimes I go with your father to meetings, but my responsibility for the moment is to my daughter.' Her expression softened. 'There is so much I have to teach her, and I want her to learn the good lessons first, before she learns fear.'

'There is no need to defend yourself to me,' Luke said gently. 'I have thought of retreating here myself. Even as a Templar, my cloak of immunity is thin at times.'

Bridget noted the word retreating, but she did not challenge him. She was sure he had not meant to imply cowardice or a shirking of obligation. 'Then perhaps you should do so?'

Luke smiled and shook his head. 'If I came to Montségur, I should want to live in a certain hut on the mountainside, and I know what can and cannot be.' Setting Magda down, he gave her a gentle push towards her mother.

Bridget looked at her cousin. There had always been an attraction between them. Occasionally she had explored the thought of deepening their relationship, but had always held back. She set great store by their friendship, but to make him her permanent consort, she would have to give him more, which she was not prepared to do.

He rose to leave. 'Don't speak,' he said with a rueful smile. 'There has never been any need for words between us.' Taking her hand, he brushed his lips across her knuckles. 'Tomorrow,' he said. 'I will call this way tomorrow before I leave Montségur for the world.'

Bridget was woken in the night by the sound of Magda's whimpering. Sleep still clouding her brain, she lifted her daughter to cuddle and soothe her. The infant's eyes were wide open. Under her hand Bridget felt the moisture of Magda's voided bladder.

'Stop!' Magda screamed. 'Mama, make it stop!' She buried

her face against Bridget's breast, her small body shuddering.
'Don't like, make it stop!'

Magda had a good vocabulary for her age, but it was the
first time she had ever strung words together. Bridget noted
this with a corner of her mind while she sought to deal with
the child's nightmare. She rocked and talked to her,
murmuring reassurances. At last the wild sobbing ceased.
Bridget changed the child's damp linens and lay down with
her, stroking her tangled blonde hair. Magda clung to her,
shuddering now and again, but finally, she relaxed and slept.

Holding her daughter's heavy warmth, Bridget wondered
if Magda had begun to experience touches of the sight. Surely
not; she was still so young. What had she seen in her dream?
What had she wanted to stop? Bridget gazed into the banked
embers of their fire, seeking out the tiny red glow at their
heart. Beneath her stare a flame began to kindle and then to
burn high.

Suddenly the whole room was shaking and filled with
choking dust raised by hundreds of horse hooves. Bridget
saw the flash and glitter of weapons against a hot morning
sky and heard the tumult of battle. Men were shouting in
Spanish, Catalan and Occitan. There was a triumphant battle
howl in the accent of northern France. A golden spotted stallion pivoted so close to her pallet that she covered Magda
with her body to protect her. The horse reared and its rider
hit the ground only inches from where she lay. The man
turned his head and his sea-blue eyes met hers for an instant
before she lost sight of him as horses plunged around him.
She saw the legs of a bright red bay stallion, saw the spatter
of blood. Advancing out of the battle fog came a warrior on
a white destrier, his shield bearing the fork-tailed lion of de
Montfort. Her frantic gaze found Raoul again, and he was
standing in de Montfort's path. She heard her own voice
crying, 'Make it stop!' But de Montfort's sword swung in a
killing arc and her vision darkened.

*   *   *

Someone was shaking her shoulder. 'Bridget, Bridget, wake up.'

Raising groggy lids she saw Luke bending over her, his dark eyes full of concern. He was wearing his Templar travelling cloak and his sword was girded at his hip. Her head was throbbing as if she had drunk an entire flagon of Gascon wine. She became aware that Magda was missing and looked round wildly.

'It's all right, she's only outside stroking Ronsorel. He's gentle, he won't harm her. What's wrong?'

Bridget sat up, rubbing her arms. Outside she could hear birdsong and Magda chattering brightly to Luke's horse. 'Last night I saw a great battle; it seemed to be here in this very room, and Simon de Montfort was carrying the victory banner.'

'Do Montfort's been in difficulty of late.' Luke poured her a cup of wine from the pitcher on the trestle. 'Pedro of Aragon has allied a huge army of southern lords against him, and there is real optimism that the northerners will be driven out. Are you saying de Montfort has won against the odds?'

Feeling cold, Bridget laced her fingers round the cup and sipped. 'I do not know. My vision didn't tell me where or even when the battle took place. It might not have happened yet. Indeed it might never be.' She looked at him. 'Luke, will you do something for me?'

'You need but ask, you know that.'

Bridget rose and went to lean against the doorpost. Magda's small hand was pressed fearlessly upon Ronsorel's foreleg, and the horse had lowered his head to snuffle the child's hair. 'I want you to find a southern noble for me. His name is Raoul de Montvallant. He is . . . he helped me to escape from de Montfort once, and I owe him a debt.'

'Raoul de Montvallant?' Luke joined her, a look of surprise on his face. 'You know Raoul de Montvallant?'

'Yes, why?'

'We are kin through my mother – distant cousins only. I

met him at Saint-Gilles the year that Pierre de Castelnau was murdered. Of course I will find him for you if I can. What do you want me to say?'

Bridget chewed her lip. 'Warn him to be on his guard against de Montfort,' she said after a moment, 'and tell him . . . ' She shook her head, and looked into her almost empty cup. Tell him what? That there were times when she still felt the heat of the fire they had kindled between them that night? 'Just tell him he is in my thoughts, that I have not forgotten. He will understand.'

'Do you want him to know that you are here at Montségur?'

'No!' Bridget said in alarm. 'That would be unwise.'

Luke's expression remained unaltered, but she sensed his curiosity. 'If that is your wish,' he said, and kissed her cheek. 'I must go if I'm to reach Mirepoix by nightfall.'

After he had ridden away, Bridget carried Magda back inside the hut. She tried to put the night's dream-vision from her mind, but throughout the day it returned to haunt her.

Stinging sweat ran into Raoul's eyes, which were already half-blinded by the constrictions of his helm. His sword grip was slippery with blood, his own and other men's. The sword itself seemed to be fashioned of lead, not the balanced Lombardy steel of an hour ago. Two waves of de Montfort's cavalry following close upon each other had swept aside the men of Foix like so many wooden skittles and then ploughed into the Aragonese with unstoppable momentum. The cry had gone up that King Pedro had been killed, and the Spanish line had fragmented in disarray.

Raoul had been near Pedro of Aragon when he fell, the King in his false humility wearing the armour of an ordinary knight with no distinguishing features to save him from the blades that tore out his heart. It had been impossible to go to his aid, so fierce was the impact of the northern assault. Before Raoul realised what was happening, their lines had been overwhelmed and surrounded, cut up into small pockets and cut up again. Now, against all hope, he and such of his men as remained were struggling to fight themselves free of the press and escape. Giles was still in position on his left, but Roland had gone down with most of the Montvallant knights on Raoul's right flank.

Raoul parried a blow. A crusader struck at him with a flail. The chain spiralled rapidly around his hauberk sleeve and Raoul was dragged from the saddle. The impact as he hit the ground punched the air from his lungs. Bausan reared and plunged, wild now that he was riderless. The shod hooves danced close and Raoul knew if he stayed down, he would be trampled to death. For an instant Bridget's face flashed before his eyes and he felt her with him, willing him to his feet.

He struggled upright, stared round, but saw only enemies. A crusader leaned down from his high saddle, aiming to decapitate him. His sword hacked into Raoul's shield, throwing him down again. He tasted dust and knew he was going to die. The legs of a red Spanish stallion flurried close. As its rider turned and prepared to strike, Raoul gathered himself and lunged and snatched. The knight cried out as he struck the ground. Seizing crupper and pommel, Raul hauled himself astride the red destrier.

Too late he sensed an attack from the side, and having lost his shield, tried to deflect the blow on his blade. The shock of the impact ran all the way up his arm. He lost control of his fingers, the weapon fell from his grip, and his enemy followed through, hacking through mail, gambeson and flesh. Raoul saw a steel cask helm plumed with scarlet feathers. He saw the fork-tailed lion on shield and surcoat. *Behold a pale horse and his name that sat upon him was death.*

Numbness welled from the wound and destroyed Raoul's every conscious function, but even in extremity, instinct made him grip the pommel and squeeze with his thighs. The red destrier reared, striking out, and the knight on the ground screamed as he was kicked. Someone grabbed the destrier's reins and Raoul knew that in a moment he would be dead; he knew also that he no longer cared, just wanted it to be over.

He thought he heard a southern tongue blaspheming amid the scrape and clash of weapons. The destrier changed pace, the plunging short strides of the battlefield stretching out to a canter. There was pain now. Each stride jolted agony through Raoul's chest. He began sliding towards darkness, but before he lost his grip upon consciousness, he was revived by the icy shock of water flowing over his thighs as the horse plunged into the River Louge.

'For the love of God, my lord, do not let go now!' he heard Giles mutter as if from a distance.

'I've got him,' Mir said close to his ear, and he became aware of the support of another horse and rider beside him in the water. His lids felt as if they were weighted with stones, but he forced them open. Through the slits in his helm the world seesawed and tilted. He saw his hands on the pommel and they were red with blood. More was dripping into the destrier's mane. The horse started to strain up the opposite bank of the river and he swayed in the saddle. Mir lost his grip, but Raoul was saved from falling into the river by the support of a Templar knight who rode up fast from behind. Just before consciousness finally went out like a snuffed candle, Raoul recognised Luke de Béziers.

CHAPTER 25

TOULOUSE, SEPTEMBER 1213

'Will he live?' asked Giles.

Luke de Béziers folded his arms and, after a long time, looked reluctantly from the patient to the anxious knight. 'He is very sick,' he said. 'The wound is poisoned beyond what I can do for him with my small training.'

Giles bit his lip and stared down at his lord – the waxen features, the fever-cracked lips, the muscular warrior's body from which the flesh was melting with alarming rapidity. The site of the wound was a suppurating, swollen porridge. Red streaks like finger marks spread out from the injury, invading the surrounding good tissue. It was two days since Count Raymond's cavalry had taken refuge behind the walls of Toulouse along with the tattered remnants of the armies that had borne the brunt of de Montfort's charge. Luke de Béziers had brought the Montvallant knights to a 'safe' house in the city close to the Pont Vieux and the suburb of Saint-Cyprien. The dwelling was owned by the Templars, and it was here, while the town negotiated for its life with the wolf outside its walls, that Raoul was fighting for his, and at the moment, both appeared to be losing.

'What were you doing in the heart of the battle?' Luke bestowed Giles a perplexed look. 'The rest of the Toulouse contingent didn't come within a mile of the fighting.'

Giles laughed sourly. 'We were representing them. My lord was trying to explain Count Raymond's viewpoint to

Foix – trying to make the old fool see the facts beyond his sword point, when de Montfort charged. We had no time to retreat even had we wished.'

'And when it came to the confrontation, he did not wish to, I think.' Luke inclined his head at Raoul.

'No.' Giles tightened his lips.

'If it comes to the end, do you want one of the Perfecti to be in attendance? It can be arranged.'

Giles gave a tired shrug. 'I do not think it matters to him either way.'

'Then permit me to send into the city for one?'

Giles made a gesture both assenting and dismissive and sat down on a stool next to Mir. The squire was knuckling his eyes and sniffing. Before he left, Luke paused at the coffer by the bed to light the oil lamp and his attention was caught by an enamelled disc lying on the coffer beside Raoul's knife and seal ring. Staring, the young Templar picked it up and rubbed his thumb over the dove and chalice symbol engraved within the six-pointed star.

'Where did you get this?' he demanded.

Giles took the token, turning it this way and that. 'I don't know. It was around his neck when we undressed him, but I've not seen it before.' He passed it to the squire. 'What about you? You're the one who helps him to arm and disrobe.'

Mir examined the disc and frowned. 'It was after we went to Foix with the Cathars that I first saw it on him – after he returned from that journey with the lady Bridget.'

'What?' Luke stared at the squire. 'Tell me!' he commanded.

'We – we rescued three Cathars from Lavaur. I – I—' Mir stammered, frightened by the Templar's reaction and over-wrought to the state of incoherence.

'One of them was your father, the lord Chretien,' Giles took over, patting the boy's arm. 'He had an older man with him, a scribe of sorts, and the lady Bridget. We took them to Foix, and Lord Raoul took her on another journey she desired to make.'

'And that was when he obtained this?' Luke took the disc back from the squire.

'I . . . I think so,' Mir said.

'Why do you ask?' Giles wanted to know.

'This one belonged to my aunt Magda. Such tokens are rare and not casually given. Bridget must have chosen him to—' He broke off.

'Chosen him?' Giles repeated on a rising note. 'Chosen him to what?'

Luke replaced the disc on the coffer. 'Forget that I spoke,' he said. 'I'll go and find a Cathar Good Man.' He hastened from the room.

Giles whistled out and sat down at the bedside. He looked at Mir. 'Can you swim, lad?'

Mir blinked at him. 'Why?'

'Because I suspect we're wading way out of our depth.' Picking up a bowl of herb-infused water, Giles wrung out the cloth that had been soaking in it and began to wipe Raoul's burning body. His lord rolled his head from side to side on the bolster and muttered, the sound rising to a cry.

'What's he saying?' Mir rubbed his hands nervously on his tunic.

Giles refreshed the cloth. 'Something about Dominic and fire as far as I can tell.'

'Dominic Guzmán the black friar?'

'That's the only Dominic I know of.'

Mir shivered and, looking at Giles, crossed himself.

'For pity's sake, Mir, go and find some wine,' Giles said gruffly. 'The stronger the better. We'll have to change this dressing soon.'

Raoul was teetering on a precarious ledge of stone, his sword in his right hand, but no shield to balance him. Frost crunched beneath his boots and the sky was crystalline with stars, the air so cold it cut his lungs. A chasm gaped below him, black and wide like an open mouth waiting to be fed, its jaws lined with jagged stone fangs. On the ramparts above, torches blazed, outlining his sword edge as he raised it and braced his wrist for the final time. Two men, faceless and dark-robed, came at him. His blade clashed on steel and was beaten down in a quenched blue spark. The pain ripped through his chest and he felt himself falling away into darkness, the abyss engulfing him. He clawed at the walls, trying to find a handhold, but they were as smooth as black glass and so cold that their chill invaded his body until he was frozen.

From a long distance he heard someone call his name. He ignored the sound, but whoever it was persisted and approached. A woman, he thought sluggishly . . . not Claire. Sudden brilliance pained his eyelids, and he parted them and saw Bridget, her body haloed with light, her hair blowing around her face. Reaching out, she grasped his hand and pulled him back towards the light. He flinched and hung back. It was safe in the darkness, but she would not relinquish her grip and she was stronger than him. He had no choice but to follow her out of the depths.

And then he was in a strange room, looking from a height on three men who were bending over a fourth lying motionless in a bed. He recognised Giles and Luke de Béziers, but not the dark-robed man beside them. To one side, Mir, his face hidden in his shaking hands, was weeping. None of them appeared to notice Bridget walk to the head of the bed, although to Raoul she was as solid as the coffer and the clothing pole beside it. Leaning over the patient, she placed her hand on his chest and pressed her mouth to his, filling him with her breath, and in that moment Raoul recognised his own self and the ground came rushing up to meet him.

'Wait,' said Giles sharply as the Templar started to pull the sheet over Raoul's body and the Cathar Good Man closed his prayer book. 'Wait, I thought I saw him move.'

'No more than the final spasms of muscle,' Luke said compassionately. 'Surely you have seen it before in your trade.'

'No, I'm sure I . . . '

Raoul forced open his eyelids. Bridget was standing among the men and watching him, but when he stretched his hand towards her, she avoided him and, with a smile, left the room. His reaching hand was caught instead by Giles, whose eyes were wondering, a little afraid.

'Lord Raoul?'

'Did you see her?' Raoul whispered weakly.

'See who, my lord?'

'Bridget . . . '

Giles exchanged glances with the other men. 'There has been no one here but ourselves.'

'She was here . . . ' Raoul tried to swallow. His throat felt like a tube of dried-out leather.

'I can well believe she was,' Luke murmured. 'I would have sworn on my Templar's vow that I was about to cover the face of a dead man.'

With a shaking hand, Giles poured watered wine into a cup and offered it to his lord.

Raoul drank thirstily then lay back against the bolster and pillows. He felt exhausted and disoriented. The Cathar Good Man quietly took his leave. With the remnants of the southern army trapped inside Toulouse, there were many more injured and dying who required his services.

'He didn't console me?' Raoul asked as Luke set about unwrapping the bindings around his wound.

'No. You were not conscious to make the responses, but he prayed your soul would find a good body to dwell in when it left you.'

If Raoul had owned the strength, he would have laughed, but he was as weak as a newborn and in pain. He could remember nothing of the past few days but dark dreams full of fire and bloodshed. 'Where am I?'

'Toulouse, my lord,' said Giles. 'We brought you here after the battle. Count Raymond is negotiating for terms. We can't fight on, but neither can we be defeated while we hold the city. It is a stand-off.'

Luke eased away the last unguent-smeared bandage. Raoul groaned and the Templar apologised.

'It's all right,' Raoul croaked. 'It hurts, but not like it did before.'

'No, the wound has begun to heal.' Luke's voice was distracted. Three hours ago Raoul's injury had been an evil-smelling mess bubbling with pus. Now all Luke saw were clean pink edges and a minor degree of swelling. The red streaks, although still present, were greatly diminished, and the flesh was cool to the touch. Here, if he had needed any more evidence, was proof of Bridget's skills.

'You almost killed de Montfort's son in the battle.' Giles fussed around Raoul like a mother hen. 'It saved your life. Mir, go and fetch a bowl of broth; perhaps my lord will drink some in a moment.'

'What do you mean it saved my life?' Raoul knew he would have to disappoint Giles's feverish optimism. He was nauseous with the need for sleep.

'De Montfort was so busy protecting his whelp and making sure he was unharmed that he didn't bother to finish you off. By the time he was free again, we had dragged you out.'

'His son?' Raoul's lids drooped. He was dimly aware of Luke smearing herbal ointment on the wound and applying a fresh dressing.

'Guy, the middle one. You escaped on his horse. You lost Bausan, but the red's a real beauty . . . My lord?' A note of panic in his voice, Giles leaned over the bed.

Luke touched the knight gently on the shoulder. 'He's only sleeping, don't worry.' His glance darted to the talisman on the coffer. 'He will heal now; I can say that for certain.'

'Here's the broth!' Mir trotted back into the room with a

steaming bowl and a horn spoon. Then he stopped and stared, for Giles was weeping unashamedly. The youth's horrified gaze flew to the bed and then to the Templar.

Luke smiled in reassurance. 'No cause for concern.' He held out his hand for the broth. 'Here, I'll take that, I'm starving. Go and fetch another one for Sir Giles. He'll be all right presently, and so will your lord.'

CHAPTER 26

Claire sat on the turf seat in the garden at Castelnaudry, her hands folded in her lap, her eyes on a distance far beyond the herb beds that she was supposed to be tending. She was permitted the occasional moment of solitude, usually when de Montfort and his sons were home from war to occupy Alais and her ladies. Today the entire castle was in a fervour of celebration over the great northern victory at Muret. Claire had closed her ears to their obscene joy and sought the solitude of the garden. Hate, as Geralda had been wont to say, was not a tenet of the Cathar faith. So she must not hate them for taking away her home, for depriving her of her husband and son. She must not hate them for forcing her to watch Montvallant's Cathars burn. She must not hate Simon de Montfort for raping her on her own solar floor and planting his child in her womb, or for taking that child away from her.

She dug her nails into her palms. Sweet Christ, it was impossible! How did she find forgiveness in her heart for such crimes? Jerkily she rose from the seat, and picking up her basket and shears began attacking the stems of the nearby lavender bushes. The aromatic scent of the herb, the motion of her hands and the silence gradually calmed her turmoil. If she could not find forgiveness in her heart now, then perhaps it would come to her tomorrow. She had to view each day not as a setback, but as a milestone on the road to her goal.

She had almost filled her basket when she heard the garden

door squeak open, and turned to see Simon's huge fawn
alaunt lumber through the entrance. Black jowls slavering,
it bounded straight across the herb beds and launched itself
boisterously at her. Claire screamed and raised her arms to
protect herself. The basket flew from her arm and lavender
scattered in all directions.

'Brutus, lie down!'

The boarhound dropped to its belly, crushing the herb
stems, releasing more of their powerful scent. Claire's
stomach dissolved in terror as Simon approached with a
measured, powerful tread. Today he wore a jewelled robe
and belt; his boots were made of kidskin, gilded with small
lions. Rings sparkled on his great square hands, which held
a bundle wrapped in waxed cloth. He set it down on a turf
seat and studied her with brooding eyes.

Unwilling but compelled despite herself, she lifted her
gaze to his. He might be robed for a feast, might be weapon-
less apart from the meat dagger at his hip, but it changed
nothing. She could still see him astride his white warhorse,
his stare impassive as Montvallant's Cathars burned to death
in the town marketplace. She could still feel the subjugating
pressure of his body, his tongue thrusting in her mouth, his
engorged penis stabbing between her thighs.

'You are like a butterfly.' His voice was gentle with a husky
edge, as if it had been roughened by the smoke of his victims.
He came to her and, reaching one callused palm, touched
her thick, russet braid. 'What a pity to crush you.'

Claire pushed his hand away and took a swift step backward. 'Don't touch me!' She half raised her fist, the shears
clenched in them.

His eyelids tensed; there was no more warning than that.
His lunge was so swift she had no time to defend herself.
He wrenched the shears from her grasp and hurled them
across the garden, twisting her wrist so hard that she
screamed and sagged to her knees. The dog sprang to its feet
and bared its fangs within a fraction of her face.

'Please!' she sobbed. 'Oh please, no!' She hated herself for her weakness.

He controlled the dog with a terse word. It dropped to the ground, but continued to growl. Simon dragged Claire upright and pulled her roughly against him. 'You are more foolish than I thought,' he said with disdain. 'Or else very slow to learn the level of my tolerance!' Seizing her face between his palms, he angled his head and kissed her savagely. Claire tried to kick him. Her hands became claws, but he grabbed her arms and forced them down at her sides.

The alaunt began to bark in the direction of the garden door. Simon glanced, saw his squire standing there, and pushed Claire brutally away. She fell to her knees, head bowed. Her mouth was swollen and numb. She spat into the grass, trying to rid herself of the taste of him.

'I sought you out to bring you these from Muret,' Simon said curtly. 'Widows should have a focus for their mourning.' He unwrapped the cloth on the bench to reveal the splintered remnants of a shield and a blunt, badly nicked sword.

Claire stared at the mangled design of interlaced chevronels decorating the face of the shield. Raoul had painted it himself during the first winter of their marriage. She could still remember his painstaking care, the bright Italian dyes, the satisfaction in his eyes as he stepped back to examine the finished result.

'I killed him myself,' Simon said as the colour drained from her face and her stare widened and widened. 'He lies in an unmarked grave on the battle plain with all the other fools who never knew what hit them – apart from the wrath of God.' His lips curved in an arid smile. 'At least he has an heir to inherit his lands – one who is being raised in good Catholic traditions.'

'You are of the devil!' Claire whispered, her gorge rising as she took his meaning.

Simon drew himself up to his full, proud height. 'I serve

my God faithfully,' he said. 'You are the traitor, and I have been lenient thus far . . . but all that can change.'

She flung away from him with a cry and hung over one of the flower beds, vomiting.

He watched her for a moment, and the frown on his face gradually became a grimace of self-disgust. Snapping his fingers at the dog, commanding it to his side, he turned on his heel and left the garden.

Claire collapsed on to the grass beside the seat and sobbed her heart out. Her grief, terror and revulsion were a raw pain. His God, not hers. She saw the distinction most clearly. Rex Mundi, eater of souls.

For a wild instant she contemplated suicide using the dull, damaged sword he had left on the bench. She set her hand to the leather grip and felt the ridges indented by the regular pressure of Raoul's fingers. How many men had this instrument killed before it had led him to the moment of his own destruction? Shivering with revulsion, she released the hilt and touched instead the broken shield beside it. Her fingers traced the bold, black design with loving sorrow and tears coursed down her face, but within herself, at her deepest core, she was aware of a transformation, as if she had woven herself a chrysalis out of her experience and only now was it complete.

Leaving the lavender strewn where it had fallen, leaving the shears and the broken weapons, she went out of the garden, and although she still wept, she carried her head high. From this day forth she would walk in the Light of the Cathar way, and no one would stop her.

CHAPTER 27

MONTSÉGUR, THE MOUNTAINS OF THE ARIÈGE, SUMMER 1215

'Do you remember what this plant is for?' Bridget asked Magda, who was sitting beside her in the dappled sunshine among the pines.

'To stop coughs, Mama.'

'That's right. And what do you do with it?'

'Pour hot water on the leaves and leave it to stand until it's as warm as new milk, then it will be ready to drink,' the child repeated faithfully. 'We don't want this leaf; a caterpillar's chewed it.'

'No.' Bridget smiled and watched her daughter select the best leaves from the white horehound and place them in the basket. 'Magda, what about this plant?' she persisted gently after a moment. 'What do we do with this?'

The little girl frowned at the clump of common plantain for a moment and then her brow cleared. 'The leaves make burns better,' she said brightly.

'Well done!' Bridget praised, hugging her. Magda was not yet four years old but her aptitude for learning was prodigious.

'Mama, why does this . . . ' Magda stopped, for her mother's attention was upon the path that could just be seen through the feathery sweep of the trees.

Hoofbeats thudded on the beaten soil and echoed in Bridget's heart. For a moment she tried to deceive herself that they heralded soldiers looking to be hired, or a supply train of mules from the foot of the mountain. But the deception was thinner than the leaf between her fingers. She knew who came. The leading horse was a striking red chestnut and, not counting a sickroom in Toulouse, the last time she had seen his rider was sleeping in a cave in the aftermath of Magda's begetting. At his side rode the knight Giles, balding and dour, and a little behind them the squire kept a watchful eye on a slender boy of about six years old.

'Who are they, Mama?' whispered Magda, to whom visitors were a novelty.

Bridget hesitated. The distant future she had foreseen, but not the manner of this meeting. Indeed, she had tried to keep her presence at Montségur a secret. Now, without warning, she needed to collect herself for what might be a rite of passage as stormy as the night on which Magda had been conceived. 'Messengers from Foix,' she answered shortly. 'Put the plants in the basket; we have to go home.'

Magda thrust out her lower lip. 'I don't want to; I like it here!'

'Do as I say!' Bridget snapped.

Magda stared at her mother in astonishment, tears filling her eyes.

The bewilderment in Magda's face stopped Bridget like a slap. Aghast at her own behaviour, she gathered Magda in her arms and kissed her. 'Ah, sweetheart, I didn't mean to shout at you.' She stroked the fair hair that was part of Raoul's legacy. Magda's rigidity melted, but when Bridget released her, and looked at her to make sure she was all right, the trust in Magda's gaze also held question.

'I know the knight on the red horse,' Bridget said. 'I had not expected to see him here, not so soon anyway.'

'Don't you like him, Mama?'

'I like him very much. He is a good man.' Bridget looked pensive. 'I don't want to hurt him . . . not any more than he has been hurt already.'

Magda screwed up her face. 'But you're a healer, Mama . . . '

Bridget gave a tired smile. 'If only that were the beginning and the end,' she said, fixing her gaze on the slope above them where the party of horsemen could still be heard.

It was in the afternoon, the hottest part of the day when everyone was asleep, that Magda heard the horse on the track above the hut that she and her mother shared. Bridget was inside, resting, but Magda, even as a tiny baby, had never slept except for the darkest hours of the night. Currently she was occupied in arranging a collection of white shells and stones in one of the sacred spiral patterns her mother had shown her.

The sound of hooves grew louder, approaching at a canter. Magda set the keystone into the pattern and stood up. Squinting against the sharpness of the sunlight, she saw a chestnut pony coming directly towards her, its shoulders and flanks dark with sweat, its nostrils wide red caverns. Astride it was the boy she had seen earlier with the knights. He was clinging to his mount's back like a burr, his expression a tense mixture of exhilaration and fear. Behind him the towers of Montségur were on fire. The pony became a warhorse, its hide grooved with muscle, and the boy became a man in armour, a sword shimmering in his hand, his expression gaunt and terrible. Other men were with him, one with eyes of winter blue and wind-blown dark hair. Out of the shadows stepped a creature in a long black robe, a dagger glittering in its thin fingers. Magda screamed and pressed her fingers across her eyes.

Her shrieks brought Bridget running from the depths of the hut, her loose hair streaming around her shoulders and her feet bare.

Peeping through a gap in her fingers, Magda saw the pony had stumbled and the boy had fallen off. He lay so still she thought he was dead. His mount was limping and uttering small grunts of distress. The sun shimmered on the pines and the shadows were somnolent and empty.

Her mother knelt beside the boy and gently probed his skull.

Magda began to cry. 'Will he be all right, Mama?'

'I think so. He's bumped his head, but nothing is broken as far as I can tell.' Bridget glanced at the sweating, trembling pony. 'This is what comes of abusing the life force,' she muttered.

'It wasn't his fault, Mama; I was in his way. I saw . . . I saw him . . . ' She broke off, shivering.

'What did you see?' Bridget demanded.

'He was grown up . . . on a big black horse with a sword in his hand . . . and the castle was on fire . . . There was a man with a knife.' She gave a frightened whimper and clutched her mother. 'A bad man; he was coming for me.'

She was overly young to be having the visions so powerfully, Bridget thought as she soothed and rocked her. 'It was a kind of dream with your eyes open,' she murmured in reassurance. 'I will teach you to have control over them. Now, do you think you can fetch me the comfrey lotion and the marigold salve? We'll talk about the dream later and what it could have meant.'

'Yes, Mama.' Magda hurried down towards the hut, and Bridget frowned after her. In Magda the sight was very strong. There had been several incidents like this, going back as far as her father's wounding at Muret, but this was the most powerful yet. She looked down at the injured boy. His eyes had opened and she noted that although his lids were heavy and his complexion ghastly pale, his pupils had reacted to the light.

'What happened?' he mumbled.

'You were galloping your pony when you should have known better,' she said sternly.

His breathing caught and he sat up, looking wildly around until he located his trembling mount.

'He's strained his shoulder to look at him. I'll see to him in a moment.'

The boy's eyes filled with tears. 'I didn't mean to,' he said in a choked voice. 'The slope was steeper than I thought.' He set his hand to the lump on his head. 'Are you a Cathar?'

'No, but I live among them. I am Bridget, and this is my daughter, Magda, whom you nearly rode down.'

'I couldn't help it.' He thrust out his lower lip. 'She just stood there in front of me.'

'Were you running away?' Magda asked forthrightly as she gave her mother the remedies she had requested.

'Of course not!' He scowled. 'I came out for a ride on my own, that's all!'

Bridget considered him. Perhaps not running away, but seeking release, she thought. Let a pup off the leash and its first energy was usually expended in a bout of frantic gambolling. 'Do you think you can walk over to that tree?'

He nodded and made the effort, although his legs were groggy and he had to hold tightly to Bridget as she led him to the shade offered by the whitebeam's branches. Magda followed them, clutching a waterskin she had thought to bring from the hut along with the salves. Bridget settled the boy against the tree trunk and left him while she caught the pony. He propped his head against the smooth, grey bark, his complexion a nauseous yellow.

'You will feel sick for some while,' Bridget warned him when she returned. 'Best if you try and sleep while I fetch your father from the castle.'

His lids flew open. 'How did you know that my fath—?'

'I saw all of you on the path this morning, and I recognised him. He helped me escape from some priests a long time ago.' She smiled. 'I even know that your name is Guillaume because I held you in my arms when you were still in swaddling and your mother brought you to one of our meetings in Toulouse.' While she spoke, she poured a small amount of comfrey lotion on to a pad and pressed it against the lump on his forehead. He flinched, and Bridget felt his muscles tighten as he steeled himself to resist more than just physical pain. She sent out waves of healing calm to penetrate his troubled aura. Gradually, under the soothing influence of her touch, his lids drooped and he fell asleep.

'Where is his mama now?' asked Magda. 'Is she at the castle?'

'No, sweetheart, she is a prisoner in another place far away.'

'Oh.' Magda looked thoughtful, not quite sure that she understood, but knowing that their patient was in sore need of comfort. She watched her mother go down to the hut and return with one of their blankets to tuck around the sleeping boy.

'Magda, I want you to do something for me,' Bridget said. 'I have to go to the fortress and tell his father what has happened. Do you think you can look after him until I return?'

Magda nodded solemnly, feeling slightly afraid, but also very important. She had helped her mother tend the sick before, had sat with them for short periods while herbs were ground and potions mixed, so this was just a small extension of that responsibility.

Bridget kissed her. 'I won't be long,' she promised, 'and you know how to summon me if anything happens.'

'Yes, Mama,' Magda replied dutifully, then ruined her serious demeanour by scurrying up the path to pick up her collection of shells and stones so that she could play with them to pass the time. An involuntary glance at the trees showed her only soft green shadows, protecting and benevolent.

The seigneur de Perella, commander of Montségur's garrison and the man responsible for building the fortress into its current formidable state, looked at Raoul who was standing beside him in the castle's crowded bailey.

'Are you travelling to Rome, too?'

Raoul gave a sour smile. De Perella was referring to the council that had been called by Pope Innocent to discuss various issues troubling the Christian world – the continuing crusade in the Languedoc being one of them. The Count of Foix would be attending to make his views known, as would the other interested parties, the exiled Count of Toulouse among them. 'Yes, I'll be in Rome, funds permitting.'

'Do I detect a note of bitterness?' de Perella asked, looking at Raoul sidelong.

Raoul shook his head. 'Not against Count Raymond himself. God knows, he must feel the taking of charity far more keenly than I do. Once he was the peer of kings; now he's reduced to begging from them.' He rested his hands on his worn sword belt, its gilding mere memory. 'If I am bitter, it is because I'm forced to sell my sword in order to eat. I run messages for Foix in exchange for the cloak on my back and a place in his hall. I watch my son growing up and wonder how he will make a living when the time comes.' His jaw clenched. 'No, that's wrong; I don't wonder, I know. By the lute or the sword he will earn his crust, and probably find an early grave. I doubt the Pope will use this council to revoke the powers of the men who have bled us dry in the name of Christ.' He expelled his breath harshly. 'Rome will only set the seal on de Montfort's theft!'

'I thought that the Pope was annoyed with de Montfort for quarrelling with Cîteaux.'

Raoul shrugged. 'A storm in a puddle. In matters of broader policy and intent, they all think the same.' He stared across the courtyard without seeing its bustle. It was two years since the defeat at Muret, two years spent on the tourney circuits and at the courts of other men, living on the crumbs of their charity. He had disbanded those of his men who had survived the disaster at Muret, retaining only Giles and Mir. While convalescing with Claire's mother at Agen, he had deliberated whether to leave Guillaume with her, but had decided against it. The boy was all he had and just as safe, if not safer, living an itinerant, nomad life than he was dwelling in a city rife with volatile rebel sympathies.

For a year they had dwelt in England among the entourage of Raymond of Toulouse at the court of King John, but Raoul had pined for the warmer climate of his homeland, for the sight of vines and olives and the ripe southern sun. He had returned to the Languedoc and taken up the offer of employment that Foix had once extended to him. He was a *faidit* in truth now, a dispossessed mercenary.

'I've done my best to make this place impervious to siege,' de Perella said, gazing round the austere grey walls as if checking the substance of every stone, every trowel-load of mortar. 'No French or Roman whoreson will do to my Cathars what they did to Aimery's at Lavaur. A sanctuary, this is, and will remain as long as I have breath to defend it. These are good people, and the Light has to be protected.' Suddenly self-conscious, he slapped Raoul's shoulder. 'I talk too much. Come and look at the new winding gear on the portcullis and give me a soldier's opinion.'

They began walking towards the stone tower housing the equipment, but were only halfway across the courtyard when Raoul stopped and stared. 'Bridget . . . ' he breathed.

De Perella followed the direction of Raoul's gaze. 'You didn't tell me you knew our healer.'

Without answering, Raoul made a distracted excuse and started across the ward.

She raised her head, looked at him, and took a step forward. His sense of the unreal increased, for he had thoroughly expected her to run away – or perhaps walk through a wall. Instead they came face to face, and she took his hands in a warm, sure grip.

'Your son fell off his pony outside our hut,' she said, cutting across his exclamation. 'He hit his head and concussed himself, but there is no lasting damage. I left him sleeping and came to fetch you.'

Questions, hundreds of them, flashed through Raoul's mind and robbed him of the ability to think or speak. All he could do was stare at her, open-mouthed, taking in every aspect of her appearance, from her braided black hair and clear grey eyes, to the plain robe and clogs on her feet. She started to withdraw her hands and he curled his fingers and gripped.

'I am real,' she said with gentle amusement. 'And I promise not to vanish on a whim. Your son will need you when he wakes up.'

Raoul shook his head. 'There is so much I need to ask you,' he said, but relinquished his hold and forced himself to pay attention to what she was trying to tell him. 'My son? He's supposed to be with Mir.'

'Well, he's given him the slip and come a cropper for the prank. Come, I do not want to leave him for too long.'

'He is alone?'

She stood to one side to allow a mule train of firewood to enter the courtyard. 'No, my daughter is watching over him, but she is young for the task.'

'Your daughter?' Raoul followed her past the huts of the Perfecti that were clustered outside the walls of the fortress. 'So you got your wish?'

'Yes, she was born here at Montségur.' Bridget bent her concentration upon the stony path before them.

Raoul walked beside her, trying to see her face, but she averted it from him. 'Why did you leave after that night?'

The scent of pine resin wafted over them with each hot ripple of breeze. 'Our lives were not destined to go forward together from that point.'

'That is not an answer.'

She looked at him then, her eyes sharp as glass. 'Why I left and where I went are not your concern. Yes, I shared my body with you once; you knew the reason and you were willing. Do not seek now to place a halter at my neck.'

Raoul's lip curled. 'So I have to stand back and humbly adore like all the rest?'

Her look crystallised, freezing him. She quickened her pace. Cursing, he hastened to catch up, and she let him.

'No one has to stand back and humbly adore,' she said in a tone less fierce. 'It is a step too close to being enslaved.'

Raoul gestured ruefully, making his own compromise. 'I owe you my life, do I not?'

She looked a question, wariness in her expression now.

'After Muret, when I was mortally sick, you came to me. Giles said I was raving with fever, but I knew you were there.' He looked over his shoulder. 'And it was this place I saw, but on a winter's night, I think.'

She shivered. 'You must try to forget. Sometimes we are permitted glances through windows that should be shuttered. Did your wound heal cleanly?'

'There's a scar that pains me sometimes, and occasionally I dream, but on the whole, I barely notice.' He half smiled. 'Few men can boast to have taken a sword blow from Simon de Montfort in the thick of battle and survived it.'

'And do you boast?' she asked neutrally.

Raoul eyed her. 'Not to Cathars,' he said with a straight face, and she was surprised into laughter. He laughed with her, the expression altering the structure of his face, revealing the young man still clinging to a tenuous existence beneath the warrior's embittered shell. He took her arm to steady her over a patch of rough ground, and the vibration of their bodies, one upon the other, blended to become one harmonious chord. His hand tightened and he pulled her round to face him.

'Thin air or lightning?' he murmured, and kissed her. Out of time, the moment hung suspended. Longing, aching; question upon question without coherent answer. As they drew apart, Bridget's certainty was shaken to the core. Without a word, she pressed herself out of his arms and continued down the path.

Magda came running towards them as they approached the hut. 'He's awake again!' she cried excitedly. 'I've given him a drink of water.' Her gaze flashed over Raoul. 'Are you Guillaume's papa?'

'Yes, I am,' he said. The little girl was Bridget in miniature with the same paradox of sturdiness and fragility. But Bridget's hair was midnight-black, and the child's was paler than ripe barley, fairer even than Guillaume's. His daughter, by the Light.

'He says that you're the bravest knight in the world!'

'Did he also mention that I'm the poorest?' Raoul smiled.

'What's poor?' She gave him a look of such puzzled innocence that he felt a lump come to his throat.

'Poor is not understanding what wealth really is,' he said wryly, and went down the path to Guillaume.

They spent the remainder of the day and the night at Bridget's hut on the mountainside. Mir came looking for them, directed by de Perella and half-mad with worry. He was reassured, fed bread and soup by Bridget, and sent back to Montségur with instructions to return on the morrow with Raoul's horse.

Mostly Guillaume just wanted to sleep away his headache, but for a while he played a game with Magda, using her white stones for counters. She proved herself adept, with a level of concentration far in advance of her tender years, and he was the first one to tire.

The children were put to bed in the smaller second room of the hut. Bridget dropped the thick, woven curtain that served as a partition, quenched the oil lamp, and returned to Raoul at the central hearth of the main room.

He arranged more twigs on the fire with unnecessary care. She watched the movement of his hands and remembered their touch on her body. A small shiver rippled through her. He should not be here. She should have made him stay at the fortress. Her throat was dry and her loins were liquid. Tonight there was no thunderstorm to charge the air; tonight there was only the sighing of the wind in the pines and the stamping of the pony outside the hut, but the human tensions were the same.

He looked up from the fire and it was as if he had absorbed the heat into his body, for his stare burned. Then he came to her. One arm curved around her shoulders, the other plucked at the simple drawstring of her gown.

'Please,' he said when she hesitated, holding him off. 'Please, I need you . . .'

Often people said need when they meant want, but she knew that was her downfall, not his. She wanted him badly, but she did not need him. Pushing his fingers aside, she unlaced the drawstring of the gown herself, and went into his arms.

This time when Raoul opened his eyes, she was still beside him, her body pressed close to his. The fire glowed in the hearth like a forge, and dawn was a long way off. He lazed in elusive pleasure. He had not lain with a woman since losing Claire. Thinking of his wife touched off a sudden sadness and a feeling of guilt within him. He still thought about her, but her memory had to compete with the everyday struggle to live and eat and raise Guillaume, and it was inevitable that it should fade into a background ache.

Awake herself, Bridget tensed as she caught the trace of what was in his mind. With a soft sigh, she withdrew from their intimacy and began to dress.

'Why the haste?' he asked, a warm languor in his voice. 'We have all night.'

'Would you have Magda or Guillaume wake up and stumble upon us like this?'

He turned towards her and slid a coil of her hair through his fingers. 'I do not see that it would cause harm.' He gave her an assessing look. 'If you let me stay here awhile to mend my wounded heart and soul, they might even grow accustomed to such a sight.'

Bridget stiffened. How easy it would be to agree, but in all conscience she knew she must tell him what she knew, and in so doing, perhaps lose his friendship. 'You cannot stay,' she said. 'Your wife still lives. She is locked up at Beaucaire on the Rhône.'

Raoul stared at her. Soundlessly his lips formed his wife's name.

Leaving his side, Bridget crouched to mend the fire, and remained there, staring into its deep red heart.

'Can you see her?' he croaked.

She rubbed her arms. 'Not tonight. My sight is weak, my body holds the mastery, but I know she is there. Your mother died from the coughing sickness soon after they were captured.'

He was silent. Then she heard the whisper of cloth and the clink of his belt buckle as he pulled on his garments. 'How long have you known?'

She bent her head and briefly closed her eyes. Now came the most difficult part, the cup from which she would rather not drink. 'Since before Lavaur.'

'Then in the name of Christ, why didn't you tell me!' The words were softly spoken, for there were two children a mere partition away, but they were raw with anguish.

She turned to look at him. 'You would have returned to Montvallant with your troops and have been killed outright. Your wife would still have been captured by de Montfort. Nothing would have changed except your death and my . . . ' She did not finish the sentence. Her hair curtained her face, and behind it she hid her vulnerability. 'You will be reunited, I promise you. At least this way Guillaume has a father.'

'Am I supposed to thank you for that?' His voice was flat.

'I did not know we would meet again so soon. I thought that you and Claire would be together before you came to Montségur, I thought—'

'Then your power is fallible,' he interrupted scathingly.

'I never realised how fallible until now.' She met his scorn with a miserable glance.

Without another word he went to the door, raised the bar, and stepped into the night.

Shivering despite the heat of the fire, Bridget hung her head, feeling utterly wretched. Gradually she calmed, reminding herself that everything had its pattern, its meas-ured rhythm even in the act of change. A permanent bond with Raoul was untenable. They had little in common except the lightning spark that struck between their bodies and made them briefly one white-hot flesh. He wanted to know the mystery when he hardly understood a word of its language. Giving a deep sigh, she rose from the hearth and went out to him.

He was bending beside the pony, checking the poultice that had been applied to its shoulder. She knew he was aware of her presence, but he did not turn round.

'I cannot give you what you ask of me,' she said to the starlit curve of his spine, 'I can heal your body, I can soothe your mind, but I cannot make you understand. That has to come from within. I am sorry I did not tell you about your wife, but there was nothing you could have done.'

He was silent for a long time, but at last he stood straight and turned round, and she saw that his face was wet. 'Sometimes I think I have nothing left inside of me,' he said wearily.

She grasped his hands, disturbed by what she saw in his face. 'You must not lose your spirit; there is much more within you than you realise!'

Raoul looked down at their linked fingers. 'If it is this painful to draw it out, then I do not think I want to know,' he replied. 'I'll take Guillaume back to the castle tomorrow. There's no point in prolonging the torture.' With gentle determination, he removed his hands from hers. 'It's late,' he said, 'and I'm very tired.'

She watched him return to the hut, but did not go there

herself for her emotions were in turmoil. Instead she took the track towards a large, flat boulder that stood among the trees above the hut. Seeking tranquillity, she sat upon its cold, smooth surface and raised her face to the quiet silver moon, but although its cool muted light soothed her body, she could not prevent the old images of fire and lightning from troubling her mind.

CHAPTER 28

TOULOUSE, WINTER 1215-1216

A bitter rain was falling on Toulouse, sky, stone and human emotions blending into one bleak environment. Murderous glances were cast by the citizens in the direction of the Château Narbonnais, from which their new Count imposed his iron rule.

Simon had little regard for their opinion. His was the power, his the choice to caress or to strike as the mood took him. Today in the overcast dawn, he was drinking mulled wine while his squires dressed him for the journey north. Each rivet of his hauberk had been burnished. His spurs glittered, his boots were gilded, and his woollen tunic was a strong brasil-red as befitted a lord who officially owned all the land between Toulouse and the Rhône.

The ecumenical council in Rome had found in his favour. Count Raymond was to live in exile on a pension of four hundred marks, having been judged incapable of ruling his hereditary lands. Simon thought it a pity that his son, Rai, was to have for his portion the Marquisate of Provence on the eastern side of the Rhône when he came of age, and that the Count of Foix had managed somehow to slip off the hook and retain his lands intact, but they were only minor flaws in Simon's design. What did they matter when he had the main part?

Alais advanced on him, a garment draped over her arm. She was dressed for travelling in her warmest gown and mantle, the latter edged with ermine tails and fastened with a heavy amethyst brooch. A gold circlet bound her wimple to her brow. Their journey was to be a victory procession, a slow progress north to do homage to King Philip of France for Toulouse and its environs and to accept the adulation of their French homeland.

'I made you a new surcoat for the occasion,' she said, unfolding the gold silk, appliquéd front and back with the snarling fork-tailed lion of de Montfort. 'The best Montpellier silk.' Pride shone in her eyes as she helped him don it and stood back to admire the result. 'How far we have come,' she breathed, and closed the distance again, her fingers greedy on the rich fabric and the bulge of his muscles beneath the thick mail shirt and padding.

Simon gestured and Giffard brought his sword belt. Taking it from the youth, he gave it to his wife. 'Buckle it on,' he commanded. She met him stare for stare, and lifting it out of his hands, slowly passed it around his waist, latched it, then knelt to attach his scabbard. The pressure of her fingers, the look in her eyes, the language of her body, aroused him, but he gave no outward sign, holding himself motionless until she stood up again. Impassively he held out his hand for his cloak. 'Is everything ready?'

'Yes, my lord,' she murmured with lowered eyes, her colour high. 'We but await your pleasure.'

Simon grunted, forced the pin through the thick wool and fur of his cloak and, taking his gauntlets from the squire, preceded her out of the door.

In the courtyard, Gentian, one of the nursemaids employed to keep the younger de Montfort children from being an inconvenience to their noble parents, was wringing her hands and biting her lip. The instant Alais appeared, she descended on her, almost weeping.

'Oh, madam, madam, something terrible has happened! I took my eyes off him for a moment and he was gone. I've searched and searched, but I can't find him anywhere!'

'Who?' snapped Alais. 'And stop snivelling. I cannot understand a word you're saying!'

Simon, one foot in the stirrup, made an impatient sound at the women.

'Master Dominic, madam. I swear I only spoke to Elise about a spare cloak and he gave me the slip!'

Alais cast her eyes heavenward and slapped the maid sharply when she continued to blubber. 'Then go and look again; he can't have gone far!'

Simon gained the saddle and adjusted his stirrup straps, his expression stony. Alais pursed her lips. 'I swear that child has a devil in him!' she declared. 'If ever there is trouble, he is always at the root of it!'

He heard the petulance in her tone and knew that its source was not so much Dominic's behaviour as the boy's uncanny resemblance to himself. The child was officially known as the son of Raoul de Montvallant but all could see for themselves the true direction of his siring. Alais had made it her business to remove the temptation of Claire de Montvallant from the household, and to that end she was kept under house arrest at Beaucaire on the Rhône. Simon had neither questioned nor contradicted the move; indeed it was a relief not to have the thorn of Claire's presence in his household. Nothing had been said between him and Alais; the partnership of their marriage remained as staunch as ever, but in the deepest corners there were shadows.

The child's name rang around the courtyard as the maids shouted and searched in vain. A man-at-arms went to investigate the well. Another squelched in the direction of the stables and the midden heap.

'Oh, let the brat rot here in Toulouse if he won't come!' snapped young Guy de Montfort, his voice rough with adolescence and the remnants of a heavy cold. He wiped his dripping nose on his sleeve. 'I don't know what all the fuss is about! He's only another rebel heretic's whelp!'

A brown-haired boy of about eight dismounted from his

pony. 'I'll check the kennels,' he said. 'Dom was mad keen on those brach pups born a few weeks ago.'

'Jesu God, Simon, not those whelped by Douce!' Guy's face took on a look of loathing as his younger brother started across the courtyard. 'Misbegotten, the lot of them!'

'Guy!' Alais's voice was as sharp as a whip.

Totally insensitive to atmospheres and quite without imagination except when it came to swearing, Guy continued to rub salt into an open wound. 'Well, it's true!' he protested. 'They should all have been drowned at birth. They're part wolf at least!'

'I would have drowned you at birth,' Simon said in a caustic tone, 'if I had guessed the difference in size between your mouth and your brain.'

Guy stared at his father in bewilderment, wondering what he had said. Unable to think of anything, and being too fond of his own hide to argue, he sulked into the fur collar of his cloak.

As the younger Simon suspected, Dominic was in the kennels, crouched in the straw with Douce and her three pups. The bitch was a brach, elegant and lean with a smooth coat the colour of clotted cream. Her pups were a motley collection of leftover scraps from every other breed within Christendom, and a few outside it, too, for their yellow eyes and long, fuzzy limbs were decidedly lupine. Douce and the kennel boy who had left her unattended at the critical moment of conception were in disgrace for the crime. That the pups had not been drowned at birth owed more to the kennel-keeper's curiosity to see the grown result than any misplaced softness. Dominic had taken to the pups as he had never taken to anything or anyone in his entire small life, as if recognising that they, too, were misfits.

'Dom, come on, they're looking for you. Gentian's nearly wetting herself! They'll beat you witless if you don't make haste!' Simon warned.

The child raised his eyes to the older boy and thrust out

a stubborn lower lip. 'Don't want to.' His scowl outdid
Guy's. Grasping one of the pups, he hugged it ferociously.

'You've got to.'

'I won't,' Dominic repeated, but then his head tilted and
he prepared to bargain. 'Not unless Loup comes too.'

'Dominic, he can't! You know Elise doesn't like dogs,
and he's not even trained. He'll piss all over the litter
cushions!'

'Don't like Elise,' he said as if that were the end of the
matter, and continued to cuddle the pup while it licked him
frantically.

Simon didn't like Elise much either. He also knew his
father was less than impressed with the maid, and decided
to take the risk. At worst Dominic would throw a tantrum,
but if they were in the courtyard, it would be the women's
task to deal with it, and at best Dominic would get his desire
and Elise's haughty nose would be put out of joint.

The older boy returned to the bailey five minutes later,
complete with his small half-brother and a leggy pup
frolicking and snapping at the string attached to Dominic's
wrist. Elise began to squawk her displeasure but was
silenced by Lord Simon himself with a furious command
that sent her scurrying into the litter like a flustered hen
into a coop.

Simon rested his eyes briefly on his namesake's innocent
expression before gesturing him to remount his pony. He
flickered an even more perfunctory glance over the little
boy wriggling away from his nurse as she tried to fasten
his cloak and avoid the pup at the same time. Straight hair
as black as his own before it had greyed, sea-storm eyes,
and the promise of bold Norman bones: Dominic de
Montvallant was the living proof of one wild moment of
lost control.

Simon heeled his palfrey's flanks. Mud spattered up from
the hooves. A groom dodged, but not before he had been
well splashed. Simon fixed his stare on the road flanked by

the towers of the Château Narbonnais, on the grey sky and the bright silk banners rippling against it, until the sight of the black-haired child and the dog had vanished from his mind's eye.

Chapter 29

Provence, Spring 1216

The soldier shook his fist, blew on his knuckles and flung the dice into the centre of the circle. They clicked together and fell in the dust. Amid cheers and curses, a fine cambric shirt changed hands.

A short distance from the gambling mercenaries, Raoul groomed his red stallion, teasing out the last of the winter coat until the hide reflected the sun like a mirror. Nearby Guillaume was practising his horsemanship with a group of young squires. Raoul paused to rest his arm and watched his son with pride in his eyes. Guillaume took a running leap at his pony, grasped the coarse mane and vaulted across its back in a single lithe movement.

'Your lad's a fine rider,' Rai commented, strolling to Raoul's side. He was lightly clad in shirtsleeves and hose, the day being hot, but nevertheless managed to look as elegant as a cat. Behind him on a leading rein plodded a dun cob – a plain workhorse with saddle galls and an expression of weary docility on its broad face. Raoul eyed it dubiously, for it was scarcely a mount worthy of the Marquis of Provence and leader of the southern army.

Rai had landed at Marseilles at the beginning of the month to gather a rebel army of Provençals and dispossessed southerners to his banner. He was the Languedoc's rising star. His father had diverted to Spain to raise a second army to strike at the northern garrisons, leaving Rai to reap the adulation of

Marseilles, Avignon, Orange and every Rhône town through which his growing army had passed. He was poised now to march on de Montfort's stronghold of Beaucaire. The lord Simon was still conducting his victory parade throughout the North, secure in his belief that the South was defeated. What did he have to fear from a broken old man and a feckless youth?

'He's fearless,' Raoul said somewhat wryly. 'He took a bad fall last year at Montségur, but it doesn't seem to have knocked much sense into him.' He was smiling as he spoke.

Rai chuckled. 'Ah, but he has courage and that is a good thing. Caution will come later, hmmm?'

'I hope so.' Raoul watched Guillaume for a moment longer – the wiry agility, the nimbus around his sun-bleached hair, then returned to grooming the stallion.

'I want you to do something for me,' Rai said.

Raoul worked his way down his mount's powerful haunch. 'It concerns that nag of yours, I think?'

Rai's teeth flashed. 'How did you guess?'

'Pure mischance,' Raoul retorted. 'If it's a sweetener to get me to do your will, you'll have to do better than that!'

Rai's grin became outright laughter. He slapped the dun's neck and tethered it at Raoul's horse line beside two pack mules. 'Do what I ask of you, and you can name your price,' he said.

'You know my price,' Raoul answered with quiet intensity, all humour flown. 'Montvallant and my wife.' He rested his gaze on the distant walls of Beaucaire on its high rock above the Rhône.

Rai followed the direction of Raoul's stare. 'I'll give you them both if you but trust me.'

'What would you have me do?'

'Take a message to the citizens of Beaucaire, giving them the where and when of our attack. There's a goldsmith, Pierre the Saracen, with a workshop near Saint-Paque. He's our contact, and he'll organise the people to repel the garrison and open the gates to us.' Rai indicated the dun cob. 'You'll ride into town as a labourer.'

Raoul eyed the spavined nag, and rubbed the back of his neck to ease the beat of the sun.

'You can leave tonight,' Rai added. 'That way you'll be ready to enter the town at dawn. I'll give you detailed instructions later.' Then he slapped Raoul's arm the way he had slapped the dun's neck and nonchalantly strolled off.

Raoul crouched in a doorway, a shield propped to one side and a sword balanced across his thighs. Both weapons had been borrowed from the rebels in the town. To have borne his own into Beaucaire beneath the suspicious gaze of the northern gate guards would have doomed him at the outset. They had stopped him entering the town and made him empty his pack on the ground. It had revealed nothing more incriminating than some patched undergarments, a tatty spare tunic, a hunk of stale bread and an onion. Not satisfied, they had examined his palms. Fortunately, Raoul had spent two hours in camp roughening his hands on a grindstone and then rubbing them into the soil, a precaution that had paid its reward. The soldiers had let him pass, mocking the *ac* and *az* sounds of his southern accent and jabbing their lances at the old dun nag in a vain attempt to make it sidle. His anger had boiled up, but he had managed to prevent it from overflowing. He could feel it now, trickling through his veins as he waited in the doorway, dressed like a peasant – a wolf in sheep's clothing.

Two other men waited with him – Thomas and Geoffrey, the sons of Pierre the Saracen. Their father was at the city gates, ensuring a trouble-free welcome for Rai's knights when they attacked.

Thomas gave a retching cough. He had been sick twice already that morning. 'How much longer?' he croaked.

Raoul glanced at him. He was a gangly youth with the baby down of a first beard on his jaw. It was the waiting that was getting to the young man as much as the fear of what might happen once the fighting began. From what Raoul had seen, the people were eager for battle. The citizens of Beaucaire were fiercely cosmopolitan, and de Montfort's attempts to rule them by the feudal laws of the North had fanned a bitter resentment. 'Not long,' he said with a glance at the luminescent rim of the eastern sky.

'Is your wife really locked up in the castle?' Jeffrey asked, curiosity overcoming prudence.

Raoul rubbed his forefinger gently back and forth over the sword grip. 'I have heard it is so,' he said neutrally.

'Our sister had to take some gold buckles up to the castle for the Countess de Montfort a few years ago, and she told me that there was a southern lady among her women. Hair like an autumn forest, she said.'

Raoul lowered his gaze to the motion of his finger. In his mind's eye he saw his hands webbed by Claire's glorious russet hair.

'She was greensick,' Jeffrey added. 'My sister said that you could tell she was with child.'

'With child?' Raoul went cold.

'Yes, she . . . ' Jeffrey stopped, his garrulousness arrested by the expression on Raoul's face. 'I . . . ' he stammered as Raoul rose jerkily to his feet. Whatever else Jeffrey had been about to say was drowned out by the clamour of the tocsin that suddenly started clanging from the castle walls.

Ignoring it, Raoul seized a fistful of Jeffrey's padded leather jerkin. 'Do you tell me my wife was pregnant?'

'My sister said so, but she might have been wrong.' Half-choking, he tried to push Raoul away. 'Perhaps it was one of the Countess's other women. It was a long time ago.'

'My lord, the alarm!' Thomas grabbed at Raoul, his young voice cracking with anxiety.

Breathing hard, Raoul opened his fingers. Cold dread seeped through him. Claire bearing the burden of pregnancy and childbirth in the den of the enemy, isolated and afraid. She had said nothing of pregnancy to him in the days before

Lavaur, so if the child was not his . . . He voided the thought in the rapidity of sudden physical action. There was a garrison in that castle, a garrison that had to be prevented from reaching the town gates.

Claire sat on her pallet and listened to the bell that was summoning everyone to mass. Prayer had been as much in evidence recently as food had not. Yesterday's ration had consisted of the end of a loaf and the lees from the last tun of wine. Yesterday, too, they had slaughtered one of the knights' horses. Claire had been allotted some thin slices of the tough, undercooked meat, but in revulsion had given it away. Cathars did not eat meat, and she knew herself to be one now in all but the final confirmation. Mind and spirit held the certainty; only the body was afraid.

It seemed an aeon since Rai's knights had galloped through the gates that the people of Beaucaire had so willingly opened for them. The crusader garrison had belatedly realised what was happening and rushed into the city to repel the southern troops. They had reached no farther than the northern quarter by the church of Saint-Paque, for the people were out in the streets and in search of revenge. The garrison was met by a barrage of arrows and stones. Deciding that discretion was better than death, the crusaders had fought their way back to the keep to secure it against the citizens. Now the castle of Beaucaire was moated by a massive southern army, and its garrison praying in desperation for Simon de Montfort to come to their aid.

Hollow-eyed with hunger and lack of sleep, the people trapped inside the castle endured the daily pounding of the walls by Rai's trebuchets and perriers. Most of the upper defence works were gone. From what remained of the battlements, the hopelessness of the crusaders' situation was plain. The rotting corpses of northern soldiers dangled from the branches of the olive trees in the town vineyards. De Montfort's relief army could not get near the castle, for Rai had learned from the disaster at Muret and refused to be drawn into a pitched battle on open ground. Instead he had constructed extra defence works to the west of the castle, and behind these he kept Simon at bay.

Claire heard the gloomy reports and she saw the growing frustration and despair of the garrison as, day by day, week by week, their hope was whittled away. Last night, as so many nights before, she had slept in her clothes. She had no change of garments now. Her spare shift had been torn up to make bandages, and someone had stolen her other gown. Once she would have been horrified to appear in public looking dirty or unkempt. Now it did not seem to matter; indeed, in some ways it was a comfort. Men no longer looked at her as if they would like to eat her alive.

What would it be like to be free? To come and go as she pleased? That thought until recently had been an exotic flight of fancy. Now, with each passing day, it became more feasible. In her imagination she set one foot outside her cage, then the other, taking cautious steps. She would go to Agen, to her mother, and she would see Guillaume again, her beautiful little boy. For a while she would stay there, regaining her strength, and when she felt ready, she would go to the hills of the Ariège to serve the Cathars and become worthy of the title of Perfect.

But then her thoughts would take a darker turn. What if her mother was dead? What if Guillaume had never reached her and his bones lay bleaching somewhere on the road between Montvallant and Agen as Raoul's bones did on the plain of Muret? The doubts rushed at her like a pack of harpies and she fled back to her cage, locking herself inside it, terrified that, like a bird with clipped wings, she had lost the power to fly.

Rai's surcoat was a confection of wine-dark silk, extravagantly adorned with thread-of-gold. It well suited his olive complexion, which was further enhanced by the dazzle of his smile. Smug with triumph, he regarded his enemy across the trestle. A hot wind gusted his hair, but it was Simon de Montfort who was being forced to squint into the sun.

Standing among Rai's commanders, Raoul stared at the northern warlord with a hatred so strong it stung his eyes. Even in defeat, de Montfort wore a look of superior arrogance, as if he were condescending to yield, and not being forced.

'We are agreed, then,' Rai said. 'You withdraw your army and yield me Beaucaire, and in return I let your garrison depart intact with their families and possessions.'

Simon glared at Rai as if he had spoken out in front of his betters. 'Agreed,' he said curtly, his lips barely accommodating the word. Inking the quill, he signed the document of surrender with bitter, forceful strokes and thrust the parchment back at Rai. Declining the offered wine, he levered himself up from the trestle. 'We have nothing more to say to each other; let the bargain be fulfilled. Amaury, my horse.' He reached for his gauntlets and glared at the knights surrounding Rai as if marking each one for future retribution.

The moment came when his stare collided with Raoul's like a lance striking a shield on a tourney field. Both men recoiled from the impact and then sought each other again. Raoul tightened his fist on the cheekstrap of the red destrier that had originally belonged to de Montfort's son.

De Montfort raised a superior eyebrow before turning his back in a gesture of supreme contempt, but not before Raoul had seen a glimmer of turmoil in his eyes.

Claire huddled in a corner of the chapel and prayed. The silence that had fallen after the garrison had departed had been eerie, a hiatus in time. Terrified that the troops might take her with them and hand her over to de Montfort, she had hidden here, behind the altar, the last place they would think to look for her.

There had been a terrifying moment when some soldiers had come to remove the candlesticks, pyx and altar cloth. She had realised that her foot was protruding from the edge of the stone and it was too late to tuck it under her, but they had been in far too much of a hurry to notice.

Now she could hear voices again, and this time the footsteps approaching her sanctuary were unhurried and casual. '. . . very generous of you, my lord, to donate new furnishings for the chapel,' she heard someone say, and daring to peep around the altar stone, saw a priest talking to a slender young man wearing a crimson and gold surcoat.

'I have appreciated your prayers and good offices among my men,' the latter replied gracefully, and walked towards the altar. Claire curled up behind it again, afraid that the thud of her heart and the shake of her breathing would give her away.

A sword chape scraped on the flags as the young man knelt, and the priest must have knelt with him, for she heard his voice intoning in Latin the words she herself had learned by rote as a small child; words that revolted her now – not for their meaning, but for the memories they evoked. Alais de Montfort and Friar Bernard forcing them at her, stuffing them into every orifice . . . eyes upon the cross, wafer on her tongue, incense in her nostrils, the devil's spear reaming her body, *Credo*. Claire bit into the fleshy side of her palm and squeezed her lids tightly shut until her vision was filled with bright starbursts of colour.

At last it was quiet. She dared to remove the improvised gag of her own hand and opened her eyes. Beeswax candles now flickered on the altar, a cross casting its long shadow between them, and staring down at her over the top of the altar table were the priest and the young man.

'Sweet Jesu!' The latter came around the side of the stone and, crouching, extended his hand as if to a wary animal. She shrank from him with a whimper.

'Claire?' whispered a horrified voice she had thought never to hear again. Behind the priest and the man in the surcoat, she saw someone else. The light glimmered on his fair hair and gaunt bones. His spurs clinked on the floor tiles, and as he advanced, his link mail flashed. 'Claire?' he said again, his throat working. 'Dear Christ, what have they done to you?'

The one who had discovered her cleared his throat and, making a tactful excuse, drew the staring priest away with him out of the chapel.

An echoing silence descended. Raoul advanced and knelt beside her. She felt his tentative touch on her snarled, matted braid. The days when she had taken a pride in her appearance were long gone, but her hair had been her vanity and Raoul's particular pleasure. She could feel the grief in his fingertips. She raised dull, haunted eyes to his face. 'They have done nothing to me,' she whispered, 'nothing. What they did was to her. After you die they cannot touch you . . .' Her eyes slipped from his. 'But sometimes, despite yourself, you remember.'

Raoul's face showed fear. He set his hand to her shoulder and shook her. 'Claire, in God's name, stop it; don't look at me like that!'

She flopped back and forth without resistance. 'In God's name?' she said in a faraway voice. 'He said that it was in God's name, when he came on his white horse, but I know which God he meant.' With an effort she focused on him. 'He told me that you were dead, that he had killed you.'

'He lied,' Raoul said, knowing only too well which 'he' she meant. He gathered her to him and she sagged in his arms like a child's cloth doll. 'I was only wounded. Beaucaire is ours, and you are no longer his prisoner. Did you hear me, no longer his prisoner!' He clutched her tightly.

Riven by tremors, Claire shut her eyes so she would not see the gilded ornaments belonging to the false God.

Raoul removed his cloak and wrapped her in it. 'We can't stay here, beloved; they'll be needing the chapel for the services. I've a house in the town where you can rest and eat.'

She felt nothing at his touch or his words. When he pulled her to her feet, she swayed against him, weak as a kitten. 'I'll always be his prisoner; don't you understand?' she whispered in a forlorn voice. The chapel whirled before her eyes, the candle flames becoming an intermittent wheel of fire, quartered by the cross. Faster and faster, brighter and brighter. Light burned behind her eyes, searing through her body. Raoul's voice came from far away, edged with panic, but she fled him for the safety of oblivion.

Claire woke to a strange room pervaded by a smell that seemed familiar but which she could not immediately identify. Bunches of drying herbs and flowers hung from the rafters, and molten sunshine bathed the floor and slanted across the bed in which she lay. On a coffer beside the bed stood a candle pricket and a bowl of fruit – pears, oranges and green figs. Belatedly she recognised the smell as that of freshly laundered linen.

Her gaze returned to the brightness of the window and she stared at the man sitting in the embrasure looking out through the open shutters . . . Open shutters? How long since she had been permitted such a dangerous luxury? She frowned and put her hand to her forehead. The scent of Castilian white soap filled her nostrils. She sniffed her wrist and stared at the clean linen chemise clothing her arm. A thin thread of memory began to unravel.

'Raoul?' she said faintly.

The man turned, and she saw that indeed she had not been hallucinating in Beaucaire's chapel. It was Raoul, a hard-boned sinewy version of the Raoul of her memories, and his mouth no longer wore a smile in repose.

'Where am I?'

He came to the bed, his expression one of mingled anxiety and relief. 'In the house of Pierre the Saracen in the town – of Beaucaire,' he added, unsure how confused she still was. 'Are you hungry? You haven't eaten anything in three days except an egg posset, and we had to force that down you.'

Claire examined the familiar, hollow feeling in the pit of her stomach. Was it hunger, or an emptiness of a different kind? She did not remember the egg posset, but neither did she remember the three days.

Taking her silence for assent, Raoul fetched half a loaf and a crock of honey from the sideboard and, with his eating knife, cut and smeared a slice.

Claire sat up, her head swimming. Raoul's face blurred and cleared by turns. She took the bread from him and bit into it. Saliva filled her mouth and the feeling in her stomach resolved itself into ravenous hunger. The anxiety in his eyes softened as he watched her devour the food, before turning to pour wine into two cups.

'You slept almost solidly,' he said. 'You hardly even roused when we bathed you . . . I'm sorry about your hair. Pierre's wife says it will grow again, but it was so matted and louse-infested she could do nothing with it.'

Claire put her free hand to her scalp and discovered herself as closely shorn as a midsummer sheep . . . or a nun. 'It doesn't matter.' She gave a brittle laugh. 'I've long outgrown vanity of that kind. When you stand to lose your soul, your body does not matter.' She pushed away the last of the bread and honey. Unaccustomed to such bounty, she felt queasy.

'De Montfort has retreated,' Raoul said awkwardly. 'The town is safely ours for the time being.' He hesitated, obviously floundering. Several times he started to speak, then, with a grimace, stopped himself. 'God's life,' he finally burst out, 'I should never have ridden to Lavaur!'

Claire shook her head. 'It would not have made a difference to the outcome; there were too many of them, and your duty was not to me alone.'

'No.' He turned his head aside and said in voice rife with guilt, 'I swear I won't leave you again.'

'Nothing can ever be the same,' she said with weary resignation. 'Too much has changed. I may love you, but I am not the girl you married, and for a long time you have been a stranger to me . . . since before Lavaur.'

Raoul rolled his goblet between his hands and did not

contradict her. She saw the way he was frowning, the set of his mouth, and her damaged heart ached. He rose to his feet and paced to the window. For a long time he stared out, saying nothing, but at last he turned round to her.

'Pierre's nephew told me that while you were kept prisoner here, you were with child. Is it true?'

Claire closed her eyes. Dear God of Light, how was she going to bear this? 'Yes, it's true,' she said in a choked voice. 'Four years ago at Castres, I bore Simon de Montfort's son.' Raoul made a stifled sound but she could not tell what it expressed, nor at whom it was directed. 'Simon de Montfort took Montvallant, and when he realised you had eluded him, he turned his rage upon me. Then he gave me to his wife so that I could be taught the error of my ways and become a good Catholic again. When I started to be sick in the mornings and my gowns grew tight, I let Alais believe the child was yours, conceived before Montvallant was captured, but it wasn't true.' She swallowed, fighting her nausea. 'They took him away from me the moment he was born, and all that I know of him is that he is named Dominic and they are bringing him up in their ways – as the true heir to Montvallant.' She put her face in her hands. 'I wished so hard to die that part of me did.'

Raoul strode to the bed and pulled her fiercely against him. 'Ah, God, Claire,' he said hoarsely, one hand upon her cropped hair, the other around her pitifully thin body.

At first she struggled against him, against the liquid burning of her eyes and the pain of dissolving from stone back into flesh. His warmth and closeness evoked bittersweet memories and suddenly tears were running freely down her face. The last time she had cried had been in the garden at Castelnaudry when Simon de Montfort had violated her again with Raoul's sword and broken shield.

Raoul murmured her name over and over, interspersed with endearments, while she clung and shivered. His own thoughts were tortured with guilt. While she had been enduring the hell of rape, he had been begetting a child, too, not in rape but nevertheless in lust and with never a thought for his wife.

'It is over now,' he said with bleak determination. 'We have to build on what remains. If we keep looking back, we'll be destroyed.'

What did remain? Claire wondered. The changes in each of them were too great to build an edifice out of the debris, but for the moment she was too weak and tired to fight him. She let him hold her and closed her eyes.

The door opened and a boy danced into the room. 'Papa, Lord Rai wants to talk to you about—' He stopped in midflow and stared.

Claire stared back at her son. She had carried the memory of his soft, blond hair, pudgy limbs and baby smile throughout her trials. The child eyeing her now was slender and tanned, and possessed the wily grace of a young wolf.

'Guillaume,' she breathed, a world of pain in that one word. 'I would not have known you.'

He nodded in response to his name, and after only the briefest hesitation, and a flicker of a glance at Raoul, advanced to the bed. Fresh tears filled Claire's eyes, blurring his image. 'Last time I saw you, you were barely walking . . . Oh God, how many years have I lost?'

'I'm nearly seven,' Guillaume obliged. 'Papa's going to give me a new pony and teach me to joust.' He cocked his head on one side and pushed his sun-streaked hair off his brow. 'Are you feeling better now?'

'Yes, much better,' Claire whispered. In fact, she felt worse. She had lost both her children. The baby conceived in rape had been taken away at birth, and this child of her heart was now a self-assured individual, already aping the behaviour of the older boys who were pages and squires. A knife hung at his belt and his liquid brown gaze was worldly-wise.

'Your mother is very tired; she needs to rest,' Raoul said with a quick look between them. 'Perhaps we can all talk later. Did you say that Rai wanted to see me?'

'Yes, Papa. About a foraging party, I think. Can I come, too?'

Raoul, tousled the boy's hair. 'I don't see why not.' He grinned at Claire. 'You should see him on horseback!'

She managed a wan smile. 'I am not surprised. It used to bring me out in a cold sweat of terror to watch you gallop him round the tiltyard at Montvallant.'

The unspoken words hung between them like beads dangling precariously on a broken necklace. One careless move and they would be scattered abroad without hope of ever being restrung.

'Yes, I remember.' His grin faded. He squeezed her hands. 'I'll stay if you want me to. Rai can always find someone else to do his foraging.'

'No.' Claire shook her head. 'Go, both of you. I am indeed very tired.'

Raoul hesitated, then kissed her brow and went to the door. Guillaume kissed her, too, performing his duty to a stranger, and followed his father.

She heard them speaking below in the yard – Guillaume's voice loud with excitement at the prospect of accompanying the men, Raoul's response amused and chiding at the same time. Sunlight upon bright, shallow water. She sought the peaceful depths of the sacred word.

Truly, truly, unless one is born anew, he cannot see the kingdom of God. Unless one is born of water and the spirit, he cannot enter the kingdom of God. That which is born of the flesh is flesh, and that which is born of the spirit is spirit.

She decided that when Raoul returned, she would ask him if there were any Cathars in Beaucaire who would be willing to visit her.

CHAPTER 30

TOULOUSE, SPRING 1217

Dominic tensed his narrow shoulders as Friar Bernard leaned over his work to examine what he had written. The results were not impressive. The five-year-old had an excellent degree of control for his age when he was allowed to use his left hand, but Friar Bernard said the left hand belonged to the Devil and he must not use it for eating or writing, nor in practice swordplay. Especially he must not use it for genuflecting in church. However, Dominic frequently chose to use it behind Father Bernard's back, signing gestures at his tutor that were far from holy, for he hated the friar with a concentrated passion. The musty smell of Friar Bernard's black robes, the fanatical sparkle in the black eyes, the whiskery black hairs growing out of the priest's nostrils fascinated and repelled him. Most of all, however, he was terrified by the willow switch that Friar Bernard carried everywhere and with which, in tyranny, he ruled his domain.

Fiat voluntas Tua . . . Thy will be done. The words straggled across the wax tablet, barely legible. Dominic bit his lip, not daring to look up into the icy, judgemental stare.

'Do you see that spider above your head?' Friar Bernard jabbed his stick at a web in the corner of the room. 'Do you? Answer me, boy!'

'Yes, Friar Bernard.' Dominic squirmed on the bench, only too aware of the bony white hand clenched and quivering with anticipation on the switch.

'That spider could write a better hand than I see on your tablet! You do this deliberately to test me . . .'

'I don't, Father, I can't use my—'

'Silence, boy! Are you insolent as well as stupid?'

Dominic's bottom lip quivered. He stiffened it, knowing full well that the friar wanted to make him cry in front of the other boys so he could further taunt him. Some of them, the sons of de Montfort's knights and retainers, had bullied him before now, calling him a heretic and a whoreson, although they made sure never to do it in front of the adults. Dominic knew what happened to the odd one out in a dog pack – either it was harassed to death by the other dogs, or it became their leader. He did his best to appear indifferent to the taunts and ridicule when they came his way, but his best was not always equal to the occasion – and never good enough for the fanatical Friar Bernard.

The priest picked up Dominic's tablet and held it with the tips of his fingers as if what it contained were contagious. 'Write this again,' he said coldly. 'Three times.' And he pushed the slate back into Dominic's hands, bruising him with the force of the thrust.

Dominic swallowed the painful lump in his throat, hatred shuddering through his small frame. Beside him on the bench, Simon, four years his senior, gave him a sympathetic nudge and a swift look. Dominic risked a grimace through the suspicion of tears.

Friar Bernard turned away, his jaw grinding, and went to stare out of the window. Dominic eyed the switch tapping impatiently behind his tutor's back. He willed it to jerk from the priest's fingers and belabour its owner about the head and shoulders. So strong was the emotion concentrated in his stare that he saw Friar Bernard begin to turn his head. Hastily Dominic bent over the dreaded tablet and fumbled with his stylus. His right hand refused to cooperate, and the lettering it produced was twofold more clumsy than before. After another furtive glance at the friar, he changed the stylus to his left hand. A transformation took place. The words flowed across the wax, and the pained expression left Dominic's face.

As if gifted with eyes in the back of his head, Bernard whirled round. His expression blazing with righteous fury, he took three strides across the room and brought his stick swishing down across the knuckles of Dominic's left hand. The stylus flew from Dominic's fingers and he screamed. Again and again the enraged friar struck him, the blows landing upon Dominic's shoulders and head, stinging across his face. Dominic curled himself into a defensive ball. After the first shriek of pain had been surprised out of him, he did not utter another sound. The tablet lay on the floor, the words *Fiat voluntas Tua* flawlessly executed. 'If you weren't Lord Simon's own son, I'd break every one of your fingers!' Bernard panted as his arm rose and fell. 'I'll drive the Devil out of you, I swear by Jesu's blood I will!' He raised the switch on high to strike again, but the blow never descended. In the shocked silence, Dominic peered through his fingers and saw the lord de Montfort himself watching the proceedings with a frozen expression on his face.

Slowly Bernard lowered the switch. 'My lord, I did not know you were here.' After stating the obvious, he licked his lips.

'I think the boys can be excused from their lessons for the rest of the day,' Simon said quietly. Without waiting for the friar's leave, he jerked his head at the children. 'Out.'

One and all, they fled with alacrity, except for the younger Simon, who paused to persuade Dominic out of his fetal ball and to his feet.

De Montfort looked at the boy's face, at the scarlet stripe branded upon the pallor of shock, at the rigid mouth and jaw, but it was the eyes that bore the most eloquent testimony to what had just been accomplished. Tears brimmed in them, but so did the pride and the hatred. His father's face wearing his mother's expression.

'Take him to the women and get one of them to put some salve on that bruise,' Simon instructed his son brusquely. When the boy had led Dominic away, he turned to Friar Bernard. 'I hope you have a good explanation for what I saw just now.'

'Dominic was using his left hand again, my lord, and he defied me before the others.'

Simon stopped and picked up the tablet at his feet. He looked at the childish characters, perfectly formed in the wax. 'There is a world of difference between breaking and schooling. Ask the meanest of my grooms.' And then the soft voice curled like a whip, and struck. 'If you ever open your mouth before your mind again in front of an audience, I'll cut out your tongue. I do not acknowledge him as mine. He is heir to the lands of Montvallant; is that understood?'

'Yes, my lord,' Bernard said stiffly.

'I hope that you do.' Simon turned on his heel. 'Because I never threaten, I promise.'

Dominic crouched against the wall in a corner of the bailey, his arms around Loup, the hot tears he had refused to shed earlier now darkening the hound's wiry silver coat. He touched the throbbing place on his cheek where Friar Bernard's whip had slashed him, and then looked at his fingertip, which was shiny with the lady Alais's goose-grease salve. He had desired neither salve nor attention, only to be left alone to cry in peace. Instead there had been an inquest with all the grisly details laid before the women by Sim, whose desire to comprehend was as insatiable as his curiosity. Not that any answers had been forthcoming from Alais, whose response had been positively glacial.

Dominic tightened his fingers in the dog's ruff. Loup might not understand, but he was loyal, big and warm, and made no demands of intellect as Sim did. Did the priest's words mean that he and Sim were half-brothers? Was he a bastard like the children born to the soldiers' women? He had heard the word often enough to know that it stemmed from some irregularity of birth. Loup licked him exuberantly and whined. Friar Bernard said that Loup was a dog of the Devil's creation, but Dominic knew that for a falsehood. Young as he was, he understood that his hated tutor was capable of seeing the Devil in a bucket of water or a horse dropping if the mood was upon him. He even claimed to have encountered the Virgin Mary in a blizzard.

Gradually, as he cuddled the dog, Dominic started to feel better. Like a snail withdrawing into its shell at moments of danger, Dominic had the ability to retreat within himself, thereby surviving the crisis. He had recovered enough to be thinking of visiting the kitchens to see if Hubert, one of the apprentice cooks, would spare him a bone for Loup and a piece of marchpane for himself if he pleaded hard enough, when some soldiers entered the bailey, dragging three men and a woman in their wake. All the prisoners were roped together and in consequence stumbling and staggering off balance. The soldiers were poking and prodding the captives and making ribald remarks.

The foremost man wore a handsome green tunic and hose, and his greying hair and beard had been curled with irons and slicked with pomade. His three companions, in contrast, wore the garments of Cathar Perfecti – unembellished hooded robes of dark blue wool, relieved only by the silver buckles on their girdles. Their faces reminded Dominic of Father Bernard – undernourished and fanatical – but, unlike his tutor, he felt no threat from these people.

He had seen these sorts of prisoners on several previous occasions, and in a relatively short space of time. It had been autumn when the de Montfort household had come to Toulouse, after the defeat at Beaucaire. Sim had told him that his father believed the citizens of Toulouse were traitors who had supplied arms and money to the rebels and they had to be punished. Occasionally he and Sim had sneaked down to the dungeons to peek at the people who had been arrested by the troops. Sometimes the blue robes were amongst them, but they never lasted very long. Dominic Guzman, the leader of the black friars, would come and talk to them, then he would either weep or become very angry at their obstinacy, but the end result was always the same. The ones who called themselves 'Perfecti' were taken out and burned. Friar Bernard said they were bad people, but then he said that Dominic was bad, and Loup also. What was good? Was it the stench of Cathars roasting? If the wind was in the wrong direction, they could smell it sometimes in the Countess's rooms, and she would make them all kneel and pray.

A flurry of activity near the main door caught Dominic's eye and he froze, cowering against the wall, his stomach clenching as Friar Dominic and Friar Bernard issued from the keep and approached the prisoners. The fat man in the green tunic fell to his knees and wept at the feet of the churchmen, crossing himself, kissing the dusty hems of their robes. Dominic saw the switch tremble in Father Bernard's thin fingers, saw the cadaverous expression on his face, and knew that all the captive's tears and pleadings were for naught. A whimper clogged his own throat, and he pressed his lips together so that no sound should betray him into another beating.

The Cathars neither begged nor wept, reacting with indifference bordering on disdain. Dominic admired their courage. Heretic was suddenly a word plucked from a vague awareness in his vocabulary and elevated to the shining levels of knight and chivalry and honour.

He watched as they were dragged away to the dungeons, watched until the glint of the last soldier's hauberk was quenched in shadow, and the black robes of the friars no longer endangered the courtyard. At his heels, Loup whined and pawed him beseechingly. The look of narrow concentration vanished from Dominic's eyes and once more he was a small boy in a dusty tunic, his mind diverted by thoughts

of marchpane and marrowbones – but only diverted.
Memory was as strong as the pulse beat in the throbbing
weal on his cheek.

Simon raised his eyes from the pile of parchments and tallies
in front of him – paperwork concerned with the war he was
preparing to open again in Provence – and stared at Friar
Dominic Guzman with ill-concealed irritation. 'You wished
to speak with me?' He noticed a blotchy rash welting
Guzman's throat and assumed the friar was wearing a hair
shirt again.

Guzman interlaced his fingers and bent his thoughtful,
sorrowful gaze on Simon. 'A brief word, if you please. It was
wrong of Friar Bernard to say what he did this afternoon in
front of so many young ears. I have spoken to him most
strongly, and I hope it will be the end of the matter.'

'I have warned him myself,' Simon said flatly. 'You are
right about it being the end of the matter.'

Guzman sighed. 'Bernard's zeal sometimes carries him
further than is wise, but he has a genuine concern for the
child's continued defiance, not to mention the persistent use
of his left hand.'

Simon ceased writing and scowled at Guzman. 'Better to
let it remain,' he said. 'If it were just his calligraphy at stake,
I would say do your utmost to correct him, but since he is
to wield sword and lance, he will perform better by doing
what comes to his nature.'

A look of surprise crossed Guzman's face. 'You intend
him being a soldier, my lord? I thought under the circumstances you would want to give him to the Church.'

'What circumstances?' Simon asked softly.

'Those of his begetting . . . I think you know what I mean,
my lord.'

'As far as I'm concerned, Guzman, the child is the rightful
heir to the estates of Montvallant, a position he can hardly
claim and keep if he takes holy orders.' Simon's gaze was

bone-chilling. 'He is to be given a thorough grounding in the military arts the better to serve God.' Having dipped his quill in the ink horn, he started scratching at the parchment, indicating that their interview was terminated.

'You will not officially acknowledge him, my lord?' Guzman persisted.

'No.' Simon did not look up. 'I will not. Do you not have work of your own to pursue?'

'Indeed, my lord . . . God's work,' Guzman replied in a voice as cold as chapel flagstones on a midwinter evening, and strode from the chamber.

Simon stared at the blot of ink spreading on to the parchment from the quill he had split with the pressure of his grip. He ripped the parchment across and across. Reaching to the wine flagon on the trestle, he was not pleased to discover that his hands were shaking.

CHAPTER 31

Bridget watched her daughter examining the shepherd boy's swollen knee. Magda's fingers moved quickly and lightly. 'The pain is worst here?' she asked, looking at the youth.

He nodded, biting his lip.

Magda glanced at her mother for permission, and Bridget nodded. It was only through the experience of touch that Magda would learn to control the healing energy.

Magda closed her eyes and put the tips of her fingers to the core of the shepherd boy's pain. Bridget felt Magda's concentration and knew the moment when the bright river of gold rose in her body and flooded out of her and into the youth. It was too much; Magda did not yet have the fine control. The boy would not be hurt – indeed, it was much to his benefit – but Magda would be drained. Bridget moved to break the contact, but even before she did so, Magda herself disengaged.

Her face was as pale as flour and her hands were trembling. Her gaze, however, was steady and filled with a new understanding. 'How do I make it do what I want?' she asked.

'That will come in time. You must think of a steady, soothing flow, not a river in full spate.'

'But I tried to do that.'

'Have patience,' Bridget said. 'You have done very well; I'm proud of you.' She kissed Magda and examined the youth herself. Beneath her gentle probing, he scarcely winced, and she could see that the swelling was much diminished.

Bridget and Magda shared a meal of pottage and bread with the shepherd lad's family; then, accepting more bread and a flask of wine to sustain them on the road, they went on their way.

Bridget noted that Magda was still a little pale and subdued and decided not to press too far that day. It was a month since they had left Montségur to travel the mountains, their direction leading them northward towards Toulouse. Bridget knew it was important for them to go there; of late she had dreamed of the city spires, of the River Garonne, of Raoul and Simon de Montfort. The dreams were vague and half-formed, but they were persistent. Magda had been dreaming again, too. On several occasions before they left Montségur, she had woken screaming in terror from a nightmare about a dark-robed spectre hiding in the pines of the mountain slope, a long dagger in its hand. Once, in her sleep, she had sobbed the name Dominic as if her heart were breaking.

Bridget had decided it was time to leave Montségur for a while at least. Once on the road, she and Magda had slept more soundly and been more at peace. With Simon de Montfort's fortunes in war on the ebb, travel was safer than it had been for several years. Magda had to know that a world of both good and evil lay beyond the boundaries of Montségur.

'Mama, will I ever have a husband and children?' Magda asked, jolting Bridget out of her reverie.

She looked at the child's earnest face. 'If that is what you wish, then surely it will be so,' she answered with a smile.

'But you don't have a husband.' Magda frowned. 'Didn't you want one?'

'Not enough to make it happen,' Bridget said, on her guard now.

'What about my father?'

'He was already someone else's husband. I had no right

to keep him. One day, when you are older, I will tell you about him.'

Magda nodded, a thoughtful expression in her eyes. 'I am going to find someone to marry, and I'm going to keep him,' she said with determination.

Bridget sighed, knowing conflict. She hoped Magda would find a husband, but he would have to be more than special to accept her gifts and the heritage that went with them. And such men were rarer than enlightenment. With the exception of Luke, who came very close, Bridget had yet to meet one.

In the very first glimmer of an autumn morning, Raoul lay on his pallet in the small tent and listened to the growing mélange of sounds as an army came to life. Soldiers on horseback and on foot, knights and squires, archers and arbalesters, ox carts laden with baggage; all were on the move, heading for the last obstacle between themselves and Toulouse – the ford on the Garonne at Bazacle. Today the city was to be liberated from de Montfort's rule and returned to the governance of its rightful lord.

Raoul touched his lips to his sleeping wife's temple, his eyes bright with desire, although not for her. These days all such urges were channelled into making war on de Montfort, where vigour and passion were permitted and bitterness could be purged on the edge of a sword. For Claire, he dared feel only a grieving compassion.

She was studying hard to become a Cathar Perfect. Frequently her apprenticeship took her away from him to other parts of the camp where she attended meetings and found the companionship of ideas in common. She had spoken to him of drinking from a deep well of tranquillity, and her face had reflected the peace of mind she was tentatively beginning to discover. He did not begrudge her that spiritual grace, but it saddened him to see her drifting ever further from his grasp.

The bond between Claire and Guillaume had never been re-established either. Claire was ill at ease in the presence of her slender, predatory son, and Guillaume himself had made little attempt to form bridges across the chasm. Indeed, sometimes in defiance, almost as if he resented her presence, he would show off his riding skills and swagger in front of her, imitating the soldiers, knowing how much the Cathars disapproved. She would pretend not to notice, but Raoul would see her eyelids tense and her mouth compress.

Her head was pillowed on his arm. She had continued to crop her hair, but the lustre and rich colour had returned. It still gave him sad pleasure to touch it, but she preferred him not to. Indeed, were it not for the chains of obligation still binding her to him and the fact that in an army camp it was unsafe for a woman, even a holy one, to sleep alone, he knew she would not be sharing his tent at all.

Mir poked his head through the loose laces of the entrance flap. 'My lord, I've saddled up the horses.' His voice was a loud whisper. His cloak was grey with water droplets, for there was a thick river mist enclosing the encampment. 'Guillaume's with me.'

Raoul nodded and gently set about rousing his wife – but not gently enough. Thrashing wildly, she screamed at him to let her go.

'No, no! Ah, God, no!' She screamed with such terror and pain that it brought Mir back to the tent flap, his eyes full of alarm. Behind him, unseen, a boy's voice questioned, the sound coming indistinctly as if through a mouthful of food.

'She's dreaming again!' Raoul said over his shoulder. 'They're always worst just before she wakens. Claire, beloved, you're all right, no one's going to hurt you. Hush now.' Mir retreated again and Raoul heard him speaking to Guillaume. Their voices receded. 'Claire?' She had ceased to struggle. Gingerly he released her.

She sat up and put her head in her hands. 'I was shut up in a darkened room,' she panted. 'And he was there with me and he said I had to tell him where you were, and when I said I did not know, he . . .' She desisted on a sob.

It was always 'he', never 'de Montfort', Raoul had noticed, and her nightmares were always about what he had done to her. Over and again, a hundred different ways, she relived the violation that not even her new faith was strong enough to purge from the unquiet corridors of her mind.

'Is it time?' She made a visible effort to collect herself, wiping her eyes on the back of her hand, setting a resolute expression on her face.

Raoul avoided her eyes. Some wounds went too deep for words or a touch to heal. 'Yes, it's time,' he said, a hint of unutterable weariness in his tone.

Through the fog the army of the former Count of Toulouse moved in shadowy formation, row upon row. Armour and harness jingled. Muffled hoofbeats thudded into the soft autumn soil, conversations were brief and whispered. Men from Aragon, from Bigorre and Comminges marched and rode with the dispossessed of the Toulousain. Astride a dappled grey Andalusian stallion at their head was the most important *faidit* of them all – Raymond of Toulouse.

For the first time since the judgement in Rome of two winters past had gone against him, Raoul saw that his overlord's head was carried high. The glow from Raymond's ruby cabochon thumb ring was reflected in his eyes, albeit that those eyes were sunken deep in their sockets and the once smooth skin surrounding them was webbed with wrinkles. He had led his small army by unfrequented roads and crossed rivers at minor fording places rather than using main bridges. It was also the reason he had avoided the towns that were populated by de Montfort's garrisons, and had waited until his intelligence reports put the hated usurper firmly out of the way on the other side of the Rhône at Crest.

The fog rising from the Garonne and drifting across the land was as thick as a horse blanket, obscuring everything.

Raoul could remember other entries into the city in times of peace and war – the heralds, the panoply, the buntings and celebration; wine running in the streets, gold coins showering upon the crowds in display of Raymond's largesse. And now the secretive return, cloaked in cloud and silence. Raoul could tell from the glow in Raymond's eyes that his blood was singing with triumph, but then Toulouse belonged to the house of Saint-Gilles. The possession was bred into them blood and bone, countless generations deep, and no northern soldier, no matter his expertise and brutality in war, was going to usurp it on the bought word of a meddling priest in Rome.

On this day Toulouse, Raoul thought, tomorrow Montvallant.

Chin propped on his right hand, Dominic used his left to toy with a piece of bread, for he was no longer hungry. Beneath the trestle, Loup waited hopefully for whatever morsels might come his way, one eye cocked upon his master's swinging legs, the other watching Amice's snappy little terrier for any treacherous sudden moves.

The Château Narbonnais was gloomy even in the fierce clarity of high summer. In autumn when the whole of the city was swallowed in a grainy, thick fog, it was unutterably damp and dark; even brightened by hangings, the walls seemed to ooze depression.

From the corner of his eye, Dominic watched the lady Alais dab her mouth with a napkin and reach to her goblet. Rings twinkled on her elegant fingers. She sent him a glower. Guiltily he stopped swinging his legs and removed his hand from the bread, knowing that she abhorred anyone fidgeting at table. Still, Dominic found it difficult to sit still knowing that as soon as the household had finished breaking fast, he was due to attend weapons practice, something that he enjoyed immensely. He was allowed to use his left hand, and was proving so adept, he was almost as good as Sim, who was a full four years older. Sir Henri Lemagne, the knight who tutored him, was delighted with Dominic's progress, and had promised that if his skills continued apace until Christmas, he could start practising with a proper sword after the festival.

Following weapons practice came lessons with Friar Bernard, but even these were tolerable now. Since the incident in the springtime, the priest had kept a rein on his tongue and his stick. Only once had Dominic been thrashed – for putting a ladder snake in Friar Bernard's hat following a lesson about the serpent in Eden. It had been worth it just to see the look of horror on his tutor's cadaverous features. Dominic smiled at the memory and his fingers crept out to play with the bread again.

Beside him, ten-year-old Sim suddenly tugged on his sleeve. 'Listen, what's that noise?'

Dominic raised his head and looked at the door. Everyone in the hall had stopped eating. The sounds came vaguely, but once noticed, could not be ignored. Not just the everyday shout and rattle of men at drill, but the wilder, higher clamour of battle and of a mob.

Alais commanded a knight to go outside and find out what was happening.

The man had not even risen from the trestle when her inquiry was answered with terse brutality by Nicholas de Riems, a knight billeted in the town, who staggered into the hall and half-collapsed, half-knelt at her feet. Blood welled from an ugly cut on his cheek, and his sword hand was lacerated to the bone.

'Madam, grave news! Raymond of Toulouse has invaded the city with an army of *faidits* and the people have risen to greet him. We have been overwhelmed . . . destroyed.'

Alais's complexion turned as white as her napkin. She grasped the jewelled cross that hung from her neck on a gold chain. 'And the château?' she asked through lips that barely moved to encompass the words.

'Safe for the moment, madam; we can hold out against them here, but the city is lost. You must send to Lord Simon immediately.'

Eyes flashing, she drew herself up. 'I know what I must do. Do not presume to lecture me!' She turned to snap her fingers at a scribe who was still holding a piece of bread, one cheek bulging in arrested mastication. 'Fetch quill and parchment!' she ordered. 'Henri, find me some messengers! I'll not be held to ransom by a heretic rabble!' Her eyes narrowed. Hastily Dominic avoided their sweeping glare.

'My lord will come,' she said, her voice low and furious. 'And then we shall see once and for all who is the master of Toulouse.'

CHAPTER 32

The siege machine known as 'the Cat' towered against the
summer sky like a creature from the Revelation. Its lair was
the carpenter's compound of the Château Narbonnais, and
it had been designed for the sole purpose of battering a breach
in Toulouse's eastern city wall.

The core of the Cat was an enormous tree trunk rigged
up in a pair of uprights, with crossbeams on top of each pair.
The trunk was slung on ropes from the crossbeams and
between the uprights. One end of it had been sharpened to
a point and reinforced with iron plates. The entire contrap-
tion was contained within the ribs of a wooden shed with an
upper housing to hold the archers. Its roof was thatched with
green hides to protect the men who would have to work for
hours on end, thrusting the iron head against the stones in
the city wall. The carpenters had nicknamed it 'Lord Simon's
prick', a title they kept to themselves in view of de Montfort's
current unstable temperament.

For nine months Toulouse had resisted Simon, and he was
scarcely any closer to breaching the city defences than he
had been at the beginning. His only advantage was that the
Château Narbonnais remained in his hands, and because of
its position, had open access to the outside world. Toulouse
was still virgo intacta, and Simon's frustration was under-
mining his judgement.

The June morning was already oven-hot as Simon, his

advisers and his adjutants inspected the siege machine after its final fettling. Dominic and Sim had tagged along, although the boys stayed well out of their elders' way.

Simon examined the Cat thoroughly before going to look at another siege machine across the compound. While the men were thus occupied, Dominic stepped curiously inside the wooden housing and imagined himself as a soldier working it. The smell of new wood and untanned hides was so powerful that it almost cut off his breath. He sat down on the oak trunk, then bounced on it several times.

'Will this really break down the wall?' he asked Sim, who was exploring the machine as gravely as the adults had done.

'My father says so.'

Dominic looked doubtful. He had been brought up to regard Lord Simon's will as law and, until recently, had looked upon him with the awe he knew should be reserved for God. Then, last month, a trebuchet stone had crashed into the chapel of the Château Narbonnais while they were at mass, killing one of the cardinal legate's chaplains. The immediacy of death, the bright splash of blood, the dust of fallen masonry hanging in the sunshine – these things held far more weight than the Count's command. He had learned to dread the whump of the counterweight, the pause and then the heavy crash of the stone missile against its target.

'Dom, stop bouncing!' the older boy said impatiently. 'If you don't behave, you'll be sent back to the women. Look, do you understand why the head is tipped with iron?'

'Course I do!' Dominic sniffed scornfully. 'If it was wood alone, it would just splinter against the walls!' He jumped off the trunk, his nose wrinkling. 'It stinks in here.' He ran back outside.

One of the carpenters, a rough, jovial man, winked at Dominic and offered him a drink of wine from his skin. 'What do you think of it then, lad? Will it breach a hole in the heretics' wall?' His eyes flashed with innuendo beyond Dominic's comprehension.

'It's very big,' Dominic said politely, and the man laughed. Dominic laughed, too, although he did not understand why. Then he ran across the compound to where a wiry-coated hound was dozing in the shade. Loup raised his head from his forepaws and wagged his tail at his young master. Dominic made a fuss of him and, seeing that no one was watching, decided to escape for a while. Loup needed a run, and on a fine day like this, Dominic could not bear the thought of returning to the gloomy darkness of the women's rooms in the château and the tongues sharp as needles with anxiety. Untethering his pony, he mounted up, told the groom that he was going home, and set off in that direction. As soon as he was out of sight, however, he doubled back and trotted his small cob in the direction of the river, Loup moving springily at the pony's heels.

Claire wiped the brow of the heavily pregnant woman and made her drink from the cup of water a passer-by had fetched.

'You should not be working so hard in this heat with your time so close,' she admonished. 'It is small wonder you fainted.'

'I'm all right, my lady,' the woman said. 'Give me a minute and I'll be back on my feet. The men have to eat.'

Claire glanced at the laden baskets of food the woman had been delivering to the soldiers on duty at the city walls. This was probably her third or fourth journey thus encumbered. She was not young. Her congested face wore the lines of early middle age, and the frizzy hair escaping her wimple was more grey than black. 'You must rest or you will do yourself harm. Let me take the baskets to the men. Isabelle will see you home and cared for.' She gestured at her maid.

The woman paused for a moment, then capitulated and pressed Claire's hand between her own. 'Thank you, my lady, God bless you. My man's in charge of the stone-thrower near the Montoulieu gate; his name's Isarn. Tell him I'm all right. The basket on the left's for the next crew along.'

Claire nodded and picked up both baskets. The entire town was determined to hold out against de Montfort, and everyone from the smallest child to the frailest octogenarian was doing what they could. Claire mostly tended the sick and wounded, although she had also carried supplies to the walls and run messages. She kept herself busy and when she was not busy, she prayed, but although her ghosts retreated from the foreground, they never left her alone.

The sun beat down and her skin prickled with sweat inside her shift and heavy Cathar robe as she climbed towards the trebuchet posts on the eastern city wall by the Montoulieu gate. Small wonder that the pregnant woman had collapsed. Perhaps they were in for an early thunderstorm. A glance at the sky showed her only a fierce, clear blue, and because she was not looking where she was going, she stumbled.

'Careful, mistress.' A soldier grabbed her arm to steady her.

Claire thanked him but quickly freed herself from his grasp. Ever since de Montfort's violation of her body, she disliked to be touched, even in concern and courtesy. He was small and wiry with twinkling brown eyes and a dark beard salted with grey.

'I'm looking for someone called Isarn,' she said as she regained her breath from the climb.

'Then look no further.' He took her arm again to steer her aside from a pulley load of rocks that two panting labourers were unloading. 'Ammunition for the old girl.' Fondly he patted the huge trebuchet at his side. 'There ain't much left of anyone she kisses!' Then he noticed the Cathar robes and sobered. 'I know you don't hold with killing, but I can't say I'm sorry to send any of them bastards to hell!'

'We don't believe in hell either,' she said and indicated the basket. 'Your wife sent provisions for you and the men. She was suffering in the heat, so I made her go home to rest.'

He shook his head. 'That's my Garsenda – she'll work until she drops. I've told her to slow down, but she'll not heed me. Her first man was killed by de Montfort's soldiers a few years ago. Hates them, the bastards.' He wiped his hands on his filthy chausses and stooped to the food.

Claire said nothing. Learning not to hate and not to fear were the most difficult lessons of her new religion – too difficult at the moment for her to surmount.

'So where do the wicked go if not to hell?' Isarn asked as his men gathered round to plunder their share from the basket.

'Into another human or animal body so that they may work out their sin in another life. Those that come to understanding become pure souls, no longer enslaved by matter and the God of matter.'

Isarn chewed thoughtfully, His eyes gleamed. 'So one day Simon de Montfort might become a worm feeding upon his own former body?'

'It is possible.' Claire tried to match his lightness with a smile, but she could not. Even the mention of the name made her nauseous.

'I've offended you now.'

She shook her head. 'It's not that. Do you mind if I have some of your wine?'

'Help yourself.'

Gratefully Claire unstoppered one of the skins and drank. Her panic subsided and she was able to thank him in a more natural tone. Putting the wineskin down, she reached for the other basket, which she had still to deliver along the ramparts. She was just taking its weight when Isarn showered out a mouthful of half-chewed meat and pastry. 'God's bleeding eyes, what the hell's that!'

His companions came running and leaned over the walls to look. Abandoning the basket, Claire ran to the parapet and stared at the huge siege engine that was rolling ponderously towards their section of wall. It consisted of a wooden housing covered with iron plates and thatched with raw hides, and seemed almost to be moving of its own accord, for the men propelling it forward were concealed within its bowels.

'The whoreson, it's a Cat! Helias, Rob, help me load la Catin!' Wiping his mouth on the back of his hand, Isarn thrust past Claire to the trebuchet, muttering the word bastard under his breath in a continuous litany.

The enormous ram crept nearer to the walls. Rooted to the ground, Claire watched it approach. Riding behind it was a man on a white stallion. He was wearing his battle helm, three red plumes tossing on its crest, and he was surrounded by a host of adjutants and squires, but she would have known him anywhere. Her belly heaved and she clapped her hand to her mouth. Something swished past her head and thrummed into the wooden structure of the trebuchet. The sky overhead was suddenly dark and there was a noise like a hundred birds in flight. She was seized from behind and, in the sweaty grip of one of the labourers, was dragged down to the wooden flooring upon which the trebuchet stood.

Claire lay too winded and shocked to move. The labourer ran at a crouch to the trebuchet and began turning the windlass frantically to lower the sling on the long end and wedge it so that Isarn and Helias could load it with a rock.

'All right, Rob, let her go!' Isarn bellowed. Rob knocked the wedge out of the fastening on the arm, the counterweight smacked down, and the loaded long end whipped through the arc of a circle, flinging the stone missile with great force out towards the enemy. It fell short, landing with an earth-shaking thud. All along the town wall other trebuchets hurled ammunition, but were not close enough to do anything but threaten. The Cat continued to creep towards the ditches, closer and closer, while the arrows whirred overhead. Claire huddled on the ground, sick with terror. Around her the men worked feverishly to reload the trebuchet. The smell of hot stone dust and tarred wood over-powered the air. Again a stone was launched and again came the groans of disappointment. Isarn's voice was hoarse as he directed his crew to reload. The weight came down and was pegged. Into the sling went the stone.

'Wait for it, lads, wait for it . . .' Isarn raised his arm. An arrow burned past his ear and he ducked. 'Now, now!' he shrieked, his arm chopping down. Out came the peg, down slammed the counterweight, over the wall sailed the huge stone. This time a different, crunching, splintering sound hit their ears. Isarn ran to the wall and peered over. A massive cheer went up from the trebuchet crews on either side of la Catin.

'It's a hit!' bellowed Helias, capering around the stone-thrower and hugging the other men. 'Up yours, Montfort! Up your arse!' He gestured eloquently. All along the wall soldiers jeered and gesticulated at the crusaders below and the broken Cat. The trunk itself had not sustained damage, but part of the housing was crushed and some of the supporting ropes had snapped. A soldier was carried out of the interior, his leg mangled and pouring blood. Under cover of more arrow-rain de Montfort's siege engine withdrew.

Isarn and his crew clustered around their trebuchet, all talking at once and capping jest with jest as they released their tensions. Claire stood up. Her knees were weak and she still felt sick. She dared not look over the wall lest she glimpse de Montfort.

Isarn noticed her plight and picked up a wineskin. 'You're as white as my wife's new-washed linen.'

Claire shook her head and grasped the second basket. 'I'm all right, and I'll be better if I give myself something to do. Besides, until I arrive, your friends have nothing with which to toast your victory.' She found a genuine smile for him and moved off along the wall, stepping over the arrows littering the ground like so many dead twigs. As she walked, she timed her footsteps to the mental chanting of a prayer, and gradually her fear of de Montfort faded to a dull but persistent niggle like a rotten tooth.

Absorbed within himself, Dominic rode much farther from the château than was wise or than he had intended, but when he realised his folly and made to turn back, Loup was nowhere to be seen. Shouting and whistling were unproductive and the confidence of his voice had started to waver and develop an edge of panic when he heard a whine from a clump of reeds and sedge close to the water's edge. Heeling his pony forward, he saw a movement among the tall stems. He also thought he heard a voice. His hand went to the small eating knife at his belt.

'Who's there?' he demanded, trying to make his voice as deep and assertive as Lord Simon's.

There was a long hesitation during which his hand tightened on the hilt of the knife. He had even started to ease it from its sheath when a girl of about his own age rose up from the rushes and faced him. Loup was with her. Her hand rested lightly on his collar, but the dog was making no effort to free himself.

'Who are you?' Dominic demanded, his tone rude because he had been frightened.

'Magda,' she answered simply, as if that were explanation enough, and flicked her hair away from her face. It was the colour of ripe barley – a shade that Alais's women were always trying to achieve out of an alchemist's bottle with limited success. Her eyes were a clear, steady grey, and full of curiosity.

'What are you doing with my dog?'

'He had a thorn in his paw, so I drew it out for him.' She smiled. Her front teeth were missing. River mud daubed one cheek and the front of her gown.

'Loup doesn't like strangers.' Dominic dismounted and clicked his fingers, summoning his pet.

'He likes me.' She patted the dog and released his collar.

Loup licked her hand and stayed where he was. She had to use her voice and point before he would return to his master.

Dominic felt betrayed. Loup's loyalty had always been singularly for him. 'What are you doing here?' he challenged, jaw thrusting in a fair imitation of Lord Simon's.

'Helping my mother pick herbs. These marsh marigolds have more flowers on this side of the river.' She showed him a basket filled with an assortment of plants. 'Why are you so angry?'

Dominic scowled. 'I'm not.'

She gave him a long look, and he dropped his gaze and scuffed his toes. Loup pushed his moist muzzle into his hand, but he ignored the perfidious hound. When he looked up again, his eye was caught by a dark, oblongish shape half-concealed among the rushes, which he suddenly realised was a small boat.

'You're from the rebels, aren't you?'

Her poise slipped and she looked quickly over her shoulder as if searching for someone.

'Are you a heretic?'

She faced him again, her shoulders tense. 'I am not a Catholic, if that is what you mean,' she said with dignity.

'Friar Dominic burns heretics,' he said. 'I'm named after him.'

Although the words might have been construed as a threat, the girl did not take them as such, and the tension left her body, as if whatever danger there was had passed. 'So your name is Dominic,' she said. When he did not answer, she scooped her hair behind her ears and set about plucking some more stems of marsh marigold. 'Mine's Magda. Do you want to help me?'

Dominic hesitated. The proud, masculine side of his nature, affronted by her easy mastery of Loup, wanted to say something scornful and ride away. His reasoning mind and his imagination bade him override his hostility and remain. He had never spoken to a real heretic before, and with her white-gold hair, river-grey eyes and delicate features, she reminded him of a faerie creature from a troubadour's tale. 'All right,' he said gruffly. 'What do I have to do?'

She showed him. Gradually his hostility melted and they came to a companionable silence, curiously adult in its quality. The pony grazed. Loup explored the reed beds, startling a heron into heavy flight and disturbing a family of grebes. He splashed in the shallows, sending up silver sprays of water, and shook himself unsociably close to the children so that they winced away, arms upheld, and broke into the common bond of laughter.

'What sort of dog is he?' Magda brushed water droplets from her gown.

'I don't know, a mongrel. Sim says he's got wolf blood, so that's how he got his name. They were going to drown him, but the Count let me keep him.'

'Who's Sim?'

'Simon, Lord de Montfort's son. He's older than me and he bosses me a bit, but we're friends really.'

'Do you live with him, then?'

'Yes.' Dominic peeled away the green outer casing of a reed stem, his movements jerky. 'They say de Montfort's my father, too.'

Magda gave him a searching look. 'Do you believe them?'

He shrugged and started shredding the white pith with his thumbnail. 'I suppose so. Sometimes they tell me my father is a southern noble, a *faidit*, and that his lands really belong to me, but I know they're lying. Lord Simon took me to see his castle once, at a place called Montvallant. The people stood in silence when we rode past and then they spat in our dust. Lord Simon had the ringleaders whipped, but it made no difference to what they thought.' He tossed the reed aside, his brows drawn down in a frown. 'I'm like Loup, I don't belong anywhere.'

'No,' said another voice, gentle and adult. 'You are yourself, and that is your strength.'

Dominic turned round quickly and found himself looking up at a slender black-haired woman with the same grey gaze as the girl. She was carrying a large, shallow basket full of plants, and her gown was kilted to midcalf, the hem dark with moisture.

'Mama, this is Dominic, and his dog's called Loup. We've picked all these for you.' Magda showed her mother the fruits of their efforts.

'You have been working hard, both of you.' The woman smiled. Dominic felt as if he were being pulled inside out and examined piece by little piece. For a moment he resisted, then changed his mind and opened himself to her stare. It was not cold like the lady Alais's, but encompassing and warm. Around her he thought he perceived a faint glow, and around Magda, too, and then he was drawn into it. It was extremely pleasant, like basking in sunshine. He sensed approval from the older woman, something very rarely meted out to him at the château, and he felt himself stretching and expanding to absorb it. But suddenly there was disturbance in the golden field. Turning his head, Dominic saw a horseman riding towards them, his own halo a murky black with pulsing red edges. The sensations of pleasure and contentment vanished with the speed of a snuffed candle.

'Mama, who is that?' Magda pointed towards the rider.

'It is the lord Simon,' Dominic said dully. 'Probably he's come looking for me. I'll be in trouble now.'

'No, he is seeking solitude.' Bridget bit her lip as all the rage, pain, frustration and hatred engulfed her in a fetid miasma.

'Look at his life force.' Magda shuddered. 'It's horrible . . . Why can I see death?'

Dominic began to feel sick and cold. Loup was growling, his hackles standing on end.

'Quickly, Magda, go to the boat!' Bridget gave her daughter a push.

'Mama . . .'

'Go!' Bridget cried urgently and, as Magda raised her skirts to her knees and hurried to their small craft, Bridget stood beside Dominic and faced the brooding, dreadful darkness of his father. A brief glance showed her that the boy's aura remained steady and confident. He was apprehensive, but he did not fear the approaching man, and that was all to the good.

De Montfort saw them, recognised Dominic, and put his already blowing horse into a renewed gallop. Dominic took a single step back and then stood his ground, his shoulders square and straight.

'What in the name of Christ's ten toes are you doing here!' Simon demanded in a congested voice, and drew rein bare inches from Dominic and Bridget. Foam spattered from the bit hinges and the stallion sidled, rolling its eyes and stamping its hooves. The man's face was dark with the temper that was swelling up in him like rapidly proving bread.

'I brought Loup out for some exercise, sir,' Dominic said. Behind his back, his hands were clenched one upon the other, squeezing tightly.

'That was not what you told the groom at the carpenter's compound!'

'I . . . I changed my mind.'

'By the rood, I should have let Friar Bernard have his will with you!' Simon manoeuvred the horse closer and leaned down from the saddle to grab Dominic's arm. As his fingers closed, Loup snarled and attacked. His teeth sank into the Count's hand, puncturing skin, drawing blood. Simon's rage erupted and he dragged his sword from the scabbard.

'No!' Dominic shrieked, protecting Loup with his own body. Simon reversed the weapon, intending to club the boy away from the dog, but suddenly let out a roar of pain. His fingers opened and the sword slid over the stallion's withers and flashed in the grass. Gasping, Simon clutched his wrist, agony writhing across his face. His horse reared and threw him. Simon struck the ground at Dominic's feet and the stallion galloped away in the direction of the château as though it were morning-fresh and had not been pushed for half the day.

Simon threshed on the ground, clutching his midriff. Bridget stood over him. 'What you give to others has been turned back upon yourself,' she said with impartial calm. 'It will destroy you unless you stop what you are doing and seek the Light.'

'Who are you?' Simon gasped through clenched teeth, his body shaking.

Bridget drew herself up. 'Who am I? Do you not recognise the radiant illuminatrix in all beings?' The light danced all around her, lifting the ends of her hair, gilding her. 'I am Bridget, of the line of the Magdalene and the blessed Queen of Heaven.' Simon's eyes widened. Then he cried out again, lost consciousness, and was still.

'Mama!' Magda emerged from the boat and ran to clutch her mother, tears pouring down her face. Bridget put her arms around her daughter, but her gaze remained sombrely on de Montfort. His aura was still murky, but the most destructive flashes had drained away, channelled through his own body.

'Is he dead?' Dominic asked. His face was ashen.

'No, just stunned.' Bridget freed one hand to set it comfortingly upon Dominic's shoulder. He felt a pleasant tingling, and the rapid pounding of his heart subsided.

'Best, I think, if we go and you let his grooms find him. They'll think he took a fall from his horse . . . and so will he. He won't remember the rest – his belief won't let him.'

Dominic looked at her anxiously. 'What if he remembers that Loup bit him?'

'He won't. Do you trust me?'

Dominic's glance flickered towards Magda and he nodded. 'Yes.'

She brushed the damp black hair off his forehead in a tender gesture. 'And it is not something given lightly, I can tell,' she murmured. 'Go now, quickly.'

Feeling stunned and disoriented, Dominic went to his peacefully cropping pony. Simon twitched and groaned and he made haste to mount. Magda and her mother were already in their boat and rowing towards the other side. The girl raised her hand in farewell, and Dominic responded before whistling Loup to heel and setting off at a gallop.

Bridget ceased pounding herbs and grease into ointment in her mortar and looked at her daughter with troubled eyes.

'You were dreaming again last night,' Bridget said, touching Magda's arm. 'Was it the same one as before?'

Magda shook her head and continued to strip the leaves from the plants they had gathered.

'Then what?'

'I don't remember, except that I was hurting here so badly that I couldn't breathe.' She fanned her hands over her belly, in the space between her navel and the juncture of her thighs. 'It was at Montségur, though, and the dark presence was there.' She shivered, and one hand left her stomach and travelled to the reassurance of the dove and chalice medallion she wore around her neck.

Bridget resumed pounding the ointment, feeling worried. She, too, had dreamed recently of Montségur. Magda had been lying upon a pallet as still as death, and for the first time, Bridget had felt the presence, too – the dark, hollow hunger of an unbalanced mind. She had tried to reach Magda and protect her from its searching greed, but had been powerless. Instead, it was a black-haired young man who had stepped forward and offered himself as a shield.

And today they had encountered Simon de Montfort's bastard son, begotten upon Claire de Montvallant – a black-haired child with an aura as powerful as his father's, but clear and pure and fierce. She suspected that his fate was closely interwoven with Magda's – that he was the reason they had been drawn to Toulouse. But the threads of life and death were so narrowly blended in this instance that she could not separate one from the other.

Concussed, head bandaged, limping from a twisted ankle, Simon refused to do as his physicians suggested and remain abed. Alais had no better success, and when Simon threatened to convince her of his determination with his fist, she abandoned him to his temper. He stumped around the carpenter's compound, swearing at all and sundry, kicking at tools and pieces of wood, and reviling the workmen when they told him that the damage to the Cat and the extra strengthening required to its structure would take them at least ten days to make good.

At first Dominic was afraid that despite what the woman had said, Simon would remember what had happened on the banks of the Garonne and connect the healing bite mark on his hand with Loup, but it was as the woman had said: Simon appeared to have blanked the incident from his mind. Only his hatred of the rebels remained. Sometimes Dominic would see it as a red-edged cloud encircling him, destroying balance and judgement. And as the great Cat grew closer to restoration, so did the intensity of that cloud, until it was a miasma.

CHAPTER 33

'Something has got to be done about that siege machine,'
Rai said. 'He's serious about reinforcing it, and we can't
depend on another hit like the last one.'

Since his arrival from Provence, Rai had taken over the
command of military operations in Toulouse from his father.
He had the youth and vigour Raymond lacked, and a better
grasp of warfare. A signal brought his youngest squire,
Raoul's son, Guillaume, hastening to refill his cup and take
away what was left of the meal.

'How long have we got?' Raymond-Roger of Foix leaned
on his folded elbows.

'A couple of days at most. I don't want him getting any
closer to the Montoulieu gate than he did last week . . . and
that was too close.' Rai's dark gaze crossed the room. 'Raoul,
you're the most experienced at quick in-and-out fighting.
Will you command a raid?'

'Willingly, my lord.' Raoul rose from his bench to look
at the plans laid out on the trestle.

Drawing his meat dagger, Rai used it as a pointer. 'We
have to break into the carpenter's compound here, preferably when as few people as possible are about.'

'Morning mass, then.'

'Ideal.'

Raoul nodded. 'A decoy attack just before the main one
to draw off the guards would be useful.'

'We can arrange that,' Rai said.

'I'll need some pots of Greek fire and some tar-soaked brands. That thing has to be set alight in the shortest time possible. We dare not linger.'

'Whatever you need is yours,' Rai confirmed. 'I'll let you organise it, just keep me abreast of the details.' Looking round, he stretched his arms above his head. 'Any other business? Otherwise I'm for my bed.' Which was currently filled by a luscious merchant's daughter, and Rai could not be blamed for wanting to retire early.

When Raoul departed, Guillaume held his horse for him while he mounted.

'Does Lord Rai keep you on your toes?' Raoul asked his son with a smile.

The boy responded with a good-natured grimace. 'He works me to the bone.'

'What else are squires for?' Raoul laughed. It had not really surprised him when Rai had offered to take Guillaume into his household to train to arms. The Raymonds owed the Montvallants a debt for their unwavering support, a debt that could hardly be repaid in money or land given present circumstances, and instead Guillaume had been favoured with a position in Rai's own mesnie that might lead to better things.

Guillaume returned the laugh. 'I'm not really complaining. I'd rather have a lot to do and people around me all the time.'

Rather than what? Raoul wondered as he gathered the reins. Rather than enduring the strained silence between parents who had grown so far apart that they seldom looked each other in the eye?

'Good luck with the Cat,' Guillaume said.

Raoul saw through the boy's smile to the underlying anxiety. 'Watch for the smoke.' He grinned, and tousled the sleek blond hair.

* * *

Isarn's wife, Garsenda, groaned and twisted on her pallet in the throes of another fierce labour contraction. Moistening the woman's lips with a sponge soaked in watered wine, Claire wished the midwife would hasten back from attending another patient. It seemed that every pregnant woman in Toulouse had decided to have her baby tonight. Claire had been summoned from her slumber to this particular bedside because the midwife could not be in ten places at once, and Garsenda, remembering Claire from the previous week when she had helped her in the street, had asked for her.

Raoul had not returned from his military briefing when she left the house in response to the summons. She knew he was going on a raid at dawn and was worried about him. For all the differences between them, for all the heartache, she still loved him and would have liked to wish him the talisman of walking in the Light.

'Ah . . . ah!' groaned Garsenda. 'I want to push!' Naked, she squatted on the bed, grey hair hanging down, sweat rolling off her unwieldy bulk. The thought of Raoul slipped from Claire's mind, and she gave all her attention to the labouring woman, wishing again that the midwife would return. Bearing two children was not the same as delivering one, but it was rapidly becoming obvious she had no choice.

Garsenda gasped and wailed aloud to God and the saints to help her, and in the next breath swore the vilest blasphemies against those to whom she had just been pleading. The mucus-wet crown of the baby's head started to bulge at the entrance of the birth passage, and Claire had no time to panic. 'You must pant,' she commanded Garsenda firmly, 'or else you will tear yourself!'

Garsenda sobbed and swore, but withheld from pushing down too hard. Claire bent over her and, with a moistened cloth, cleaned the baby's face as it was born. On the next contraction, amid a gush of fluid, blood and slime, the infant slipped out on to the bedstraw, a bluish-red bedraggled scrap, as wrinkled as one of last season's apples.

'Is it all right, my lady? What is it, a boy or a girl, what is it?' Garsenda cried.

The infant wailed lustily, arms and legs thrashing like windmill sails, the cord still attached and pulsing. The sound echoed in Claire's head. 'A boy,' she heard herself say. 'And he's perfect.' Where had she heard those words before? Alais de Montfort with malice in her eyes.

'Let me have him, oh, let me have him, he's so beautiful!' Garsenda stretched out plump arms to the baby, tears of joy streaming down her face, mingling with the sweat of her travail. She took the baby on to her breast, crooning in absorption to the slippery, blood-streaked little body.

A new soul trapped in flesh, Claire thought, but her own weepiness stemmed from a feeling of loss. She had never been able to grieve for the child conceived in rape and taken away the instant that the cord was cut. The wound still festered, and she knew it would never heal.

The midwife returned in time to deliver and examine the afterbirth, and hear Garsenda's praise for Claire.

'I couldn't have done it without you, my lady,' Garsenda declared, smoothing a gentle forefinger over the baby's damp hair. 'My Isarn's on watch until prime. Will you take him a bite to eat and give him the good tidings? He'll be so proud!' She put her new son to her breast, cradling him tenderly.

Swallowing the lump in her throat, Claire prepared a basket of provisions to take to the men. She was glad to perform the task, for she knew if she returned home, she would only worry about Raoul or fall asleep and endure nightmares.

When she stepped into the street, the sky was paling towards dawn over the suburb of Saint-Cyprien. People were stirring from their beds – those who had not been on night watch. The smell of fresh bread filled the air, and on the walls and among the dunghills the cockerels crowed to greet the morning. It was the hour of stillness before the streets filled with the rumble and bustle of activity. Claire slowed her walk to suit the moment, taking advantage of the cool half-light as she strolled towards the Montoulieu gate.

Raoul gave Rai's knights five minutes to draw off the guards with an attack on de Montfort's camp, then led his own assault upon the carpenter's compound.

The soldiers posted around the Cat rallied swiftly and put up a spirited resistance. Raoul realised after the first vicious exchange of blows that here were no raw, expendable troops, but hand-picked professionals, nursemaiding their commander's last hope of conquering the city. It was still half-dark, hard to judge when to strike and when to duck, or identify whether it was ally or enemy who screamed under his blade. From his eye corner Raoul saw Mir lob two clay bombs of Greek fire at the giant Cat. One missed and burst like a fiery marigold on the compound floor. The other hit the green hides and cracked open. As its volatile burden dripped in shreds of silver flame down the sides of the weapon, Raoul cut beneath his enemy's guard, leaped over the falling soldier, and ran to help the youth. Seizing a pitch-soaked torch, he hurled it through the open mouth of the Cat where the tree trunk protruded like a tongue.

The sun burst over the horizon and leached the colour from the flames, giving it instead to mail and surcoats, to wood and stone and steel. 'À Montfort! À Montfort!' came the furious rallying cry, and crusaders started to pour into the compound from the camp around the château.

'Sound the retreat!' Raoul bellowed at Giles, knowing they couldn't hope to hold off the full tide of the counter-attack. Fighting hard, they backed towards the safety of the Montoulieu gate. When they reached the defensive ditches before the walls, the trebuchets began to hurl stones into the northern troops, and arbalest bolts whizzed overhead, proving a hazard to both sides.

Raoul slashed and thrust and struck, all the time retreating towards the safety of the gate. He was challenged by a thickset knight who kept bellowing, 'À Montfort!' through the slits in his helm to rally and direct the crusaders. One of Simon's senior battle commanders, Raoul surmised through the roaring of blood in his ears and the harsh draw and release of breath as he continued to back away. The knight pursued him grimly. Smoke gouted from the direction of the siege machine, blinding and choking, spangled with heat. Raoul almost lost his sword to a twisting motion made by the knight, but recovered and retorted. An arbalest bolt whined past his helm and sank into his opponent's upper arm. The knight buckled to his knees and Raoul raised his sword on high to finish him, only to be engaged by another warrior who had forced himself forward out of the northern mêlée. This time there was no doubting his identity. Three red plumes danced on the crest of the helm, and the fork-tailed lion snarled across his shield. Once more Raoul found himself staring death in the face.

As the light brightened with the dawn, Claire stood beside la Catin on the wall at the Montoulieu gate, her view of the fighting clear. She saw the bursts of flame explode on the Cat and flare upon the barricades protecting it.

'Look at them!' Isarn smacked the wall. 'Proper ants' nest! Go on, lads, show them who's master!' His eyes were dark-rimmed with tiredness, but his expression was exultant.

'My husband is down there,' Claire said, her hands clasped so hard together that the knuckles showed bone-white. 'He was coordinating the raid.'

Isarn's gaze turned to her and his voice softened. 'He's a right brave man, my lady.'

'Yes,' she said. 'Yes, he is . . . he deserves better.'

'I do not under—'

'Look sharp, lads!' yelled Helias. 'Counter-attack!' He stood by the peg on the windlass as the crusaders began pouring into the compound. Arbalesters ran to man the walls either side of la Catin and aimed their bolts as best they could.

The area below became a confusion of struggling men –
the knights in mail and brightly dyed surcoats, the ordinary
soldiers in leather hauberks and padded gambesons.
Weapons clashed amid a cacophony of shouts and screams.
Along the walls the stone-throwers cast their missiles into
the far reaches of the mêlée. La Catin hurled its first stone.
Helias and Rob hastened to reload, not waiting to see if they
had done any damage.

Claire stared into the mêlée and saw the familiar shield
and helm of de Montfort in the forefront. She watched the
muscular mail-clad arm sweep down in a killing blow. A
soldier crumpled and died. Sickened, cold, but unable to
look away, she followed de Montfort's progress through the
mêlée, and suddenly screamed and clutched the wall because
Raoul was blocking de Montfort's way and refusing to give
ground.

Rob ran to help Isarn wind the empty sling back down.
The latter was muttering his usual litany of 'bastards' beneath
his breath, with a few choice epithets besides. There was a
thud. Rob staggered and cried out, a crossbow quarrel
protruding from his chest. He collapsed on all fours, then
keeled over, blood trickling from the corner of his mouth.
Isarn ran around the trebuchet and, raising Rob's shoulders,
cradled him, slapping his face and shouting, but to no avail;
the young man was dead.

Claire watched Raoul and de Montfort exchanging blows.
Being less powerfully developed, Raoul was taking a terrible
hammering. 'Run!' she screamed at him but, even as the
words left her mouth, knew he could not hear her and that
he would not back down, for he and a small core of his men
were protecting the retreat of the others into the safety of
the city.

'Come on!' Isarn snarled, grabbing her arm, his eyes wild.
'Help me prime her. This one's for Rob!'

'What do I have to do?' She knuckled tears from her eyes.

'Just turn the windlass, fast as you can . . . Hurry!'

Feverishly Claire grabbed the handle as if snatching at sanity. It was a machine of war, of destruction, but it was something to occupy her hands and mind, prayer being no solace. The wood burned against her hand, her shoulders nearly tore from their sockets, but the sling came down and Isarn pegged it before running to help Helias load the stone.

'When I shout, pull out the peg!' he cried to Claire.

Face white with strain, she nodded. Over the wall she heard the increased howling from the crusader mob and the diminishing cries of 'Toulouse!'

'Now!' bellowed Isarn.

The peg resisted her tug. She set both hands to it and yanked with all her might. It flew out, gouging a deep splinter into her palm, and she fell backward, hitting the platform at the same time as the counterweight whumped down and the boulder shot over the walls in the direction of the ditch. She heard the crash as it hit, and then a strange, hollow silence. Slowly that silence was filled by cries of disbelief and ragged cheers. Claire crawled to her knees and, clutching the wall for support, staggered to her feet and looked over the parapet. The fighting had stopped. Raoul was standing alone, his sword and shield both lowered, and no one was making any attempt to come at him. Instead the crusaders were retreating, dragging something with them – a man's body, but even from here she could see the blood, the flattened helm encasing a red pulp.

'God's eyes!' croaked Helias. 'You've hit de Montfort!' And then, voice growing stronger as belief took hold, he cried over his shoulder to Isarn, 'Here's revenge for Rob; de Montfort's dead!'

The word spread along the walls like wildfire. Fists punched the air. The ragged cheering rose in volume to a sea-like roar of jubilation.

The words 'de Montfort' and 'dead' unlocked a door in Claire's mind. She glimpsed light and air and suddenly recognised the moment in her dreams when she set foot outside her cage and advanced to make her own life . . . or else retreated into the darkest corner of her cell. The cheering reached out to her like a lifeline. Looking over the parapet, she sought her husband. He was limping towards the gate, his shoulders slumped. As she watched, he stumbled and almost fell. Whirling round, gathering her skirts, she left the trebuchet and pelted along the wall and down to the gate. She had to fight against and through a seething crowd of citizens. Several times she was grabbed and hugged and once was drawn into a wild dance. Euphoria crested, broke, and surged anew, wave upon wave.

> *'Montfort est mort!*
> *Montfort est mort!*
> *Montfort est mort!*
> *Est mort, est mort!'*

In the middle of the crowd, sitting on an upturned barrel, his head in his hands, was Raoul. When only a yard separated her from him, she spoke his name and he raised his head. A deep scratch was beaded between eye corner and jaw where a fragment of the exploding stone had caught him. The rest of his face was colourless.

'It's true,' he said woodenly. 'He's dead. I saw him hit . . . like a ripe plum struck by a mallet.' He clenched his teeth, fighting his gorge. 'If I hadn't given ground a moment before, it would have been me . . .' He looked her in the eyes, his expression bewildered and weary. 'How is it possible not to believe the truth?'

'Oh, Raoul!' Weeping, she threw herself into his arms. He caught her and they clung together as if to save each other from drowning, while around them the sea of euphoria roared towards a full-blown storm. De Montfort dead was like having a constant plucked out of the firmament. Everything had to be readjusted, realigned, and in the meantime there was a frightening void.

'I was helping to man the stone thrower that killed him – la Catin,' Claire wept. She was assaulted by terrifying, conflicting emotions. She had violated the Cathar creed of non-violence and was sick and ashamed of the surge of exultation that had coursed through her vitals as the stone flung over the wall. It still ran strongly in her veins now, knowing Simon de Montfort was dead. It seemed only just she should have a hand in killing him. But whose justice? The Cathar God was above the creed of an eye for an eye. That doctrine belonged to the crusaders' God, Rex Mundi.

She heard the rejoicing, the howls that seemed like bloodlust. The scent of war and destruction was in her nostrils. She held Raoul tightly in her arms and felt his shuddering through her own body. They wept together, and although there was release in their tears, there was a terrible grief too, for all that was lost and could never be regained.

CHAPTER 34

After the darkness of the chapel, the bright sunshine was a shock to Dominic. He blinked and squinted and raised his hand to shade his eyes. The courtyard was packed with wains and carts, sumpter horses, destriers and palfreys. Six dappled grey horses champed between the shafts of the ladies' litter, and six black cobs were harnessed to the sumptuous open cart that bore Lord Simon's pall-covered coffin.

Dominic admired the gold tassels fringing the pall, the bright limewood and linen shields nailed to the side of the cart, the silk banners and richly decorated harness and trappings. What lay beneath the gilding was not so pretty. He had seen Lord Simon's corpse when the knights brought it back from beneath the city walls – the torso unmarked, the helmet crushed into the head and oozing bloody matter. Sim had been sick, and Amice hysterical. To Dominic, the sight of the body had been unpleasant, but there had been nothing to frighten him now that the awful black cloud had dissipated from around it. It was only a body, no different from a butcher's carcass on a block.

Friar Bernard, the priests and chaplains said that Count Simon's soul was now in heaven, its bliss assured by the great service he had performed for Jesus Christ. Dominic wondered what Jesus Christ really thought of it all. He even asked Him in the chapel when he was supposed to be praying for Lord Simon's soul, but there had been no reply except for silence itself.

A month had passed since the stone had crushed Simon's skull, a month in which the siege of Toulouse had been half-heartedly pursued by Amaury de Montfort and then abandoned. A month of disbelief and indecision for the adults, a month of wandering freedom for Dominic and Loup. They had visited the place where they had encountered the heretic woman and her daughter, and Dominic had stared across the river until his eyes ached, but there had been nothing to see except the glitter of the sun on the water and the breeze stirring the reeds.

This morning at dawn, the main camp had been razed to destroy everything that might be of use to their enemy, the gutted frame of the huge Cat included – a pyre marking the departure of Simon de Montfort to Carcassonne for burial.

Friar Bernard was travelling with the entourage. Dominic eyed him sidelong and contemplated putting a burr beneath his saddlecloth. As if reading his thoughts, his tutor turned and fixed Dominic with an icy stare. Dominic returned the look, but not for long enough to bring retribution down on himself, and busily adjusted his stirrup strap.

Alais emerged from the château with Amice and the maids. She was sombrely gowned and wore no jewellery apart from a gold cross on her breast. She still walked as if she owned the world, her voice autocratic and powerful, but Dominic had seen behind the mask with which she faced the world, had seen her straggle-haired, a wine flask in her hand, her face bloated with weeping. Her night-time alone face, the price paid for showing pride to the world when all her pride was rotting beneath a pall of crimson silk.

They left Toulouse behind, the ancient château and muscular sweep of river, the gold and pink town scarred but secure behind its ditches and ramparts. Simon's triumph and Simon's downfall. Of them all, only Dominic looked back, and he was not thinking of Toulouse, but of two people he had met upon the banks of the Garonne.

At the crossroads upon the hill, Raoul rested his hands on the raised saddle pommel and looked out over his Montvallant lands. A broken wain lay at the roadside and some peasants were picking it clean. It had belonged to the crusaders, but they had abandoned it in their haste to leave. All over the Toulousain and the Agenais, the northerners were departing, retreating into towns that they knew they could hold for certain, slipping away north. The second siege of Montvallant had been as rapid as the first, only this time it was Raoul who had appeared beneath the castle walls with troops in overwhelming numbers and offered the defenders surrender or death.

The northern commander had been sour but sensible, and Montvallant once more belonged to a seigneur of that name, but, like an insecure child, Raoul kept looking over his shoulder, expecting at any moment to see a crusader force marching down on him. Rumours clustered thicker than a cloud of flies in fresh dung – Amaury de Montfort was coming from Carcassonne with fresh troops; the Pope had called a new crusade. Philip of France was coming to put an end to Rai's string of successes. Beware, be on guard, do not relax for an instant. Hold the soil in your fist, the clay of which you were made, and let no one take it from you.

And Claire said let everything go. The spirit is what matters.

She joined Raoul now where the road branched. Isabelle followed at a discreet distance on her palfrey, and behind her rode the soldiers whose task it was to escort the two women on their chosen road. Raoul turned his gaze from his lands to his wife. 'Are you sure?' he asked.

She returned his stare, her eyes travelling slowly over his face as if memorising every feature. 'Yes, I am. I have to leave for both our sakes, or else we will bleed for ever. I wish I could make you understand.'

Stretching across the horse, he took her hand in his. Her fingers were brown and firm, devoid of rings, testimony to her commitment to the Cathar way. He sighed deeply. 'I have tried being blind, I have tried being angry, but I have been blocking out the truth, not destroying it. Take your path; I will not stop you.'

Her eyes were luminous with tears, but she was smiling. 'Oh, Raoul,' she said softly.

Raoul kissed her fingertips. 'Walk in the Light, Claire,' he said huskily. 'And think of me sometimes.' Abruptly he released her, and turning his horse around, set him to a canter in the direction of Montvallant.

Tears spilled down Claire's face as she watched him go. A warm wind tumbled and gusted, billowing her cloak, drying the moisture to salt on her cheeks. 'Walk in the Light,' she repeated softly. The wind took her words and danced away with them. She turned her mare southward.

Raoul rode towards his castle, its walls golden-red in the autumn sunshine. He felt the sleek power of the glossy courser beneath him, the leather in his fingers, the sun on his face, and the desolation of having no one with whom to share them.

He forded the river, low now after the hot summer. Brown-skinned children played in the shallows, and women pounded their linen on white stones beside the bank. Difficult to imagine from this scene that there had ever been a war or foreign occupation, but the scars were there all the same, deep and bitter. One of the women glanced up from her laundry. She had copper hair of a similar shade to Claire's, a winsome smile, and abundant curves, accentuated by the damp patches on her gown. Slowing the horse, he approached her, seeking solace.

CHAPTER 35

TOULOUSE, SUMMER 1234

Half opening his eyes, the young man squinted against the intrusion of daylight from the window embrasure. Linen sheets and a rumpled coverlet were tangled around his long body. An unaccustomed warmth pressed against his spine, and fingers smoothed over his ribs then investigated lower. Normally he would have responded with alacrity to such an invitation, but after last night's excesses, all inclination was subjugated by the pain hammering within his skull and the gurgling pit where his stomach should have been.

Undaunted, the woman persisted and was rewarded with a token response, his body functioning on the raw, physical level of young manhood. 'You want me again, Lord Dominic?' she purred.

Her accent was Catalan. Gingerly he rolled over to face her and in the light from the embrasure saw that she had a mass of dark curls, magnificent dark eyes and even more magnificent breasts. What was her name? Peronelle? Williametta? He couldn't remember, didn't want to. Last night, his first in Toulouse for more than fifteen years, had been passed in convivial celebration – wine, song, gambling, more wine, and then the woman. At the time, it had seemed an excellent idea. The area below his waist still thought it was, but his stomach threatened to react violently against any such prospect.

'No,' he muttered, shoving aside her busily kneading hand. 'Just . . . just go away.'

'You didn't say that last night.' She poked her tongue in his ear.

'I wasn't sick last night,' he groaned. 'Please, just . . . just go.'

Tossing her head, she sat up, torn between petulance and sympathy. For five years, ever since the treaty of Meaux when the young Count Raymond had submitted to King Philip Augustus of France, the Château Narbonnais had been occupied by French troops. Business was always brisk when there was a change of garrison, the homeward-bound men celebrating their release, the incoming ones drowning their sorrows.

Lord Dominic was a young knight attached to the new garrison, and a very personable one at that, better than the smelly greybeard who had taken her for his regular bedmate last time. Her new partner still possessed all of his teeth, and his undergarments showed signs of recent laundering. He was darkly avised like the native southern men, and the bold expression in his eyes as he had looked her up and down proclaimed him an heir to the troubadours. His payment had been generous, too, although that might just have been the drink. What a pity his home was the Île-de-France, his allegiance to the North, and that he would not be staying at the château above a few months.

'Shall I come back tonight?' Reluctantly she started to dress.

Hovering on a very delicate brink, knowing that if he did vomit, his head would explode, Dominic made an inarticulate sound. She took it to mean yes, because that was the best way to do business, and, having shunned the temptation of extracting whatever coins were left in his pouch, kissed him lightly and tiptoed out of the room.

Dominic heard the door close behind her and, with a suffering groan, buried his head beneath the bolster. It was not often that he drank to excess, but last night he had needed the oblivion. The Château Narbonnais held too many memories, and to have them land on him all at once had been too much to bear . . . but then so was this headache, and he thanked Christ that his duties did not officially begin until the morrow.

When finally he dared to move, the hot southern sun had burned away the first cool of the morning. In the château, however, the shadows were as dingy as he remembered, and everywhere the ghosts whispered at him. A small boy with a red weal burning on his cheek and a young and eager mongrel dog trotting at his heels escorted him through the various chambers. Passing the chamber where he had learned his letters, the echoes were at their darkest. It was still occupied by children struggling with their Latin and tutored by a Dominican friar – a young man with a fluffy red tonsure and an eager, freckled face. Not all of them were bad, he told himself, but the memory of pain and humiliation kept him from being convinced.

The chapel was dark and cold, busy with priests. The smell of incense hit his nostrils and threatened to upset his slowly settling stomach. Here, too, were memories – his father lying in state, although, of course, they could not display his face in blessed repose because there had been no face left to display. A swift death, and an inglorious one. Live by the sword, die by it, but there were worse ends. He had his own share of battle scars, but these days no one flung at him the taunts of bastard and whoreson. No longer was he Dominic de Montvallant or Dominic FitzSimon, but Dominic le Couchefeu – the banked fire. His was a nature of smouldering coals over intense heat. The doubt, insecurity and misery of an unloved child drove his ambitions. He acknowledged it, knew his failings, and kept them on a tight rein lest he become like his father, which was both his hunger and his dread.

The breaking of fast in the hall was long over; the trestles had been cleared and stacked against the walls, and people were going about their daily business. Some young knights with whom he had been carousing the night before had gathered in a morose huddle near the hearth to nurse their fragile heads and stomachs. Not relishing the prospect of recounting last night's follies, Dominic edged around them, avoided two Dominican friars with a perfunctory right-handed signing of the cross, and headed for the kitchens to rekindle a certain old acquaintance.

Hubert, who had been an apprentice during Dominic's boyhood, was now a fully fledged cook in his late twenties, red of face with close-set eyes that displayed an alarming tendency to cross when he concentrated. He looked Dominic dubiously up and down and wiped his hands on his apron.

'Can I be of service, my lord?'

'Don't recognise me, do you?' Dominic grinned, lounging against the doorpost. 'Would it make things easier if I begged a piece of marchpane and a marrowbone? I haven't got Loup with me. He died last year and I've yet to find a pup to replace him.'

'Master Dominic?' Hubert's eyes grew as round as tart cutters and the pupils shot towards each other. 'By all the saints!' He hesitated, obviously wondering whether to bow or adopt the familiarity of their former relationship.

'I'm not sure that the saints have anything to do with it!' Dominic laughed and, slapping the cook on his heavy dough-kneader's arm, peered into the dark, hot depths of the kitchen. 'I missed the breaking of fast. I don't suppose you can spare me a crust of bread and some wine?'

'At least your appetite hasn't changed!' Hubert laughed, deciding on familiarity. Ushering Dominic inside, he tipped a sleeping tabby cat off a spare stool.

'It's only just returning to life,' Dominic confessed ruefully. 'I made a night of it and my gut's as sour as the bottom of an English vintner's barrel!' He sat down on the stool. The cat, a champion mouser and thus permitted the run of the kitchens, glared balefully at him and stalked off to inspect the trestle next door where an apprentice was gutting fish.

Hubert set a brimming cup before his visitor, a loaf of bread, and some goat's cheese. 'Get outside of that,' he said cheerfully. 'You'll soon feel better.'

Dominic eyed the cheese dubiously, but cut a weighty chunk from the loaf with his eating knife.

'I remember you sitting there when your eyes scarce reached above the level of that table.' Hubert shook his head. 'You'd make two of me now!' He returned to chopping herbs with rapid, unthinking expertise.

'I'm not as tall as Simon or Amaury.' Dominic raised his cup.

Hubert eyed him, not deceived by the light tone. The quiet, self-contained child had not suddenly become a garrulous extrovert, unless by way of a shield. 'So how are the other boys?' he asked.

Dominic swallowed a mouthful of wine. 'Amaury's King Louis's constable now, although you probably know that already. He arranged for me to be taken into the royal household as a squire after the lady Alais died, and of course, he's ceded all rights in the South to the French Crown – nor can I blame him. He had a rough time after the siege of Toulouse. It's hard to live in the shadow of a dead paragon, particularly when he's your own father, and your every movement is compared and found lacking.' He shrugged and drank again.

'Is that your problem, too?'

'God no!' Dominic laughed sourly. 'I'm just the overlooked bastard, and tainted with southern blood at that. They expect me to be trouble, and I don't disappoint them. Amaury sent me down here, you know – decided that posting me to Toulouse was the quickest way to settle the dust.'

Hubert stretched across the table for a bundle of tarragon. 'What did you do?'

'Dallied with a lute and someone else's wife and got caught by her husband.'

Hubert clucked his tongue against the roof of his mouth with censorious amusement.

'I was transferred to the garrison here, and Clémence was packed off to a nunnery. Not that she minded. Her husband was sixty years old and as odious as they come, but Amaury didn't like the scandal.' A spark of devilry bordering on relish glowed in Dominic's eyes.

Hubert gave a reluctant chuckle.

Dominic lifted his shoulders. 'Simon's doing well for himself,' he said.

'Yes?'

'He's been able to claim the earldom of Leicester because of a kinship link. I've an offer of employment there any time I want it.'

'Leicester?' Hubert fumbled his tongue around the name and looked blank.

'It's in England,' Dominic said. 'Farther north even than the Île-de-France.'

'Will you go?'

'I might.' He broke off another chunk of loaf. 'I haven't decided what to do with my glittering future. Amaury would always keep me – I've got better manners than a mercenary when I think to use them, and a family connection. The same goes for Simon's offer . . . I don't know.' He grinned. 'I'm like raw wine; I need time to mature.'

'Hmmph,' Hubert muttered and, brows puckered, returned to chopping herbs, the sound blocking off all conversation.

When he had finished and swept the results into a bowl, Dominic asked, 'What about Toulouse? What's been happening here?'

Crossing his ankles, Hubert leaned one arm on the trestle and rested the other against his hip. 'Well, the new Pope's certainly keen on rooting out the heretics, and Guzman might be dead, but his kind are everywhere. You can't take a step these days without tripping over a friar with his ear to the ground and his nose on a scent. It's no wonder they call them the dogs of God.' He tut-tutted for a moment. 'At least the Cathars let you make up your own mind. If you disagree with the black friars, they take you away for questioning and you're never seen again, unless it's chained to a stake or tied to a whipping post outside the basilica.'

'I remember.' Dominic made a face as the image of Friar Bernard crossed his mind.

'You don't,' Hubert contradicted grimly. 'It's more vicious these days than it was when you dwelt here. Have you been out in the streets yet?'

'Only ridden through them yesterday.'

'Well, take a good look. Black robes everywhere and folk wearing cloaks sewn with yellow crosses to show that they're repentant heretics, and for no greater crime than passing a true heretic in the street. These days it is best to be seen going to mass every day and adoring the cross. Wear one round your neck and stitched to your surcoat. Sign your breast when you're out and make sure you're seen doing it.' Hubert pinched his upper lip. 'Do you know what else?'

Dominic shook his head.

'They won't give permission for old Count Raymond to be buried in consecrated ground. Twelve years his coffin has lain in the precincts of the Hospital of Saint John, and he was never even convicted of heresy.' The cook grimaced. 'I'm a good Catholic, wouldn't want anyone to think otherwise, but they have taken matters too far.' He pointed his knife at Dominic. 'Don't go using that left hand unless you're forced; it'll be seen as the Devil's mark, and the Count ain't here now to throttle the opposition.'

'I can look after myself,' Dominic replied defensively and, draining the cup, rose to his feet.

Hubert studied him with pessimism. 'How old are you, lad?'

'Two and twenty last Candlemas.'

'Well, if you want to live to be three and twenty, better gentle your attitude.'

'Don't worry, I'll be as meek as a washed lamb,' Dominic said in a tone that did nothing to reassure the cook and, thanking him for the food, strolled from the kitchens.

The city of Toulouse beckoned him and he left the gloomy environs of the château for its busy streets. The walls and ditches that had ringed the town during his previous sojourn had been demolished or filled in, in accordance with the treaty of Meaux. Some dwellings for the Dominican friars donated by a pious citizen of Toulouse stood sentinel directly opposite the château, and black-robed figures could be seen industriously entering and departing like swarming ants.

Everywhere towers thrust at the sky, armouring and enhancing the private homes of the rich, or proclaiming the pride of the Roman religion – the square towers of Saint-Etienne, the Romanesque spires of the basilica of Saint-Sernin. In every quarter, from the city to the burg, to the sprawling suburbs on the west bank, the bells called the faithful to bear witness.

Dominic allowed the city to seep into his pores. Memories competed with the hot dazzle of the present. New buildings had appeared in places he remembered as grassland or decimated by war. Urban bustle had returned, and prosperity, but the hatred and fear were still present. He could sense the wounds festering beneath the superficial bandages. People noted his fine tunic and the sword at his hip with speculative suspicion. Was he one of them, or a northern oppressor? If he opened his mouth, he knew his accent would damn him, thus he did not pause to listen to the troubadours in the marketplaces or inspect the wares in the merchants' booths, nor did he stop to hear a Dominican friar haranguing the crowds from a podium outside the ancient church of Notre-Dame de la Daurade, but hastened to complete his circuit of the city and return to the château.

Before the great gate, a crowd had gathered to witness a

spirited brawl between two of the château's guards, a friar and one of the townsmen, although it took Dominic a moment to discern exact numbers because of the entanglement of arms and legs. The friar flew backward and landed almost at his feet, blue-veined shins exposed, his dignity in tatters. A soldier followed him to the floor, his mouth and nose a scarlet smudge.

The townsman stood his ground, brown eyes blazing, blond hair ruffling like feathers. His shoulders were heaving, not just with exertion, but with the force of his dry sobbing. 'Good God!' he choked. 'Can't you even leave the dead in peace, you black kites!'

The other soldier drew his blade. Glancing around, Dominic saw that members of the crowd had picked up stones, and the atmosphere was volcanic.

'Hold your sword!' he snapped to the soldier.

The man turned with a curse on his lips, recognised Dominic's rank and accent, and protested instead. 'He's to be arrested, my lord.'

'What for?'

'Interfering with the lawful progression of justice and God's law!' snapped the friar, struggling to his feet and dusting himself down.

'God's law!' spat the young townsman. 'Is it truly God's law to dig up the dead and burn them? What's the matter, haven't you got enough living heretics to keep your fires fed?'

'Blasphemy!' squawked the friar, pointing a bony finger. 'Arrest him now!'

Fear coiled and tightened in Dominic's gut as he recognised Friar Bernard, his former tutor. The priest had changed little except to become more cadaverous, flesh drawn tight and ivory-pale over his skull and bony beak of a nose.

The injured guard sat up, wiped at the blood pouring from his nose, and looked in surprise at his red hand. The crowd began closing in. From the direction of the château, Dominic heard the clash of pikes as reinforcements hastened to contain the disturbance. The townsman was seized, the first stone flew, and the brawl renewed itself on a greater scale. Dominic raised his arm to protect his face and a sharp stone slashed his hand to the bone. Friar Bernard, his lips curled back from his teeth, incited the crowd to new heights of bitter violence by howling hellfire and damnation at them.

'By the rood, shut your foolish mouth!' Dominic bellowed. 'You will get us all killed!'

Friar Bernard stopped in mid-tirade and stared at Dominic. His pupils contracted and, as recognition tardily dawned, he silently mouthed his former pupil's name.

Dominic snarled a mirthless grin. 'Deliver us from evil!' he mocked, dodging another stone.

The arbalesters arrived then, crossbows primed at the crowd, and the townspeople gave up the fight, retreating in a last defiance of flung stones and insults. The prisoner was manhandled roughly into the château and dragged away to the cells.

Friar Bernard gave Dominic a basilisk glare as he beat dust from his robes and sought to reassume his dignity. 'What are you doing here?'

'Being stoned,' Dominic retorted flippantly because inside himself he was quailing beneath that flat, black stare. 'Look, it's my left hand.' The blood dripped steadily into the dirt like a sacrifice. 'Would you not say there was judgement somewhere?'

Bernard's eyes narrowed. 'Take care,' he hissed. 'You're no longer a child; I'm no longer your tutor. You're a man answerable for your sins, and I'm an inquisitor.'

'*Fiat voluntas Tua,*' Dominic said, crossing his breast, and, with a look of cold scorn, stalked off in the direction of the leech's quarters to seek attention for his hand.

Later, in the cool of the evening, Dominic ventured down to the banks of the Garonne to pay a poignant homage to the place and the day from his childhood that he had never forgotten. Little had changed. He stood, breathing in the scent of river and meadow. Among the reeds, a herd of brown and white cows stood knee-deep in the shallows, swishing their tails and snatching at succulent green shoots on the bank. Slender marsh marigolds grew in abundance. Half-smiling, Dominic plucked one with his good hand and thought of the fair-haired girl. How long it had been, and how powerfully she still tugged at his soul. A golden moment amongst so many dark ones.

He wondered what had become of her. Had she survived to grow up like himself, or had she been caught and killed as a heretic? He stared out across the river to the opposite bank; the reeds and grasses gilded by a flamboyant crimson sunset. It was here that he had first discovered his ability to see the life force that dwelt in all living things. The tones of harmony, soft and rich; the more intense hues of power and determination, and the jagged, dirty shades of imbalance, madness and evil.

It was a fickle gift. He was often too preoccupied to be receptive and was unable to summon the faculty at will, but sometimes it came upon him so strongly that he was always surprised to learn that others saw nothing. These days, he kept it to himself. Tonight it was strong. He could see a soft golden haze rising from the backs of the cattle, from the grasses, from the heron, even from the flower in his hand.

He was back in Toulouse. He could not call it home, and yet the place exerted a powerful pull on his soul, and this plain stretch of riverbank, the strongest tug of all. He cast the marsh marigold into the water and watched the slow-flowing water spin his offering around then bear it away in the direction of the water mills downstream.

The following morning saw Dominic established at a trestle in the great hall, a scribe to one side of him and a mountain of paperwork to the other. As he was the youngest knight of the relieving garrison, the most mundane and tiresome tasks were quickly foisted upon him, nor did his bandaged left hand provide any excuse, for he still had the use of his fingers.

He scrawled with rapid impatience, now and then pausing to ask the scribe a question or clarify a point. Sometimes the pauses were longer because the more experienced men kept directing external queries to Dominic's trestle and he would have to stop and deal with them – demands for payment of kitchen supplies, of ox cart hire; an irate father looking for the soldier who had got his daughter with child. As the morning wore on, so did the pressure of Dominic's fingers on his quill, and on a hard downward stroke it snapped, spraying ink across the close-written sheet of vellum.

Cursing through his teeth, Dominic trimmed a fresh pen, then sat back, opening and closing his aching fist. A servant put a cup of wine down in front of him and made to move on. 'Leave the flagon,' Dominic said.

'But, my lord . . .' The servant caught the look in Dominic's eyes and did as he was told. Sighing, Dominic took a deep swallow from the cup. In the corner of his vision, he saw a helpful official directing yet another query in his direction, and swore again. The scribe smothered a grin behind his hand and bent diligently over his parchment.

The man who came to Dominic's trestle was tall and lean, with a face too old for the proud, athletic carriage of his body. An embroidered tunic, gilded belt and rings upon his fingers professed his nobility; a musty smell informed Dominic that the finery was not habitual.

'I have come to enquire about my son,' the southern noble said, and nodded over his shoulder. 'They directed me to you.'

Dominic took another swallow of wine. 'They would.' He grimaced. 'I'm today's scapecoat. Have a stool.'

'I prefer to stand.'

Dominic put the cup down. His ears grew hot as he was neatly put in his place, which was not even on the lowest rung of the southerner's ladder. He thinks I'm a bored upstart; probably he's right. And I think he's a pain in the backside. A hint of wry amusement curved Dominic's lips. 'Your son?' he said.

'He is locked up in your cells for fomenting a riot yesterday noon, or so I understand. I want to see him.'

Dominic met the piercing sea-blue gaze with a kindling of interest. 'As a matter of fact, I was there.' He held up his bandaged hand. 'I'll warn you now, he's not just clapped up for brawling in the street. He said some rather unpalatable things to a Dominican friar and knocked him to the ground. It is likely he'll be charged with heresy.' Dominic indicated the stool again. 'Sit, I pray you.'

The man did so, but slowly, as if a swifter motion would break the shell of his pride. 'What precisely did he say?'

Dominic appropriated the scribe's empty cup and poured the noble a measure of wine. 'I didn't hear all of it, but the gist was that the friars had no right to go about digging up corpses and burning them because their owners had been heretics in life.'

The older man closed his eyes tightly for a moment, as if he were in mortal pain. Then, opening them, he took the wine Dominic offered. 'They did that to his grandfather last year,' he said wearily. 'He died a Cathar, so they came and took his body from the crypt and burned it in the centre of the town. We had to pay a heavy fine. Guillaume would rather run a black friar through on the tip of a lance than defer to him.'

Dominic smiled without humour. So would I, he thought, and realised the southerner was staring at him with a strange, almost painful intensity. 'I wasn't laughing,' he said quickly, thinking perhaps his expression had been misconstrued. 'I have no love for the friars myself.'

'And no inkling of what we have suffered!' The noble's complexion flushed. He waved a contemptuous hand. 'Ach, go home, lad; you don't belong here. Get out and play your knighthood games where it's safe.'

Dominic tightened his lips. 'Don't judge me by my appearance,' he said curtly and, drawing forward a fresh sheet of parchment, began rapidly to write. 'My mother was . . . or is from the Agenais, and I spent my childhood in Toulouse.' He dipped the quill in the ink horn. 'Your son's name?'

'Guillaume de Montvallant, son of Raoul.'

Dominic wrote the name on the parchment in a fierce burst of pressure. The quill split again, and raising his head, he met the blue stare and saw his own recognition mirrored.

'Holy Christ,' whispered Raoul de Montvallant, gripping the trestle with both hands. 'You're Claire's son, aren't you?'

'They never told me her name.' Dominic was surprised to hear his own voice emerge level and calm, as if he were discussing the price of wine or an ox-load of faggots. 'How did you know?'

'Just now . . . the way you smiled, and what you said about her being from the Agenais.'

He tried to stay detached, but something he could not control was gathering at the periphery. 'I was raised by Alais de Montfort and fostered at the French court by Amaury when she died . . . They used to tell me my father was a rebel southern lord and that his estates belonged of right to me.'

'You are not mine,' Raoul said harshly. 'I grant you no claims on the Montvallant lands!'

'Christ, do you think I want them!' Dominic snarled.

'Your true father didn't care upon whom he trampled to take what he wanted!'

'No, he didn't,' Dominic agreed, 'so that's reason enough to cover me with the same fleece, isn't it?'

'What are you doing in Toulouse, if not examining the possibilities?'

'I was posted by my half-brother for being troublesome at home. That's the problem with mongrels; they don't conform to the ways of thoroughbreds.' Jerkily he sanded the document he had just completed and stood up. 'Come with me.'

De Montvallant stared at him. 'Where?'

'To the cells, of course. This is a warrant for your son's release. I might have to do some browbeating to get him out . . . but then, I'm not Simon de Montfort's bastard for nothing.' He glinted the southerner a malicious look.

The older man looked uncomfortable. 'I'm sorry, I should not have been so swift to judge.'

Dominic shrugged. 'I'm used to it.' He set off purposefully across the hall, aware that de Montvallant was having to lengthen his stride to keep up. In a gloomy, unguarded corridor, he slowed his pace and made an effort to control himself, to maintain his detachment in the face of his shock.

'My mother,' he said carefully. 'Does she still live?'

Raoul de Montvallant slowed, too. The bitterness in his expression softened with compassion. 'Yes, she still lives, although perhaps for you it would be better if she did not. She is one of the Perfecti, a preacher of the Cathar faith.'

Dominic stopped and faced the older man. 'Tell me about her,' he said. 'I need to understand.'

Raoul gave him a hard look, as if measuring whether Dominic was capable of shouldering the truth. 'Your father captured Montvallant. It was me he wanted, but I was absent in Foix, so he took out his frustration on my wife – raped her and gave what remained to the lady Alais to do with as she pleased. She tried to turn Claire into a good Catholic, but after you were born, she realised why she would never succeed and had her locked up in Beaucaire. Poor Claire,' he said grimly. 'She wept for losing you, but she could not forgive or forget the violation.'

Dominic was silent for a long time. 'I didn't know,' he said at last. 'I was never allowed to ask questions about her. The little I do know has come from my half-brother Simon. I thought perhaps she had been his mistress.' It took a tremendous effort, but he looked Raoul in the eyes. 'You must have hated him.'

'Yes.'

There was another silence. Dominic looked away. What could he say? That he was sorry for his father's sins? That he wished he had never been born?

Finally it was Raoul who placed his hand lightly on Dominic's arm. 'We cannot bury the past when the priests keep digging it up, but perhaps we can see some of it in a different light,' he said gruffly. 'I lay no blame at your door. You are as much a victim as any of us who are left from that time.'

Dominic shook his head. 'I came to Toulouse to escape, and find that instead I'm caught fast!' He gave a shaken laugh and, pulling away from Raoul, strode out again. 'Dallying here solves nothing. Let us go and secure the release of your . . . of my brother.'

Dominic reached out from the saddle and took a lance from the stack propped against the tiltyard wall. In the centre of the practice ground, Guillaume was hanging a wooden ring on the quintain post, his expression one of careful neutrality.

Dominic knew that Guillaume's feelings towards him were ambivalent. His half-brother bore an implacable hatred for the northern invaders who had ruined his life, and he reviled the de Montforts in particular. Dominic was a de Montfort, yet they were kin by blood and Guillaume owed him his life. If not for Dominic, he would still be fettered in the cells of the Château Narbonnais, awaiting trial for heresy.

Vividly aware of Guillaume's critical scrutiny, Dominic couched the lance, collected his horse to a steady canter, and assaulted the quintain. To his relief, he succeeded in lifting the ring off the post as delicately as a lover lifting a lock of his lady's hair. At the time all the hours of training had seemed tiresome, but now he was glad of Henri Lemagne's insistence on the mastery of technique.

'Good!' Guillaume applauded with grudging appreciation and placed another ring on the quintain. 'My turn now.' He ran lightly to his horse and vaulted nimbly into the saddle. When he took the lance from the stack, he twirled the shaft, his dexterity making the tip a silver blur. Before he charged down the tilt, he made the horse perform rear, back-kick and side-step, using only his thighs for guidance. If Dominic's touch had been delicate, Guillaume's was positively ethereal as he lifted the ring off the hook.

Flushed with achievement, a challenge in his hot, brown eyes, Guillaume faced Dominic. 'Want to run a tilt against me?'

Dominic grimaced and handed his lance to a squire. 'I think not,' he said quietly.

'What's the matter, scared of losing?'

'It wouldn't just be to prove valour, would it? If you unseated me, you would be insufferable with victory; if I unseated you, you'd bear a grudge far greater than the one you bear me now.' Dominic dismounted.

'Coward,' Guillaume hissed through his teeth.

'I'm not the one running away,' Dominic said in a voice that his de Montfort half-brothers would have recognised; its quiescent power was identical to their father's.

Turning away, Dominic stripped his gauntlets. The look on the groom's face warned him and he spun and ducked, but Guillaume, with the suppleness of a born athlete and the killer instinct bred in the nomadic life of an army camp, adjusted the blow even as he launched it.

Dominic went down, the air bursting from his lungs, and Guillaume was immediately on top of him, hands digging into the embroidered collar of Dominic's tunic, raising him up, slamming his head back down on the tiltyard floor, once and then again. Dominic's knees arched. He twisted, got his arm under Guillaume's and, with a sudden spurt of pressure, threw him over and scrambled to his feet, his breath coming in short, painful gasps.

Guillaume made a fluid recovery and drove his fist straight at Dominic's face. Dominic blocked the move with his right forearm and punched with his left. The blow literally stopped Guillaume in his tracks, for he had not been expecting a retaliation from that direction. Blood dripped from his split lip. He touched the damage with the back of his hand, looked at the red smudge, and then at Dominic, who was nursing his grazed knuckles.

'If I hit you again,' Dominic panted, 'I'll not be able to sign any more releases, and I certainly don't want you to hit me. You've got a punch like a mule!'

Guillaume eyed him suspiciously, his body still keyed up to fight, but the explosive tension draining away. He discovered he no longer wished to murder Dominic. A test had been passed, and new parameters set. 'You're left-handed!' he accused.

'It doesn't do to take me for granted,' Dominic agreed and held out his right hand. Guillaume shook his head and, with a reluctant grin, extended his own across the space separating them.

The two young men sat their horses on the hilltop, the lands of Montvallant spread out before them, fields and vines baking in the sun.

'Truly,' said Dominic, 'I lay no claim to any of this. I can have lands in the North for the asking – one day I probably will.'

Guillaume gave Dominic a sidelong glance. 'Lands for the asking,' he said with a bitter note in his voice. 'I suppose it makes a difference to lands for the taking.'

Dominic managed not to rise to Guillaume's bait. He had been trying to conciliate, but realised he had not been tactful. The Montvallants' own struggle for their lands was written in sweat and blood.

'My father fought a battle down there against the crusaders,' Guillaume said after a moment, and pointed towards a meadow of bleached yellow hay, 'and he won. He told me about it. It was the day I was born.' He narrowed his eyes at Dominic. 'By the time I was two years old, your father had possession of Montvallant, and mine was reduced to a life in our army camps, fighting for our bread. I lived with my grandmother for a while, and then I lived on the road with him. When we regained Montvallant I did not know how to call it home any more. I still don't.' He guided his horse down the goat track leading towards the river. 'I'm lost,' he said. 'Where do I belong?'

'I have asked that question a hundred times myself and been drawn into more trouble seeking the answer than most men would find in a lifetime,' Dominic replied, following him down the twisting path. He screwed up his face, partly against the strength of the sun, partly in self-mockery. 'I've sought it in all the wrong beds, hoping to find the right one . . . That's one of the reasons I'm in Toulouse now, avoiding a furious husband.'

Guillaume snorted with scornful amusement.

'I've sought throughout all the taverns in Normandy and France, on battlefields and in castle and camp, and the restlessness only increases. I understand what you mean – about belonging.'

They paused again at the foot of the hill to drink from their waterskins. 'I have thought about joining the garrison at Montségur,' Guillaume said. 'Prayer alone won't keep the Cathars safe from the Pope and the French King. Montvallant is becoming dangerous for me. That black friar of yours would love to roast me at the stake.'

'He is not my friar,' Dominic said with revulsion. 'He used to be my tutor, and would beat me black and blue for the smallest misdemeanour. He would love to roast me at the stake, too, and I do not speak in jest.'

Guillaume's smile was mocking as he pushed the stopper back into his waterskin. 'Yet another thing we have in common,' he said with mordant humour.

Magda checked her satchel of herbs for omissions and reached on tiptoe to the shelf above her head for the vial of lavender oil. 'I think that is everything,' she said.

Bridget smiled, but Magda could see she was afraid. She knew her mother hated it when she went away from

Montségur, even when she was in the safe hands of her great-uncle Chretien.

'You have given me your wisdom. Now I have to learn my own.' Magda put the satchel to one side and crossed the fire to kiss her mother's cheek.

'Yes, I know that,' Bridget answered quietly, 'nor will tomorrow be the first time of your leaving. It is only a mother's anxiety for her fledgling in a world of predators. Here, sit and eat; the food is ready.'

Magda and her mother shared a loaf and bowl of thick herb and vegetable stew in companionable silence, savouring the food and each other's company, knowing it would be the last time they would be together until the first winter snows powdered the mountain passes.

When they had finished and cleared away their bowls, they sat beside the fire, preparing freshly gathered herbs for storage, as if this were an ordinary evening. 'I must make some more rub for Matthias,' Bridget murmured, more than half to herself. 'His joints are so stiff and sore these days. I can ease them a little with my touch, but I have no cure for old age.'

Magda watched her mother's deft fingers strip the leaves from a stem of sage. Her vision was briefly overlaid with the sight of those hands illuminated in lightning, outlined in fire. She pushed the image away, for it bore echoes of the nightmare that had haunted her for as long as she could remember.

Her mother looked at her sharply. 'What do you see?'

'You were in a cave with a man, and a storm was all around you. And then I saw you on the battlements of Montségur calling out to the lightning.'

Bridget's gaze grew intent. 'And have you seen this before?'

'No.' Magda shook her head. 'This is the first time . . . although the other vision, the dark dream, is very close.' She gnawed her lip and said hesitantly, 'The man in the cave . . . I saw him when I was a little girl. He came to Montségur with his son.'

'You remember it?' Bridget asked with surprise. 'You were not yet four years old.'

'It was the first time I had the dark vision. And the man said to me that being poor was not knowing what wealth really was.'

Her mother's gaze brooded on her. She drew a deep breath. 'He is your father,' she said. 'His name is Raoul de Mont-vallant, and he is a seigneur of estates close to Toulouse. He is a fine man, an honourable one, but we never had enough in common to make a life together, and besides, he was already married.'

'But enough in common to lie together?'

'Do you moralise, daughter?'

Magda shook her head and lowered her eyes. 'No, Mama.'

'Your father had a vitality about him, a spark that I wanted my daughter to have.'

'I have often wondered who my father is,' Magda said. 'I thought perhaps he was one of the Cathar men on the mountain, but I know that they are sworn to celibacy.'

'Perhaps I should have told you before, but you never asked, and you seemed content with what you had – your uncle Chretien and Matthias, and sometimes Luke.'

'I have not been unhappy,' Magda said quickly, not wishing to upset her mother over what could not be changed. 'I have never lacked for love and I have always had a sense of belonging – to you, to Montségur, and everyone here.' She looked pensive. 'Does he know about me?'

'He knows. I told him on the night you were conceived, and when he came to Montségur, he saw you, and he was proud.'

Magda wondered if she would have greeted him any differently if she had known he was her father, if she would have looked at him more closely or fixed his image more firmly in her mind. Strange to think that she had a half-brother, too, and that he was a grown man.

There is something else I have not told you,' Bridget said, 'but since you know the one, you might as well know the whole. Your father's wife dwells here at Montségur – Sister Claire.'

Magda stared at her mother with widening eyes. 'Sister Claire?' she repeated, thinking of the quiet, chestnut-haired woman who spent so much time in prayer, and who had dwelt at Montségur for the past fifteen years at least.

'She came to us after the final siege of Toulouse. Your father and she had been separated by the war, and by the time they were reunited, they had each journeyed too far in different directions. Claire took the consolamentum and became a practising Cathar.'

'Does she know about me?'

Bridget frowned. 'No, daughter. I have wondered whether to tell her, but what purpose would it serve? She has scars enough already from the war. Do you remember that day by the river outside Toulouse when you met the dark-haired boy?'

Magda's lips curved. 'Yes, I remember.' A soft note entered her voice. 'His name was Dominic.'

'His father was Simon de Montfort, and his mother is Claire de Montvallant. De Montfort took her body by force when she was his prisoner.'

Magda looked at her mother with a mingling of horror and compassion. How could such knots ever be untangled and made smooth enough to weave into life's tapestry? She thought of the boy, trying to shrug and pretend his parentage did not matter. She thought of the suffering of Claire de Montvallant. Then she thought of the walls of Montségur ablaze with lightning, and a shiver ran through her.

CHAPTER 37

Dominic had just begun to realise he was lost when his horse went lame. Cursing, he dismounted and ran his hand down the chestnut's foreleg. The animal flinched and sidled as he touched the hot, slightly swollen knee. Further examination revealed that the shoe was loose, too, missing a nail. Dominic cursed again. Cobweb drifts of mist were thickening in the direction of fog, and the sun had vanished from a grainy sky. It had been shining brilliantly that morning when he had bidden farewell to Guillaume and set out for Toulouse. Only somewhere he had taken the wrong path, and instead of approaching the outskirts of the city as the afternoon drew on, he was in the middle of nowhere, with not so much as the clonk of a goat bell to tell him that he was near civilisation.

Following a period of convivial exploration of the taverns and stews of Toulouse, the two young men had gone hunting in the purer air of the mountains, seeking more of the common ground that Guillaume said they shared. Dominic was not sure he agreed with him. Certainly they had found many grounds for differences of opinion and taste. Even with the best will in the world, suspicion and envy still lurked in the shadows of the campfires they made. But each had learned from the other. Guillaume had begun to think a little before he opened his mouth, and some of his spontaneity had rubbed off on Dominic's cautiousness. They had parted on wary but friendly terms, Guillaume riding off to visit acquaintances of his father's from the old days of the war, Dominic taking the road – the wrong road – to Toulouse.

Grasping the chestnut's bridle, Dominic started to lead the horse along the track. Downward, he told himself with a grimace at the deepening mist, go downward. People lived in valleys, not on the top of mountains, and he had to find some kind of shelter for the night.

The mist drifting up the river valley had gradually thickened during the day into a moist fog, enclosing the village and concealing it from prying eyes. The settlement lay off the Toulouse road between Foix and Palmiers, a hamlet of the Plantaurel foothills, red-tiled roofs swaddling squat amber stone and tightly barred shutters.

Magda was glad of the roaring fire in the hearth of the shoemaker's cottage, and the bowl of hot bean soup cupped in her hands. She sipped with relish. A meeting had been held earlier that evening, and two of the villagers had taken the final Cathar vows from her uncle Chretien. One of the converts had been so old and weak that his relatives had to carry him into the cottage, and it was obvious that the consolamentum was but a deathbed comfort. The other, however, had been a widow of middle years, healthy and strong, with a need to devote her life elsewhere now that her husband had gone.

There were many believers in the village, and Magda and Chretien had been welcomed with open arms and invitations to stay for as long as they wanted. That, of course, was unsafe. Even in a village of believers, there were those who would betray a Cathar to the Inquisition for the bounty payment of a mark per head, and the Dominican friars had their spies and informers everywhere.

Magda knew her heritage made her especially vulnerable to persecution and that if she was caught, she would be subjected to inquisition, torture and death at the stake. She and her mother stood accused of heresy and witchcraft. All the priests of Rome saw was the blaze of their own bigotry in the flames to which they committed those of different beliefs. Anger surged within her, but she quashed it. Love, not rage, was the ultimate immolator.

There was a momentary lull in the conversation around the hearth. The fire crackled and the sound of the ladle being stirred in the cauldron by the shoemaker's wife was as loud as an oar on a rowing boat. Outside, a horse whinnied.

'Hola!' shouted an impatient voice. 'Is anybody there?'

Magda felt a powerful tingling in her veins. The traveller was impatient because he had tried several houses in the village already and found them empty; she could read his thoughts as if they were her own.

The shoemaker, his face paling, went to the door and opened it the merest crack. 'What do you want?' he muttered, his attitude at complete odds with the Cathar doctrine of love to every man.

'A farrier to shoe my lame horse, a bed for the night and directions to Toulouse in the morning,' came the irritated reply. 'A little courtesy would not go amiss either. If it's dependent on silver, I'll pay.'

The tongue was southern, but horribly mangled by a northern French accent. As wide-eyed as a trapped rabbit, the shoemaker turned to his guests for guidance.

'There is no danger,' Magda said with quiet certainty and, setting down her bowl, stood up.

'No danger, madonna, but . . . ?'

'I promise you.' She fixed the gibbering craftsman with a steady, grey gaze.

'If you want, we will leave,' Chretien offered. 'We can always make do with the goat shed or the threshing floor.'

'No, no, I wouldn't dream of turning you out!' The shoemaker shook his head.

'And if the Christ came knocking at your abode?'

Shamefaced, their host widened the gap in the door by a

thumb width. 'There's stabling at the back,' he said gruffly to the stranger. 'I've no room in the house, you'll have to sleep with your horse, but I'll bring you a bowl of soup.'

'My thanks,' came the ironic response, followed by the slow clop of hooves and the jingle of harness. Magda saw the firelit chestnut hide and the plain but high-quality saddle trappings as the horse was led across the ribbon of light from the doorway and around to the dilapidated goat shed at the back of the dwelling.

Pushing through the uneasy throng of villagers to the hearth, Magda ladled some steaming bean soup into a wooden bowl. Chretien watched her with a mixture of apprehension and approval. She cast him a reassuring glance. 'It is all right, truly,' she murmured. 'You know that my sense is as keen as my mother's.'

'Yes, child, if not keener,' Chretien replied, 'but you are also very beautiful.'

Magda was touched and amused. 'I have nothing to fear from him,' she said and briefly squeezed his hand. 'Do you go and talk some charity into these people while I administer some to our guest.'

He was unsaddling his horse and swearing softly beneath his breath. Magda hung a lantern on the hook provided and put the soup bowl down on the milking stool. Separated from the first section of the shed by a rickety partition, the shoe-maker's goat flock milled and bleated.

'The villagers do not mean to be rude,' she said. 'They are just afraid.'

He set his saddle down in a corner and turned to face her. 'Small wonder if this is how skilfully they cover up illicit meetings.' He unrolled a blanket from his pack to throw over the horse. 'If I wasn't suspicious before, I'd certainly convict them now.' Crouching, he ran his hand down the courser's foreleg and clicked his tongue with annoyance. 'I'll have to walk him tomorrow, even with a new shoe.'

'Let me look at his leg; I'm a healer,' Magda offered. 'And you can drink your soup before it goes cold.'

'I don't need to be a healer to know what's wrong!' he snapped, but stood aside to let her pass and, picking up the bowl, sat down.

Magda felt the swelling just above the cannon on the chestnut's near foreleg. Gently she curled her hands around it, closed her eyes, and concentrated. The horse snorted and plunged once, then, quivering, stood still. Heat flowed from her fingertips into the damaged tissues. Once, she had doubted her ability to control this force within her, but now it came as easily and unconsciously as breathing.

She felt the man's gaze upon her spine, knew that he had yet to recognise her and was eyeing her as he would any peasant girl in a stable at night. She sensed that there had been many such moments and many such girls, and because she had come out alone to bring him the soup, he thought that she was one, too. Smiling into her hood, she finished with the horse and, rising from her crouch, turned round.

'The leg will be better by the morning,' she said. 'He'll carry you safely to Toulouse.'

One corner of his mouth tilted cynically. 'Impressive. Perhaps I could persuade you to lay your hands on an old war wound of mine and appease the ache.' His aura flickered with glints of vitality and small, impatient sparkles. She projected her own to meet it and saw him register the challenge with a rapid blink of surprise. He set the bowl down beside the stool and stood up, his eyes intent on her cowl-shadowed face.

'What's your name?' His voice was as intimate as the space within a set of bed hangings. He raised his hand to touch her cheek and at the same time gently pushed down the hood of her cloak. In the wake of his fingertips Magda's skin tingled and warmth suffused her body.

'It is Magda,' she said. 'Do you not remember?'

His hand left her face, his breathing faltered, and she knew with a quickening at her core that he did indeed remember. 'Magda?' he whispered, looking her up and down. 'Holy Mary!'

She smiled at his choice of oath. If only he knew . . .

He gazed and gazed, drinking her in. 'I've never forgotten that afternoon. I even went down to the river when I returned to Toulouse – made a wish and threw a flower into the current, but I never thought it would come true.' He broke off and shook his head in bemusement. 'Jesu, you're beautiful!'

'You didn't think that last time.' A dimple appeared at the corner of her mouth. 'I was a muddy heretic girl who had stolen your dog.'

'And I was the son of the most powerful man in the Languedoc.' His eyelids tensed. 'I've never forgotten that part of it either – what happened to him. I knew he was going to die when I saw him on the ground at your mother's feet. It was his only way of escape.'

'He had a choice,' Magda said.

He shook his head. 'For my father there was only the power of the sword. Sometimes I see myself following him down that same road. He is in front of me, leading me on, and I know that when he turns round, he won't have a face.' He turned to his horse and stroked its satin chestnut hide.

Magda watched him, sensing his complexity and tension, the hair-thin line he trod between darkness and light. He reminded her of a caged lynx that she and her mother had seen on a feast day in Foix.

'Are you one of the Perfecti?' he asked on a more level note.

'Not in the orthodox sense.'

'What does that mean?'

Magda hesitated, bemused, a little frightened by the speed at which events were moving. 'My mother and I live among the Cathars, but our beliefs are not the same. Our bloodline carries the blessing . . . or curse of adept skills, and it is my duty, as it was my mother's, to continue it.'

'Are you spoken for?'

Warmth rippled through her body in response to the timbre of his voice. He was swift, decisive, going straight to the heart of what he wanted to know. 'The women of my line speak for themselves,' she said proudly.

He left the horse and came to stand in front of her. 'And how say you?'

Between their bodies was a resistant barrier of physical heat, demanding to be broken and reforged. There had been temptations for Magda before as her womanhood came upon her and she started to notice men, but no one had ever attracted her with this kind of intensity. Was this how it had been for her parents? 'That I am no man's property, nor ever will be except of my own desiring.' She stepped away from him. 'And you? How say you?'

He released his breath and his tension relaxed, but she was aware of the predatory gleam in his eyes. 'I have no pledges to break.'

She regarded him warily. How easy it would be to seek an hour of gratification. The moon phase was perfect; she was assured of conceiving, but a deeper concern held her back. She wanted to know more of the man than a single carnal moment. The road branched here. She could have this one night, or a lifetime. The path her mother had trodden, or one of her own choosing. 'You could travel with us awhile,' she suggested, and held her breath.

'Travel with you?' he said slowly. 'To make of me a Cathar?'

She looked at him steadily, willing him to understand, not to turn away, and then because she knew the power of her own mind, lowered her gaze and blanked out that will. Whatever his decision, he had to make for himself. Once before they had stood like this in a water meadow, she offering, and he at war with himself.

He inhaled to speak, but said nothing, his gaze leaving hers to fix on the crude shed doorway.

'Uncle Chretien,' Magda said with a mixture of relief and disappointment.

Chretien's deep-set eyes raked over her and Dominic while he assessed the situation. 'Are you coming back within, Magda?' His voice was more of a command than a question. 'It is time to bolt the door.'

'Yes, Uncle,' she replied so meekly that his brows lifted in speculation as she brushed past him into the cold night. She looked round once at Dominic, an unspoken question hanging in her eyes.

'Demoiselle,' he saluted, then added softly, 'until tomorrow.'

She caught her breath and smiled at him before she turned away, decently drawing up the hood of her cloak.

The glow left Dominic's eyes as he faced Chretien. 'Are you her guardian?'

'I am.' Chretien handed him a coarse blanket. 'Here, it is going to be a cold night out here – alone.' Emphasis pressured the final word.

Dominic laughed shortly and took the blanket. 'You are right to be suspicious,' he said. 'She is beautiful, but then you Cathars would say that beauty is just another snare of the Devil.'

Chretien considered him thoughtfully. 'The beauty of the soul we do not deny, just its fleshly covering. Without love, there is naught but corruption.'

Dominic spread the blanket on the dirty straw of the stable floor. 'Then I have led a very corrupt life,' he said lightly, but the remark itself was not light at all.

'You are young; you have time. All you have to do is open yourself to the truth.'

'The truth?' Dominic lifted a cynical brow. 'If you are going to preach to me about good Gods and evil Gods and spirit and matter, you will be wasting your breath.'

Chretien looked amused. 'The breath is wasted anyway

unless it bears witness,' he said. 'The core of the message is simple enough – deed, not word; example, not hypocrisy.' His eyes lit upon the sword, shield and rolled-up hauberk propped against the harness.

Dominic followed his glance. 'I am not of your creed even while I applaud its merits,' he retorted with amusement of his own, and sat down on the blanket.

'You're a good French Catholic then?'

'Hah, none of those!'

Chretien stared at him, and Dominic laughed. 'Well, I never claimed to be good, and I'm only half-French – my mother's from Agen. As to being a good Catholic . . .' He spread his hands. 'My tutor was a black friar and he was convinced that I was a minion of the Antichrist. Whatever devotion I had to offer was beaten out of me at a tender age. I render lip service, no more.' A pensive, almost defiant expression crossed his face. 'Magda asked if I would travel with you for a while.'

Chretien sucked in his breath and almost looked dismayed. 'And how did you reply?'

'I more or less accepted. I have no commitments in Toulouse . . . well, none that matter. I left my post with the garrison more than a month ago.'

The older man frowned. 'If you came with us, it would be because of your interest in her, would it not?'

'I would be lying if I said I was driven by religious fervour,' Dominic said drily. He met the Cathar's stern gaze with candour. 'But if I agree to travel your road, I will be making a commitment far beyond idle dalliance, and at her behest.'

'Magda is no ordinary young woman. There is a blood price on her head way beyond that upon any Cathar, indeed way beyond mine. I advise you most strongly to think with your head, not your loins.'

'I am thinking,' Dominic said softly, 'with my heart.'

* * *

In the morning the chestnut's foreleg was cool beneath Dominic's hand, and there was no evidence of swelling. 'I do not suppose that you can conjure a horseshoe out of thin air?' he enquired of Magda when she brought him a bowl of hot, honey-sweetened gruel and a cup of wine to break his fast.

Her eyes sparkled. 'I have never tried,' she said laughing, and sat down on the stool to watch him eat. 'But there is a smith in the village. He'll be here as soon as he's broken his fast.' She crossed her ankles. 'Uncle Chretien doesn't know whether or not to approve of you.'

Dominic sampled the gruel and found it more appetising than it looked. Besides, he was starving. 'I hope you set his mind at rest.'

'That is something you will have to do yourself – if you have not changed your mind?'

'Why should I do that?'

Colour flooded her face. 'Last night you were not given much time to decide.'

'I have not changed my mind, unless you have changed yours,' he said. 'It doesn't matter how quickly things happened, only that they did. And for all your cleverness, you are wrong.'

Magda raised her brows. He pointed his spoon at her. 'Sixteen years,' he said. 'I have been waiting sixteen years. There is nothing swift about that.'

She laughed and then she grew solemn. Their eyes met and held. 'No,' she said. 'There is nothing swift about that.'

They rode together that day, side by side, sometimes in animated conversation, sometimes united by a silence more profound than the speaking of words. He told her about northern France – the cooler, unpredictable summers; the grey, heavy winters – about life at Montfort l'Amaury, and then later at the French court – although he was somewhat circumspect about his adventures there, particularly with respect to women. And Magda told him about her childhood at Montségur among the Cathars, and a little about her upbringing – and she, too, was circumspect.

As evening fell, they came to the next village on their path and were welcomed with food and lodging. Sidelong glances were cast at Dominic, for Cathars did not usually journey in the company of armed soldiers, but Chretien explained that the young man was a fellow traveller, a friend who had joined them for a while on the road, and Dominic was accepted.

Chretien preached to a gathering of villagers, his deep, mellifluous voice filling them with his vision of a purer life. Such was his gift for oratory that even Dominic, who had learned the power of the sermon from the black friars and grown cynical and disillusioned, felt a spark of optimism.

After Chretien had spoken, bread and soup were served and the people came to Magda, asking for her healing touch, for potions and balms and advice. Dominic watched and listened, absorbing this, too. He saw how they trusted her, and how she gave of herself unstintingly until she was white and drained. He thought about sending away those who still waited their turn, but checked himself. It was not his place to do so, it was hers.

She raised her eyes to his and gave him a brief smile of approbation. Unobtrusively he brought her a cup of sweetened wine, pressed it into her hand, and, with a light touch on her shoulder, went and sat down next to Chretien.

'It is always like this,' Chretien said to him. 'News of our coming travels ahead and the village numbers swell to twice their size.'

'The French court is the same,' Dominic said with a shrug. 'But of course, the people wait on the King's pleasure, not he on theirs.'

'Are you saying we should do the same?'

Dominic met the straightforward dark stare. 'No, sir,' he answered quietly. 'There is a difference between being the taker and being the giver. I do not think that the King of France would recognise it.'

A half-smile relaxed the severity of Chretien's mouth. 'Have you never thought about taking up preaching yourself?'

Dominic chuckled and shook his head. 'That is for other men with a deeper conviction than mine – and a greater skill. To give people belief, that is a very great power, but I do not trust it. Each person's own truth is different from the truth of his neighbour.'

Chretien's half-smile faded, but not with disapproval. 'There is more to you than meets the eye,' he said, glancing at Magda.

Dominic followed the direction of his stare. His own eyes settled on her willow-slim body and need flickered within him. The desert wanderer discovering an oasis. 'There is more to everyone than meets the eye,' he said.

Two nights later, between villages, the travellers made camp beneath the stars. Encroaching autumn had put a nip in the air. They had been gathering firewood along the road as they journeyed, and while Dominic picketed the chestnut and the pack horse, Chretien prepared the fire. The tinder had little inclination to light. Although the day had been fine and the evening sky was clear, the misty weather of the last week had dampened the firewood. Dominic finished tending the horses and came to help Chretien, kneeling down to blow beneath the tenuous flicker of the last of Chretien's tinder.

Magda came over and, setting aside the loaf and wine she had been carrying, knelt before the fire. She spread her fingers over the damp branches and feeble guttering of tinder. Drawing a deep breath, she then released it slowly. The flame steadied, wearing a single eye like a candle, and then, before Dominic's astonished eyes, yellow flowers bloomed among the caverns of firewood. Heat spread outward in a golden aura amid the crackle and spit of a living fire.

'How did you do that?' He gazed at her in astonishment. That she was a healer of considerable talent he had accepted, but that she could kindle a fire out of damp wood set her abilities in a different dimension.

'My mother taught me to control it, but it is something I have always been able to do. It's not really much different from laying my hands on a sick person.'

She spoke so normally that Dominic's skin prickled. What other skills did she take for granted? Perhaps, as he had once thought as a child, she was indeed of the faerie kind. She scooped her hair behind her ears and turned to the food. 'Bread,' she said, breaking the loaf, 'and wine. It is all we have until we reach the next village.'

Uneasily Dominic consumed the food of the sacrament, and pondered what he had seen, measuring his strength to cope with it. As if sensing how disturbed he was, Chretien announced that he was tired and rolled himself in his blanket early, leaving him and Magda to watch over the fire.

'You are troubled,' Magda said to him as the sound of Chretien's breathing grew deep and even.

'It is nothing,' he lied, and avoided her eyes, which would draw the thoughts straight out of his own.

'It is because I raised the fire, is it not?'

He tossed another branch on the flames and listened to the hiss and spark, guarding his thoughts while he mustered them. Finally he looked at her. 'Most women bake and spin, tend the household and the vegetable plot. Do you do those things, too?'

She pursed her lips and asked a question of her own. 'Most women? How many have you known?'

Dominic shrugged. 'More than I can count, or even remember their names. Life at the French court when you are Simon de Montfort's son is akin to being a bee in a garden full of flowers.'

'Truly known? I mean beyond flesh?'

'I doubt any of them,' he said. 'But then I did not want

to know them beyond flesh, or else they could not give me what I needed.'

Magda studied him gravely. 'Yes,' she said. 'I can bake and spin and tend vegetables like other women.' She leaned towards him, touching her heart for emphasis. 'I am a woman, ordinary in most senses of the word. I would not be set on a pedestal. I accept you as you are, as you must accept me.'

'What do you expect me to do when out of nowhere you stretch your hand above damp branches and cause them to light?' he snorted.

She looked sad. 'The way you speak, to return to Toulouse.'

Dominic gazed into the fire she had raised. Why not take one of the safe, ordinary heiresses his brother Simon was always offering him? Why not, as Magda said, return to Toulouse, report for another stint of garrison duty, and seek out Peronelle and her abundant breasts. Pillow his head on them. Then he looked at Magda and knew his reason for staying.

'There is nothing for me in Toulouse,' he said. 'All I want is here with you. All I need.' He set his arm around her waist and drew her towards him. She came into his arms, eager and shy, her faced raised. Dominic kissed her brow, her eyelids, her cheeks and chin, returning finally to the soft cushion of her lips. As if he were kindling to her touch, he felt the fire lick through his body and centre at his core.

The kiss broke for want of breath, and was renewed. He wove his hands in the silk of her hair. She pressed herself against him, the formerly unfocused yearnings of her body now given sharp clarity. This man. For ever.

Again they broke apart to breathe and recover. Dominic swallowed. 'Sixteen years,' he said in a constricted voice. 'A while longer will not matter. I want to know you, Magda, all of you, little by little. Everything at once would overwhelm me.' He stroked her cheek, tracing the outline of her face with a wondering forefinger.

'It is the same for me,' she whispered in reply. 'It frightens me – to feel so much, so strongly.'

Sobered, they remained staring at each other until the fire choked on a knot of resin and spat out a shower of sparks. Both of them jumped. Chretien sat up, looked at Magda and Dominic with the eyes of a dreamer, and lay back down.

Magda leaned towards Dominic, kissed him gently, and, after a final lingering study of his features, rolled herself in her cloak. 'Good night,' she whispered.

Dominic smiled and answered her the same, but he made no attempt to sleep himself, preferring to remain awake, watching the fire and the stars, distilling from the open night a sense of power, calm and great, great joy.

CHAPTER 38

Tiny flakes of snow danced in the air, starring the travellers' cloaks and ticklishly settling on their faces. The powdery ground muffled the chestnut's hoofbeats and recorded each imprint of shod hoof and human foot on the village road. Winter had come early this year to the Plantaurels, and although the cloud was not thick, the snow was a portent of what was to follow. This journey was Chretien's last before returning to Montségur for the harshest winter months.

Behind Dominic, sharing the chestnut, Magda dozed, her cheek against his spine, her hands beneath his cloak, taking purchase in his belt and drawing comfort from the heat of his body. He smiled to feel her presence, and bore the bitter wind with equanimity.

For two months he had been travelling with her and Chretien, but it seemed as if it had been for ever, so quickly had he become attuned to their way of life. He had been wary of pursuing a dream, of revealing too much of himself, but gradually, as the dream took on texture and reality, he had become absorbed into it, opening to Magda's scrutiny his heart and his soul, something that even his half-brother Simon, who had come closer to him than anyone, had never been permitted.

The physical tension was still present; he had only to look at her, or feel her looking at him, for his breath to grow short and heat to quicken his loins, but he was willing to wait upon a time that was ripe, rather than slaking something that was pure appetite. The fact that he had proved he was not about to pounce on Magda and ravish her behind the nearest rock had much improved his standing with Chretien, as had his perseverance. He was well aware that the elderly Cathar had half expected him to tire of waiting, make his excuses and leave in search of easier game. These days Chretien was less reserved with him and more willing to trust.

When they arrived in the village it was almost dusk. The headman, Jean le Picou, a wool merchant, welcomed them into his house and served them bread and a rich vegetable stew, fussing obsequiously over them. His nervous manner was more than Dominic could stand and, on the pretext of emptying his bladder, he excused himself and went outside.

Le Picou's goat flock was penned in a ramshackle shelter close to the house. The beasts had grazed well all summer and were sleek and strong. Their breath steamed in the night-blue air, and their horns gleamed as they moved. It had stopped snowing and the first stars glimmered on a turquoise horizon. Dominic inhaled the frozen tranquillity and gazed at the dark humps of the surrounding mountains while he waited. When he heard the sound of the door latch clicking, his eye corners tensed with amusement. Turning his head, he watched Magda walk up the path to join him.

'What's your excuse?' He grinned, unfolding his arms.

'You.' She reached on tiptoe to kiss him, her hands stealing beneath his cloak. He kissed her back, his body suffusing with exquisite warmth. They held each other, their embrace deepening, losing its playfulness, while above them the sky darkened and the stars glittered like distant salt crystals.

A door slammed and a dog barked. Breaking the kiss, Dominic raised his head. Magda swayed against him, her eyes half-closed, her lips parted, the bodice of her gown undone beneath her cloak. Dominic stroked her breasts, remembering other such occasions with different women.

Snatched moments in dark corners, one ear cocked for a footfall.

> *A wonderful gift she gave to me*
> *her love, her ring. God end the strain*
> *Beneath her mantle my hand will be*
> *If yet enough of time I gain.*

'Magda?' he said gently, and found the strength to remove his hand.

Her eyes lost their blind look and she raised her head. 'Why did you stop?' she said.

'Where would we go? In with the goats? Up against the wall? Sneak past your uncle and our host?' His voice was full of wry amusement and not a little frustration.

She glanced round and acknowledged with a soft sigh the truth of what he said. 'It will be different when we reach Montségur,' she murmured, rubbing her cheek against his hand.

'Montségur,' he repeated, and withdrew into himself a little. Magda was overjoyed to be returning to her mother and her people, bringing with her the man with whom she had chosen to share herself, but for him it was not so simple.

'You are worried about meeting your mother, aren't you?' He lifted one shoulder. 'It will not be easy.'

Magda leaned against him, offering comfort. 'No,' she agreed. 'But you have the strength, and so does she.'

'You know her well, then?'

'I was only a child when she came to Montségur, but my mother often visited her. She was much troubled with nightmares and a burden of guilt and grief that she should not have been carrying. I think she recovered from them enough to find a measure of peace and take the consolamentum, but I do not believe that she has ever been really happy. If she could come to terms with what happened in the past . . .'

'Stare it straight in the eyes, you mean,' Dominic said grimly. 'I am told I look like my father.'

'Looking is not being.' She sought his hands and squeezed them. 'I think that once she has seen you, she will be cleansed . . . and so will you.'

'Where would I be without you?'

Her arms encircled his neck. A glint of light caught the corner of his eye and he turned, half expecting to see Chretien in his role of chaperone. Instead he saw the cloaked figure of a woman leading a pack mule down the village street. She wore stout leather shoes, and the nailed soles clicked loudly in the silence and created a pattern of sound that wove in and out between the clop of the mule's small hooves.

Magda craned over his shoulder and her hands suddenly gripped upon him. 'It is my mother!' she said in surprise. 'I felt she was close to me, but I thought it was because we were on our way to Montségur!'

The mule and the footsteps ceased. The cloaked figure turned in a half-circle and looked directly at the lovers.

'Mama!' Grasping Dominic's hand in hers, Magda tugged him towards Bridget.

She was as he remembered, her grey eyes warm and bright, her smile tender. When she put down her hood, he saw that her once black hair was ribboned by a wide moonbeam of silver.

'It is but a few days' journey to Montségur,' she said as she kissed Magda and held her close. 'I decided to come down and meet you. I knew this time your homecoming would be special.' Her gaze went to Dominic and once more he felt the cleansing glow of her scrutiny.

'Be welcome,' she said, and embraced him, too. 'Magda has chosen wisely and well.'

He felt how lightly boned she was, her frame birdlike beneath his hands, whereas Magda's was sturdy. He could almost see the flame of her spirit within the shell of her flesh. 'I will strive to be worthy,' he said.

Magda smiled and folded her arm through his. 'So will I.' She looked up at him with such radiance in her eyes that it took his breath and prickled his lids. His early years had been so bereft of affection that to have it poured upon him now was almost too much for his heart to bear, and he thought that it would burst.

The wool merchant delightedly welcomed Bridget into his house, and his nervous hand-rubbing increased three-fold. He insisted on going out to fetch more bread and wine, and when Bridget protested that what they had was entirely adequate, he fluffed up like a cockerel, declaring that it would be slacking his duty as a host to do otherwise.

Magda sensed Dominic's irritation, although it did not show on his face, which remained impassive. Feeling unsettled herself, she looked anxiously at her mother.

'Yes,' Bridget said softly. 'It will be wise to travel on fast tomorrow.'

'We have been little troubled thus far,' Chretien said. 'An armed escort has seen to that, although a Cathar journeying in such company is a sight to behold.'

Dominic gave an uncomfortable shrug. 'I know you would rather I discarded my sword, but it has been a part of me since infancy. One day I might indeed beat it into a ploughshare, but for the moment it remains, especially if there is danger.' He rose to his feet. 'Le Picou's been gone a long time. I'm going to look for him.' His scabbarded weapon was leaning against the doorpost and, on his way out, he paused to take it with him.

Magda stared at the door he had just gently closed. 'When we reach Montségur, the moon time will be right,' she said, and laid her hand upon her flat, taut belly.

'You have not lain with him yet?' Bridget asked curiously.

Magda shook her head. 'In the beginning I was afraid of losing him – he has had many women before.' Her chin came up in defiance. 'I did not want him for just one night of

rutting fever even if it would better have served our bloodline. And if that is heresy, so be it.'

'Even so, I do not believe you would have lost him.'

'Neither do I now, but at the time I was unsure.'

Chretien cleared his throat and, muttering something
about relieving himself, went out of the door.

Mother and daughter exchanged rueful glances. The
Cathar belief that celibacy was a prerequisite of spiritual
enlightenment did not sit easily with their own belief in celebrating the life force at the given time.

'Does he know about us, about the Virgin and the
Magdalene?' Bridget asked.

'A little. He has seen I have the gifts to raise the fire and
heal the sick. I will tell him the full story of our bloodline
when we arrive at Montségur. I—' She stopped speaking
and her head jerked up as they heard a commotion outside
the house. The door burst open and Chretien hurtled in on
a draught of frozen air.

'Quickly!' he panted. 'Le Picou has betrayed us. The
Dominican Inquisition is here in the village with soldiers!'

Weapons clashed outside the house. Magda heard a
scream, and then Dominic was in the room with them, his
sword stained red. She ran to him. His lips touched hers in
a single hard kiss, and then he was pushing her away. 'Go
with Chretien,' he commanded. 'I'll join you later!'

'You will be killed!'

'Go!'

Bridget grabbed her daughter's arm and jerked her away
towards the low door that led through into the merchant's
stables.

'In the name of our Lord Jesus Christ, I command you
stay where you are!' A black friar loomed upon the
threshold, a bony forefinger pointing at the occupants of
the room.

Magda froze, all her childhood nightmares suddenly
solidifying as she stared upon the face of the dark presence

of her dreams. She was powerless against it, could feel her will being subjugated by terror. It was her mother who spoke, her voice more terrible than Magda had ever heard it. 'Perhaps you should invoke the Virgin Mary, since you claim she saved your life on the road to Carcassonne one winter's night,' she said, giving him stare for stare. 'If it were not against my teaching, I would have left you to die.'

The friar blenched. His eyes were blacker than a void. He tried to articulate, but no sound came from his working throat. Bridget dragged Magda through into the stables.

Dominic raised his sword and blocked the advance of two soldiers who had ranged themselves on either side of the stuttering Friar Bernard.

'Get out of our way, you accursed heretic,' snarled one of the men.

Dominic heard the neigh of his chestnut horse and the thud of hooves in the dirt yard behind the house. The soldier attacked.

The shriek of sword upon sword carried across the frosty night. Blue-white sparks flashed off the blade edges as they slid along each other. Dominic twisted and cut. His opponent, trained to deal with a right-handed adversary, made the wrong parry and paid for it with his life. Dominic leaped over his falling body and engaged the second man, feinted right and struck low and left, ripping open his leg. He lunged at Friar Bernard, but a knight caught and deflected Dominic's sword on his shield, and behind the knight was a crossbowman with his weapon cocked at Dominic's breast.

Defeated, Dominic lowered his sword and opened his hand to let it fall. Magda, Bridget and Chretien were safely away; it didn't matter what happened now.

Friar Bernard pointed an accusing forefinger at him. 'If it is the last thing I do,' he panted, 'I am going to hold you up to the world for the filthy heretic you are! Take him!'

The soldiers handled him roughly, but Dominic didn't respond. He retreated within himself, closed the drawbridge, and presented the foaming Friar Bernard with an impervious façade.

CHAPTER 39

TOULOUSE, SPRING 1235

Torchlight. Voices. A key screeching in the lock. Those occupants of the cell who were capable scuttled away from these portents like insects panicked from beneath an overturned stone.

Dominic curled his left fist, testing the pain of his raw nail beds against his palm. At the time that they ripped out his fingernails, it had not seemed too difficult to bear because he had been locked in a trance, backed against the far wall of his snail shell of retreat. Magda had come to him through the door and past the priests; they had not seen her and she had taken him away, leaving only the husk of his body to the inquisitors. But the moment had arrived when he had had to return to reality and face the pain. Suddenly and sharply, with no time to accustom himself.

Time had lost all meaning. He might have been in the cells of the Château Narbonnais for three days, three months, or three years. He had been beaten, tortured, pushed and pushed to confess to heresy by Friar Bernard, whose assaults, both physical and mental, had increased in viciousness as Dominic refused to yield even a grain of ground. They were back in the schoolroom, will locking with will. *Fiat voluntas Tua.*

The soldiers picked their way across the musty straw, searching the darkest corners of the cell and the cowering rags of life until at last they located Dominic hunched against

a dank wall, staring at nothing. They hauled him to his feet
when he ignored their order to rise, and dragged him out of
the cells and up the twisting stairway. He concentrated upon
summoning the light, upon reaching out to Magda; he could
sense her, but he was weak and she was so far away.

Fear and privation had enfeebled him. He had no control
over his chattering jaw and the guards had to support most
of his weight as they mounted another set of stairs. Through
a haze of pain, Dominic slowly realised they were not taking
the usual direction to the inquisitor's rooms, but were
entering the private chambers belonging to the garrison
commander and his officers, a place that Dominic himself
had much frequented in the past, in another life, his fingers
stained with ink, not blood.

'Good God!' he heard a shocked voice say. Squinting
through gummy lids, he recognised Henri Lemagne, his
former tutor in arms. 'Give the lad a blanket and pour him
some of that double-strength wine . . . Quickly, man, don't
just stand there!'

Dominic swayed. A hand held out a blanket towards him.
He took it with his right hand, could not hold it, and it slid
to the ground. 'Henri,' he said hoarsely, and his knees
buckled.

Swearing, Lemagne knelt beside Dominic. He was still
conscious, but that was all that could be said. His bones
protruded through his pallid skin and terrible sores marked
his wrists and ankles where the iron fetters had chafed him
raw. The left hand was the worst, and Lemagne's oaths became
yet more blasphemous as he realised what the priests had done
to it.

Dominic managed the mirthless travesty of a smile.
'Don't let Friar Bernard hear you say that. He'll have you
in thumbscrews faster than a whore lifting her skirts for
business . . .' He squeezed his eyes shut, gasping with effort
and nausea. 'Have you come to watch me burn?'

'You're not going to burn, lad!' Lemagne declared, his

voice ragged with pity and rage. 'I'd light a torch beneath the black friar who did this to you if I could! Can you sit up?'

Grimacing with pain, Dominic struggled to raise himself. Lemagne watched him, a lump thickening in his throat. Left-handed himself, his skill proven by the fact that at the age of five and forty he was still alive and barely scarred by a life of fighting, Lemagne had been responsible for much of Dominic's early training in the use of weapons. The good wages paid by the Count de Montfort and a genuine affection for Dominic had bound Lemagne to that employment for more than ten years. To see his handiwork thus abused was like seeing a beloved blade that had been deliberately broken.

The wine arrived. Dominic extended his left hand, remembered, and used the right. 'What are you doing here if not witnessing my execution?' His speech was slow and difficult, for his lips were cut and swollen where he had been struck across the mouth. Two of his teeth were loose.

'Simon sent me to get you out. What else would I be doing in this godforsaken cesspit?'

'Simon did?'

'And Amaury. The de Montforts look after their own. Your half-brothers are powerful men.' Lemagne took a roll of parchment from the trestle and waved it at Dominic. 'This is your release. You've been signed into my custody by Friar Seilha himself, senior inquisitor for the district.'

'So I'm not a heretic?' Dominic said bitterly, and took a shuddering drink of the wine. 'God pity me if one of my brothers were not the high constable of France, and the other an earl.'

'God pity you indeed.' Lemagne frowned, and twisted his beard between his fingers. 'They say you were caught travelling with some Cathars in the mountains and that you killed an inquisitor's guard so that the Cathars could escape. What were you thinking of?'

Dominic dropped his gaze. 'If they had caught her, she would have burned,' he said huskily.

Lemagne's tight mouth relaxed. He made an exasperated gesture. 'Dominic, Dominic! A woman. I should have known! Those friars almost had me thinking you truly had taken to heresy. God's sweet love, will you never learn? Women are trouble – more than any man can handle! Look what happened in Paris when you tangled with Clemence de Veyran. You were lucky to be banished to Toulouse with your jewels intact. Didn't you learn any discretion?'

Dominic knew it was pointless explaining his motives to Lemagne. The man had about as much imagination as a loaf of bread. Let him believe it was the folly of hot blood. Easier for everyone. The warmth of the room was bringing his injuries back to throbbing life as the cold receded from his bones. He gritted his teeth against a red wave of pain. 'What about Friar Bernard?'

'What about him?'

'Didn't he protest about my release?'

Lemagne shrugged. 'He's away at a council in Albi. Seilha's zealous, but he's not blind to reason when it knocks on his door bearing the seal of France's constable. Don't let it concern you.' He splashed more wine into Dominic's cup. 'Once you're out of this place, your paths won't cross again.'

Dominic kept his eyes down and held his tongue, but Lemagne was a seasoned soldier and saw straight through him.

'If you were thinking of riding out of Toulouse and straight back into trouble, let me disabuse you of the notion now. There are terms to your release,' he growled.

'Terms?' Dominic's gut clenched.

'You're to remain in my custody until handed over to Amaury or Simon; you're to wear the yellow cross of a repentant heretic on your garments for a period of three years, and you're to take an oath to go on crusade as soon as you are sufficiently recovered.' He lowered his brows at

Dominic's obdurate expression. 'Forget her, lad. You're playing with fire, the real thing, not the mush that troubadours peddle through their lute strings. Do you want to burn in hell?'

Dominic bent his head, assailed by violent wingbeats of pain that threatened to make him scream. He was to be released from prison but still kept within the shackles of Friar Bernard's forging, and doubtless closely observed – for his own good, they would say. He dared not endanger Magda or her family by making contact, not yet at least. 'This is hell,' he muttered, his eyes blinded by scalding salt. He curled his fingers around the goblet and, with the last of his strength, abandoned control and hurled the cup across the room. The sound of it shattering against the wall, his accompanying howl of anguish and Lemagne's exclamation were the last things he heard for a very long time.

CHAPTER 40

MONTSÉGUR, SPRING 1242

They said that he was dead, but staring out on a landscape of green spring buds, Magda knew it was not true. She would have felt the emptiness in her soul. In the early months of their parting, she had found him in the dungeons of the Château Narbonnais in Toulouse, and had done what she could to help him endure. It was for her sake and her mother's that they were breaking him, and watching him suffer had filled her with guilt and grief. Then one day, when she sought him, he was gone, and in his place she found the wall. One of their number who was able to move freely in Toulouse had made discreet enquiries at the Château Narbonnais. He had been told by the guards that Dominic le Couchefeu was dead, but Magda refused to believe such a thing.

She wiped the tears from her cheeks and rubbed her eyes with the back of one hand. She could see one of the women from the fortress coming towards her through the trees, and did not want to be discovered weeping.

As the visitor came closer, Magda saw that it was Claire de Montvallant, and she was carrying Sancha, her two-year-old granddaughter, in her arms. The child was the result of a liaison between her son Guillaume and a capricious Spanish mercenary's daughter who cooked for Monstégur's garrison.

Magda put aside her tribulations and went to meet them, a smile on her face. She was always pleased to see Claire, for she was a tenuous link with Dominic. Sometimes Magda could see him so clearly in the Cathar woman that her heart would clench with pleasure and pain.

Whimpering, the little girl curled against her grandmother, her hair a snarled mass of dark curls, her eyes a huge, liquid brown. One cheek was bright red.

'She is teething, poor lamb,' Claire said as Magda led her down to the hut that she and Bridget shared. 'Constanza says she kept her and Guillaume awake all night with her crying. I thought that you might be able to ease her pain.'

'Give her to me.' Magda took the little girl's warm weight in her arms, and settled her on her knee. Sancha thought about screaming, but her wails were only half-hearted, and after a moment, she forgot them and peeped a shy smile at Magda from beneath coquettish black lashes. Magda laid the palm of her hand to Sancha's burning cheek and summoned the healing flow in the gentlest trickle to soothe the tender gum. 'I will give you some ointment of honey and cloves to rub on it,' she said, and enquired politely after Claire's well-being and that of Guillaume and Constanza.

'I fear for my son,' Claire said sadly. 'Today he rode out of Montségur with Pierre-Roger and some others and they were all dressed for war and spoiling for a fight. He feeds on his hatred of the French. I know why he came to Montségur. Toulouse and Montvallant were no longer safe for him. Here, he has the protection of Pierre-Roger and the wherewithal to make war. Many times I have tried to reach him and make him understand that what he is doing is wrong, but we speak a different language.'

'His conscience is not in your keeping,' Magda warned gently. 'If you goad him, you will drive him further away.'

Claire sighed helplessly. 'Yes, I know. Your mother told me as much about Raoul once. She predicted that Guillaume would reach manhood with many roads open before him. It breaks my heart to see the one he is choosing. Is there nothing I can do?'

'Listen to the voice of your own soul,' Magda said. 'Look

at the paths of your own choosing.' She gave Claire a sad smile. 'That was what I was doing myself when I saw you coming towards me. A part of me says it is time to leave the old road for a new one before it is too late. But another part lingers, waiting for someone else to catch up.' She tightened her arms around the child and, brushing her lips over the silky curls, imagined that Sancha was her own. Sometimes the emptiness in her loins and breasts was a physical ache. I have been fallow for too long, she thought.

They say he is dead. I do not believe it.

Guillaume kissed Constanza, squeezed her rump, drank from his goblet, and sat down beside his mother, who was watching Sancha sleep, free of teething pain. Guillaume's blood was still up. Claire could almost hear it fizzing in his veins. Eyes bright with drink and excitement, he seemed not her son, but a stranger, one of the false God's servants.

'You'll be able to travel the roads in peace now,' he told her proudly. 'Safe from the black-robes!'

'What have you done?' Her stomach turned over at the taint of wine and meat on his breath. It was one of her denial days and only water had passed her own lips.

'You've heard me mention Alfaro? He's Rai's bailiff in Avignonet and married to Rai's half-sister?'

'I . . . I think so.'

'Well, he hates the Dominicans and the French as much as I do, so when an inquisition of eleven of them turned up in Avignonet, he sent word here straightaway . . . and we rode out and dealt with them.' He patted the sword on his hip and held out his empty cup for Constanza to refill. 'I've got a fine new horse and harness out of it, and a spare hauberk.' Grinning, he addressed his mistress. 'They'll fetch enough money to keep you in silk gowns . . . or perhaps you'd like a necklace of Byzantine gold, hmmm?' He snatched a fondle and a kiss.

Claire heaved and had to swallow her gorge. Raoul had

wept when he killed men, had used his sword with reluctance. Guillaume was openly bragging. Oh God, how he had been twisted by this lifetime of war. Occasionally she glimpsed the remnants of the decent young man he could have been staring through a chink in Rex Mundi's black armour, imprisoned, bewildered. It was the way she remembered her own past before the salvation of the consolamentum. But Guillaume was unable to see the shining light beyond his desperately outstretched fingers. All he saw was a killing darkness.

'Do you think such an act will stop them?' she asked tiredly. 'Fighting evil with evil only begets evil.'

Guillaume's eyes flashed. 'You are content to have the soldiers protect you up here on your sacred mountain!' he sneered. 'What do you think would happen to this community without a garrison of sinning souls to guard it?'

'I am not content, but I tolerate it,' she replied, and smoothed her hands over her knees in a repetitive motion, struggling to remain calm. 'What disturbs me is when you ride out to kill and return gloating over what you have done. It frightens me. Your soul will be lost.'

Guillaume cut off her concern with a harsh laugh, grasped his goblet, and walked unsteadily away. Grief wrapped its tentacles around Claire until the pain was too great for her to contain and she let out the wail of a woman mourning for the dead. But Cathars did not mourn the dead. They sang with joy for their release, or prayed that in the next life they would find the enlightenment that had eluded them in this.

CHAPTER 41

GASCONY, SUMMER 1243

A competitive chess game was in progress, the atmosphere less than brotherly. Dominic picked up the ebony knight between forefinger and thumb, hovered for an instant, then set it suddenly and decisively down.

'You underhanded, sly . . .'

'Bastard?' suggested Dominic, grinning at Simon. Leaning back, he stretched his arms above his head. His shirt, transparent with perspiration, clung to his lean, muscular body. He wore braies and chausses, but had long since discarded hose and shoes. The heat was stultifying, without so much as a hint of a storm to clear the dusty air, the clouds high and distant, out of reach.

'That as well.' Simon glowered at the board and then at Dominic. 'Ach, it's too hot to play chess!' He waved dismissively.

'Too hot to do anything else. Do you concede?'

Simon was saved from an ignominious declaration by the approach of one of his squires. Trailing in his wake came a jongleur and two dusty, exhausted-looking women.

'Luck of the devil,' Dominic muttered, and lowered his arms. One hand descended to fondle the silky ears of the dozing young wolfhound near his feet while he appraised the women and found them as appetising as two barnyard hens in moult. Frayed robes drab with dust; worn shoes; worn faces. The man was a draggled cockerel, faded ribbons twisted in a limp bunch at the neck of his lute, and a cap set askew on his dyed yellow curls.

The news had continued to spread in widening rings from the original impact that King Henry of England was lingering at his court in Gascony and spending money as if it were water. Every juggler, tumbler, sword swallower, huckster, buffoon, trickster and troubadour in the world had made his or her way here in the hopes of a share in the largesse. Most numerous were the men of the Languedoc, where the living was no longer easy and well patronised – where frequently there was no living at all because the nobility there were impoverished and struggling to survive. As one of the most powerful men at court, Simon was constantly being approached by such creatures in search of employment and charity.

'We already have troubadours coming out of our ears,' Dominic said indifferently, 'although the soldiers might pay them for a ditty or two.'

Looking exhausted, near to tears, the women slumped against each other. They were hardly the kind of fare to tempt the appetites of men jaded by a life of idle good living for the worst part of four months. Pity stirred Dominic's conscience, together with disgust for the indolent stagnation of his life, feeding on itself like a Celtish circle, teeth devouring tail.

'My lord Earl, we have news,' declared the minstrel, flourishing a performer's bow, obviously forcing the effort through his weariness. 'All the way from Toulouse!'

Simon looked mildly interested. Dominic's heart quickened as it always did when the South was mentioned. He ceased fondling Lynx's ears and beckoned a squire. 'Bring wine and food,' he ordered. The squire's lip curled, displaying what he thought of being sent on an errand for such riffraff, but he was not so foolish as to refuse.

'News?' Simon motioned the three to be seated on the floor near his chair. 'Tell me.' He lifted a silver penny off the gambling pile beside him and flipped it to the trouba-dour. The musician caught it in midair faster than the snap of a starving fox.

His news was commonplace and some of it was stale. Simon's hazel eyes began to narrow and he raised his hand, preparing to dismiss the motley trio. Then the word Montségur dropped into the narrative. It meant nothing to Simon and he clicked his fingers.

'Wait.' Dominic arrested his brother and leaned forward. 'What about Monségur?' he asked in a keen voice.

'My lord, an army is marching from Carcassonne to take it once and for all.' Sweat trickled down the minstrel's cheeks. 'The Cathars are to be burned if they don't recant, each and every one. It's true, I swear it. We were in Carcassonne when the troops were assembling, at least a thousand men. It's because of what happened at Avignonet, when the holy friars were massacred. The Cathars don't really want peace, they just employ other people to do their killing for them!'

'Well informed about them, are you?' Dominic said silkily, causing Simon's to look at him in sudden speculation.

The troubadour had not missed the threat in Dominic's gliding tones. 'I don't know anything about them, my lord. I'm a good Catholic, I am! I go to mass every week!'

'Then do not go making judgements you cannot uphold,' Dominic bit out. 'Who's commanding the army?'

'Hugh d'Arcis, my lord.'

'The seneschal of Carcassonne,' Simon said. 'He's a mastiff. Once his teeth sink in, he doesn't let go until his opponent is dead.'

The squire returned with the food. Dominic abruptly rose from the chessboard and went to stand in the window embra-sure. Thrusting his shoulder against the cold stone, he stared down into the pleasance below. Under the watchful eyes of their nursemaid, Simon's two small sons, Henry and Simon, were romping with a ball. Some gaily bedecked women were clustered around another of their number who was playing a lute. The notes drifted up, as sweet and light as one of the King's angel wafers, and as superficial. Dominic examined his left hand – the lean brown fingers, a jagged white scar where a falcon had once clawed him . . . the ridged, misshapen fingernails that had never properly grown back, the thickened skin. He became aware of his half-brother's silent presence beside him.

'Simon, I have to go to Montségur,' he said without turning round.

'Oh yes?' Simon said neutrally.

'My mother is there . . . and someone else. If there is the slightest chance of getting them out, then I have to take it. I thought they were safer without contact from me. I was wrong. I should have gone there years ago.'

Simon gripped and raised the irrevocably damaged left hand. 'And if fortune fails you? It won't just be your fingers, Dom, it'll be your life and your soul. I can't protect you again.'

'My life and soul will be forfeit anyway if I don't try.'

Simon made a perplexed sound in his throat and released him.

'Have you ever wondered why I have turned down offers of marriage over the years?' Dominic asked.

'It had crossed my mind. I thought you were mad to reject that Breton heiress. Educated, handsome, a superb dowry, and all you did was shrug and reject the offer cold.'

'Lukewarm,' Dominic protested. 'I did consider it for a moment, but there is someone else and she has lived in my heart a long time.'

Simon was swift to pick up on the repetition of 'someone else'. 'A Cathar!' he surmised on a falling cadence. 'So Henri Lemagne was right. Jesu, Dominic!'

He smiled ruefully. He was always Dominic, never Dom, when he did things of which the more responsible Simon disapproved. 'No, not a Cathar, but living among them. She has the sight and healing skills and other gifts that I'm not even going to try to explain to you. Don't stare at me as though I'm contagious; I am not possessed – well, no more than you are by your wife and sons.' He looked out of the window at the bright gathering below, and sighed. 'I want a woman I desire to call wife, and children by her to inherit the English lands you have bestowed on me. You wanted Eleanor from the moment you laid eyes on her. Do not deny the same feeling in me for Magda.'

'Eleanor is the King's sister,' Simon pointed out drily.

'And you're a de Montfort out of a Montmorency!' Dominic retorted. 'The rules are different for you. I can mate where I choose. My mind is made up. I'm riding out at first light. If you won't give me leave from my command, I'll resign it.'

Simon rubbed his fingertip up and down the sweaty groove of his upper lip. 'You mean it, don't you? All right, gather what you need, we'll leave at first light.'

'We?' Dominic twisted in the embrasure and stared. 'You can't enter the Languedoc with your retinue.'

'I mean you and I alone, perhaps one squire.'

Dominic's eyes narrowed suspiciously. 'Why?'

Simon shifted uneasily and cleared his throat. 'I'm not sure I know the answer to that. Perhaps because I'm bored stiff dancing attendance on Henry day in and day out. It's bound to be cooler in the mountains, and the hunting should be good and . . .'

'And?'

Simon rubbed the back of his neck. 'Ah, Christ, I don't know. I was four years old when you were born, but I remember it clearly. Your mother was beautiful and I was love-lorn. The other women spurned her and I knew she was unhappy, but she always had a smile for me. My mother gave you to a wet nurse and eventually banished Lady Claire from her household. I was bereft at first, but then I realised I could at least look out for you. She was greatly wronged, Dom, and it needs to be redressed.'

Dominic shouldered out of the embrasure and clicked his fingers at Lynx, who was attending hopefully on the three entertainers for scraps, with little success. 'You will never redress what has gone before.'

'But I can ensure that the future is more evenly weighted,' Simon said.

'Then thank you.' Dominic inclined his head. 'I'll welcome your company . . . but just now I'd rather be on my own for a while.'

For the first time in many nights, Dominic went to bed sober. Despite the news of the danger to Montségur, he felt more settled than he had done in an age. The barrier that had led him to bury the past and live an exemplary Christian life for the eyes of the Dominican friars who spied upon him was redundant and he could let it tumble.

He closed his eyes and opened his mind and she came to him, crying his name like a stumbling pilgrim out of the desert. He grasped her, and she clung to him. Joy and grief mingled so powerfully he could not tell where one began and the other ended.

'I am coming to you now,' he told her, but even as he tightened his hold, her image began to fade. Their finger-tips touched as he stretched out to try and keep hold of her. He received the image of flames and death, of terrible danger, of an army encamped at the foot of a steep mountain and a dark beast hunting. Lightning sparked and he opened his eyes with a jolt to the fading echo of his own voice crying out her name and the sound of thundery rain sluicing off the tiles and into the courtyard.

CHAPTER 42

Montségur at dusk: the pines a vivid green just on the visible side of darkness, their scent distilling on the summer air, making it as resinous as Greek wine. The powerful silence was broken by the husky calls of hoopoes and the rustle of the wind through the trees. The metallic clop and scrape of shod hooves and the champing of horses sounded a note of discord.

The hairs lifted at Raoul's nape. He felt as if he were in a vast cathedral in the presence of some dark being with a thousand invisible eyes. The Old Testament God of war, the Cathars' Rex Mundi laying siege to the tiny point of clarity and light crowning the mountain. His horse sidled and, behind him, one of his knights muttered something about the atmosphere being haunted.

The sky darkened; swags of cloud like witches' tresses drifted across the moonrise. The men continued to climb, drawn by the comforting pinpricks of light above, driven by the heaving darkness that surrounded them. Raoul almost leaped out of his skin when the trees rustled at the side of the path, and a slight figure emerged to stand in shadows and silver before them.

He gasped with relief and released his instinctive grip on his sword hilt when he saw that it was a young woman with unbound flaxen hair. She wore a pale robe that gleamed in the darkness, and around her neck a medallion flashed. In this bad light, he could not see its design, but he knew instinctively that it would bear the dove and chalice symbol. 'Magda?'

'My mother said you would come when you heard about the army they are sending to destroy us.' She stroked his mount's nose, calming the horse with the skill in her hands.

Raoul stared at his daughter. She had Bridget's wonderful eyes and grace, but her build and colouring were his. He wondered if she knew. 'She sent you here to wait for us, on the mountainside?' he asked with a hint of reproval.

'No, I was seeking someone else, and I heard your horses. Come, I'll take you up.' She felt his concern for her, and heard the question that he did not ask. Her father; the man her mother had chosen above other men, but not for a permanent life-mate. His lined face was handsome and his aura glowed with a steady strength, but she saw great sadness there, too, and his eyes were weary, as if they had seen too much.

'I do not know whom you were seeking,' he said. 'There is no one here except us. We have seen scarcely a soul since leaving Foix, and we are the only ones on the mountain path tonight.'

'The man I am hunting is beyond physical reach for the moment.' A mischievous note crept into her voice. 'He is in Gascony, and it is easier to call to him in the open than it is surrounded by walls.'

'In Gascony?' Raoul looked askance.

'I knew he wasn't dead.' She smiled at Raoul and stepped on lightly before him and his troop, her pale hair and robe glimmering almost like a lantern to guide their way up the steep southwestern approach to the fortress.

Guillaume's attention diverted from his dice game as the horses entered the bailey. His eyes narrowed on the newcomers and he rose from his crouch. 'Papa?' he queried to himself with surprise and not a little trepidation. He hurried from the shadows to grasp his father's bridle. 'It is you! What are you doing here!' His gaze flickered to Magda. She looked between him and Raoul, hesitated for a moment, then excused herself.

Raoul dismounted and he and Guillaume clasped each other hard, then harder still, saying in the embrace all that words could not. "There is trouble afoot. I'm here to talk to de Perella and my family. Ah, God, Guillaume, it's good to see you!'

Guillaume stepped back. His stomach swooped and he wished that he had not drunk so deeply from the leather wine bottle that had been passing from hand to hand around the circle of gamblers. 'What sort of trouble?'

'I'd rather talk to de Perella and Pierre-Roger first.'

Guillaume scowled. His father still seemed to think of him as a child who had no business in the world of men. 'I'm a senior knight, you know,' he said resentfully. 'I'll be in on anything you tell them.'

'As you were in on Avignonet,' Raoul retorted. 'Rai of Toulouse told me you were involved in the murders, and what was going to happen as a consequence. That's why I'm here.'

Guillaume jutted his jaw. 'I'm not sorry we killed those inquisitors. Given the opportunity, I'd do it again without remorse. 'Did the Count say anything about sending us more troops?'

'Just take me to de Perella,' Raouol said wearily.

Guillaume shrugged as if he did not care, and lengthened his stride.

Ramón de Perella and his nephew and coorganiser of Montségur's defences, Pierre-Roger of Mirepoix, were talking in the hall over a late supper of bread and the local cured donkey sausage. Raoul was greeted warmly but with an underlying anxiety and furnished with a chair, a portion of the meal and a cup of wine. Uninvited but not rebuffed apart from a single sharp glance from de Perella, Guillaume drew up a stool and sat down, too.

'What brings you to Montségur?' asked the commander. 'Must be more than twenty years since last you were here. A family visit perchance?' The deep-set eyes flicked between father and son.

Raoul gave a brusque nod. 'In part. Mainly I came to bring you a warning. An army is gathering in Carcassonne under Hugh d'Arcis – a thousand men at least, with the object of destroying Montségur and everyone in it.'

'That's dung!' Guillaume spat, fear blazing in his eyes.

Pierre-Roger wiped grease from his lips on the back of his hand and lifted his cup. 'For the sake of your pride, I would not have put it as bluntly as your son, Lord Raoul, but I've heard this kind of rumour many times before.'

'This is no rumour, but the truth!' Raoul said irritably. 'Do you think I would have ridden all this way for the sake of a rumour!' His gaze cut to Guillaume. 'Or perhaps you do!' He pushed the food impatiently aside. 'I came because Count Rai himself gave me the warning, knowing that I have family and friends here.'

'Count Rai?' De Perella's cup stopped halfway to his mouth. 'He would never permit such a thing. If this army marches, he will come immediately to our aid!'

'He won't,' Raoul said with finality. 'He's angry at being excommunicated for Avignonet, which was none of his doing. He wants to be buried in consecrated ground when his time comes, not left to moulder in his coffin in a corridor like his father. He needs to ingratiate himself with the French. They suspect him of plotting against the Crown, and he doesn't want another army ravaging what lands and dignity remain to him. You, all of you, are to be the sacrifice – a symbol of southern resistance that's not going to cost too much to yield up. It'll satisfy France and remove the problem of the Cathars from Rai's attempts at reconciliation with the Church.' He glared round the trestle. 'Now do you see?'

De Perella and Pierre-Roger looked at each other with the beginnings of dismay.

'It isn't true!' Guillaume said hoarsely. 'Rai will keep faith.'

'You're not a child any more; I can't make your nightmares go away!' Raoul snapped. 'Especially not those of your own making. How can Rai ignore something of the magnitude of Avignonet? Already that inquisitor is a martyr of saintly proportions. His canonisation sings in the corridors of Rome. Cut off one head and a thousand more grow to replace it.' He put his face in his hands for a moment and then rubbed it wearily. 'If your mother will come, I want to take her away before the army arrives – and two others if they can be persuaded.'

De Perella said slowly, 'If this is true, we will need to make arrangements for all the money and books to be taken out to safety.'

'We can hold out!' Guillaume protested. 'We've fought off intruders before!'

De Perella looked at his nephew and Guillaume. 'Let the valuables be removed to a secure place as a precaution,' he said, and bared his stained, war-stallion teeth. 'Then let the hordes of Beelzebub come, and let them die.'

'I cannot leave,' Bridget said when Raoul spoke to her in the infirmary some time later. 'Not while Matthias still lives and the others need me more than I need to go. I know that Chretien feels the same way, but I thank you for your offer. Magda at least must leave with you though.'

'I'm as safe here as anywhere for the moment!' Magda objected. 'I won't leave you!' She had been tending a cauldron of simmering water and herbs with Claire, but now she put her ladle aside and came to join the conversation.

'Daughter, you must,' Bridget said in a voice slow with fatigue. 'You have a sacred duty.'

'The people need me here,' Magda said stubbornly. She stood a slender head and shoulders above her mother. 'I am the one who goes among them while you tend Uncle

Matthias. If I leave, they will feel just as betrayed as if you had gone yourself.'

'That's as may be, but you still have your life before you, and it would be senseless for it to end here on this mountain.'

'I could stay and help you a while longer in the infirmary – help you build up a stock of remedies for when I am gone,' Magda said.

'It is too dangerous now!' Bridget objected.

Raoul stepped into the silence of the unequal duel and made sure of the outcome. 'There are no pressing claims of home or conscience to hold me back,' he said. 'Everything that has ever meant anything in my life is here at Montségur. My wife . . . my family. If you are all bent upon self-destruction, this is the last opportunity for me to be with you. I can take Magda wherever she wants to go when I leave. If she desires, she can dwell with me at Montvallant.'

Magda felt an overflowing gratitude towards Raoul. 'Thank you,' she said, with a look for him that acknowledged all that was known but unspoken between them. 'But someone else is coming to take me away from Montségur.'

'Who?' Bridget eyed her sharply.

Magda drew a deep breath. 'Dominic. I want to wait for him.'

It was the first time she had spoken his name in front of anyone but her mother and Chretien. Claire, whose presence at the cauldron of herbs had gone overlooked in the contest of wills between mother and daughter, gasped at the mention of the name and spun round, scalding liquid dripping unheeded down the front of her robe.

'Who is Dominic?' Raoul asked, suddenly tense.

Magda looked at Claire. 'Guillaume's half-brother. I met him a long time ago in Toulouse when we were children, and again after the treaty of Meaux. He travelled the hills with myself and Uncle Chretien until we were ambushed by inquisitors. He saved us from them at cost to his own liberty, and they put him to the torture. For a long time I thought he was dead, but it is not so, and he is coming for me.'

Claire's face was bloodless. 'It is impossible,' she whispered. 'It cannot be.'

'So you found him, my daughter?' Bridget said.

Magda nodded without taking her eyes from Claire. 'In Gascony. Suddenly the wall was not there any more.'

'I know him.' Raoul, too, was looking at his wife. 'He rescued Guillaume from rotting in the cells at the Châteaux Narbonnais. For all the sins of his father, he seemed a balanced and intelligent young man . . . more balanced than Guillaume, I sometimes think. I heard he had been imprisoned and tried for heresy; the rumour was even put about that he had died, but I am glad it was untrue.'

Claire staggered and Raoul hastened to support her with a comforting arm around her shoulders.

'Dominic.' She said the word haltingly as if it were in a foreign language, and her expression was haunted with terror, grief and guilt. 'God forgive me and show me the Light, for I have lost my way.'

'Hush, love, hush,' Raoul murmured, hugging her, his lips upon her grey-streaked hair.

'It is part of the pattern,' Magda said softly. 'De Montfort persecuted us, but his son has redressed that wrong. It is like two curves joining to make a perfect circle. One cannot be whole without the other . . . and I have been incomplete for so long.'

'So have I,' sobbed Claire softly. 'So have I.'

'In nomine Patris et Filii et Spiritus Sancti, amen,' Friar Bernard prayed, welcoming the discomfort of the hard ground upon his calloused knees. The hair shirt beneath his habit irritated his skin, which was already chafed raw, weeping in the places of constant friction. A tight cord bound the undergarment to his body, digging into his waist, creating exquisite pain. See how I suffer for thee, O Lord. He had taken a vow not to remove the hair shirt until Montségur had fallen and every last Cathar had been destroyed, and for every day that they remained in possession of the summit, he had himself publicly flogged by one of the younger friars in his entourage.

The Cathars were evil, evil. To think of the doctrines they preached made him weep and grind his teeth with rage and shame. They said the Resurrection was a lie, that the doctrine of the spilled blood of Christ buying redemption for mankind was the product of dark, corrupt minds.

All Cathars deserved to go to hell. They were so close, yet so unattainable, locked inside their fortress two thousand feet above the encamped and still-arriving army. Were they kneeling and worshipping, too? Practising their vile rites? Smearing filth upon the God whom he loved and so devoutly served? Bernard could not bear the thought; it filled his head with madness. Biting his lip until it bled, he prostrated himself before the altar in his tent and prayed with renewed fervour. Behind his lids flickered a vision of the Cathars burning in the flames of hell. And cool in the snow, the Virgin Mary mocked him with her heretic smile.

The mountain stream was as clear as glass, and even in the heat of early summer, icy with meltwater. Dominic scooped a palmful, drank, then sluiced his face. The horses dipped their muzzles and sucked up the water with thirsty pleasure. Half a day's ride was all that separated him and Simon from the army amassed at the foot of Montségur. Tonight they had made camp among the mountains a little to the west so that in the morning they could ride in fresh to the crusader assembly. It lacked an hour to dusk, but they had preparations to make for the morrow, and a good night's rest would not go amiss, for they had been riding hard.

To Simon, it had been as much pleasure as urgency that had led him to push their pace, easing out the creases of indulgent living, shedding surplus flesh. Dominic would have enjoyed it, too, had it not been for the nightmares that haunted him every time he fell asleep. Friar Bernard would chase him up and down crags, across fields and through narrow town alleyways, his eyes ablaze with a fanatical light and a dagger in his hand. Dominic would awaken sweating and terrified, his arms raised to protect himself. Dreams involving Magda were just as bad. They made him groan and toss for an entirely different reason, but the torment brought no release. Either Friar Bernard would appear with his blade at a moment close but not close enough to culmination, or Simon would dig him in the ribs and complain about the noise he was making.

Dominic filled his waterskin and stood up, inhaling the scent of pine needles and enjoying the slanting warmth of the late sun. Simon's mount raised its dripping muzzle, ears pricked towards the trees, and nickered. Dominic secured his grip on the horses and looked to his sword. The mountains were rife with wolves – both the four- and two-legged variety.

Something was moving through the dense forest on the other side of the stream. A horse answered Simon's and a knight emerged through the woods across from Dominic. He was leading a glossy roan destrier and his yellow surcoat was appliquéd with black chevronels, the device echoed on the shield hanging from the saddle. Dropping the rein, the man let his mount drink, and gazed across the stream at Dominic. 'God's greeting,' he said, without surprise.

Dominic stood motionless. 'Lord Raoul?'

The creases deepened around the other man's sea-blue eyes. 'I was not sure you would recognise me.' He crouched to drink.

Dominic released the breath he had been holding. 'What are you doing here?'

Raoul shook water from his hands and smiled at Dominic. 'Looking for you and playing escort to a certain young woman who told me where to seek.'

'Magda!' Dominic's chest tightened and suddenly it was difficult to breathe. 'Magda is with you?'

Raoul glanced over his shoulder. 'Not far away. There's a Templar knight travelling with us, too – Magda's cousin.'

'And you are looking for me?'

'And your half-brother.'

'How did you . . . ?'

'We'll come to your campfire tonight?' Raoul took up his mount's rein.

Dominic sought to muster his reeling wits with limited success. There was nothing beyond the thump of his heart reacting to the moment. 'You'll be more than welcome,' he heard himself say in a constricted voice. 'We caught a hare this morning and we have bread and olives if you don't want meat . . . We were on our way to Montségur.'

'I know,' Raoul said, 'and I believe you will still have to go there, but we can talk about that later. I'll go and fetch Luke and Magda before it grows dark.'

Dominic returned to the camp in a daze, the thought of

Magda a blinding light in his mind, obliterating all other considerations. He answered Simon's questions in monosyllabic grunts as the latter cleaned the hare and set it to roast on a spit.

'A Templar, eh?' Simon mused. 'I've heard it said more than once that their methods of worship would not stand up to scrutiny by the Inquisition.'

'The Templars make their own rules and alliances,' Dominic said distantly, his eyes upon the forest beyond their campfire. 'Within the outer ring of ordinary brethren, there's an inner, secret core.'

'How do you know that?'

'I overheard Guzman and Bernard discussing it. They were angry because their people could not search the Templar preceptories.'

'Their suspicions appear to have been borne out.'

Dominic shrugged. 'To our advantage,' he said.

Simon looked thoughtful. 'And this Raoul de Montvallant. You say he is your mother's husband? Very saintly of him not to hate your guts.'

'He would have done if I'd grown up here and usurped his lands, but I saved his son from the Inquisition and, as men, we like each other well enough.'

'How's he connected with your Magda?'

'I don't know.' Simon's relentless quest for information was irritating him, and he got up and walked away to help the squire hobble the horses.

An appetising aroma of roasting meat soon filled the air. The sky darkened into dusk, the orange fabric of sunset smudging into an indigo hem beaded with the first stars. Dominic paced to the edge of the camp, impatience trembling through him. He felt as if a layer of his skin had been peeled away, exposing him raw to the fragrant night air. Every sound, every scent, every touch of breeze and insect was magnified almost to the level of pain.

He heard the snort of a horse and saw a glimmer through

the trees – a Templar's white surcoat, perhaps. A man spoke, a woman answered, and he realised that it was her gown he had seen, for the Templar wore a dark cloak over his own robes.

'They are here,' he said over his shoulder to Simon, and went forward to meet them.

Time slowed as he greeted Raoul and was introduced to the Templar Luke de Béziers, a powerfully built warrior in his late prime. He must have made the correct responses but was not conscious of his lips moving, for every fibre of his being was concentrated upon the woman who had been sitting pillion on Raoul's stallion and was now lifted down by him.

Her hair was woven with wildwood flowers like a bride and rippled to her waist, heavy as ripe corn. A plain white woollen robe clung to her supple figure, relieved only by a cord of braided scarlet silk at her waist and the flash of an enamelled medallion at her throat. Dominic stared, transfixed.

'Dominic,' she breathed, and was at his side, her hand linking through his, her eyes shining. He felt the tingle of the connection, the quickening of already quickened blood. Uncaring of the two men, he gasped, pulled her against him and covered her mouth with his, feeling whole again for the first time since his capture by the Inquisition. The Templar smiled. Raoul's expression was wistful.

'I told Raoul and Cousin Luke we would find you here,' she said when at last they surfaced from the embrace, both of them breathing hard. 'I have been so worried, so lonely. There is terrible danger.'

'We've come to take you to safety.' He pressed his palm against hers, felt the response of her fingers playing against his like needles in the blood. The delicate lines of her face; the gleam of her collarbone; the swift rise and fall of her breasts.

'And this must be your brother Simon coming now?' she

murmured. 'He has a life force much like your father's.'

'What?' Dominic turned to regard his advancing half-brother. The glimmer surrounding Simon was like the mountain stream – pure and strongly flowing with bands of indigo and green and blue at its margins. 'It is nothing like my father's!' he protested, horrified

'No, I mean like your father's might once have been – strong and idealistic. He gets what he wants, sometimes to his own detriment. Yours is not dissimilar.' Her voice struck a more intimate chord and her fingers stroked his. Dominic responded, linking his through hers, gently closing his grip.

'Simon,' he said, 'I want you to meet Magda.'

Over a meal of bread and wine, olives, and roast hare for those whose diet permitted meat, Magda and Dominic brought each other abreast of all that had happened to them during their years of separation – years of wilderness, as Dominic thought of them. It was time also to reappraise each other, measure the changes that experience and maturity had wrought. It was sweet agony to touch and be touched, to lean shoulder to shoulder and know both the joy of being whole again and feel the turbulence and tension of desire. When Magda therefore announced she could not come with him to Gascony in the morning, Dominic could not contain himself.

'Then, God's grave, why have you come!' He sprang to his feet, his body quivering like an overstrung lute 'I broke myself for you once; what more do you want?'

Magda held out her hand towards him. 'If I only had my own desires to consider I would not put this burden on you. I would leave with you tonight, but I have to set them aside for the greater good. I need your help for all of us in Montségur.'

Breathing in shallow bursts, Dominic clenched his fists and turned away, and it was Simon who answered. 'You must know that it is impossible,' he said with a glance at his brother. 'We came out of obligation to you and to Dominic's mother, not to die for a host of heretics.'

'They are not heretics!' Magda flushed. 'They follow God's law more diligently than most of your priests!' She drew herself up and set her jaw. When she spoke again, it was to Dominic. She could feel his hurt, his anger, the undercurrents of love and lust, flashing and interlacing like a necklace in two colours of gold. 'I did not mean that you should fight for us,' she said in a measured tone. 'It is grief enough and cause of much dispute among our elders that we have soldiers to protect us at all.'

Dominic slowly turned. 'Then what do you want?'

'There are items at Montségur that have to be taken away to safety.'

'Such as?' Simon leaned slightly forward.

Magda focused on him, on the curiosity and acquisitiveness in his nature. 'Books, money, treasure . . . the Grail cup.' She felt him bite. A glance revealed that Dominic was studying her with wary eyes.

'I thought,' said Simon, the catch in his voice betraying his eagerness, 'the Cathars lived by the code that it is easier for a camel to pass through the eye of a needle than it is for a rich man to enter the gates of heaven.'

'The treasure has been bequeathed to us by wealthy people who have either become Perfecti and given all their possessions away, or by believers who want to ease their consciences and support us. You have such folk in your own Church by the thousand, do you not? We use the money to buy food and essentials for the community. We do not care about it.'

'But you pay the soldiers?' Simon pounced. 'Feeding the hand that holds the sword. Is that not as bad as holding the sword yourselves?'

Magda sighed. 'Indeed it is,' she agreed, 'but what else are we to do? Even if we did not pay them, most of the men are so committed to preserving the community at Montségur they would fight without wages. If we took away their weapons, they would use their bare hands.'

'That is so,' Raoul confirmed. 'My own son is numbered among them, and I know that money is not the reason he fights. His hatred is as dark as the love of the Perfecti is light – like the other side of a coin.' His expression hardened. 'I'm neither a theologian nor a politician. All I want is to see those I care for safe.'

Simon rubbed his chin and said in an interested voice, 'So what happens to the treasure once it's out of Montségur?'

'Oh, for God's sake, Simon!' Dominic snapped. 'I know you're short of funds, but aren't you being a little too obvious?'

Simon flushed, but did not take his eyes from Magda.

'The gold has never meant that much to us,' she said calmly. 'You are welcome to a share in it if you will undertake to remove it to safekeeping. The money will go to our communities in Lombardy, and some of the books. The remainder I will bring with me.'

'And the Grail?'

Magda looked directly at Simon. 'You have read the tales of King Arthur,' she said. 'You may search for ever and a day and never realise that all the time it lies beneath your nose. As to its symbol, that belongs to the Templars.' She touched Luke lightly on the knee and smiled.

Simon frowned. She could see he did not understand and was therefore ill at ease and still prepared to be hostile. 'These books, are they heresies?' he demanded.

'It won't damn your soul to read them, but they might change the way you look at the world,' Magda answered. 'Mostly they are Gospels translated from old scrolls and codexes by a man of learning in our community. They are teachings that have long been struck from the Roman version of the Bible, or never included in the first place.'

Simon chewed his lip. 'If I were a good son of the Church in whose service my father was killed, I would have no more to do with any of this,' he said. 'I would ride away, find the nearest church and confess and do penance.' His hazel glance brooded upon Dominic. 'However, my father left a debt that has gone unpaid for long enough. So be it, I will help.' He spoke haltingly, as if the words were being dragged out of some part of himself that it surprised him to find. 'You'll need an escape route and safe escort. Where are you planning to go?'

'England,' Dominic said. 'Your lands and power will give us security, and my own interests are there.'

Simon considered, then nodded. 'My jurisdiction only runs from Gascony. You'll still have to escape from Montségur and across the South.' He gave Magda an impatient look. 'Why can't you come with us now as Dominic wants?'

'There is still a book to be finished, and they need me there, more than ever now. There are paths known only to the local people. Even with an army of a thousand men, Hugh d'Arcis cannot surround the entire mountain. How do you think we came out?'

'What I suggest,' said the Templar, who had been silent thus far, 'is that Earl Simon organises a safe route between Gascony and England, and that you' – a look at Dominic – 'join the besieging troops and arrange the travel between Montségur and Gascony. I have contacts among the crusaders and can move easily between both camps, so I can be your message-bearer. Raoul can be trusted to get Magda and the treasure out to you at a prearranged time, and the other women if they will come, although I doubt it.'

Dominic stared beyond the campfire into the distance while he thought, and, after a short time, capitulated with a deep sigh. 'It is not what I would have chosen, but it seems sound enough to me. Simon?'

His brother gestured assent with a gleam in his eyes. Like their father, he excelled at planning and strategy. To be requested to undertake this task, with its element of mystery and risk, was a temptation impossible to refuse.

'It is settled, then.' Luke de Béziers raised his cup in salu-
tation. Everyone drank. Setting aside her empty cup, Magda
regarded Dominic across the firelight and, rising to her feet,
walked away into the darkness. Dominic did not immediately follow her. He would look a fool if she had just gone
to empty her bladder, and besides, he felt oddly nervous, as
if it were about to be his first time. He had half a mind to
run in the opposite direction.

After several minutes had passed, Simon nudged him.
'You'd better make sure she hasn't been eaten by a wolf,' he
said with amusement. 'Not afraid of the dark, are you, Dom?
Shall I go instead?'

Luke de Béziers was smiling. Raoul, his expression
knowing and sad, reached again for the wineskin. Standing
up, Dominic scowled at Simon. 'I always thought I was the
family bastard,' he said.

Simon laughed.

Magda was waiting for him near the stream, her arms
embracing her knees, her body curved like a new moon. The
water splashed over the stones in a pleasing rill of sounds
and the grass on either side was lush and damp. He hesitated for a moment before spreading his cloak and sitting
down beside her. Every fibre of his being was aware of hers
to a level verging on pain. He wanted to blend with her in
the white heat of physical release, yet he held back,
constrained by her mystery.

'Will it seem strange living with me when all your life
you have lived among Cathars?' he asked.

Magda turned her head and smiled. 'Do you mean because
I will be a baron's wife, or because you are a man with a
man's needs?'

He plucked at the grass. 'Both, I suppose.'

She tossed back her hair and looked at the sky. 'I have
lived among soldiers and their wives for my entire life, so

the first part will be simple enough. I shall found a convent in the name of the Magdalene with the money I bring from Montségur, and it shall be a sanctuary for the persecuted, whatever their need. As to you being a man . . .' Here she paused and gave a throaty chuckle. 'I do admit that although I know much of men's hearts and minds, their bodies are a mystery, and you left me with a taste to know more.' She leaned towards him.

Dominic touched her hair. It felt like silk against his fingers. It was going to be hard to see her return to the dangers of Montségur, even harder to settle down in the enemy camp and make a pretence of being a crusader, attacking what he had come to preserve while arranging a route to Gascony.

Her breathing quickened and he sensed her tension. Tenderly he plucked loose a flower from her hair and moved closer, his breath against her ear, her throat, upon her lips. The seal of a kiss, her lips parting under his. The feather touch of fingertips upon skin, the delicate unplucking of laces, yielding new areas of discovery. White breasts clefted with shadow and crowned by taut nipples. Cool, satin textures over which to glide palm and tongue. Smooth thighs, the inside skin softer than rose petals, and the heart of the rose itself, the mystery, the Grail.

Magda wrapped herself around him, making small, needful sounds as the pleasure grew within her, congesting her loins, blooming upon her skin. She arched to receive the first swollen thrust. He filled her and the pain was like scarlet fire. He murmured reassurances against her throat. A fine coating of sweat clung to his body, making his spine slippery beneath her fingers. His mouth covered hers, the kiss moving in rhythm with the motion of their bodies. Give and take and give. Magda opened her eyes to see the gleam of her lover's, the wheeling of the stars over their heads and the deep infinity of the sky. She sought his hand with hers – his damaged left one, meshing her grip through his. The flames consumed her, the stars turned; his fingers squeezed upon hers, tightening and tightening as the tension rose, and she squeezed in return, unable to gasp or cry out because his mouth was on hers. He made a sound in his throat and plunged and the scarlet fire became ripples of white heat, flashing through her body, engulfing and transfiguring her. She and Dominic were the fire. And through the burn of fulfilment, their hands remained joined, each imprinted on the other, nor did they disengage as the white light faded to the merest glimmer.

CHAPTER 44

MONTSÉGUR, AUTUMN 1243

Three weeks after returning to Montségur, Magda knew for certain that she was pregnant. Pleasure and apprehension filled her in equal quantities. The journey to safety would not be easy. By the time they reached England, she calculated that she would be entering her final three months.

She kept the news to herself – although she was aware of her mother's sharp scrutiny – and went about her duties as normal. The besieging army at the foot of their rock had swollen in number, and at night, their campfires could be seen as yellow suppurations among the trees. The sense of danger was suffocating. Wisps of fear, like thin black smoke, trickled over Montségur's battlements and infected its occupants. The sanctuary had been defiled. For all that Montségur had been her home from birth, Magda knew she would be glad to leave.

One of Raoul's men had gashed himself while cutting wood for their fires. Magda attended him, laying her hands upon the wound to stem the bleeding, then stitching it closed and smearing it with a honey salve. Raoul, who had brought the man to her, watched her work, a tender expression on his face.

'You are as gifted as your mother,' he murmured.

'I owe my gifts to her teaching,' Magda said and smiled at the soldier. 'Rest easy for the rest of the day, and tomorrow you will scarcely feel the wound.'

He grinned in return. 'I scarcely know it now, madonna.'

'Perhaps you should rest easy, too,' Raoul said to her when the soldier had gone. 'I do not like those dark shadows beneath your eyes.'

'There will be time enough for rest later.' Magda slung the strap of her satchel over her shoulder and stood up. The sudden change of position made her stagger and if Raoul had not caught her, she would have fallen. For a moment, she hung between consciousness and oblivion. Nausea churned in the pit of her stomach and cold sweat broke out on her body. She heard Raoul call out for help.

'It is nothing,' she mumbled, her lips barely forming the words. 'I am all right.'

More arms supported her and lowered her to a bench. 'Don't just stand there like a fool,' said the voice of Claire de Montvallant, 'fetch a cup of sweet wine.'

'I'm all right,' Magda repeated, 'I stood up too quickly, nothing more.'

'It will not harm you to sit for a moment,' Claire said. 'You take far too much on yourself, and will not heed to those who tell you to slow down, even your own mother.' She reached up, took the cup that Raoul handed to her, and set it against Magda's lips. 'Drink. I am playing the healer now.'

Obediently Magda sipped the wine. It was a Gascon brew, fortified with sugar, and it warmed her veins, dispelling the sweat and nausea. Her body craved the sweetness, and before she knew it, she had finished the entire cup. 'Now I truly won't be able to stand up,' she said ruefully.

'I'll carry you back to your pallet in your mother's room,' Raoul said. 'You can lie down for a while.'

'No, I cannot, I . . .'

Stooping, Raoul lifted her in his arms. 'When you reach my years and experience, you realise that there is no such word as "cannot",' he told her as he set off.

Bridget was on her way out of the tiny chamber she shared

with Magda, but when Raoul appeared, she stepped aside to let him enter, and then followed him back inside.

Magda had recovered from her faintness, but the wine had made her dizzy. Raoul laid her down on the bed. 'She collapsed,' he said.

Bridget set her hand upon Magda's forehead. 'Lie still, daughter,' she murmured.

'I am all right. I stood up too quickly.'

Bridget lifted her brows.

Magda coloured beneath her mother's knowing scrutiny. 'There is nothing the matter,' she persisted, trying to keep the fear out of her voice.

'And nothing that cannot wait for an afternoon of rest,' Bridget said. 'Besides, with a cup of Gascon wine inside you, your healing skills will be impaired, to say the least. Close your eyes and I will wake you in a while.'

Magda struggled, but her lids were like lead weights and the bed had never seemed so comfortable. Her mother's palm upon her forehead was soothing and cool. There would be no visions, it promised, only the peace of dreamless sleep.

Bridget stayed until Magda slept, then quietly left the room. Raoul was waiting for her outside the door. 'I wish she had not returned when you took her out to meet Dominic,' she said grimly. 'She should have gone with him. It would not have mattered about the rest of us.'

'It would have mattered to her,' Raoul replied. 'By the same token, I need not have come from Montvallant and volunteered to stay here. Nor yourself . . . You are not a Cathar.'

'But Montségur is my home.' She gave him a tired smile and touched his cheek. 'I suppose we all have our reasons, however foolish. I am glad that you have come.'

He shrugged. 'There was nothing left for me at Montvallant but the dust of memories. I used to think Claire was mad when she said it was the spirit that mattered and all else was dross, but now I know what she meant. I can take

the soil of Montvallant, of my life, and scatter it to the wind.'
He kissed her fingers as she withdrew them from his cheek
and, leaving her, went down to the bailey.

Claire was waiting for him, taking her turn to grind ears
of grain into coarse flour, using a small hand quern. When
she saw Raoul, she handed the task to another woman and,
dusting her hands on her gown, hurried over to him.

'How is she?'

'She's resting now, and seems all right.' He made a face
and glanced around the compound. A bitter wind was
blowing, grey clouds boiling up across the mountains to the
south, promising heavy rain. 'Bridget is worried about her.'
He drew Claire into the lee of the wall and positioned himself
to shelter her from the wind.

'Yes, I know.' She looked at him. 'I think Magda is with
child. It is not only her work and worrying about the soldiers
outside our walls that have put dark shadows beneath her
eyes. It will be a difficult journey for her when the time
comes.'

Raoul's brows drew together. 'You do not know for sure
though?'

'No, but I know the signs.' Her expression was an ambivalent mingling of pleasure and apprehension. 'She is carrying
my grandchild. As a Cathar, and Simon de Montfort's
victim, I ought not to approve, but in my heart, I wish her
well.'

'It will be my grandchild, too,' Raoul said and braced
himself for Claire's response. They had known each other all
their lives, had lived and loved and come to a parting of the
ways. If anything, that parting had deepened their bond, but
he had never told her about the night he had spent with
Bridget, and the child born of their union.

'That, too, I have strongly suspected,' Claire said wryly.
'You need not look so anxious. Once, I admit, I would have
been devoured by jealousy, but if I look back now, I can see
the reasons, both yours and mine, for Magda's existence.'

'How . . . how did you come to suspect? Raoul asked, relieved but curious. 'Did Bridget say anything?'

Claire shook her head. 'Bridget has never spoken of Magda to me, nor do I expect her to. We respect each other's privacy. No, I watched Magda grow up, and sometimes she reminded me of you, but it was not until Guillaume came to Montségur that I saw the true resemblance. When they stand side by side, it is clear to see they are brother and sister.' Her smile, although sad, was warm. 'I love Magda as if she were my own daughter.'

Autumn tightened its hold on the fortress, the bitter mountain winds and sleeting rain making life uncomfortable for besieger and besieged alike. Hugh d'Arcis, commander of the crusader camp, increased the wages and extended the periods of leave in the valley, but he held those on duty to a rigid discipline.

Within the fortress, firewood and provisions were meticulously rationed in the hopes of conserving them until the spring. On foggy days, foraging parties managed to creep out of Montségur, avoid the soldiers and obtain provisions in the valley. Occasionally the sympathetic villagers would find ways of reaching the castle with supplies, but they were only a trickle, and the danger was terrible.

Magda's pregnancy continued to sap her strength and her vitality. Even ordinary healing tasks left her exhausted. Her body rejected food; even the smell of it nauseated her, and the soothing possets brewed by her mother were all she could keep down. People watched her and worried, but there was little they could do for her except pray and allow her to rest. They protected her as best they could, but they could not protect her from the nightmares.

Friar Bernard twisted and writhed on his narrow pallet, beset by the torments of the damned that made the sores from his hair shirt and the stripes from his latest flogging seem no more than the caress of a lover's fingers. The pain was exquisite and he sucked it into himself, knowing that when it reached its crescendo, he must surely explode into a thousand particles and become one with his Saviour. Was this how Christ had suffered on the cross? Oh, to feel some of the pain and know that it linked him with the God he so devoutly served.

He was climbing the rock of Montségur barefoot like a penitent, a cross of human ashes drawn upon his forehead. The stones of the mountainside cut his feet and he felt the blood running between his toes, even as Christ's blood had run on the cross. The pain in his chest as he climbed was as cruel as the thrust of a lance, but he knew when he reached the fortress at the summit, he would find his prize.

There were guards on the walls, but he had God's protection and they did not see him walk past them, nor did they see the bloody footprints that marked his trail through the castle. The heretics were sleeping, crowded together like corpses in a charnel house, and his heart cramped with savage joy to see the level of squalor in which they dwelt. A host of them were praying in the hall, their backs stooped to make one huge monster, each individual forming a cobbled black scale.

A little to one side, a soldier was watching the beast, a bearded soldier with the cross of truth embroidering his breast. Bernard tried to gain his attention and order him to strike at the creature, but the knight neither heard nor saw the frantic signals and, with gut-lurching shock, Bernard realised that the knight was one of the heretics, too.

Raising his arm, Bernard prepared to call down destruction upon the entire hellspawn gathering, but a white-hot pain stabbed through his limbs, arresting all motion. Even his feet ceased to bleed. A dazzling brightness encircled him, separating him from the Cathars, obscuring his vision and lifting him up. He was borne upon it, his agony so intense that it was beautiful. He floated through the roof and found himself upon the battlements. It was not the direction he had intended to take and he struggled against the strands of energy meshing him fast. He was propelled rapidly to the edge of the crenellations and catapulted powerfully outward and upward like a stone from a trebuchet.

The light exploded around him in myriad rainbow spangles that gradually winked out and vanished, leaving him to wade through a filthy black murk that filled his eyes and nose and mouth, clogging and suffocating. He struggled to reach the surface, but the morass stretched in all directions and he didn't have the strength to free himself.

'Jesus Christ, help me!' he croaked with his dying breath, and woke up choking to discover his blanket was smothering his face and twisted tightly around his body. His heart was pounding so hard he thought it would leave his body. He took huge gulps of air and felt the humiliating burn of urine on his thighs.

When finally he gained sufficient control of his shaking hands, he kindled the small clay oil lamp at his bedside and sat up. His starved lungs were deprived again as he ceased breathing and stared at his feet, at the mottling of bruises and the dried blood that was caked between his toes.

Magda's eyes flung wide, and she awoke panting and sweat-drenched on her pallet. The dark terror had been so close. She had touched it, and it was so full of hatred that even its centre was black. Casting it forth from Montségur had stretched her abilities to the full.

She sat up, pushed her hair out of her eyes and reached for the cup of wine at the side of the pallet to rinse the taste of fear from her mouth. Her hands were trembling, and there was a sharp, squeezing pain through the base of her spine, lunging down into her pelvis.

'No,' she denied, and pressed a protective hand across her womb. 'Oh, by the Light, please, no!' The wine spilled into her lap, flooding her pale chemise with a red stain even as the sudden gush of blood from between her thighs reddened the mattress.

CHAPTER 45

Dominic hunched into the squirrel-fur lining of his cloak and, with his knife, slit the seal on the package that the messenger had just handed to him. Simon's seal and Simon's neat, decisive writing. No scribe had been allowed anywhere near this

Simon de Montfort, Earl of Leicester, high Steward of England, to his dearest brother Dominic, greetings.

Herein is the list of you asked me to obtain in respect of succour on your pilgrimage.

Witness myself at Portsmouth, this first day of October, year of our Lord twelve hundred and forty-three.

That was it – succinct, to the point, nothing to incriminate either himself or Dominic should the letter be intercepted. A second sheet of parchment detailed the places where they would be welcomed and no questions asked. Dominic fished in his pouch and presented the messenger with a coin.

'No reply,' he said, and rolling up the parchments, tucked them down between hauberk and gambeson. The man bowed and returned to his horse. Dominic watched the messenger pick his way carefully back down the mountain towards the main camp at its foot, then turned to look at the fortress towering over his head. Grey stone, grey sky, grey hopes of holding out. And ultimately, ash, too, was grey.

'Shall I load 'er up, then, my lord?' asked Jules, the serjeant in charge of the morning shift manning the enormous trebuchet. Hugh d'Arcis had had it dragged up the mountain in pieces and assembled within range of Montségur's outerworks. 'Cold 'un today,' he added, blowing on his hands. 'Could do with a good bonfire to warm us up.' He gave a yellow grin. 'Ever smelled heretics roasting?'

'I could keep warm all winter long on the amount of hot air that comes out of your mouth!' Dominic retorted witheringly. 'Yes, load her up. They'll be hurling stones at us soon enough.'

'Right away, my lord!'

Another soldier brought him a cup of wine and a flat loaf sliced half-open and filled with pungent goat's cheese. Dominic didn't feel like eating, but he took the food and bit unconcernedly as if his mind were on the mundane and not on the escape that was so close now, just awaiting word from Magda. His own part was fulfilled. How slowly the time was passing, and how quickly they were making progress with this damned trebuchet. A couple of times he had managed to commit minor sabotage, but dared not try again too soon for fear of raising suspicions and a corresponding level of security. Hugh d'Arcis was a cautious, hard-bitten commander who would relieve Dominic of his post in an instant rather than house so much as a single doubt. Thus far, Dominic congratulated himself sourly, he had not set a foot wrong.

Avoiding Friar Bernard in the camp below had been his most trying problem. The man was everywhere. Dominic had circumvented recognition by letting his beard and hair grow unchecked – such concealment offered protection against the mountain cold, too – and by keeping to the background as much as possible. The command of this trebuchet post had been an ideal opportunity to escape up the mountain away from potential discovery, but it had its price.

He heard the counterweight slamming down and the rico-chet of stone on stone. His gut reacted first as it always did: with a sudden contraction like the jolt of the trebuchet as the wedge was yanked out of the windlass. Then the memo-ries would whip into his skull and crash through barriers more than twenty years old to reach and pierce the small boy within. He knew the destruction of which a trebuchet was capable, could only pray that Magda, Bridget and his mother were not tending the wounded anywhere near the outer defences that were now so vulnerable to crusader attack. Each time they launched another stone, he flinched, and each time the garrison above retorted, he remembered his father. Oh Christ, this was mad, and he would go mad soon if he could not escape with Magda.

Thump. 'Stone!' bellowed Jules, and they all scuttered for cover like rabbits. Crash. Pebbles bounced away into the trees. Soldiers ran to retrieve the rock that had been hurled at them and prepared to reload it into their own trebuchet. One of them chalked a crude sketch on the boulder – a Cathar tied to a stake. A groove of muscle tightened in Dominic's jaw. As they cranked the windlass he looked away and saw Luke de Béziers riding along the track towards him. Abandoning the trebuchet, Dominic hastened to meet him.

'I've had the details from Simon,' he announced in a lowered voice as the Templar dismounted. 'Tell Magda. We can leave as soon as she's ready.'

Luke's expression was troubled as he unstrapped a bundle from his crupper. 'That might not be for a while.' He paused, his hand on a buckle and looked at Dominic. 'Did you know Magda was with child?'

Dominic's mouth was suddenly dry. There was no joy in Luke's expression. 'No, I didn't.'

'She's been taking too much on herself – tending the injured, keeping the hysterical ones calm, balancing the evil surrounding us with her own spirit. It has drained her white. We have tried our best to shield her, but in the end she . . . I'm sorry, Dominic,' Luke said. 'She started bleeding last night. Bridget couldn't stop it and she lost the child.'

Dominic thought that his heart had stopped beating, but it could not be so because he was still alive, because it hurt to breathe, and the wind was drying his open eyes, forcing him to blink.

Luke's calloused hand pressed upon Dominic's taut shoulder. 'I'm sorry.'

Thump, bellow, crash. The noises rang hollowly inside Dominic's skull. Behind him he heard the men of the trebuchet team discussing in obscene detail what they would do to the Cathar women before they were burned. Heat stung his eyes and he clenched his fists, digging his nails into his palms while he controlled himself. 'Will she be all right?'

'There is no one more skilled in the healing arts than Bridget.'

Dominic examined the Templar's face. It was indomitable and compassionate, and there were things he was not saying, terrifying things. What if Magda died? Or if she was too weak to travel when the final assault came? Darkness encroached upon him, the sense of being trapped and helpless. The thump of the trebuchet's counterweight was like a fist smashing him into the earth.

'I cannot do this any more.' He swallowed with revulsion. 'I have to see her, Luke; take me into Montségur.'

Luke regarded him with a perplexed and heavy stare. 'You and I and Raoul are the bridge between Montségur and the world over which any survivors are to cross. You have to endure.' And then his face changed. 'Company from the camp below,' he warned softly. 'Hugh d'Arcis, no less.'

Dominic turned to look and knew as it began to drizzle that his misery was complete. From all sides, thoughts and feelings clamoured for his attention and had to be denied as he projected himself into the role of competent, pragmatic battle commander.

'I'll give you these books later,' Luke murmured, restrapping the bundle to his crupper and swinging into the saddle. 'And I'll see what I can do about smuggling you into Montségur.' Leaning down, he gripped Dominic's rigid shoulder for an instant before riding off.

Bracing himself, Dominic left the Templar and walked across to the commander-in-chief of the crusading army.

Hugh d'Arcis sat astride his tall brown horse, studying the work in progress. 'Good as far as it goes,' he nodded. 'But I think we would make more headway if we moved the stone-thrower a couple of degrees to the left. We have to knock out the trebuchets on their outerworks if we're to get any closer.'

'Yes, my lord,' Dominic said woodenly. Rigors shook him and his teeth had started to chatter.

'Are you ill, messire?' D'Arcis leaned towards him.

'Something I ate,' Dominic said quickly. 'I'm all right.' The last thing he needed was to be sent back down the mountain.

D'Arcis grunted. 'Not losing your stomach for the task?' he asked shrewdly.

'No, my lord.' Christ, d'Arcis was too perceptive. 'Just sick of waiting. Day in, day out, it gets to you.'

'Aye, they're determined, all right,' d'Arcis said with grudging respect. 'You could almost admire them if they weren't so tainted with heresy.'

Dominic compressed his lips and did not reply.

'There'll be more soldiers coming up to you later this week – Basque mountain men.' D'Arcis turned his horse. 'They'll be stationed at your post, but they have their own commander and instructions.'

'Yes, my lord.'

The horse took three strides and d'Arcis drew rein and looked round. 'Is that Templar knight a friend of yours?'

Never tell a lie, Dominic thought, his mind racing. 'We met a few months ago when we were both hunting in the mountains,' he said with an indifferent shrug. 'He seeks me out sometimes by way of acquaintance but I don't know him well.'

'Has he said anything strange to you?'

Dominic prayed that the look he gave d'Arcis would pass for bewilderment. 'My lord?'

'Rumour has it that his father is a leading Cathar.'

Dominic continued to stare as if the notion were so shocking that it had robbed him of speech.

'Don't be seen in his company,' d'Arcis warned. 'It will sully your own reputation, and I don't want to dismiss a good man.' He dug in his heels and his stallion swung into its heavy stride.

A mist was descending over the mountain, obscuring everything. Dominic felt a similar fog enter his soul, as if all the evil forces of the world were gathering to strangle the light.

A bowl of broth in her hands, Claire tiptoed into the curtained-off section of the hall where Magda lay. Bridget sat at the bedside, watching her daughter's pale, barely breathing form with a troubled gaze. Magda had lost so much blood that her body had been brought to the threshold of death. Bridget had done what she could, but her daughter's life still hung in the balance.

'I have brought you some soup,' Claire said. 'How is she?'

'No better, no worse,' Bridget said. 'The bleeding has stopped and there is no fever, but her spirit is wandering the realm between this life and the next, and I cannot reach her. If only I were not so tired.' She pressed the palm of her hand to her aching forehead.

'We are all praying for her.'

Bridget forced an exhausted smile. 'I know. I have felt

your love and been comforted.' Taking the bowl of broth, she half-heartedly sipped.

Claire knew Bridget was already bearing a burden of grief. Matthias had died three nights ago. It had been a golden release for his soul to escape the pain-riddled, contorted old body, but they all mourned the loss of his wisdom.

'Shall I sit with her a while?'

'Would you?' Bridget rose to her feet. 'Hold her hand, talk to her, don't let her slip away.' After a final, lingering look at her daughter, Bridget went out into the hall.

Claire smoothed the bedclothes around Magda and rearranged her heavy blond braid. The rise and fall of her breasts barely stirred the coverlet and her skin was alabaster-pale. When she took Magda's fingers, Claire felt their iciness strike through her own warm skin. The pulse was a faint throb, barely enough to keep a shadow alive. With her free hand, she fumbled open her copy of the Gospels and started to read aloud. Magda remained cold and unresponsive, and once it seemed to Claire that her pulse faltered. Quickly she put the book down and leaned over her.

'Stay.' She squeezed Magda's cold fingers. 'You must stay!' Her thoughts scurried, seeking to forge a link between the two of them, something that would hold Magda to life. 'I know you must be in pain and I know how much you grieve for your child. She would have been mine, too . . . my grand-daughter.' Tears filled Claire's eyes and she brushed them away on the back of her hand. She had been present at the end of Magda's traumatic premature labour, had seen the baby, its hands perfectly formed and as tiny and delicate as daisy petals. A child of the Light returned to her source even before she had drawn breath.

'I lost my child, too,' she said, stroking the frozen hand in hers. 'The pain never goes away. I saw him a few times at the wet nurse's breast. They bound up my own breasts to stop my milk and they separated us. I wanted him so badly and at the same time I was so afraid I would hate him that

I was driven to the point of madness.' She stared intently at
the pale face upon the pillows, searching its stillness for a
response. 'What is he like that you should want him above
the other men you could have chosen?'

Magda made no answer, but Claire sensed she was
listening and that she had gained at least a little space of
time. And time for Montségur was running out faster than
grains of sand through a punctured sack. They still had
enough food stockpiled to hold out for months to come, and
the winter rains had started to fill the dangerously low
cisterns, but the sheer doggedness of the crusaders was
wearing them down. The trebuchet that had been erected
near the summit slammed rocks at their outerworks day in,
day out, and sometimes through the night. Conditions were
crowded, with no place to sleep in peace even during the
brief lulls in enemy activity. Nor did the crusading troops
show any signs of leaving for the winter months as had been
the case in previous campaigns. D'Arcis, it seemed, had the
support and determination to stay outside Montségur for as
long as it took to see it fall.

Claire pressed Magda's hand. They could not let him
snuff out the light. He might destroy the lamp, but the
precious flame must be preserved and found a new setting
in which to shine. She could feel it guttering beneath her
fingers. 'Don't leave us,' she implored Magda. 'You must
not give up!'

In the hall she heard the sound of prayers being led by
Bishop Bertrand Marty and Chretien de Béziers. A baby
belonging to one of the soldiers' women wailed fractiously,
and the sound sawed through the curtains and into Claire's
heart like a dull knife. She wondered if Magda could hear
it.

Male voices approached the curtain. She recognised
Raoul's and the deep rumble of Luke de Béziers, but the
third one eluded her even while it held a familiar note – deep
with a husky edge. The curtain was drawn aside and Claire

glimpsed the cramped squalor of the hall and the backs of the other Perfecti bowed in prayer, and then her view was blocked by a tall young man whose black hair and beard framed bold, rugged features. His looks, his presence, evoked such memories that the world dissolved around her and she became a terrified young wife, sprawled in the rushes of her own chamber, her raptor's weight grinding her thighs apart.

She stumbled to her feet and, in blind panic, spread her arms, shielding Magda. 'You cannot come in here!' she cried.

He ignored her, pushing past her in true de Montfort tradition in order to fulfil his own need.

'Let him.' Raoul grasped her sleeve and pulled her to one side. 'He hasn't got long and he is taking a great risk being here at all.'

For a moment Claire struggled against Raoul's grip, then capitulated and pressed herself against his comforting stability, gripping him as if he were a rock planted in an expanse of shifting quicksand.

Dominic knelt at the bedside. Magda's face held the same translucent stillness he remembered seeing on Alais de Montfort's, lying in state in her open coffin. It was a memory that had stayed with him down the years because most of the bodies he had seen had been mutilated by war, and she had seemed in contrast as pure as unflawed glass. The similarity now between her and Magda terrified him.

They had told him she had lost too much blood, that everything possible had been done to keep her alive, but it still might not be enough. They told him the child had been a girl. The words had meant nothing then. Now, he understood. Grasping her cold right hand, he pushed his fingers through the spaces between hers, weaving the link as it had been woven before in the act of creation.

'Magda, I'm here. Can you hear me? Can you feel me? Remember, remember this? You're not leaving me, I won't let you. I need you. We all need you!'

The twin notes of determination and anguish in the man's

voice caused Claire to lift her head from Raoul's shoulder. She stared at the hard brown hand pushed against Magda's, the black hair bent against the shining blond braid, and sensed the pulsing strength of the life force within him. Her son. The thought hit her in the solar plexus like a blow. Perhaps he looked like his hellspawn father, perhaps he had the latter's driving strength of will, but the direction was different. It was the memory that haunted her, not the man. But how to separate one from the other? Leaving Raoul, she knelt opposite Dominic at the bedside, and taking Magda's other hand, added her own prayers to the passion of his.

It was cold and dark and there was weakness, blood and pain. Magda felt these things and avoided them. Why should she return to such discomfort when before her rippled a field of glowing rainbow light, alive with the memory of how it had been not to have a body? Unfettered, harmonious joy. At the other side of the field was a doorway, and she knew that once she had passed through its portal, nothing of her present mortal existence would remain except the uninhabited husk of her body on a different plane.

Uncertain, she hesitated, lingering near the pain, aware that something was incomplete and, without it, she could not progress. Voices vibrated along the fragile silver thread connecting her spirit to her body. One owned a deeper resonance that struck so strong a chord that the rainbow field shimmered around her and merged into one bright light. Again and again the cry rang across the levels. Here was the part that was incomplete. Energy flowed through her, illuminating the silver cord down which she must return to the solid particles of her earthly form, and she was drawn irresistibly back towards it.

She felt the jarring sensation of soul merging with body, the heaviness and pain. Slowly she opened her eyes and saw the hall at Montségur and Dominic leaning over her, his face wet and his hand tightly laced through hers, binding her to life with his will. She breathed his name, the slightest thread of sound.

'Oh, my love!' he said hoarsely, and drew her tightly against him. The strength of his body flowed into hers and the light of the other world receded, leaving a crystal residue of heightened awareness.

She touched his face, her heart overflowing with love and grief. 'You should not be here; it is far too dangerous!' she whispered weakly. 'But I am glad, so glad.'

'Hush, it's all right.'

She held on to him for a long time, drawing on the comfort of his presence and the radiance of his life force until she knew that, for his own safety, she had to let him go. 'You cannot stay here longer,' she murmured, holding his face in her hands and looking into his eyes. 'You will be found out.'

'It is you that matters; I do not care about myself.'

'Then for my sake, go.'

Dominic started to shake his head, but when he would have spoken, she pressed her fingers across his lips. 'As soon as I'm recovered, we'll leave, I promise you.'

His eyes never left her face as he kissed her fingers and slowly stood up. Her colour was much improved and her breathing was steadier. It was he who felt drained, but then he had given unstintingly of his own energy to bring her back from the brink of death. 'Do not keep me waiting,' he said with an anxious smile. 'I love you.' He kissed her and went to the curtain, giving her a lingering look over his shoulder.

The woman who had knelt with him at Magda's side was regarding him with agitation, as if she wanted to say something but was afraid to do so. Before the moment drew out, however, she lowered her gaze and busied herself with Magda. Thinking no more of the moment and too preoccupied with other things, Dominic went out into the hall, where the Cathars were still praying, and sought Raoul and Luke. In low tones he told them about the detail of Basque climbers that was to be sent up the mountain. 'D'Arcis has a plan up his sleeve. Be on your guard against any attempt to scale the walls. We're moving the trebuchet in the morning – east-ward. I'll try and hinder matters as much as I can, but I have to be careful. D'Arcis has a keen eye.' He gave Luke a warning look. 'We were seen and remarked upon yesterday morning. D'Arcis is suspicious of you. I dare not make contact again for a while at least.'

Luke grimaced. 'It was always a risk,' he said. 'All right, we'll just have to be careful.'

Raoul said curiously to Dominic, 'How did you manage to escape your men tonight?'

'I told them I had a tryst. My serjeant thinks I'm at the foot of the mountain enjoying myself with a whore.' Dominic made a face. Some lies sullied the mouth with their telling. 'It's a good excuse to be sluggish in the morning, too.'

He followed Luke from the hall and down a dark stone corridor that led through the bowels of the castle to a small postern doorway at the rear of a storage cave. The Cathar woman who had attended the sickroom was waiting for them and, as they approached, Dominic saw that she was trem-bling violently. Nevertheless, as he drew level, the hand she set upon his arm to detain him was resolute. Luke, after one assessing glance, moved discreetly away into the depths of the storeroom, murmuring something patently fabricated about having lost his cloak pin.

'Lady?' The hair prickled at Dominic's nape, for there was a strange expression in her eyes. Hunger, he would have said, and loathing, and something else, deep and hard to define.

She studied his face intently by the flickering light of the torch in the wall bracket and slowly shook her head. 'You look so much like him,' she whispered.

'Like who?' He heard the hollow ring of his own voice and became aware of how cold it was down here, and dark, the shadows scarcely kept at bay by the fickle light of the torch.

'Like . . . like your father.'

He had to lean towards her to catch her words as her whisper sank to little more than the pressure of ordinary breath. 'He was older and greyer, more heavily set.' Her hand left his sleeve, and although her eyes remained fixed on him, it seemed to Dominic that she was looking through him at something terrible.

And then it came to him and he wondered why he had not realised it earlier at Magda's bedside. 'You are my mother,' he said. Even now, with the knowledge upon him, he did not recognise the cry of blood, only the cry itself.

'I am the one who gave you birth; that much is true,' she said in a hollow voice, 'but I never had the opportunity to be more than that, nor do I know if it would have been within me. All I can say is that I was so badly wounded by what was done to me that for a long time I wounded those around me, too, so that I would have companionship in my suffering. It was not until I came to Montségur that I truly began to heal and find peace.' She raised her chin and steadied the quiver in her voice. 'I can feel that your spirit is good . . .'

'But you cannot see it while you still see my father?'

Her gaze, meeting his, was intense. 'There is an abyss within me that stops the person I am becoming the person I want to be. All it takes is a leap of faith, but I am frightened I will not leap far enough and fall into the abyss and he will be waiting for me there.'

'I think that everyone has such a place within themselves,' Dominic answered, knowing that he would not have to feign exhaustion when he returned to his men. He had never felt so drained or uncertain as he did now. 'I cannot see a black friar without breaking out in a cold sweat of terror. I am afraid of failure; I am afraid that one day the hunger within me will consume me as it consumed my father. When I reached out to Magda, half of it was terror for myself. What would I become without her?' Shrugging, he took a step back from her. Revealing his deeper levels to this woman who had every claim on him and no claim at all was definitely setting one foot over the abyss of which she spoke. 'I have to go,' he said curtly.

She nodded and took her hand from his arm. 'I'm glad to have met you. You have haunted me for a long time.'

He smiled at her bleakly. 'As you have haunted me. I wish it could have been different.'

Her jaw was taut with effort. 'Walk in the Light, my son,' she said before turning away, and as she did so, Dominic saw the sparkle of her tears.

CHAPTER 46

The January night was brittle with cold, with no cloud cover to protect the mountaintop from the freezing, pure light of the stars. Fuel supplies were low in the fortress, and only essential watch fires burned on the heights. The ordinary people huddled together for warmth, and the Perfecti, like the rock, endured. Dying from cold was easier than dying in the fire, and of death itself, the Perfecti were not afraid.

Magda practised the discipline that Bridget had taught her for generating body heat and, as the warmth surged through her in pleasant, tingling waves, was able to unclench herself.

'Two more nights and you'll be gone,' said Raoul. He was fumbling to buckle on his sword belt, his hands made clumsy by the cold. With a pang she noticed that his hair was thinner, almost white, and his finger joints knotted. When had he grown old? All their strength was being sucked away by the greedy, devouring thing down the mountain. And her love stood in its very maw.

She came to help him attach his sword to his belt. 'A part of me will always remain here, and a part of you . . . of everyone in Montségur, will live in me for ever,' she said with quiet reassurance.

He cleared his throat twice before he spoke, and even then his voice was husky. 'More than you know.' He brushed his thickened knuckles gently across her cheek.

'But I do know,' she answered steadily. 'There is nothing you could tell me that would come as a surprise.'

A sad smile deepened the grooves between nostril and mouth corner. 'You are Bridget's daughter. It could be no other way.'

He left to check the sentries on night watch and, sighing deeply, Magda began to take stock of the items that she was bringing with her on her journey to a new life. Her portion was not great, for they were of a necessity travelling light. She had custody of the most important books, the knowledge that was her birthright, money to pay their way, to pay Dominic's brother, and to found her convent. She also had the cup that was to be given to Luke.

Tracing the engraved pattern on the cup's shining surface with her forefinger, she placed her other hand lightly over her womb. Despite having almost died at the time of her miscarriage, she had suffered no lasting harm. The time would ripen again even as season followed season, as fallow was ploughed and sown and harvested. She still mourned her lost baby, snatched untimely from her by the insidious darkness outside their walls. As her child had died, she had felt the force of the hatred growing and swelling. Daily it sucked against their barriers, seeking a way inside. Sometimes she could almost see it lurking in the shadow of the walls, waiting.

A sound of self-irritation escaped her lips. Even now it attacked, sowing doubt in the hope of reaping despair. Magda breathed deeply and concentrated her mind. The shadows surrounding the torchlight became less thick and the flame itself leaped in the sconce. She would not yield.

Raoul paced the wall walk and talked to the soldiers on duty. The air was so cold that it was like breathing broken glass. Beneath his mouflon-lined boots the wooden boards crunched with rime and the tiled roofs of the bailey sheds far below glittered like the encrustations on an archbishop's robes. A powdering of snow had fallen earlier in the day and might do so again if this crystalline weather broke. He glanced skyward and prayed that there would not be any severe falls for the next week at least in order to give Magda and Dominic sufficient time to escape.

Peering over the battlements, he could see the crusaders' campfires ringing the mountain at regular intervals like a hundred malevolent golden eyes. The slopes themselves were peppered with outposts, one of them Dominic's, and a beacon of hope among all the other portents of destruction. He walked on and tried not to think of the odds stacked against them, comforting himself with the thought that thus far Dominic had made a nonsense of all such odds and that amidst the confusion there was a pattern if only he had the vision to discern it. The sons of Simon de Montfort had been chosen as the guardians of the light that their father had fought to extinguish.

Blowing on his hands, Raoul went to inspect the eastern barbican, which commanded the outerworks of their defences. The edifice stood on a steep escarpment, attached to the main fortress by a narrow ledge of stone with horri-fying sheer drops on either side.

Guillaume was in command of the barbican guards tonight, and he greeted his father with the offer of a drink from his wine flask. The breath that swirled from him in a white vapour smelled strongly of the brew, but his balance was steady and his speech gave no hint of being slurred.

Raoul declined the proffered skin. 'Are you not being careless? A man needs his wits about him to take night duty on this wall.'

'I do have my wits,' Guillaume retorted. 'I heard you coming a mile away. If I had wanted, I could have had this skin concealed under my cloak, and you none the wiser.'

'You cannot conceal your breath,' Raoul said stiffly, and continued along the wall walk. Grimacing at his father's spine, Guillaume took another defiant swig and followed him.

Two guards were leaning against the stonework, faces hidden in shadow, voices low and intent.

'God's life!' Raoul snarled. 'Is this what you call being on duty? I've seen housewives in a marketplace better prepared than this! You two, pick up your spears and . . .' His gaze fell upon the coils of rope gleaming in the starlight, upon the flash of a grapnel biting the edge of the wall. He clawed for his sword, his gut dissolving as he recognised the terrible danger that stalked here. Every soldier of Montségur's garrison was known to him by face if not by name, and these held neither in his memory. Steel shimmered in their hands; the cold glitter reflected in their eyes. Behind Raoul, Guillaume swore and threw down the wineskin to draw his own weapon.

'Go!' Raoul snapped without taking his gaze from the men as one sidled to his left and one to his right. 'Raise the alarm. Run, damn your hide. Do as you're told for once in your life!'

Guillaume ran. The clash of sword upon sword vibrated through his skull, throbbed down into his gut and twisted his loins with sick guilt. He was brought up short on the edge of the open high stone corridor by another intruder. Near the man's feet a barbican guard lay in a widening puddle of blood.

Guillaume refused to believe this was happening, that they were being attacked by stealth in the middle of the night and, if the attack succeeded, the blame would be his for complacence and lack of attention to detail. 'No!' he roared, and leaped at the enemy soldier.

The ground underfoot was treacherous, slippery with rime, and Guillaume skidded. In trying to save himself he lost his sword over the edge of the chasm. His opponent's long knife sliced into his body, but Guillaume's unsteady momentum turned the blade aside from all vital points. He stumbled against the soldier, and the impact of his weight brought them both down, Guillaume on top, thrusting his enemy's shoulder against a bulge of rock beyond which there was nothing but the darkness of space. A knee butted his groin. The dagger flashed towards his throat. Guillaume caught the wrist in mid-motion and locked and twisted, his forearm and biceps straining. Blood ran down his side. He felt its hot burn in the silvered cold. His arm was tiring and he knew that in a moment he was going to lose his grip. 'No!' he sobbed again and, with gritted teeth, made a final effort.

The dagger clattered sideways. His opponent struggled, trying to buck him off, but Guillaume clung like lichen to a rock. He struck with his fist, felt his knuckles split upon teeth, struck again, heedless of the pain. The other man choked on blood. Guillaume wrestled his own knife from his sheath and struck a third time, and a fourth, and a fifth, until the point grated on rock and the soldier beneath him ceased to writhe. Weeping with effort and shock, Guillaume heaved his dagger free. Bracing himself on all fours, he vomited up the wine that he had so profligately consumed.

The barbican was silent. All sounds of struggle had ceased and, with a terrible awareness that he was already too late, Guillaume staggered towards the main fortress to raise the alarm.

Raoul's cheek was pressed into the slippery white frosting of the wall-walk boards. The hand that was trapped beneath his body was warm with blood; the other one gripped the planks, caught there in spasm. No strength remained within him to move it, his life draining away through the wound in his chest, which had been slashed open along the line of the old battle scar from Muret. He would already have been dead, but the severe cold had reduced the flow of blood to a thin trickle. Death encroached slowly, circling him like a beast, biding its time.

He had sold his life dearly. Three Basques sprawled in the starlight beside him, already claimed. It had made no difference to the final outcome. The barbican was lost to the defenders, and with it, the last hope for Montségur. He closed his eyes, too weary to keep them open, and besides, there was nothing to see; the stars had gone out.

Someone rolled him over. 'Dead,' he heard the rough Basque voice grunt.

'Throw him to the kites. There's no need for Christian decency toward a heretic!' growled another voice.

'Seems a pity to waste good armour. Come on, help me get this off him.'

They stripped him of his hauberk, dagger and gambeson, acquisitive as magpies. 'What's this around his neck?'

'It's one of their evil talismans; throw it away!' The voice was spiky with alarm.'

'Might be valuable, might bring me luck. You're just wishing you saw it first!' The Basque mercenary tugged at the cord of the dove-and-chalice medallion.

Raoul tried to thrust away the groping hand. At first his limbs did not answer his command, and then suddenly, as if a prison door had opened, it was easy . . . too easy. He stood up, feeling as light as thistledown. The Basques were crouching over something on the ground, a broken chrysalis that looked strangely familiar. Grunting with effort, they carried it between them to the wall. Heaving it up, they toppled it into the chasm below and leaned over the stone, looking down. A slight thud echoed up, followed by silence. In curiosity Raoul would have pursued the sound into the darkness, but he was prevented by a rippling barrier of light, shimmering with a rainbow brilliance that reached out to absorb him. It was only then, with a feeling of detachment already of the spirit, that he realised this time he truly had crossed the divide between life and death.

Within his tent, Dominic restlessly checked that everything was prepared for the journey – travelling rations, blankets, thick cloaks, waterskins. He chewed his thumbnail, his nerves taut, and wished that they had left the previous week when some of the books and treasure had been smuggled out over the side in baskets attached to ropes. That cargo was now safe in the caves of Ornolac, awaiting collection. Raoul's task and his own was going to be made that much more difficult now that the eastern barbican was crusader-occupied by some of Hugh d'Arcis's best troops. The trebuchet had been dismantled in order that it could be dragged to the summit and lodged in the barbican, where any stone fired was almost bound to score a direct hit.

Dominic sat down cross-legged on his pallet and breathed deeply in and out, emptying his mind, seeking calm, but before he had even found the thread of a shallow tranquil-lity, a young soldier burst into the tent, his expression raw with excitement and fear. 'Lord Dominic, come quickly. Jules and a Basque are killing each other!'

Dominic was more than tempted to tell the lad to let them get on with it, but the pretence had to be maintained. 'All right, I'm coming,' he said, adding irritably, 'Next time, wait outside and crave admittance before you fling in on me like that.' Without enthusiasm, he unfolded his limbs and picked up his sword.

'Yes, my lord.' The youth lowered his eyes and stood aside.

The crowd of soldiers encircling the combatants gave way smartly at Dominic's angry arrival. Jules and the Basque were circling each other, weapons poised as each sought an opening in the other's defence. Both were bleeding from superficial wounds, and neither of them displayed any incli-nation to back down.

Dominic strode between them, his own blade raised. 'Put up your weapons!' he snapped. 'You know the penalty for brawling.'

'I didn't start it!' Jules protested in a voice that was pitched high with indignant rage. 'I won the token fair and square. You can check the dice yourself, my lord; they aren't loaded!'

'Bastard, you cheated!' the Basque spat, and lunged, only

to be brought up short by the swift flicker of Dominic's sword.

'Drop your weapons, both of you!' Dominic commanded. How easy it would be to let go and give vent to all the tension pent up within him and unleash his own violence on the moment. And because it was too easy, he kept a grim rein on his control.

He could tell from the raised voices and the exaggerated gestures that both soldiers had been drinking. These disputes always followed the same monotonous course. Wine, dice, hot words, spilled blood. Even the penalties, ranging from public flogging to death on the gibbet, did not readily deter the men from brawling.

Jules rolled his eyes and slung his sword on the ground. Expression venomous, the Basque dropped his own weapon. 'He stole from me,' he reiterated as Dominic gestured and the crowd began dispersing. Jules furiously started to protest his own side of the matter again.

'Silence!' Dominic's voice was dangerous, but the look in his eyes more so. 'Precisely what are you fighting over? Show me.' He held out his hand.

Jules dared to meet his commander's wintry stare, felt it begin to draw his guts out through his body, and fumbled in the purse at his waist. 'This, my lord, it's mine. I won it fair and square!'

'Liar!' spat the Basque and was prevented from lunging by the glitter of Dominic's blade. Without relaxing his stance, Dominic looked at the talisman that Jules had just reluctantly handed to him. It was a disc of enamelled silver dangling from a grubby cord of plaited red silk, the design that of a cup, or chalice, and rising out of it, a dove in flight.

'Where did you get this?' Dominic demanded with apprehension. God's bones, what did this mean? He raised the tip of the sword to rest it in the hollow of the Basque's throat. 'Tell me, quickly now!'

The mercenary swallowed and, not surprisingly, chose to

cooperate. 'I took it from a dead Cathar on the east barbican, my lord.'

'A dead Cathar?'

'Yes, my lord. A knight, he was – fought like one possessed, but we got him in the end. I took that thing from him as a memento. He had a good hauberk, too, but me and Gaston sold that and split the money.'

Dominic's throat closed. He knew by this token that Raoul must be dead. It had been Raoul's task to inspect the sentinels, make sure they were at their posts. What was he going to do now? His fist closed over the token until the edges bit into the flesh of his palm. 'You should not have gambled with the thing if you set such store by it,' he said harshly. 'A dead heretic's token, perhaps even tainted with blasphemy. I think it best neither of you have it. If I don't mention this to the priest when he takes the next mass, you will count yourselves fortunate, as you will count yourselves fortunate to receive ten stripes of the lash apiece and keep your necks unstretched!'

That was the façade, the crisp, controlled anger of a commanding officer punishing squabbling children, but once he had seen the punishment administered and spoken to the Basque's commanding officer, Dominic retired to his tent, sat on his pallet and put his face in his hands.

Guillaume lay on his mattress, his face buried in his folded arms and angled away from the world towards the wall.

'Papa?' His small daughter patted his shoulder. 'Papa, please don't cry any more.'

Her gentle touch was a barb in Guillaume's wound. 'I'm not crying,' he croaked, and raised his head to show her dry but red-rimmed eyes. There were no tears left in him. 'Look, doucette, just leave me alone. Go and find your mother.'

The child sucked her soft pink underlip. 'Bridget sent me to find you, Papa; she wants to speak to you.' She continued to pat his shoulder.

Groaning, Guillaume sat up and rubbed his hands over his bristly face. He felt dreadful. The flesh wounds of his encounter on the east barbican were sore but healing well – bearable pain. It was the turmoil within that unmanned him, and he could not dull his ache with wine. The very thought of a brimming cup of cool, red poison made him sweat with longing and nausea.

Sancha perched on the edge of his pallet, huge brown eyes fixed on his face with anxious adoration. Trustingly she leaned her head upon his muscular arm. He had betrayed that trust in drink and carelessness, and now the enemy had access by trebuchet to every vulnerable part of Montségur. He reached for her and pulled her to his chest. There had to be a way out for her and Constanza. He dared not believe that he had caused their deaths, too.

Bridget was waiting for him in the small room where the medicinal herbs and roots were prepared and stored for use in treating the sick and wounded. Magda, Claire and Chretien de Béziers were with her.

'Have I been brought here to be judged?' Guillaume asked in a belligerent voice.

'I think that you have judged yourself already.' Advancing years had brought the hint of a quaver to Chretien's reso-nant voice.

'Then what do you want?'

'Your help,' said Bridget.

Guillaume's eyebrows rose to meet the ragged line of his fringe. 'You want my help?' he said incredulously. 'After what happened to the east barbican?' He looked at his mother, and she looked back at him with such compassion and grief in her eyes that he could not bear it.

'Perhaps because of that,' Bridget answered. 'You won't take the crusaders for granted again. You are hurting so badly that unless you make reparations, you will destroy yourself with recrimination.'

'How generous of you to seek to set my mind in order

and grant me your absolution!' Guillaume spat, and turned his back, but he did not walk out. The tears he had thought wrung dry at their source were suddenly hot behind his lids. He pinched the bridge of his nose and squeezed his eyes tightly shut, but knew his breathing was giving him away. 'What do you want me to do?' he asked in a choked voice, not turning around.

Chretien cleared his throat. 'Were you aware that your father was planning to leave Montségur?'

'No.' Guillaume's voice sank to a whisper. 'No, I wasn't. He said nothing to me, but then he wouldn't. He didn't trust me, you see. Fickle and wine-wild. I proved him right, didn't I?' The last word rose to a sob.

'Stop it!' Magda hastened to his side and drew him farther into the room. 'It was his choice to stay with us at Montségur. He could have left long ago, and no one would have prevented him or thought less of him for doing so. He did not tell you because he was sworn to secrecy.'

Guillaume shook his head and wiped his eyes on the side of his hand, but he remained silent and his body became less rigid.

'He was going to take me out of the postern and down to meet Dominic,' she continued. 'If there was trouble, your father and Luke de Béziers were going to deal with it while we made our escape. All the plans have been laid, routes, everything.'

'Dominic?' Guillaume's eyes were suddenly wider than his little daughter's. He gaped at Magda. 'You mean my half-brother? Dominic? . . . Dominic is here?'

She nodded. 'Among the crusaders. We have been soul mates for a long time, and more recently lovers. It was our child that I miscarried.'

Guillaume stared at her in astonishment. He had often wondered which man of the Montségur community she had taken to her bed, but even his wildest imaginings could not have conjured this. Her and Dominic? Jesu!

'I'm so afraid he'll be discovered; he's taking a very great risk. Luke has been his contact, but it's not safe any more. Hugh d'Arcis watches Luke too closely, and the ring of security around us is so tight that he cannot move in and out of Montségur like he used to.'

Guillaume wondered how these things could have existed beneath his nose without his knowledge. Perhaps the drink had rendered him blind to all save his own hatreds, or perhaps because he was so volatile and fickle they had been at pains to conceal their secrets from him. 'Why should your escape be so important?' he asked Magda. On seeing the look that passed between the group, he flinched. 'All right, don't tell me,' he said wearily. 'I know I don't deserve your trust. What do you want me to do?'

Bridget considered him. He had looked inside himself and been horrified at what he had found. That was always the hardest part. Some men and women never came to it, preferring to live shallowly for fear of what lay in the depths, until one day the shallows evaporated and they died of thirst. 'No,' she said in a firm, quiet voice. 'You have a right to know why you are being asked to risk your life.'

Guillaume watched Ramón de Perella knuckle his eyes in exhaustion, and with a heavy sigh, look around the gathering of his most trusted knights. 'We cannot go on,' de Perella said. 'Either we negotiate now for surrender terms while we still have a sting in our tail, or we negotiate in a month's time when we have nothing left to make it worth their while listening.'

'No!' His nephew Pierre-Roger slammed his huge fist down on the trestle like a mallet. 'We won't give them an inch of ground unless they die taking it!'

'We are the ones who are dying,' de Perella said. 'Now they have possession of the barbican, they can kill us at will. I have suffered torments even thinking of surrender. I once swore to turn the mountains red with the blood of those who dared to trespass on this holy mountain, but even I can see that to go on is to prolong our pain.'

His nephew's lip curled in disgust. 'I cannot believe you are advocating this!'

Two weeks ago, Guillaume would have leaped to his feet and taken Pierre-Roger's side in a fury. Now, tempered by grief, guilt and the burden of a terrible responsibility, he remained seated and rode out his first instinctive denial.

'There are secrets here that the Dominicans must never lay their hands upon,' he raised his voice to say, 'but the net has been drawn so tight it has become impossible to make arrangements. Negotiations would give us that opportunity.'

'Secrets?' de Perella gave him a hard look. 'Connected with the mystic women?'

'Yes, sir. My father was supposed to escort Magda to a contact on the mountain, but after what happened at the east barbican—'

'And we all know whose fault that was!' Pierre-Roger flashed nastily.

Guillaume clenched his jaw, but his voice remained level. 'You can say nothing that I have not already said to myself.'

'Don't be too sure!'

'Peace!' de Perella growled. 'Recriminations are a waste of breath. Blame Guillaume and you might as well blame yourself for Avignonet in the first place! To open negotiations will be to open a channel to the world.'

'And what of the Cathars?' Pierre-Roger flung. 'You know what Hugh d'Arcis will do to them!'

'Will it alter anything if we hold out for another month, two at the most? This way at least some of us will keep our lives.' He thrust his head forward to emphasise his words. 'I see no harm in suing for discussion, Pierre. We can always reject the terms if they prove impossible to swallow.'

'I'm choking already!' his nephew sneered.

'Then chew it over properly! There's more at stake here than your pride!'

It was very quiet in the moments after Pierre-Roger slammed out of the room – not that there was anywhere to go to vent his temper. All space and safety had shrunk to a cramped corner of the ward where the shadow of the trebuchet did not reach.

'He'll see the sense of it when he's had time to think,' de Perella said uneasily, as if he did not quite believe his own words. 'He has to.' He stretched his lips at Guillaume in a poor imitation of a smile. 'How do you feel about conducting negotiations as my chief adjutant?'

The dove-and-chalice medallion suspended before him, Dominic concentrated until his eyes started to smart and he was forced to blink, breaking the moment. There was nothing, not even the vibration of a feeling. The fortress shunned him, permitting him no access to Magda.

Dominic replaced the red cord around his neck and regarded his surroundings with loathing. The guardroom of the east barbican was more comfortable by far than a tent, but the very sight of the stones was anathema. Raoul had died here, and so had hope. A trebuchet crowned the battlements and spat stone destruction at the trapped Cathars. And he, too, was trapped.

A fist struck the guardroom door. Dominic tucked the medallion down inside his hauberk. 'Come,' he called brusquely, and stood up.

The door creaked open and Jules stood on the threshold. His recent whipping and Dominic's bad temper had both failed to make a dent in his swaggering nature. 'My lord, the heretics have sent someone out under a banner of truce,' he announced with gleaming eyes. 'They must be getting desperate, eh?'

Dominic's heart quickened. Abandoning his brooding, he shouldered past the little serjeant without a reply and ran up to the battlements. After the briefest look, he snapped a command at the men on duty and hurtled back down the twisting stairs.

Guillaume was barely recognisable. The glow of young manhood was less than a memory in a face that was all bone and cavernous hollows. He was thin to the point of emaciation, pared down to raw, burning spirit. Suffering and hardship were imprinted on his expression. So too was a terrible grief.

'I bear authorisation from Ramón de Perella and Pierre-Roger of Mirepoix to negotiate a truce with Hugh d'Arcis,' Guillaume said formally for the benefit of the men gathered around Dominic, listening. His eyes, however, told a different, more personal story.

Dominic lifted his brow. The unspoken message passed between them, and he swung to the shamelessly inquisitive crowd of soldiers and squires. 'Have you no work?' he snapped. 'Those who haven't, wait my pleasure and I'll soon find you some!' The spectators vanished as rapidly as mist in sunshine. 'Holy God, Guillaume,' he muttered, 'what's been happening up there! I've been worried sick! Magda should be long gone by now!'

'How do you expect that to happen when your soldiers are all over the barbican?' Guillaume's lips drew back from his teeth. 'Nothing moves without their eyes seeing it!'

'They are not my soldiers!' Dominic retorted in a voice no less abrasive. 'I warned your father to be on his guard for just such an assault. I do what I can, full knowing that it is not enough, but I dare not attach suspicion to myself if the escape channel is to be kept open.'

'What use is an escape channel if we cannot reach it!'

'I assume that's why you're here now?' Taking Guillaume's arm, he drew him towards the guardroom. 'Come on, we might as well flay each other in comfort.'

Guillaume's weathered skin took on a deeper hue at the remark. Gritting his teeth, he followed Dominic into the barbican's guardroom, where only a month earlier he himself had sat in comfort, a flagon within easy reach of his hand – too easy.

The warmth of a brazier beckoned him to hold out his hands and experience the luxury of heat. Since late January there had been no fuel except for cooking and the heating of water to clean wounds. Feeling like a traitor, but unable to stop himself, he revelled in the warmth. The sound of wine trickling from a flagon to a cup made him swallow nauseously, his mouth filling with saliva.

'I don't want any,' he said rapidly to Dominic, terrified that he would be unable to resist once the cup was in his hands. 'Since . . . since my father died, I've forsworn all drink except water.'

Dominic gave him a look so sharp, so perceptive that Guillaume lowered and half turned his head. 'I was in command of this barbican on the night he was killed,' he said. 'It was my fault that we were taken by surprise.'

Dominic did not speak. Guillaume risked a glance, but his brother's face was blank of expression. 'Aren't you going to condemn me?' he challenged.

'I'm walking too narrow a ledge myself to lose my balance casting stones at others.' Dominic opened one hand in a wry gesture and took a short swallow of wine. 'What we have to do is get Magda to safety before this place falls, because when it does, there'll be no quarter given.'

'I know.' An aching anxiety filled Guillaume's chest. 'I'm not only here for Magda, I'm here to negotiate for others whose lives might be saved if we surrender now. I have a woman and child in the fortress, neither of them Cathar, and it's the same for many other fighting men. There is no reason why the Church cannot let them go free. While there's a truce for negotiation, you and Magda can escape.'

'As I remember you back in Toulouse, you're hardly the material of which diplomats are made,' Dominic observed drily.

Guillaume grimaced. 'I've changed since then. It alters you irrevocably when you reach thirty years old and see a rip in the fabric of your dreams for every one of those years.

Suddenly you're threadbare to the world . . . I want my daughter to live.'

'I can understand that,' Dominic said grimly and took another hard swallow of the wine. Then he set it well out of his reach.

'Jesu, I'm sorry,' Guillaume said.

Dominic made a small gesture of negation. 'Why should you apologise for my loss? We're here for a purpose other than commiserating with each other. Stick to business; it's safer.'

Guillaume stiffened at Dominic's tone, and all contrition vanished from his eyes. 'Business,' he repeated, jaw tight. 'Bridget has a scheme set for the eve of the spring equinox if I can drag out the negotiations that long.'

'The sooner the better, I would have thought,' Dominic said with a frown.

'No, at the equinox the natural power is easier to harness. Bridget no longer has the strength to conjure a storm out of nothing.' He watched Dominic closely for signs of incredulity, but his half-brother remained undisturbed by the remark.

'So where do we go from here?' Dominic reached again for the goblet, but only to tip the wine into the rushes.

CHAPTER 47

Friar Bernard stared at the fish head on his trencher, and it stared back at him out of sightless, candle-white eyes. Rags of flesh still adhered to its backbone. He stretched out his forefinger and touched the delicate, sharp tracery. How beautiful, how stark and mortal, and how blasphemous of the Cathars to believe that a human soul could be reborn into the body of a fish. Only man had a soul, and when he died, it either entered heaven's bliss, or suffered the torments of hell. The Cathars were going to hell, every last one of them on that mountaintop. He was not going to permit a single one to recant.

'Is the fish troubling your digestion?' inquired Hugh d'Arcis with concern in his voice.

'No, my lord, the fish is excellent.' Bernard pressed his fingertip into one of the stiff, needle-sharp bones until it punctured his skin. A tiny red jewel, vein-dark, glistened. *I will make you fishers of men*. 'I am concerned over your decision to allow any recanting Cathars to survive along with the men and women of the garrison.'

'The siege has gone on far too long already,' said d'Arcis with badly concealed irritation. 'This way, the staunch Cathars will die at the stake and we will obtain the fortress without having to waste any more time or expense. Once Montségur is in our hands, the heretics will never be able to use it again for a base. I tell you, Friar Bernard, and you have seen it in the camp yourself, I cannot hold my men in the field much longer; they want to go home.'

Bernard's upper lip curled away from his teeth. 'The Cathars are concealing things from you. I know, I have seen. The ordinary heretics, yes, they will go willingly into the flames for their accursed beliefs, but there are sheltered among them people whose blasphemy is even greater than theirs. The Cathars will do everything within their power to help them escape and proliferate.'

'What power?' d'Arcis scoffed. 'They're trapped in there like lobsters in a basket!'

'Baskets can be used for escape as well as imprisonment – that breach of security the other night, for example,' Bernard said, referring to some Cathars who had escaped from the fortress with laden packs. A sentry had heard a sound and, glancing up, had seen the end of a rope snaking up the sheer wall into darkness. Although the alarm had been raised immediately and the mountainside thoroughly searched, the escapees had got clean away.

D'Arcis looked annoyed. 'Since then, security has been tightened to a stranglehold. Nothing will get past now,' he said dourly.

Bernard was not mollified. 'They do have power, I tell you, of a diabolic nature. I myself have experienced it at first hand.'

D'Arcis gave him a cold stare. 'That is for you to challenge, Friar. My own concern is military.'

'Then you should look to their negotiator. He's not to be trusted. Probably he spied out all our strengths and weaknesses before he returned to the fortress.' Bernard wiped the smear of blood from his finger on to his trencher and watched the bread absorb it the way his tongue absorbed a holy wafer. The truce ended at dawn tomorrow, two weeks from its commencement, and Montségur was honour-bound to open its gates. Tomorrow when the fires were lit and the heretics committed to the flames, he would remove his hair shirt and rejoice.

Unconcerned, d'Arcis ate from the dish of mussels in front of him. 'I would expect any soldier worth his salt to do the same.'

'And would you expect him to have aid from among your own troops?'

D'Arcis paused chewing and looked gravely at the friar. 'That is a most serious accusation. I trust you can substantiate it?'

'Do you really believe that these breaches of security are just carelessness? You must look at the men closest to the walls.'

'I do not need a meddling priest to tell me my business! I've vetted all my commanders and found none of them wanting.' D'Arcis resumed eating, grinding his food between his molars as if it were a substitute for his table guest.

Bernard's obsidian eyes narrowed. 'I have the victory of our Lord Jesus Christ at heart.'

'I know that you do,' d'Arcis answered wearily. 'So do I, but let me be the best judge of my men.' He started to rise. 'If it will ease your zeal,' he murmured, 'I'll send up the mountain to the barbican watch and tell Dominic to be on the lookout for anything out of the ordinary tonight.'

Bernard stayed where he was, his eyes upon the fish skeleton. 'Dominic, you said?'

D'Arcis shrugged. 'I believe he was named after the founder of your order by the Countess de Montfort herself. He's the bastard son of old Count Simon – God's athlete, as he used to be known.' He smiled into his beard. 'I hazard Dominic's athletics are considerably more secular where the fair sex is concerned.' His brow contracted at the look on Bernard's face. 'What's wrong?'

'I know all about Dominic FitzSimon,' said Bernard in a chill voice. 'I was his tutor in Toulouse. If you have vetted all your commanders, then you will know he is a heretic of the first order, branded with the left hand of the Devil.'

'Oh, come now!' D'Arcis laughed uneasily. 'I've known several left-handers in my time, one of them a priest. You can't hold that against a man!'

'He was arraigned for heresy and banished from the Languedoc. The only reason he did not burn was because of his family connections,' Bernard continued as if d'Arcis had not spoken. 'His mother is one of the Cathar Perfecti locked in that fortress, his mistress another, and the envoy who came to negotiate terms with you, Guillaume de Montvallant, is none other than his half-brother.'

Hugh d'Arcis turned crimson. 'I don't believe you!' he spluttered, but they were only words. He did believe him, he simply did not want to.

'Now I see the link,' Bernard muttered. 'It eluded me before. I should have known.' He pressed his fist to the centre of his forehead. 'It will be tonight; I know it will.'

The flush of chagrin on Hugh d'Arcis's face turned to choler. 'I'll put out an immediate order for Dominic's arrest,' he said furiously and strode to the tent flap to issue commands.

When d'Arcis and Friar Bernard had sat down to dine, it had been a clear, mild spring evening, but a wind had begun to ruffle the tent canvases and gust through the campfires. When Friar Bernard looked up at the sky, the stars were rapidly being swallowed in cloud.

'It comes,' said the friar in a spine-chilling voice. 'The final battle.'

D'Arcis felt his hackles rise, and discovered it was Friar Bernard of whom he was afraid, not the Cathars upon their rock.

On the battlements, Bridget sat facing eastward to the place of sunrise, her grey-streaked hair cloaking her naked back. Her body, weakened by fasting and privation, had lost all suppleness and tone, but the inner glow remained, flickering around her, more animated than the flesh containing it.

Tonight was the equinox, tonight the power of nature was open to be harnessed, and they had never had more need of it than now.

Bridget closed her eyes and concentrated. She was the conduit through which the life force would flow to its destination. Her body trembled with the strength of the forces within and without. Even in her prime she would have struggled to control such power, and now, as it started to build, she knew that this summoning would kill her.

Throughout her life she had glimpsed this night in brief visions no longer than the flicker of a single bolt of lightning. It was a sacrifice she was ready to make; for Magda, for all the women who had gone before, and all who were to come and bear the inheritance of their bloodline. There was sadness in her but no grief. She had made her farewells steadily, without tears, and Magda had suited her own responses to her mother's wishes. Besides, it was a parting of the ways, not an irrevocable sundering.

Across Montségur's battlements, the first flash of lightning ripped the sky like a glimpse of the world beyond, and the clouds billowed like steam from a giant cauldron.

Resembling an ancient goddess, the huge trebuchet on the eastern wall was both the destroyer and the giver of life; the key to freedom. Dominic eyed the grotesque siege machine with loathing and a glimmer of satisfaction for what he was about to do. From early childhood, one of these monsters had been a part of him. He could not remember a time when the thud of the counterweight and the creak of the capstan had not lived in his dreams and haunted his waking mind. His father crushed to a bloody pulp; men and women screaming. Friar Bernard's willow switch.

For a fortnight the trebuchet had stood a silent sentinel on the walls, muzzled by the two weeks of truce granted to the Cathars in order for them to mull over the terms of the surrender and review their lives. Tonight the machine would be silenced for ever, but not before it had performed one last service.

He had dismissed the men on watch to their meal in the guardroom. While the truce was in operation, vigilance was not as strict upon the trebuchet and no one had complained or even thought his action strange, for he had made this the routine for the past four nights.

After a final glance around, Dominic set his foot on the winch, his hand on a beam, and pulled himself lightly on to the main body of the weapon. Reaching beneath his cloak, he unfastened from the belt at his waist one of a dozen small clay eggs and placed it with meticulous care against a niche where two beams joined. The egg contained Greek fire – a dark liquid with spectacular burning properties, easy to ignite, almost impossible to put out. Methodically ho climbed about the trebuchet, removing the other vessels from his belt and arranging them to suit his ultimate purpose – one on the capstan, another in the leather bag that held the stones, two on the ground supports, others on the super-structure. All his concentration was encompassed by the small, volatile shells of clay that one careless move or slip of the fingers would cause to explode in a ball of searing flame.

When he had completed the task, Dominic jumped down from the trebuchet and spared a moment to heave a sigh of relief and wipe his hands on his cloak. Wind riffled through his hair and he glanced briefly skyward. A cloudy night sky was rapidly absorbing the star-twinkled dusk. He turned to the barrels of pitch lined up neatly against the battlement wall. Two of these he rolled along to the trebuchet, positioned them on their sides, before knocking out the bungs. A third one he broached and tilted to pour a shining, glutinous trail from trebuchet to stair head. He was breathing hard now with effort, but through the exertion and nausea of tension surged a sense of elation. The trebuchet had haunted his life for too long. Let it go in sacrifice.

'Benedicite,' he saluted, and plucking a wall torch from its bracket, touched the flaming tip to the edge of the trail he had laid. Then, as yellow daggers stabbed up from the pitch, he ran.

'Fire!' he bellowed, flinging open the guardroom door. 'Don't just sit there like sheep; the trebuchet's burning! Organise a bucket chain. I'll raise more help!'

Above him as he sprinted into the night, the roar of the flames was clearly audible as they were fanned by the rising wind, and upon the battlements, the first flickers of lightning dazzled the sky. Keeping to the shadows, moving as rapidly as a wolf on a scent, Dominic hastened towards Montségur's west wall.

Magda clung to the rope that was slowly being paid out over the sheer west drop of the fortress, and felt as vulnerable as a fly upon a wall, ripe for the swatting. Surely the guards would see her and Guillaume in the jagged flashes of lightning and cry the alarm; or the other thing, the black night walker, would sense the breach in Montségur's defences and come on swift, silent feet to destroy them.

Fear gnawed at the edge of Magda's composure like a rat gnawing at the rope from which she was suspended in a flimsy leather harness. She must not fear. To fear was to give the darkness a wound on which to feast.

'Not far now,' whispered Guillaume from beside her.

She could not see his face, but knew from his voice that he spoke as much for his own comfort as hers. The leather bit into her thighs, the rope swung, grazing her against the walls, and the wind howled like a demon unchained, whipping her hair across her face. The ropes securing herself and Guillaume lurched wildly as those who were lowering them, weakened by lack of food and exhaustion, struggled to hold them steady and did not succeed. She tried not to think of the drop below, concentrating all her will instead on the image of Dominic waiting for her.

The lightning tore across the battlements, reached the barbican and stabbed at the walls. In a lull of wind she heard Guillaume's triumphant cry as flames soared skyward from the barbican's summit, illuminating the trebuchet in a giant praying mantis of fire, attended by a bee swarm of molten sparks. They heard the boom of pitch barrels exploding and hugged it to their hearts, the exultation warming their wind-frozen bodies.

Suddenly there were loose stones and tufts of wiry grass beneath their feet. Guillaume, being the heavier, was marginally the first to land, and kicked himself free of the harness. A shape scudded through the darkness and he groped for his sword, then relaxed as he saw that it was Dominic.

'Good bonfire.' Guillaume nodded at the barbican, his glib remark concealing his fear.

'It'll keep them occupied for a while.' Dominic's reply was curt, all his attention for Magda, who was tangled up in her harness and struggling to rise. He helped her out of it, drew her to her feet and briefly against him. She fitted into the contours of his body as if there had never been any danger or heartache or parting, or perhaps because of it and against all the odds. Dominic spared time for a swift hard kiss, then set her free. 'Give me your pack,' he said. Rubbing the back of her neck to ease the muscles that the straps of her pack and the descent had tightened, Magda looked up at the rearing walls of the fortress. She could feel her mother, but there was no space for benediction or a final farewell. She felt Bridget's struggle to hold the power of the lightning and would instinctively have tried to help her, but Dominic barred her way.

'Come now, quickly!' He tugged at her hand.

Her gaze dropped to his fingers meshed through hers, forging the link to the future. She followed in his footsteps, the men's garments she wore feeling unfamiliar, but far more practical. No skirts hampered her legs as she ran with him through the darkness.

'Torches,' Guillaume warned, 'spreading out below us, look!'

They paused to stare down the mountain at the bobbing dots of light advancing on them through the trees.

'Down here!' Dominic's voice was raw with urgency. 'Hurry!'

Stones turned beneath their feet and rattled away down the slope. Clinging tightly to the strength of Dominic's hand, Magda skidded and slipped. If only she could stop for a moment to gain her breath and find the submerged sixth sense that would permit her to walk these slopes as if they were steeped in noontide sunshine. The illusion of the latter was briefly granted by a vicious bolt of lightning, pink and blue, that sizzled into the rocks close to the path and sent a small avalanche bouncing away into the trees below.

Dominic urged them onward and downward. They passed a deserted picket post – Dominic had earlier dismissed the soldier from his duty – and entered the shelter of the pines. Here they paused for a moment to recover their breath, every sense straining. The easy part was over. Now all they had to do was rendezvous with Luke and the horses and slip between the campfires ringing the hill.

The first drops of rain spattered on them, sharp as needles, as they started to pick their way down the slope, following goat trails through the trees, concentrating on keeping their feet. The sudden flight of an owl from a low branch gave them all a flash of fear. Far more frightening, however, was the moment when the wind died down and they heard the baying of dogs. Too close for comfort, as were the seeking torches. Behind them, the burning trebuchet was in its death throes, the walls of the barbican illuminated in a weird red light upon which the lightning fed so that the sky burned and rippled like a vast, bronze sheet.

They hastened downward and the path widened. Pale tree stumps stood to either side of the route, showing where pines had been felled and dragged down the mountain to build stockades and shelters for the besieging troops, and, more sinisterly, a compound filled with faggots and brushwood for the purpose of destroying the unrepentant Cathars in the manner decreed.

An abandoned hut stood on the edge of a clearing. Below to the left were more cut trees, but the track to the right was still cloaked in thick forest. Beside the hut, horsehide gleamed like blackened metal and Luke was waiting, holding the bridles of four restless coursers.

No words were exchanged. In rapid silence they strapped their packs to the saddles and began mounting up. As Dominic cupped his palms to boost Magda into the saddle, the first dog bounded into the clearing. Guillaume cried a warning and drew his sword, but even as he raised it, Magda screamed at him to stop.

'If you kill the dog, it will lead them straight to us as surely as if you let it live!' Leaving the horse, she stepped in front of Guillaume, one hand extended, forefinger pointing. The hound, a huge black alaunt, stopped abruptly as if it had struck an invisible wall, and staggered. Soft growls rumbled from deep in its throat. Magda kept her forefinger directed at the centre of its skull, and beneath her breath, chanted softly to herself. To the men it sounded like a spell, but it was a device to concentrate her mind and make the hound do her will above the will of those who had sent it to track them down.

As the rain seethed around them, the creature whined and, tail between its legs, ears flat to its broad skull, slunk sideways and backward, cringing. The clearing emptied. Magda lowered her arm and sighed with effort. With so much blackness surrounding them, every projection of her life force was so difficult, like rolling a boulder uphill.

'I'm all right,' she answered Dominic's anxious query as

she returned to her mount. 'They will lose our trail from here. No dog will go beyond this point – they will feel the other one's terror and the rain will wash our scent away and make us hard to see.'

Their horses, dark-coloured to blend with the night shadows, disappeared into the trees, and when, a few moments later, a group of searchers reached the old Cathar hut in the clearing, the dogs reacted with such terror that their handlers became terrified, too, and without so much as a perfunctory search for tracks and much signing of the cross, they hurried on towards the beacon of fire crowning the mountain.

Panting from his climb and soaked to the skin, Friar Bernard stared with venom-filled eyes at the trebuchet, which still burned to defy the rain, and then at the soldiers who had been detailed to search the mountain. All of them were assembled close to the summit, and none of them had anything to report, apart from the men who had come up through the clearing and experienced such anxiety that they were convinced the old hut was haunted.

'Fools, they have slipped through!' Bernard said scathingly, eyes flaying the soldiers where they stood. 'You did not look hard enough or take enough care. Why should the dogs be afraid unless one of the heretics had cursed them?'

The soldiers shuffled their feet and looked at their boots. If there were curses afoot, they had no intention of putting themselves in jeopardy.

'They have to be stopped; don't you understand?' He turned to Hugh d'Arcis, who was standing to one side, grimly regarding the remains of his trebuchet. 'We must set out after them, tonight, immediately. Give me five of your best men, my lord.'

D'Arcis chewed his lip and considered. Tomorrow Montségur surrendered. He had to oversee that, not only as a matter of duty, but as a matter of vindication and revenge. 'Yes, take them,' he said curtly.

Friar Bernard inclined his head, although there was no deference in the gesture. Hunching into his cloak like a vulture, he departed for the camp at the foot of the mountain.

CHAPTER 48

The storm was so loud that it drowned out all other sounds. Walking through Montségur, Claire felt it vibrate through her body until she herself was the thunder pursuing the tail of the lightning. She hoped Magda and Guillaume were safely away by now. The beacon in the east barbican was a testament to Dominic's determination, a funeral pyre to mark Raoul's passing. She thought of her husband, and of her sons, united by a common bond, and found within her a well of ungrieving sadness like the last autumn leaf on a threadbare tree.

Tomorrow the women and children of the garrison would walk out of the gates to the freedom. So would the Cathars, except that the door to their freedom was fashioned of fire. How long did it take to burn to death? Would she have time to know and scream? It was the false God who was putting such thoughts into her head, urging her to recant, to be free of pain at the peril of her soul. But he would not win. She was too strong!

The women of the garrison were huddled together in a corner of the hall. Sancha, undisturbed by the storm, was sound asleep in Constanza's arms. Constanza herself had been weeping. Although her relationship with Guillaume had been shallow, he had provided well for her and the child, and she had not wanted to lose him. Claire moved on. There would be time for Sancha and Constanza later; for the moment, she was seeking Bridget.

As she gained the battlements, another terrific stab of lightning struck the walls. The thunder this time sent her cowering against a merlon, her hands over her ears. The echoes rolled around the sky, growled and died away to an eerie silence, broken only by the thud of the rain. Heart pounding, Claire regained her feet and went unsteadily along the wall walk to the small platform built on the eastern tower wall to which Bridget had so often gone to view the sunrise and gather her strength.

She was there now, lying on her side. Claire approached, her hands to her mouth. She knew Bridget was dead, but even so, after she had mastered her first shock, she crouched to make sure and found her still warm, as if her heartbeat had only just ceased.

The wind keened across the battlements, and within the rain there were chips of ice that struck like stones and froze Claire through her threadbare cloak and gown. Her vision blurred by tears, she composed the body as best she could and tried to tell herself that it was but a shell; the vital spark, like the lightning itself, had dissipated into infinity.

She became aware of another living presence and, turning, saw Chretien staring at Bridget's body with a great sadness in his dark eyes. 'She is with the One Light,' he said, a tremor in his rich voice. 'I only wish that her parting from this life could have been easier.' He laid a comforting hand on Claire's shoulder, and wordlessly she leaned against him like a sapling clinging to the support of an older, stronger tree. They stood like that for a long time. The rain ceased to fall and the sky took on a paler hue behind the mountains to the east. At last there came the sound of the main gate creaking open in surrender to the crusaders and the priests.

Hugh d'Arcis clasped his hands behind his back and examined the two groups of humanity standing in the castle ward. There was not a great deal to choose between them in terms of shabby, gaunt exhaustion. It was difficult at first glance to determine hardened heretic from stray Catholic sheep. The slightly larger group consisted of the men, women and children of the garrison force who had been led into blasphemous ways but could be redeemed by re-education and penance. A woman near the front of the line was eyeing his soldiers with bold and sultry eyes. Leaning on her shoulder, a little girl with black, curly hair stared solemnly at the crusaders and sucked her thumb.

The other group faced him not with resignation and fear as he had half expected, but with a vibrant certainty that outstripped all ordinary belief, their faces aglow with what he would have sworn was a residue of last night's lightning. For these Perfecti there was not even the glimmer of a doubt. Some of them even held out their wrists for the manacles that the soldiers were roughly clamping upon them.

Their possessions had been stripped from them and thrown into a small heap in the middle of the ward – mostly copies of the Gospels in the vernacular, but the Inquisition would need to examine them before they were burned. There were a few paltry necklaces and bracelets – the Cathars had no belief in adornment, and most had been taken from recent converts who still had sentimental ties with their past. Despite the rumours of fabulous treasure that had abounded throughout the crusader camp during the winter, there was nothing worth plundering.

Leaving the soldiers to their task, d'Arcis wandered through the fortress that had taken him nine months to reduce to surrender, deserted now apart from the captives in the bailey. His footsteps rang hollowly on stone and wooden plank. He paused at a cauldron of gruel, moved on past cramped sleeping quarters of rank straw. The fortnight's truce had permitted the Cathars rations and a degree of decency they did not deserve. His trust had been abused, hence the manacles. Let them be dragged down the mountainside to their deaths like the gutter-dregs they were.

He mounted the wall walk and paced along the battlements.

The morning air was sharp after the previous night's cata-clysmic storm, but scented and soft with spring too as the world turned towards the sun.

Tomorrow they would begin the task of slighting Montségur's great walls, tearing them down until what was left could not pose a threat. Strange how the edifice was oriented to make the most of the sun. It dazzled in his eyes as he reached the end of the wall walk and arrived at the small platform where he found the body of woman. She was middle-aged and thin to the point of being emaciated, but the bone structure of her face was quite beautiful, and her face wore a look of peace. He felt an odd qualm of tender pity, which he immediately shook off. This body, too, would have to burn, the sooner the better.

Claire stumbled over the rough stones of the steep descent. She could feel the ground through the worn sides of her sandals, every footstep keen with the pain of contact, of knowing that these were the last steps she would ever take, that her view of the mountains, blue in the spring haze and dark with pines, was her final one of this world. She wanted to stop, to take a moment for farewell, but the guards, in their haste to have the thing over and done and no Cathars to trouble their consciences, hustled them forward with sticks and horsewhips and the flat of sword blades as if their captives were animals being herded to the slaughter.

At her side, Chretien stumbled and fell. Claire stooped to help him, but was dragged brutally away by a young soldier. 'Leave him, whore!' he spat in a voice that still grated with adolescence. His eyes were filled with fear. Fear of the inner self, she thought. Strip the covering to reveal the greatest terror of all. Repay hatred with love.

'May you walk in the Light,' she said softly to him, and was struck across the face for her benediction. She reeled, clutching her cheek. Abruptly the young crusader jerked Chretien to his feet and shoved him so hard that he almost fell again. 'Move!' he snarled at him, and rounded on Claire. 'You, too, bitch!' His fingers bruised her arm as he flung her forward.

As they neared the foot of the mountain, the crusaders lined the path, jeering and spitting, running out of line to prod the Cathars with sticks. She saw the black cloaks of the Dominican friars, the gorgeous encrusted silks of a bishop, the blood-red robes of a papal envoy, the altar set up in the open air with its huge cross raised on high for all to see and adore. The stink of the army camp made the smell in Montségur during the last weeks of the siege seem like the sweetest perfume by comparison. Here were the stenches of worldly corruption that she had forgotten during her years on the mountain. Now the recognition flooded back and filled the back of her throat with bile.

A stockade had been erected using felled, trimmed pines and it was filled with faggots and brushwood over which priests were sprinkling holy water and soldiers were pouring pitch. Wooden steps led up to a walkway across the top of the stockade, and she saw a man in bishop's robes standing in the centre of the walkway beside a crude wooden ladder that led down into the kindling. He waited for his victims, a cross held high before him.

Contempt and terror warred within Claire at this grotesque parody. It would have been too simple for them just to have a gate in the stockade and lead the Cathars in. No, they had to be bound in chains, dragged down the mountain and exhibited to the crusaders, spat upon, jostled and tormented, before mounting a stairway to be symbolically sent downward again to the fires of hell. Did these people not realise that hell was here? That what was coming was release, and that they had failed? No, she thought sadly, they realised nothing.

They were pushed forward, up the stairs to the ladder. When it came her turn to descend into the compound of faggots, pungent with the smell of cut wood and pine pitch, the bishop made the sign of the cross over her head. She looked him in the face and he averted his own gaze with the unease of secret fear. 'You have failed,' she told him aloud and, setting her hands on the sides of the ladder, gladly went to join her fellow Cathars. When the last Perfecti stepped into the stockade, the ladder was drawn up to prevent anyone making a dash for freedom. More than two hundred people stood waiting to die.

The bishop raised his crosier and started to speak, his words full of rhetoric, full of his own importance, of evil and delusion. Claire closed her inner ear and murmured her own simple prayer. She shut her eyes, too, so she would not have to look upon the image of the cross as she prayed.

The smell of burning invaded her nostrils – not the general aroma of campfires, but the one she had been dreading. 'For thine is the kingdom, the power and the glory, for ever and ever, amen . . .' Raising her lids, Claire watched the flames tongue upward above the level of the stockade amid resinous gouts of smoke. A few moments of pain and the waiting would be over. Another woman had told her to inhale the smoke; death would come quickly that way. She repeated the prayer again more loudly and powerfully, crying out for deliverance. And then the smoke snatched her breath and a sudden gust of fire caught the ragged hem of her gown, played with it briefly, and flashed up her body. Her lungs filled with fire, her body became a torch. The first seconds of scorching agony were replaced with cool, flowing light that cleansed and smoothed and set a barrier between her and the fires of hatred and ignorance. Her body fell, was charred and twisted by the flames, but Claire de Montvallant was finally free.

CHAPTER 49

Dominic finished rubbing down the horses, threw blankets over their backs and set about hobbling them for the night. At their tiny campfire, Guillaume busied himself gutting and skewering some trout, while Luke foraged for firewood.

The night was clear, the stars heavy and bright, but with a passive rather than illuminating glitter. Dominic glanced at them and resumed his task. Only this one more night and they would be across the Gascon border. Perhaps then the prickling sensation across his shoulder blades would cease. He had the strangest feeling they were being followed, but all his checks from heights along the way, all the scrutiny of the other two men, had revealed nothing. Magda was aware of it, too, and he knew that she was not just feeding off his unease.

'Do you want some help?' She joined him even as he thought of her. It was often the way now, the merest spark of mind enough to alert each to the other. Competently she set about hobbling her gelding. The siege had left her painfully thin, but she had still proved capable of travelling at the pace he had set. She never complained, but he knew he was pushing her hard. She would eat her rations when they stopped for the night, and then be sound asleep within minutes. He would have given her more time if he had been able, but a sense of urgency, of impending disaster, goaded him to travel hard and fast.

She removed the broad-brimmed pilgrim hat that in the daytime concealed her braid of shining hair. He longed to loosen it and feel it silky and cool between his fingers. When she stood up, he could not resist pulling her into his arms and kissing her. She laced her fingers behind his neck and responded with a mute hunger the equal of his own. Dominic groaned softly and broke away. He knew that they could satisfy themselves here and now beside the horses. Guillaume and Luke would hardly interrupt them, but amid the stirrings of his body ran a thread of warning, a heightening of the sense of unease. He released her and, thrusting his hands into his belt to resist temptation, looked sombrely at Magda. She returned his gaze, a question in her luminous eyes.

'When I was eighteen,' he said slowly, seeking the words to explain what he felt, 'I bedded every woman who came my way, be they maiden or married, lady or serf; it did not matter.' He shrugged uncomfortably. 'I was still seeking the comfort of the breast, I suppose.'

'So now you are proving your maturity by abstaining?' Magda said with a half-smile. 'Surely you have no need with me?'

'No, it isn't that, you know it isn't. I passed that test a long time ago – with Chretien breathing down my neck,' he added wryly.

'Then what?'

'I was a squire at the court of King Louis and, as usual, pulling forbidden fruit off every tree I could find and unashamedly devouring it . . .' He looked at her sidelong. 'One day I was caught with more than just my teeth in one particular apple by an irate husband. I have never forgotten that feeling – turning round and seeing a man wild with righteous fury standing over me with a drawn sword. It is with me now, as if something is just waiting for the moment I drop my guard to take revenge for my stealing what it considers theirs.'

Magda shivered. 'It is not just the legacy of your past,'

she said. 'I have felt it too. I believe we were followed from Montségur.'

'It is not over yet,' Dominic said softly, and cast his eyes towards the blue distance of the mountains.

In a grave mood they returned to the fire and drew close to its welcoming warmth.

'We'll rest the horses for a couple of hours and cross into Gascony tonight,' Dominic said to the others as they dined on the trout, flat wheat cakes and raisins. 'Does anyone object?'

As one, Luke and Guillaume shook their heads, and Dominic saw that they, too, were troubled.

Friar Bernard considered the glimmer of light that marked out the heretics' campfire. He could see the figures stretched out on the ground sleeping, the man on guard and the tethered horses. Close now, so close. Like a wolf, he lifted his nose to the wind and touched the dagger in the sheath at his waist. It was a hunting weapon, a knife of Cologne steel, full nine inches long. He had prayed over it and purified it in holy water and blessed its honed edges. Thus he knew that the heretic woman would die, and her knowledge with her. His strength was greater than hers, because his strength came from God. God had told him what he must do.

Unable to sleep, Dominic folded his blanket into a neat bundle for his saddle roll and came to crouch beside the fire where Guillaume was on watch.

'Surely not time already?'

Dominic shook his head. 'I couldn't sleep, I'm too much on edge.' Picking up a twig, he flicked it into the fire and watched the flames consume it. Then he glanced along the squirrel-fur collar of his cloak at his half-brother. 'What will you do now? After this is over, I mean?'

Guillaume moved his shoulders as if shifting a weight that chafed. 'I cannot return to Montvallant. I will be branded

an outlaw from Marseilles all the way to the cold Narrow
Sea for this.'

'You would be welcome to make your home on my English
lands. French writ does not run there.'

'I'd rather not be beholden to a de Montfort for my daily
bread,' Guillaume said stiffly. 'Perhaps there might be justice
in it somewhere, but I think I'd rather starve.'

This time Dominic remained silent, not trusting himself
to speak. The bond of blood linking himself and Guillaume
was more of a stumbling block than one to mount to a higher
understanding.

'It wouldn't work, don't you see?'

'Clearly now,' Dominic said coolly. But he knew it was the
truth, and after a moment made a wry gesture of acceptance.

'Anyway,' said Guillaume, cocking him a look, 'I've more
or less decided to go with Luke and take Templar vows.'

Dominic started to speak, studied Guillaume, and changed
his mind. Probably there were more Cathars and Cathar
sympathisers among the Templars than there had ever been
among the entire population of Montségur, and as Magda
said, they were the guardians of the Grail. Not only that, but
neither the Pope nor the Dominican friars were able to touch
them, for they wielded power and influence in all corners of
the Christian world and beyond. He nodded slowly in
approval.

Magda whimpered in her sleep and tossed. Dominic
turned his head, his attention distracted. Guillaume rose and
moved restlessly like a caged beast scenting freedom on the
breeze.

'She's my half-sister, did you know?' he said.

'I suspected it. Fair hair was a rarity in the South until
the French came, and to see you together is to know without
a doubt.' Swept by a feeling of protective tenderness,
Dominic stooped beside her.

'Yes,' Guillaume muttered with a touch of malice. 'You'd
think looking at you and me that I was the northerner.'

'Skin-deep,' Dominic said, refusing to be drawn. 'It's what lies in the heart that counts.' And he received no satisfaction when he saw Guillaume flinch.

Magda's whimpers grew louder, becoming cries, and her arms and legs thrashed as if she were trying to kick off an assailant. Dominic murmured reassurances, but they were drowned out as she started to scream.

Dark shapes attacked like wolves out of the blackness. Guillaume's sword flashed. Roused by Magda's cries, Luke had thrown off his blanket, his weapon already to hand. Dominic covered Magda with his own body to protect her and realised that this was the very position his mind had imagined, except that no lovemaking was involved, and that if he died, it would be for more than just a matter of seconds. Beneath him, Magda's eyes were dark pools of shock and fear.

'They have found us!' she gasped as sparks struck the night and blade met blade and rasped off. Guillaume lunged and was rewarded by a shriek of pain. His attacker staggered backward, tripped on a piece of kindling and fell heavily into the fire. Smoke gushed in an engulfing, choking cloud and retching coughs came from the combatants.

Dominic hauled Magda to her feet and pulled her towards the horses as Guillaume covered their escape. As they ran, he dragged his own sword from its scabbard. A soldier came at them. Dominic parried, parried and cut, pulling Magda onward. And then a black shape leaped out at them, body spread to form a black star, a silver gleam at its upper edge. Dominic felt a cold punch against his ribs and heard Magda scream. His nostrils were filled with the musty odour of wool and old incense. His mail deflected the blow but he staggered. Magda was wrenched from him. He saw the glint of steel raised on high and threw himself at her attacker with whiplash speed.

The three of them went down together. Again and again, driven by the assassin's superhuman strength, the razor-edged poniard flailed and struck, flailed and struck, the grip becoming slippery with blood as Dominic strove to disarm the man. At last he succeeded in grabbing the priest's wrist, but Magda screamed, 'Let go of him!' in a voice so wild and imperative that, against all instinct, he obeyed. He was not fast enough. The first jolt ripped through him as well as his enemy and hurled him backward in a moment of blinding agony.

There was light in his eyes, a blaze of rippling fire, but hotter than flame and colder than ice. Through it he could hear the other man screaming like a wounded rabbit, or perhaps it was he who screamed, or his father beneath the walls of Toulouse. How could a man with a crushed head scream?

The sounds diminished to a weak, hoarse crowing that Dominic could now distinguish as separate from his own harsh breathing. He opened his eyes, squinting because they were still light-dazzled. His hands were deeply gashed and pouring blood. His mail had saved him from worse damage than bruises and the odd pinprick wound. On the ground near him, Friar Bernard still moved weakly, eyes rolled up in blindness, blood frothing from his mouth, and a knife hilt protruding from the centre of his breastbone.

'He stabbed himself in his own frenzy,' Magda panted shakily. 'I turned his own evil back upon himself.'

Even as they stared at the priest in appalled horror, he ceased to breathe. The knife hilt trembled one last time and then was still. Magda looked at her blood-soaked gown and then at Dominic's lacerated hands and went convulsively into his arms. They kissed with shock and relief, this time neither of them fighting the wildness. Magda put her hands on his and concentrated until the golden strength flowed through her fingers into his. There were only scratches and superficial cuts on her own body.

'I felt him stalking us in my sleep,' she gasped as they broke apart. 'I tried to wake up and warn you, but I couldn't! He had me trapped!'

He started to smooth her hair and stopped, conscious of the state of his hands. They were still covered in blood, but it was no longer flooding out of the cuts and the pain, although raw, was bearable.

Guillaume ran up to them. 'Christ God, how badly are you hurt?' His gaze darted with growing concern over Magda's saturated garments and the dark slashes on Dominic's hands. 'Jesu!'

'It looks worse than it is,' Magda said quickly to reassure him. 'What about you?'

Guillaume pressed his palm to the stitch in his side. 'Not a mark,' he panted, and suddenly grinned. 'They'd been hanging around in an army camp for nine months and their edge was as dull as a rebated blade.' He looked over his shoulder at the shambles around the campfire. 'Too flabby and well fed to cause Luke and me any problems.'

Luke, still gasping, did not possess the wind to disagree as he wiped and sheathed his sword. All he did know was that Guillaume was going to make a formidable addition to the ranks of the Knights Templar.

Guillaume stooped to peer at the dead friar. 'I know him,' he said with a hint of surprise. 'He's a papal inquisitor.'

'Do you not remember him from Toulouse?' Dominic asked. 'He was the friar who had you arrested outside the Château Narbonnais.'

Guillaume shook his head. 'They all look alike to me.' He cleaned his sword blade on the black cloak.

'Not this one,' Dominic said with soft intensity. 'He has shadowed my life since I was born, and he'll shadow it still even though he is dead.' He took Magda's arm. 'We're not going to get any more sleep tonight. Let's ride for Gascony.'

CHAPTER 50

ENGLAND, MAY 1245

Lying in a willow basket beneath the apple trees in the garth, the baby opened and closed her fingers, trying to grasp the dappled light filtering through the leaves. By tradition, she ought still to have been swaddled, but Magda would have none of it. Her daughter would know what her hands were for from the very beginning; she would never be confined.

'Anyone would think she was talking to the trees.' Dominic sat down beside his wife on the turf seat. The day was sufficiently warm for him to have discarded his tunic, and he wore only his shirt and hose. Here, in his own domain, he could be as casual as it suited him to be. Simon had recently left for the court again, trailing chests of rich garments piled upon staggering sumpter mules and flaunting banners and panoply to suit his station. Dominic much preferred to live a quiet existence at home with his wife, his new daughter and the fraternity of masons who shared the castle with them while they constructed Magda's convent.

'She is talking to the trees,' Magda said. 'She can see their life force; it's not just the sun dapples she's trying to hold.'

Dominic set his arm across his wife's shoulder and played with the silky end of her braid. Throughout her pregnancy she had blossomed; indeed, she looked like a bloom now – pink tinted with gold, and glowing with vitality. Bridget's birth had been smooth and easy, without complication, and the child herself was a source of constant delight. Dominic did not believe that he could ever be more content, these moments given clarity and a depth of feeling beyond expression by the trauma of what had gone before.

Magda leaned into his touch and watched the shadows of leaf and sunlight, the blending ripples of his aura and hers and the baby's. 'What if I told you that I was descended from the Magdalene?'

Dominic shrugged. 'Then she must have been very beautiful.'

'Seriously . . .'

'It would make no difference to me were you to claim Hecate herself for your great-grandam. It is you I care for, not your ancestors.'

'But they have bequeathed my bloodline some strange and dangerous gifts.'

Dominic spread his hands. They bore the fading scars of a madman's dagger. 'I'll admit to that, but I still say it matters not to me.'

She held his gaze. 'Not just the Magdalene. She was married to James, brother of the Christ, and her children were the grandchildren of the Virgin Mary. The bloodline continues with our daughter.'

Involuntarily his eyes went to the gurgling infant. 'You must have proof,' he said, 'or the priests would not have been so determined to silence you.'

'Oh, yes.' Magda nodded. 'As you have seen yourself, I have the texts from Montségur. There is a copy of a Gospel written by the Magdalene herself. Her family were persecuted, so she and her children fled to southern Gaul. At first they were hounded for being Christians, and then, in later generations, as the power of the Roman Church grew, for being heretics and proclaimers of blasphemy. A branch of the family fled across the Narrow Sea to Britain. My mother was the surviving member of that branch. As you can see,' she said with a tender look at the baby, 'the line usually runs to girls. Each generation is taught to use their gifts for good

– for helping and healing.' Her eyes grew sombre. 'And for that we are hunted down and branded witches and whores.' Bending, she raised her daughter out of the basket and kissed her soft dark hair. 'It has to be nurtured quietly, in this generation at least, and perhaps for a long time to come.'

Dominic lifted on his forefinger the dove-and-chalice medallion she wore over her gown. 'So you are the Grail,' he mused. 'Yes, I see that: the bearer of the holy blood, the cup of grace.'

Magda lowered her eyes, her skin suddenly a warmer pink at the tender note in his voice.

'The bloodline is safe in my hands,' he said as he laid the medallion gently back against her gown. 'They have been scarred and mutilated enough to prove it, and I'm a part of it now, in flesh and blood and spirit.' He held out his forefinger and his daughter curled her own small fist around it, clinging tenaciously.

They sat on in the garden while the day mellowed around them and the sun changed its angle, creating around the three of them a golden nimbus of light.

Readers often ask me how much of what I write is historical fact. I tell them to imagine that my novel is a tapestry.
The real events and people form the backdrop on which I
weave the colours of my story using my own characters and
imagination. So, how much of *Daughters of the Grail* is
embroidery, and how much is historical truth?

During the twelfth and thirteenth centuries in Europe,
there was a growing dissatisfaction with the established
Church. People thought that priests had become too corrupt
and worldly. Religious sects whose aim was to 'get back to
basics' proliferated. Some, such as the Dominican movement, or the Franciscans, had the sanction of the Catholic
Church. The Pope allowed there was a place for reform, as
long as it was under Rome's control. The Cathars did not
conform to that philosophy; indeed, they rejected it outright
and thus were viewed as heretics and a threat to order.

The Cathars were dualists. They believed in two deities.
In general terms, this meant that they worshipped a good
God, benevolent and far removed from the lusts and turbulence of the world. They also believed that he had an evil
counterpart – Rex Mundi – who presided over everything
that was fleshly and materialistic. Rex Mundi, as his Latin
title suggests, was 'King of the World' and can be very
roughly equated with the God of the Old Testament.

Cathars believed that each time a human infant was

conceived, a pure spirit was dragged away from the realm of the good God and forced to enter the flesh of the child. Thus the spirit became trapped and gradually, because of the contamination of its earthly life, forgot its pure origins and became bogged down in the sins of the flesh. Only by living an exemplary life could the spirit return to its unfettered source. This involved for the Cathars the taking of strict vows. A committed Cathar was celibate, vegan in diet and owned no possessions. At a time when a chronicler could say of a leading Catholic bishop that 'his heart was a bank', the ordinary people were keen to look to the Cathars for their spiritual comfort.

The Catholic Church denounced the Cathars whose rituals were simple and whose methods of worship it viewed as downright blasphemous. Cathars, for example, worshipped wherever they gathered, not in a place especially consecrated for prayer. Women were allowed to become priests. They did not believe in baptism or marriage, and saw the idea of Christ suffering on the cross to redeem everyone's sins as both untrue and abhorrent. Their ideas were so different from those of the established Church that they were bound to come into conflict with its officials. But it was not until the Cathar movement began to gather enough devotees to threaten the power of Rome that the Pope decided to act.

The lords of what is today southern France were tolerant to Catharism. They had a more liberal outlook than their northern European counterparts, and allowed Cathars, Jews and Muslims to flourish in their communities. Their culture and society still bore vestiges of the rule of the Roman Empire, and they spoke a different language from the North – Occitan. Through trading links with the Mediterranean and the East, they were a wealthy, cosmopolitan people. Theirs was the land of troubadours, culture and courtly love. The rougher northern lords coveted such a lifestyle for themselves.

It was almost inevitable that the South's wealth, allied to its religious tolerance, should bring its lords to grief. Pope Innocent III tried to bully them into purging their towns and villages of the Cathars. When rejected, he called a crusade that the warlords of northern Europe were keen to join.

The soldier who led the crusaders to victory after victory over the southern armies was Simon de Montfort, a French baron who hungered for land and had the fighting skills to take it. A superb and energetic general, he seized control of much of the Languedoc, dispossessing its existing ruling houses to do so.

He was killed in 1218 beneath the walls of Toulouse and, as mentioned in *Daughters of the Grail*, he was indeed struck a direct hit on the skull by a missile from a stone-throwing machine operated by a woman.

The atrocities of the Cathar war are also taken from history. The entire population of Béziers was massacred, a total of between ten and fifteen thousand men, women and children, Cathar and Catholic alike. Geralda of Lavaur was thrown into a well and stoned to death. In other captured towns, Cathars were burned in their hundreds.

The final stand of Catharism in southern France took place at Montségur, a castle built upon a mountain in the Pyrenean foothills. Much has been written about the castle, the siege and the mystery surrounding the Cathars. Rumours abound that they were in possession of a fabulous treasure. This has variously been interpreted as consisting of the treasure of the temple of Solomon, or perhaps priceless books full of esoteric and cabalistic lore. There is also the speculation that the Cathars were the guardians of the holy bloodline of Jesus Christ. Whatever the truth of such matters, the Catholic Church was determined that the Cathars of Montségur be exterminated.

Following a siege lasting nine months, the garrison surrendered. More than two hundred Cathars were led down the mountainside to a field, and there they were burned to death en masse.

A memorial stone stands there now. Fresh flowers and wreaths adorn its base. The people of the Languedoc still remember. I have climbed the mountain myself in the course of my research and have explored what remains of the walls. There is a stillness and silence about the place, a tranquillity that belies its bloody past, and from its diminished battlements, the Pyrenees stretch beyond the eye's reach in colours as chameleon as the moods of the sky.

Daughters is a work of fiction, but for those who want to know more about the Cathars and the Albigensian Crusade, as it came to be known, I include a brief bibliography of some of the books I found useful to me in the course of my research.

BIBLIOGRAPHY

Baigent, Michael, Leigh, Richard, and Lincoln, Henry. *The Holy Blood and the Holy Grail*. Jonathan Cape, 1982.

Birks, Walter, and Gilbert, R.A. *The Treasure of Montségur*. Aquarian Press, 1987.

Christie-Murray, David. *A History of Heresy*. New English Library, 1976.

Foss, Michael. *Chivalry*. Michael Joseph, 1975.

Guirdham, Arthur. *The Cathars and Reincarnation*. C. W. Daniel, 1990.

Hallam, Elizabeth, ed. *Chronicles of the Crusades*. Weidenfeld & Nicolson, 1989.

Labarge, Margaret Wade. *Simon de Montfort*. Cedric Chivers, 1972.

Ladurie, Emmanuel le Roy. *Montaillou: Cathars and Catholics in a French Village 1294–1324*. Scolar, 1978.

Paul, Richard. 'Heresy and Holy War in Languedoc.' *France* magazine, Spring 1990.

Riley-Smith, Jonathan. *The Atlas of the Crusades*. Guild Publishing, 1991.

Strayer, Joseph R. *The Albigensian Crusades*. Dial, 1971.

Sumption, Jonathan. *The Albigensian Crusade*. Faber, 1978.

Wakefield, W. L. *Heresy, Crusade and Inquisition in Southern France 1100–1250*. Allen & Unwin, 1974.

Walker, Barbara. *The Women's Dictionary of Symbols and Sacred Objects*. Harper & Row, 1988.

Walker, Benjamin. *Gnosticism: Its History and Influence*. Aquarian Press, 1983.